LIS MCDERMOTT spent thirty-four yea
latterly as a schools adviser and OFST
education in 2008 to set up her own phc
last she might be catching up with her frie

In the 90s, during her time in educati
a series of books to support the classroom music curriculum. She published her first solo book in 2014, a photography book called *Headshot Diva: why your business profile affects your bottom line.*

Having awoken another passion, she has now published an autobiography – a book of short stories and four poetry anthologies. She also mentors others to write their books.

Lis lives in Royal Wootton Bassett with her husband Conrad, with whom she shares a love of music and films.

HE IS NOT WORTHY

LIS McDERMOTT

SilverWood

Published in 2022 by SilverWood Books

SilverWood Books Ltd
14 Small Street, Bristol, BS1 1DE, United Kingdom
www.silverwoodbooks.co.uk

Copyright © Lis McDermott 2022

The right of Lis McDermott to be identified as the author of this work
has been asserted in accordance with the Copyright, Designs
and Patents Act 1988 Sections 77 and 78.

ISBN 978-1-80042-193-6 (paperback)
ISBN 978-1-80042-194-3 (ebook)

British Library Cataloguing in Publication Data
A CIP catalogue record for this book is
available from the British Library

Page design and typesetting by SilverWood Books

This is dedicated to the love of my life, Conrad.

PROLOGUE

The principal was speaking, but the boy had stopped listening several moments ago, after hearing the words, 'I'm sorry, but your father is dead.' He was aware that the man's lips were moving, but there was a rushing sound in his ears, and the room was beginning to turn dark.

He felt arms holding him and someone pressing a glass of water to his lips. He drank slowly and the room began to come back into focus. It felt as if he were watching a film. One of those dreary European art films shot in sepia, where a scene showed someone had been given terrible news, and the people talk in hushed tones.

"Sit here for a while until you feel able to move. Your aunt is driving up to take you to visit your mum in hospital. So, I'll leave you alone for a while, but if you want anything I'll be in the office next door." Then the principal turned and walked through an adjoining door into another office, leaving the door ajar.

Slowly drinking the water that he had been given, the boy remained seated for some time. Finally, he was beginning to breathe more easily. The rushing sound had quietened, although it had moved to the inside of his head. Then, for no reason, he suddenly didn't want to be in this room anymore, so he walked out of the principal's office completely unnoticed.

Once outside in the corridor, he stood for a while, trying to decide where to go. In the end, he chose to sit on the floor beneath the stairs. He didn't think anyone would notice him. This corridor wasn't the busiest area, and only a few students had walked past since he sat down. Without warning he started to cry, finding he couldn't stop. He put his hand over his mouth, as he didn't want to make a noise and attract attention to himself.

A girl's voice asked, "Are you OK?" He didn't look up. "Sorry, that's a silly question. You're obviously not. What I meant was, can I help?" He still didn't look up.

To his embarrassment, the girl sat down beside him. At last, he looked up at her. Even in this saddest moment of his young life so far, he noticed how beautiful she was.

"What's happened?"

Trying not to snivel but failing miserably, he said, "My dad has died."

The girl put her arms around him, pulling him towards her and saying, "I'm so sorry."

He leaned into her jumper, which he was now making wet with his tears, and closed his eyes. Then letting go, he sobbed uncontrollably. Still, the girl held him tight as if she would never let him go. The boy felt loved. His mother hardly ever held him this physically. He had rarely felt as much love from her as he did now from this stranger.

Eventually, his sobbing calmed, and after searching in her bag, the girl handed him some tissues. She still held him, and he was happy to remain within that beautiful, physical hug. He knew it sounded dramatic, but he felt as if an angel had appeared to give him comfort in his hour of need.

CHAPTER 1

RHI

It was unseasonably chilly, and the cold air had been blowing in from the sea all day. So, to keep warm, I snuggled into the low and extremely soft, squashy sofa in a dark corner of the local pub we all frequented on a Monday night for a meal and a quick drink, listening to the chatter of the rest of my work team.

Outside it was typical British weather. You know, the type where you can never tell what it will be like from one day to the next. Usually, if it weren't too cold, we would sit outside, where we could be a little more raucous, not offending any of the older clientele who have been coming to the pub for years. However, today, none of us fancied braving the weather, so we had come inside and taken over a corner section of the bar. At least on a Monday, the pub wasn't too busy, so Jack, the owner, was always pleased with our custom.

The team included Ali, my best friend and the head of music, and Megan, Ali's second – a very young twenty-three-year-old. Then there was Jon, the drama teacher, far too confident for his own good, and Mark, my second in the department. Plus, me, Rhi Dobbs, head of art. I'm only in my fourth year of teaching, and proud to have made a department head. We all teach at Whittingbury Academy, a secondary school at the edge of Whittingbury. We are fortunate that the school grounds have a fantastic view of the sea. Not many schools can boast of such, I'm sure.

You are probably wondering why we are out for a meal and drink on a Monday evening. Most teams go out on a Friday night to start the weekend. We tried that, but people didn't turn up for one reason or another, so we kept missing our nights out. After that, we decided we'd have a 'start-the-week-Monday' night out instead. But, of course, meeting up on a Monday does have its drawbacks. It means you must be careful about how much you drink, as trying to contain a class of teenagers when you're suffering a hangover from hell and not on top form can be a complete disaster.

Jon and Mark had started a discussion to see who had dated the youngest girl but keeping it legal. However, Ali and Megan were starting to get quite heated by their male-chauvinist attitudes, so Megan decided to play them at their own game. Turning towards us, she asked Ali and me if we'd noticed Matthew Greening.

"You mean that fit one in Year Ten with the mop of blond hair and very blue eyes?" asked Ali, laying it on thick.

"Yeah, he's going to be a real looker when he's older," Megan continued.

"Baby-snatcher," I said, smiling to myself.

"It's more normal for younger women to go out with older guys," Jon remarked.

"Says who?" Megan asked.

"Well, women don't age as well as men. That's a fact."

"Do you really want to go down that route, Jon?" Ali glared at him.

"I'm just saying that, usually, the age difference is the man being older. It's historical, isn't it? Women used to die in childbirth, so the younger they were, the more likely they were to survive," Jon replied, looking smug.

"But we're living now, and we're not talking about having babies, we're just talking about dating," Ali replied.

"And sex," Megan added.

Mark cut in. "Yeah, there are some good reasons to go out with an older woman, or so I've been told."

"And they are?" I asked.

"Well, you know, they can teach you things."

"Like embroidery? Cooking?" Ali suggested.

"Come on, you know what I mean. Sexually!" He whispered the last word in a very camp way, exaggerating the pronunciation with his mouth and lips. It reminded me of the way some older adults speak about someone else sitting in the same room, but don't think they'll notice if they say it in a whisper.

The three of us girls just stared at him, before all of us, Jon and Mark included, burst out laughing. After which, we all sat quietly drinking, waiting for our food to arrive.

However, Jon did not appear to want to let things go, as he asked, "So, who else have you got your eyes on then, girls? Have any of you ever been out with anyone younger than you?"

"No," replied Ali and Megan, almost in unison.

I hadn't replied, mainly because I was trying hard to clear my mind of the younger man who had instantly sprung into it. I hadn't been out with him, but he had been in my thoughts a lot of the time recently.

Jon noticed I'd remained silent. "So, what are you smiling about, Rhi?"

"Nothing, erm…no, in answer to your question, I've not either."

"Methinks maybe you took too long to answer that." Jon gave me a stare, and without being able to control it, I flushed. Hopefully, though, in the low lighting, he hadn't noticed.

"OK, who wants another round to go with the food?" Mark interrupted, standing up ready to go to the bar. We all put in our orders, and Ali talked to Megan about the next day's lessons. Jon joined Mark at the bar, and I quietly finished my drink.

Tomorrow I'd be teaching the young man who had been invading my mind over the last few months. It had happened very gradually. Initially, I'd noticed him because of his artistic talent, which was impressive for someone his age. He had found a style already, which was precocious for someone who hadn't even attended a college course yet. At the beginning of the year, I'd invited a few of my upper-sixth A-level group to come to my studio on Saturday mornings to explore artistic mediums that weren't on the curriculum we followed in school. It was all above board as I'd checked with Janice, the headteacher, before inviting them. Josh Campbell was among the group, along with Gemma Smith, who was also very talented. I had a good group this year, and along with Josh and Gemma, Steven and Georgia also came for the Saturday morning sessions.

It was Josh who I found myself thinking about, particularly his beautiful eyes: a deep dark brown. And his smile...his smile was just so captivating. The mixture of the smile and eyes just made my heart pump that little bit faster than it should. When he and Gemma first joined my group, I thought they were together, but soon learned they were just best mates. They always struck me as an odd mix but thinking about it, and as I got to know them better, I realised that their shared love of art was what had cemented their friendship.

Gemma had a strongly individual style, and character. However, she didn't suffer fools. She was a bit of an outsider, tending to keep to herself at school, although it seemed she frequented a few pubs and bars at weekends. Josh had only joined the Academy in his lower sixth year, after moving from London. He was the only mixed-race pupil in the whole school, so he could quite easily have become an outsider too. However, due to his easy-going character, he had fitted in well. He and Gemma were very different in many ways, but their shared humour and passion for art had created a strong bond between them.

"Here you go, Rhi!" Mark was standing in front of me, handing me my drink.

"Sorry, Mark, I was miles away."

At the same time, our food arrived, and there was a moment of silence while everyone got stuck into their meals.

Between mouthfuls, Ali asked, "Are we all ready for this term and the exams?" Being the head of the arts team, she had to ensure everything in the department ran smoothly. Compared to many other schools in the area, we were a young team considering the amount of responsibility we had. Still, the good thing about the Academy was that Janice always supported us.

A little over a year ago, the first person I told was Ali when I heard I'd got the job. It was thanks to her that I'd even applied for the post. Later, she had turned up on my front doorstep with a bottle of Prosecco to celebrate my success. "Hey, did you send me flowers as well?" I asked, hugging Ali when she arrived.

"Er, no, I'm not that generous. You know me, I'd only bring something I can share." We both laughed because we knew this was true. Ali did like her wine, Prosecco, and cocktails when she had the chance.

"Well, I don't know who they're from, but they're beautiful."

"You must have a secret admirer," Ali said, giving me a shove. "Come on, let's get this bottle open and start the celebrations. Whoever it was could have been here too if they'd signed their name. Too bad! All the more for us!"

Ali and I had met when we were teenagers, and I had come to Whittingbury Bay for my annual stay with my aunt Jinny for the summer holidays. Ali lived a little way out of the bay, on the road to town. It took her about twenty minutes cycling, with the wind behind her, to reach the sea. The first time we'd met was on the beach. Ali had been clambering around the rock pools with a small shrimping net, trying to catch anything alive. Finally, she walked around a larger rock formation and met me. I was dangling my toes in the water, a sketchpad balanced on my knees, drawing what looked, according to Ali, like weird squiggles. We'd started talking after she had managed to spray water all over my drawing.

I'd told her I was staying with my aunt who lived in the cottage above the beach. I can still remember Ali's face when I said that. She suddenly became very animated. It seemed that she was fascinated by Aunt Jinny's cottage. In her mind, she had created all sorts of stories about the place. But the thing she loved most was its name, Starfish Cottage. We'd wandered around the beach for a while, me with my sketchpad and pencils stuffed in my backpack, and Ali clinging on to her shrimp net. Then, together we'd gone to look for starfish in the little rock pools. Ali was disappointed because she had never found one, telling me all she typically caught were tiny crabs and seaweed!

During our walk, I'd discovered that she lived on a farm with her parents and two brothers. I told her I lived in Didsbury, in Manchester, where there wasn't any sea. It was a big city, nothing but houses. I thought she was lucky living by the sea. I didn't mention my parents, feeling uncomfortable when she had asked if they were on holiday too. However, I was saved from answering because, to our amazement, we found a starfish. He was bright orange, and although we shouldn't have missed him, we nearly did. He had been hiding under a small overhang of rocks. Ali was so excited. She had started jumping around and, holding my hands, began dancing with me. She kept telling me I was her good luck charm.

We spent the rest of that summer together, becoming inseparable. As an adult, she had become my good luck charm on more than one occasion. As time went by, we had developed different passions in life but had remained firm friends. By the time we both went to college, we knew we would be best friends for life. I couldn't believe that had been fourteen years ago. Look at us now! Ali was leading the team while I was head of my department. I don't think either of us would have believed it when we met on the beach all those years ago.

After we'd finished our meals, people gradually started to drift off, leaving Ali and me. We decided to stay on for a coffee and a catch-up after the weekend.

"Have you had any flowers this week?" she asked.

"Yes, I got some on Friday. I still never manage to see who delivers them, and there is nothing on them to say where they're from. It's bizarre."

"Yeah, it is weird; I mean who on earth would be sending flowers to a 'ginger'?" Ali was always rude about my red hair. When people first met me, they would assume being a redhead meant I would have a temper, so it came as a bit of a surprise when I didn't fit the stereotype, even with the addition of green eyes. Secretly, I think Ali was jealous of my hair, but she wouldn't admit it.

Since moving into Starfish Cottage when I got the job, I'd been receiving flowers weekly. The flowers would suddenly appear. A courier or a local florist didn't deliver them, and I hadn't heard a car engine. They were just there. To start with, I'd felt a little uncomfortable, especially after all the trouble I'd gone through with Paul, my ex-boyfriend. I'd hoped that I wasn't going to end up with someone making my life hell again. However, there had never been anything sinister. The beautiful flowers appeared, with no notes, or even threats. It seemed I had an admirer. I just couldn't work out who it was.

"What did you do at the weekend?" I asked Ali.

"I went to see my brother Ian. They've just had another baby, so I'm an aunty, yet again."

"Lucky you, more presents to buy."

"I know. The only thing is, whenever my brothers take girlfriends home, or get married and have babies, my mum asks me when I'm settling down. It really gets on my nerves." Ali had a quick slurp of her coffee. "I don't know why she wants me tied down so quickly. Do you think she's worried I'm going to end up an old spinster?"

"Hardly that!" We both laughed at the idea. That was something Ali would never be. A spinster. It wasn't that she didn't have boyfriends and she certainly wasn't virtuous; luckily, her mother didn't know the latter part.

It was funny, though, because Ali was always nagging me about getting out and meeting people. She didn't think I was having as much fun as I should. Since Paul, I'd had a few casual relationships, but I certainly wasn't looking to get serious about anybody or get tied down again anytime soon. Then, of course, there had been the odd one-night stand, and I'd even been out with a parent of a pupil from school, which, in hindsight, hadn't been a particularly good move. But, overall, I was coping without a man in my life.

Tuesday morning, I made my way through the throng of sweaty teenagers towards the Art Hub. I don't know why, but schools all have that same scent. I had decided long ago it must be the mix of the disinfectant used by the cleaners, along with the smell of trainers and PE kits kept too long in lockers. Whatever it was, visit any school and the same fragrance eventually meets your nose.

Nearly every pupil I met nodded or said, 'good morning', which had happened almost from my first day. It made me feel I belonged. At least, I had never been mistaken for a student by any other teacher, which had happened to Jonesy, the PE teacher. When he first arrived at the school, a senior staff member had shouted at him for being late for lessons and not being in uniform! He had been dressed in the standard PE teacher attire – a tracksuit. It made me smile just thinking about it.

Finally, I arrived at the Art Hub. Making the trek to the other side of the school to the staff room for the short breaks of the day seemed a complete waste of time. I preferred to make my coffee in the art storeroom-with-study I'd created within the Art Hub, although Mark, my second, much preferred the staff room. The storeroom was a long, thin space. A window just above my head level allowed some much-needed light into the room, but it also meant that pupils couldn't spend their time gawping inside when I was relaxing.

At the room's far end, there was a low cupboard with several coffee mugs, with a kettle sitting on top. Next to the cabinet was a mini fridge that housed milk and sometimes my lunch when I needed to work through. There were two Ikea Poang chairs that feel like rocking chairs when you sit on them because of their slight bounce. Great for catching a relaxing five or ten minutes' peace whenever possible. Art paraphernalia packed the remainder of the storeroom. There was another storeroom in Mark's room, which was even fuller than mine. After the fifteen-minute break, the upper sixth would arrive – with the morning ending well. Until then, I could settle down to relax and daydream with my coffee.

Over the last few days, I'd been thinking a lot about Mum. It was coming up to the anniversary of her death. I'm not someone who dwells on the past, nor am I particularly nostalgic, but I always remember the day of her death. She had died from cancer when I was ten. It had been quite sudden. She hadn't been ill for long, but it had been the worst time of my young life. My dad didn't know how to cope with me, which is why I had spent so much time with Aunty Jinny, Mum's sister. She had almost become my surrogate mum. Over time, Dad had gradually pulled himself together, and we'd rattled along together in the house from day to day. But I missed Mum's laugh and her carefree spirit. She'd been strict when she needed to be, but most of the time easy-going.

When I was in the sixth form, Dad had met Karen, who eventually became my step-mum. I didn't hit it off with her that well, which caused plenty of rows with Dad, and living with her was a nightmare. She was everything Mum wasn't. Karen was much louder than Mum, what many would refer to as 'high maintenance', mostly getting her way in any discussion between the three of us. I was relieved to get away from home and go to college.

During my second year, they sold up and moved to Alicante in Spain. Just like that. I was angry that Dad had just upped sticks and started a new life. I couldn't forgive him for acting as though Mum had never existed. The saddest part of it all was that we'd never had the chance to make up because he died a year after they moved to Spain. Karen didn't even tell me until after the funeral. I never forgave her for that. Finally, however, I came to the decision that Dad probably had taken on more than he had bargained for with Karen, and lately, I had begun to feel sorry for him. All he probably wanted was some company.

The bell rang loudly, interrupting my thoughts and denoting the end of the break. I quickly finished my coffee and walked into the classroom, just as some of the sixth formers started to arrive. They were going to tackle life drawing today, as quite a few wanted to brush up on their drawing skills. Coming into the room, they greeted me, then each of them went to put their bags and belongings in their cubicles.

A large part of the room was set out with a semi-circle of chairs and easels around a single chair on a small, raised dais where the model they would draw would sit. A couple of weeks ago, I'd asked Josh Campbell to be the model because his drawing skills were excellent. But I'd decided – he would gain more by being on the other side of the easels, seeing how hard it is to sit still for a couple of hours! The norm for the model was to wear a PE kit because this meant that the arms and legs of the sitter would be bare. It was the closest you could get to drawing a nude, which, of course, would certainly not have been allowed – although I did know of a couple of private schools that employed nudes for life drawing.

"OK, everyone. Josh, can you come and sit on the chair, please?"

Josh walked out from his cubicle wearing, as requested, his PE kit. However, he had removed his T-shirt, wearing only his shorts, due to the room's warmth. Inwardly, I took a breath. I hadn't realised how fit he was!

"Ooh, get you, Josh. Mr Lean and Mean." Gemma laughed as Josh walked in. "We won't be able to concentrate." And she laughed again.

"It's a good job we're not drawing you then, isn't it, Gem? We'd have to draw your tats as well as your mad hair! And I don't think I've ever seen you do PE – do you even have the kit?" Josh responded. She made a rude gesture at him while the rest of the group joined in the laughter. I couldn't help but laugh too at the banter between them.

"Come on, guys, let's get on with it. Have you all got the view you want?" I received nods and affirmative replies from the group.

"Josh, are you comfortable sat like that – can you stay still in that position for a couple of hours?"

"Yeah, I think so, miss." He gave me one of his glorious smiles, which always had more of an impact on me than it should as a grown woman and teacher.

Initially, I moved around the room, making comments here and there and giving advice when needed. Finally, I decided I'd join the group, and taking up my sketchpad, I perched myself at the back of the room. With the pad balanced on my knees, I had a good view of Josh. He was so beautiful to draw, being tall, having dark brown eyes and an athletic body, as I could now see. I was glad to be sitting behind the group, feeling myself blush as I was gazing a little too intently at his body. At one point, I thought Josh had caught me out, as he happened to gaze my way, so I quickly looked down at my drawing, continuing to concentrate on the markings my pencil was making. When the lesson ended, Josh stood up and stretched, elongating his tall, slender body even further. I was relieved when he collected and put on his T-shirt.

I encouraged the class to share their drawings with Josh and each other. They were excellent. Some hadn't quite managed to capture Josh completely but had got an overall feel for how he was sitting. Gemma and Steven had achieved a remarkable likeness and captured the light and shade of his skin as the sun fell on his body during the morning. I was pleased with their results and the progress made, which, looking back to when they had started two years ago, was terrific. However, I didn't share my drawing – I kept it for myself.

After they had all left, while I was clearing up, I found myself thinking about Josh's taut, muscled body. I'd never noticed how fit he was when he was wearing his school uniform. At the weekends when he and the others had come to the studio, he always wore jeans and baggy T-shirts. Recalling my moment of self-embarrassment during the lesson, I wondered how I had even managed to concentrate or remain professional while teaching the rest of the group. My lips curled into a smile as, for a moment, I let myself imagine drawing his naked body, which was so unlike me. What was I doing?

"Oh my God! I've got a crush on one of my students!"

CHAPTER 2

BEN

While preparing tea, Ben glanced up at the photo on the wall. Happier times. It was a birthday party. He was sitting at the table with his parents standing on either side, both smiling down at him with their 'proud' parent faces. In front of him, on the table, was an ornate birthday cake with many lit candles. He couldn't remember how old he was, and the number of candles, which seemed excessive, didn't give a clue.

They had been a close family, the three of them. His mother was at the centre of both his and his father's love; while he, Ben, was at the hub of hers. She loved him almost too much, and as he grew older, he began to resent it. It was a cloying, demanding love, which, although he returned it, made him feel continually guilty. Guilty he wasn't good enough, clever enough, or handsome enough. Despite this, he knew she loved him, almost obsessively, to the point of ignoring her husband. His father seemingly accepted this, doing everything with her happiness in mind. She was a beautiful woman, tall and slender with long dark hair, and, unusual for that colouring, blue eyes. She had always been the centre of attention. Ben had always been proud to be seen out with his stunning mum, thinking how she was so much prettier than all of the other mothers. This attention had made her shine like a star.

She was still the centre of attention.

Ben walked up the stairs, carrying the tray of food. "Come on,

Mum, let's sit you up. Your tea's ready for you."

The bedroom had been her pride and joy – her sanctuary when she had one of her migraines and wanted to be alone. Ben had realised early in his teens that the migraines were often an excuse to escape what she didn't want to face. Ben was only allowed inside her bedroom occasionally. He remembered how it always held an atmosphere of opulence. The scent of her perfume lingered in the air and her wardrobe door was always slightly open. Inside, he could see the wonderful colours and materials bursting to escape their wooden prison.

Now, as he looked around, the bedroom was more like a hospital room. His mum was hooked up to a mishmash of wires and tubes, all attached to different machines, which were taking up space around her bed. The overriding smell now was one of hospital sanitising chemicals, but especially of illness.

After setting the tray down on the bedside table, Ben helped her into a more comfortable sitting position, propping the pillows up behind her. He tucked a napkin into the top of her nightie and, picking up the bowl of soup, started to feed her. "It's a lovely day outside today – cool, but sunny, and the sea's glistening in the sunlight."

He leaned forwards to wipe a little dribble of soup that had missed her mouth and was trickling down her neck. "I saw Rhi when I walked down to the beach. She was busy painting, so I didn't stop to talk to her. I didn't want to disturb her."

The look in his mother's eyes said it all. She didn't believe he knew a girl. She didn't think any other woman apart from her would look at him. Ignoring the cynicism her eyes conveyed, he continued to feed her carefully. When she had drunk as much as she could manage of the soup, Ben helped her find the most comfortable position against her pillows. He picked up the book on her bedside table. "Are you ready for the next chapter?"

His mum nodded. Well, he knew she had, even though the actual physical movement she made was minimal. Since the accident and during the last two years, her movements had become far more restricted.

Ben began reading from *Wuthering Heights*, a book he had read several times over the last eight years: 'While leading the way upstairs, she recommended that I should hide the candle, and not make a noise; for her master had an odd notion about the chamber she would put me in, and never let anybody lodge there willingly.'

He glanced up. His mum looked peaceful, though not asleep as yet, so he continued reading. Finally, she fell asleep, and he crept out of her room with the tray.

Back downstairs, he cleared away all evidence of tea, and after making a quick coffee for himself, he went into his room. This was one of the two large sitting rooms situated on either side of the oak-panelled hallway leading to the front door. His room had a bay window in which his large TV stood. A comfy sofa was placed opposite the TV and behind that his bed and wardrobe. To the left of the door into the room stood his work desk. The interior was dark, mainly because the blinds were continually kept drawn, but it was not helped by the deep navy painted colour of the walls.

On the wall behind the desk containing his twenty-seven-inch Mac was a large, framed paper cutting of a girl with curly, red hair. A girl called Rhi. It was the photo from the local newspaper, celebrating her appointment as head of the art department at Whittingbury Academy. Ben logged on to Facebook and opened his fake profile, which he'd set up some time ago. Due to his ability to use social media well, he had managed to 'friend' some of the other teachers where Rhi taught, and had recently managed to connect with her, too. He had purposely not posted anything on her page, but because they were friends, he could now see what was going on in her life – at least to a certain extent. He noticed she was very careful what she posted. Not wanting any pupils to see what she was doing or give a bad impression to any parents who might check her out. Ben spent some time copying some of his favourite images of her from the page, saving them into a special *Rhi* file on his Mac. He planned on printing them out and sticking them on the wall alongside the large paper cutting.

He was so intent on what he was doing, he hadn't realised the time. Hearing the front door open, he knew Pam, his mum's carer, had arrived to settle her for the night. Ben popped his head around the door. "Hi, Pam, she was asleep earlier, and I haven't heard anything from her since. Do you want a hot drink? I'm making myself one."

"No thanks, Ben, I'm fine. I'll give you a knock when I'm leaving." And she disappeared upstairs.

Ben couldn't have coped without Pam and the carers who had come before her. His mum could be very hard work. Over the years she had scared away several of the carers with her rude and awkward behaviour, but Pam seemed to have got his mum's behaviour sussed, and could deal with her easily. Each day, Pam would arrive in the morning to take care of his mum's needs in terms of the different equipment that needed checking – sorting out the different bags that required changing and giving her a bed wash. She would do the same in the evening, so his mum could get a good night's sleep. In the early days, Ben had been able to support his mum far more, but he had always needed help with the complicated equipment required to keep her alive.

He went into the kitchen but decided against another hot drink, getting himself a beer instead from the fridge, before going back to his room and settling down to listen to music and do some work on his computer. After about an hour, Pam knocked on his door. She never came into his room, respecting his privacy, which he appreciated.

"See you in the morning, Ben. Take care." He heard the front door shut quietly.

Tomorrow was Saturday and a new day. He would take a walk into town, and maybe down to the beach to see if he could catch a glimpse of Rhi.

CHAPTER 3

BEN

Leaving the house, he called out 'goodbye' to his mum, although he knew she wouldn't hear or respond. It was a habit he had fallen into. She was probably dozing. That was what she did more and more these days. The only good thing about that was, he didn't feel as guilty as he might once have done about leaving her alone. He had set up a monitor linked to his phone, so he would be alerted if there were any problems. After that, he felt confident he could spend a few hours out and about on his own.

Walking away from the house, he glanced back. It didn't look too bad – not too uncared for in a street that was very much about 'keeping up with the Joneses'. When his dad, Alex, was alive, he had been a keen gardener, at least when he had time. For his sake, Ben had tried to keep the front garden tidy. He didn't want their house to stand out for the wrong reasons. At least each house was a unique design, unlike many new housing estates, where each property looked like its neighbour. Ben's parents' house seemed quite foreboding in its way. It was a large, double-fronted detached house, surrounded by several very tall fir trees, appearing dark and uninviting.

As he walked down the hill into town, Ben felt a slight chill, which compared sadly to the day before when he had seen Rhi out painting on the beach. However, it made the air considerably cooler. Typical British summer weather – cool, then warm, then even cooler the next day! He decided he'd get a coffee to warm himself up. Watson's Café on the high street, which had opened recently, already had a good reputation, so he thought he would give it a try. As he entered the café, something familiar caught his eye – red hair. Rhi was sitting at a table by herself as if waiting for someone.

This was the first time he had come face to face with her in years. He stopped in his tracks, undecided whether to turn around and make a quick exit or stay and approach her. Finally, she made his mind up for him. Hearing the door open, she looked up, expectantly, and waved. Ben couldn't believe his eyes. She had recognised him. His heart beat faster, and smiling broadly, he began walking towards her. He was just about to open his mouth to speak when someone pushing past bumped into him, and he heard another female voice saying:

"Sorry I'm late. Hadn't got enough change for parking!"

Ben's body slumped in disappointment. He hoped Rhi hadn't noticed his elation when he'd thought she was greeting him. For a few seconds, he couldn't move but had to when another customer said, "Excuse me," as they wanted to get past him so they could leave. Feeling deflated, he decided he still needed warming up, but he now needed some warmth in his heart too. He walked past Rhi and her friend, who had finished hugging and were starting to chat. Then, feeling exposed after the gaffe, which only he knew about, he stood at the counter where the food and drinks were displayed.

"What's it going to be?" the young man wearing the name badge *Ryan* asked him.

Ben was still feeling annoyed at his own mistake in thinking that Rhi was pleased to see him, so he hadn't thought about what he was going to drink. "Er…a hot chocolate please, and one of those cookies." He pointed to some delicious homemade peanut butter biscuits.

As he took Ben's money, Ryan asked, "Where are you sitting, so I can bring them over for you?"

Ben looked around and chose a table where he knew he would hear and see Rhi and her friend without them noticing him. As he went to sit down, he picked up a magazine from a pile at the end of the counter, which the café left for customers to read while relaxing. Then, taking off his coat, he made himself comfortable. Ben started to browse the magazine while surreptitiously glancing in Rhi's direction. She looked beautiful, just as he'd always remembered her. Her hair was a little longer than last time he'd seen her, and he hadn't realised just how red it was. She was wearing a green jumper, jeans, and ankle boots. She also wore a patterned scarf. As he was watching, she removed it and hung it over the back of the chair on top of her coat. Her friend was dark-haired and was also wearing a jumper and jeans, but Ben wasn't interested in her or her attire. They both had extra-large pieces of cake and were drinking coffee.

Rhi's friend began to talk about the 'hot' date she had been on the night before, with some guy she met in a bar.

"What was his name?"

"James, I think."

"What are you like!" Rhi pretended to be shocked.

"Nothing happened. We didn't hook up completely – just a lot of tongue hockey."

"You are gross, Ali! Are you seeing him again?"

"No, he's not really my type."

"You know all the time I've known you. I haven't yet worked out what your type is. I just think as long as men have functioning bits, you don't care."

"I like a man with a brain too, but it seems hard to find them, at least in Whittingbury." They both laughed.

"Tell me about it," Rhi agreed.

They both stopped to devour their food and drink. Ali asked, "So, did you go on a date with that dad – what's his name?"

"Matt. No, I just didn't fancy him."

"But you could have had a good night out," Ali interjected.

"Yeah, but I want more, and I don't want another Paul. I just couldn't live with that amount of control again. It makes me nervous when I think about getting involved. You don't know how people are going to turn out, do you?"

"I understand that. It certainly wasn't a good time. I could have killed Paul over how he treated you. But you've got to start somewhere. Otherwise, you'll never trust anyone."

They touched hands across the table. Rhi said, "I know. I wouldn't have got through all of that without you."

"That's what friends are for," Ali replied. "Anyway, I thought you had a crush on someone?"

"Mmm, not going to happen. He's not the right person, and as you've just reminded me, I'm not good at picking the right guy."

"I didn't say that. I said you were unlucky. Anyway, there's nothing wrong with dreaming." They returned to their cake and coffee. There was silence for a bit, as they were both lost, musing, in their own worlds.

Ben, listening to the discussion, was fascinated. He had no idea what women talked about. He had gone to an all-boys school. His perception from their conversation was that her friend, who he now knew was Ali, was a bit of a tart. On the other hand, Rhi had been badly wronged by some guy, and now she had a crush but no boyfriend. He was collecting great intel, which was probably even better than he would have gained had he sat and conversed with Rhi.

Two mums came into the café pushing buggies. What had been a space of mumbling voices suddenly became a screeching horror house! Ben was relieved when he heard Ryan asking the mums to leave the buggies outside. Everyone listened to the young mums' reactions.

"You expect us to leave them outside – they'll get nicked. And where are the kids going to sit?"

"You're welcome to use the high-chairs, or you can set the children on your knee, but I'm sorry, we don't want buggies taking up space. Also, some of our more elderly customers need room to get around," Ryan explained, keeping his voice even-tempered.

"Well, you can stuff your bloody coffee, mate. We'll go somewhere else. We won't be coming here again," one of the two mums shouted with vehemence. The pair made a lot of noise while leaving, slamming the door for extra measure to ensure everyone could share their outrage. Inside the café, there was an almost palpable sigh of relief.

Averting his gaze from Rhi and Ali, Ben noticed that the café was mainly full of older people or young, professional businesspeople. He had failed to notice the lack of children when he came in but now recognised why the café was popular with certain sections of the community. However, when he turned his attention back to Ali and Rhi, the former was trying to convince Rhi to go to a speed-dating event.

"It'll be fun. I'm not expecting to meet Mr Right, but we can have a laugh and a good night out together. What d'you think?"

Rhi, who was on her second coffee, which Ali had been getting when 'kid-gate' happened, was thinking about it. She eventually replied, "Oh, go on then, let's have a laugh. At least it'll take my mind off my Mr Wrong." They both laughed, loudly.

Ben was making a note in his head to look for speed-dating events locally. Then, amazingly, Rhi asked the question he wanted to be answered.

"When is it then?"

"A week next Friday, at the Plough Inn. New people have taken over, and they're trying to get more people in and change the pub's reputation. They want to get a wider age range in there, rather than just older men. They're starting to do food too, and not just the iffy bar snacks."

Ben made a quick note on his phone. Maybe that would be his chance to meet Rhi properly.

Suddenly, Ali leapt to her feet. "Oh, shit! I'd better go. My parking's about to run out."

"I'll come too. I've still got some more bits to get before going home, but I'll walk back to the car park with you."

They both stood up. Rhi grabbed her coat, her scarf falling to the floor. In her rush, she didn't notice. Ben was about to get up to tell her, but she and Ali had reached the door. They were off before he could say anything. He stooped to pick up the scarf, quickly putting it into his pocket, hoping nobody would notice.

Walking home, his hands in his pockets, Ben could feel the softness of Rhi's scarf in his fingers. Why on earth hadn't he introduced himself at the beginning? Ben knew why. He hadn't wanted to share that moment with anyone else. He had often thought about meeting Rhi again and the unspoken intimacy between them. How he would pull her into his arms and thank her for her comfort. But he hadn't. He hadn't even said hello. But, what could he have said? 'It's great to see you after all this time. I've thought about you every day.' That was true, but he hadn't seen her for eight years since their first meeting. And perhaps saying he had thought about her every day might make him sound a little creepy.

In his head, he could hear his mother berating him for his lack of confidence. He could almost hear the 'I told you so' tone of her voice. Again, he felt the scarf in his hand. It brought him warmth and a feeling of closeness to Rhi.

Once home and in his room, Ben held the scarf against his nose, inhaling her perfume and almost crying with happiness.

CHAPTER 4

JOSH

Standing at the school gates waiting for his friend, Gemma, Josh still couldn't believe the difference in surroundings compared to his last school. Arriving at Whittingbury Academy had, in so many ways, been like going back to primary school. The other kids in his year were so immature, what his mates back in London would have called 'country yokels'.

At least that's what he had thought when he had arrived until he got to know some of them – particularly Gemma. They had ended up sitting near each other in the first art session of the lower sixth and had hit it off straight away. However, had he seen her and not conversed with her, he would probably have dismissed her as a 'Goth' due to her clothes, piercings, and tattoos. He thought they would have nothing in common. He was so wrong! Art was the thing they were both passionate about and could talk about for hours. Then he found that she had a mad sense of humour, often saying what she thought. No skirting around issues, she went straight for the jugular. After that first meeting, they had become best buddies, which had lasted for the last year and a half. He hoped it would continue when they went away to college.

As well as having a friend who was very different from anyone he had known before, Whittingbury was distinct from his school in Islington. There, whichever way you turned, you were surrounded by buildings, and it seemed that everyone in that school was into something slightly dodgy. He knew several of the lads in his year were making money on the side from selling pills or running errands for older guys. His mates had made fun of him when he told them he was moving to the country.

Initially, he had found the area too quiet, and he missed talking to his mates about music. Now, he had got used to the peacefulness, realising it gave him time to think. As for his music, well, he could listen to that anywhere. Looking at the landscape around the school, it was the difference between the earth and the moon. He was growing to love what he saw.

Now he was nearly at the end of his second year and the last term at Whittingbury, he understood why his parents had moved from London. Here, Josh had been able to concentrate on his art, and not worry about outside pressures, such as his mates trying to entice him along on their night-time jaunts. The year he left, two lads in the year above him were involved in a knife attack; one had died, stabbed for no apparent reason. He recalled his parents having, what was for them, a heated discussion about moving after they had heard about the recent knife attack.

"I can't face living here any longer, Patrick. What if that was Josh? It's getting worse all the time," said his mum, Sue, tears in her eyes, desperation creeping into her voice.

"I know, love, but I've got to find a job – it's not that easy, you know. Not these days. And where would we move to?" Patrick had put his arms around his wife, holding her close. "I'll look into it and see if any transfers are going. It's all I can do now. It's not like he's a bad boy. He doesn't go around with the wrong crew."

Shrugging out of Patrick's arms, she had almost shouted. "That's not the point, is it? Look at Stephen Lawrence; he wasn't a bad boy either. I'm not losing my boy." The tears that had been bubbling fell. Patrick had quickly pulled her back into his arms.

Several months later, Patrick hadn't managed to find a job transfer but had got a new job, based in the south-west. He was in sales, and travelling was an integral part of the job, so they could choose where to live, within reason. Sue had done some research online, finding out about

Whittingbury Academy and the reputation of the art department. Josh remembered being shocked when the three of them visited. He hadn't seen a school with so much land around it. He was further impressed when he saw the amount of space set aside for the art department. The school in Islington had been an older building with smaller rooms for each subject area.

Patrick and Sue had a good look around the area, finding a house they liked, which was much bigger than expected. They had anticipated that house prices would be lower but hadn't realised just how far their money would go, especially considering their proximity to the coast. The house they found had four bedrooms, compared to the three they had in Islington. It was certainly more modern, having been built in the eighties, when compared to their old Victorian terrace. Patrick was particularly excited, because they had a garage where he could keep all of his tools and what he had previously kept in a garden shed. Unfortunately, the house didn't have a good view of the sea, but if you stood on tiptoe and leaned out of one of the back-bedroom windows, you could catch a glimpse of it in the distance. A couple of months after moving, Sue's mum, Lizzie, also moved into a small flat in the same area.

Josh hadn't wanted to move away from his mates and his girlfriend, but he had to admit that he often felt nervous when he was out late at night. You could be completely innocent of any wrongdoing, not even mixing with the wrong people. Knife attacks could happen to anyone and appear to be random. You could put yourself in a dangerous situation just by looking at someone in what they considered to be the 'wrong way'. He knew what he wanted in life, and if it meant moving away from friends for a safer environment and better school, then it was worth it. Besides, he could easily keep in touch with friends.

It was going to be more challenging keeping in touch with his girlfriend, Dee. She was a friend of his sister's, and the fact they were going out was something they had kept quiet from both her and his parents. It wasn't as though it was serious, and it was more of a physical relationship than anything else. Josh didn't think there was enough connection between them even to bother suggesting they kept in touch after the move. If he were honest, he had been quite relieved it was over. When he told her they were moving, she had just shrugged. His reading of the situation had been correct. Over a year and a half ago now, he and his parents had moved to Whittingbury, leaving his older sister, Alisha, behind.

"I'm not moving! I don't see why my life should be disrupted, just because he needs a better school. I mean, I love Josh, but this is my life. So, I'm staying here, *and* I'm moving in with Sam," Alisha had yelled at her parents when they had initially mentioned the idea of moving. She wasn't impressed.

"You're moving in with Sam?" Patrick yelled back. "This is the first I'm hearing of it. I don't think so, my girl. We need to talk about this."

"You can't tell me what I can do, Dad. I'm old enough to make up my mind. Besides, you obviously didn't consider me when you were thinking about this move. So, I don't think you have any right to criticise me!"

Patrick had his mouth open, about to answer, when Sue had cut in. "Patrick, calm down. Alisha, Sam is a lovely young man, but you have only been together for a short time. Are you sure you're ready for such a commitment?"

"Oh, my, God! Mum, Dad." She sighed. "You're more worried about me moving in with Sam than leaving me behind?"

Almost together, they had replied, "Noooo!"

Then, Sue answered for them both. "We understand you don't want to leave such a good job, but for the same reason we are moving to keep Josh safe, we want to make sure you're going to be safe too." Patrick was nodding in agreement, although still frowning at the idea of his 'little girl' moving in with a man.

Josh and his sister were close. They rarely fell out, and although they still had the typical sibling rivalry, he understood why she didn't want to leave. She had a good job working in a bank in the City, and he knew she had good prospects there. Sam, her boyfriend, was also in finance but earning at least twice as much as her. He had an apartment in Battersea and had recently asked Alisha to move in with him. Josh liked Sam and knew he would look after Alisha. However, she hadn't got around to telling their parents until they sprung 'the move' on her.

After the initial shock on all sides, the family soon calmed down. Following a good talk with her parents and then Sam, they decided that Alisha would move in with him a couple of months before Sue, Patrick, and Josh moved away, just in case there were any hiccups.

Josh heard Gemma before he saw her. She was running towards him, slightly out of breath, due to being later than she intended. "Hiya." She slapped him on the arm. "You have a good weekend?"

"Yeah, didn't do much. I was doing some research for my art project."

"You're such a creep! Is that all you did?"

"No. I spoke to my sis – she's doing well; she just had another promotion. I went to see my nan. Ah, yeah, and I went to the cinema with my dad. What did you get up to? Did you manage to 'pull' Saturday night?"

"Good news about Alisha. No, I didn't manage to pull anyone – well, not this weekend. The music was good, though. A new band – The Albino Zombies. They were awesome."

"Er, you think every band's awesome."

Gemma made a sign with her middle finger. "So, you going to be getting your kit off again in art?" Gemma prodded his chest.

"No, not this week. Don't you remember, we're going to be working on our exam prep? It's the last lesson before exams, and I hate the writing stuff."

"Yeah, I remember. Just joshing you." She had recently found the phrase while working on a project in English and found it hilarious that Josh's name was also slang for 'joke'.

Josh pulled a face at her, then asked, "Are you getting nervous about the exams?"

"A bit, but to be honest, but I'm sicker of all the planning stuff – I just want to get on with it, don't you?"

"Big time!"

Gemma thumped him again. "Come on. We'd better get in for registration. Otherwise, we'll be in trouble. See you later."

"Yeah, see yah," Josh said, walking towards his tutor room.

After tutor group, Josh wandered into the Art Hub and went into his cubicle. No one was teaching in the room today until his group, the two sessions before lunch. He'd wondered if Mr Jones might be in there, although he didn't usually teach in that room as much as Miss Dobbs. Josh was relieved, as he had the space to himself. He got out his sketchpad and notebook, continuing to think about his art project.

A couple of minutes later, he was distracted, and his thoughts went back to the first time he was in a class Rhi taught. He had instantly liked her, her style, manner, and above all, the way she taught. Although the group had been to her cottage for extra work at weekends, he had always found her so easy to talk to outside the school. Besides admiring her as an artist, he also thought she was beautiful. The most beautiful woman he knew. Her red hair glistened when the sun caught her curls, and she had the most amazing green eyes. He often made quick sketches of her when no one was looking. It had been coming across one of these in the sketchpad that had distracted him from his work.

Recently he had been fantasising about Rhi as a woman rather than a teacher. During one of the art lessons, she had leaned forwards to point out a section on the drawing on which he was working. He had smelled her perfume, and as she leaned further forwards, he had caught a glimpse of her cleavage. Since then, every time she entered a room, or he caught sight of her around school, he had felt a stirring deep inside his stomach. Sometimes, moving between lessons, if he saw her further down the corridor, he had to stop and watch her. He knew it was more than a schoolboy crush; his feelings were more profound than that.

During the sitting in the previous lesson where he had been the model, he had the opportunity to watch everyone else in the class as they concentrated on their work. Gemma had made him smile because she had a habit of biting her lip whenever she was concentrating, and it looked as though she was pulling a face. Although she was good at drawing, it wasn't her main skill. Her talent was sculpture. Steven was totally engrossed in what he was doing, as were most of the others. What they couldn't see, but he could, was Rhi. After she had settled everyone down and checked on their progress a few times, she had perched herself on a desk at the back of the room.

Josh had caught her looking at him intently and smiling to herself. He didn't think she had noticed him returning her gaze, but the look on her face hadn't been what he expected to see. Thinking back now and remembering her face, the only word he could come up with to describe how she looked was enjoyment. It gave him hope. Part of him knew it unlikely, but just maybe, she found him attractive. As soon as he thought this, the little voice in his head told him he was being stupid – he was just a student as far as she was concerned. However, Josh felt something had changed. There had been a difference between them during the rest of the lessons that week. Perhaps it was how he was feeling, but an optimistic part of him remained hopeful.

Looking down at his sketchpad and notebook, he saw he hadn't done a thing; he'd wasted most of his time daydreaming. His hope that Rhi would arrive before the rest of the group so he would have time with her alone was utterly squashed when Gemma flounced into the room.

"Oh, my, God! I've just had the most boring English lesson! Mr Jones talks a load of crap sometimes. He's just ruined 'Leda and the Swan' for me. *Forever!*"

"Who and the swan?" Josh asked, laughing at her dramatic entrance, despite his disappointment that she wasn't Rhi.

"It's a poem by Yeats, don't worry about it. I'll get over it. What have you been doing?"

Josh paused. "Not as much as I should." Gemma walked over to her workspace. He wasn't going to tell her about his feelings for Rhi – not yet. Gemma was his best friend, but he wasn't sure even she'd understand. Josh wished he could be more like her.

Gemma somehow managed to keep any romantic urges in check, at least in school. He remembered her telling him when they were first friends. She didn't go out with anyone from school. She wasn't wasting her time getting serious because she was getting away from Whittingbury as soon as possible. College couldn't come early enough for her. Josh smiled to himself, recalling the conversation about *who* it was that she did go out with. She had told him, "I find guys at the pub at weekends. Just one-night stands. I'm not interested in relationships, just their bodies!" Gemma had laughed as she said this. Probably because Josh had looked a bit shocked, although he tried not to appear a prude – he wasn't, but he hadn't expected this admission from his, then, new friend.

He had asked her, "Don't you worry about being safe? I mean, if you pick them up at the pub, how well do you know them?"

"I talk to them first. Get to know them a bit, and generally, I think I'm a good judge of character. You're my best buddy, aren't you?"

"Yeah, but even so, you need to be careful. Have you ever had any problems with any of them?"

"Not that I can't handle, no," she had answered confidently.

Since then, she had often regaled him with stories of her conquests after the weekends – that is, when she felt like sharing.

At that moment, Rhi walked in and started preparing her notes, without noticing the pair of them at the other end of the room. The rest of the group followed her, arriving in dribs and drabs until everyone had arrived. The lesson began. After they each had shared how they were getting on with their preparation for the exam, they went back to their cubicles to continue working on their final plans. Rhi spent time with each of them in turn to check their progress.

Josh set to work. The theme they were each working on was 'freedom and limitation'. Josh, linking to his ancestry, had decided to take the theme of 'slavery' as his starting point. He was researching African and Jamaican artists for inspiration, particularly in their use of vibrant colours. Josh was planning a large piece of work, wanting to paint on metal, a rigid material to convey the concept of the slaves' lack of freedom. Rhi had discussed this with him previously and was trying to find where he could source some metal for his work. He had been busy over the last couple of weeks, creating colour sketches, and exploring the mixture of colours he finally wanted for his larger pieces of art. Josh also had to write a commentary explaining the thinking behind his work. He needed some help, as he wasn't always able to express what he wanted when putting it in writing. He would have been fine if he could talk to the examiner, but you didn't get that opportunity. He was deep in thought and hadn't noticed Rhi until she was next to him, in his cubicle.

"I've got some good news, Josh. I've found someone in Barnstaple who will give you some aluminium. Isn't that brilliant?" He noticed how green her eyes were as her enthusiasm bubbled over.

"Thank you, miss. That's great. How did you manage to persuade them?"

"My good looks and charm," she joked but then unusually looked a little embarrassed. She quickly continued, bending to look at his work. "So, how are you getting on with your commentary and ideas?"

Unexpectedly, Josh felt a little flustered. The space in the cubicle was small because of some sheets of metal, early experiments, leaning against one of the walls. That meant Rhi was so close to him. Her arm brushed against him each time she took a closer look at his sketches and writing. He felt hot. Finally, he managed, "I'm OK with the ideas. It's just the writing I'm not good at."

Rhi smiled, and again he felt that flutter in his stomach. "You can do it, Josh. Imagine you're explaining it to someone else and then write it. You need to finish it today. I'll read it through later and give you some feedback."

He watched her walk over to Steven, and he began to breathe normally again. Pretending to work but watching without making it obvious, he noticed Rhi didn't appear to lean in so closely to Steven. She didn't seem to smile at him quite as much, and she didn't look at all embarrassed. Everything was going too fast. The exams were in a couple of weeks, and once they were finished, he wouldn't see her. He had to do something before it was too late.

At the end of the lesson, Rhi asked for a volunteer to help her move some heavy stuff in the art cupboard.

"I'll help, miss, no problem," Josh answered before anyone else could. After that, he'd be alone with her and could make his move. Leaving his bags in the cubicle, he followed Rhi into the art storeroom.

CHAPTER 5

RHI

Walking towards the art room, I was busy rummaging through my bag, not looking where I was going. Where the hell is my diary? I can't have left it somewhere. It wasn't as though it was the end of the world because I'd got all my appointments on my phone calendar, but it was the other stuff I didn't want to lose. I often created quick sketches when I was out and about without my sketchbook. So, where on earth have I put it?

After the recent life drawing lesson when Josh had been the model, I couldn't get the image of his fit body out of my mind. He was muscular without being too big, and his smooth skin was a beautiful light, golden brown. He looked far more mature than most of the other lads in the sixth form. The thought brought a smile to my lips. It's not surprising I'm losing things! I continued searching through my bag, becoming more irritated with myself by the minute for being so careless.

During this last week, I'd taught Josh on four occasions, and I had felt awkward on each occasion. I was certain I was behaving differently towards him and was sure he must have noticed. In the past, we'd always had a great teacher–student relationship, although more relaxed than a formal one. I need to get my act together. I'm a grown woman, for goodness' sake. Yet, I'm behaving like an immature teenager!

Normally I shared everything with Ali, but this time, for some reason, I couldn't bring myself to talk to her about what was going on in my head. I knew Ali would be sensible. I could hear her telling me to get over it and have a cold shower. The words made me smile. My mind was flitting about so much, I nearly walked past the art room. Walking into the room, I was beginning to feel nervous. This lesson was with the upper sixth, which meant I would see Josh again. There was a feeling of what Mum always referred to as butterflies beginning in my stomach. I needed to calm down.

Because I was so engrossed in my thoughts, I didn't notice Josh working in his cubicle. Instead, a few other students rushed into the room, busy chatting and generally being the lively bunch. "Morning, miss, morning all," Gemma shouted. There were replies from different parts of the room as the students all greeted each other. "Morning, Gemma. Hiya. Hi, babes."

I grabbed my teaching notes from my bag, looked around, but meeting Josh's gaze, I quickly looked away. "Right, you lot. So, today is the last session before your practical exam starting on 10 June for three days. You need to finish your commentaries and supporting written work. I can give you feedback to get it completed if I receive it by Friday. Are you listening?" I said, giving extra emphasis to the last three words. There were mumbled replies and nods from the students who were listening.

Later during the lesson, I moved around the room talking to each student, aware it would soon be Josh's turn. When I got to his cubicle, he was busy working on his exam prep and hadn't heard me arrive. There was a look of surprise on his face when he saw me standing next to him. I was excited to tell him the good news – I had managed to find a local business owner who would provide the metal he needed for his project. But then I completely embarrassed myself with a joke, which generally I would have managed easily. There was something going on between us. Even when I leaned forwards to look at his drawing and my arm touched his, I instantly felt an electric shock run through my body. I pulled my arm away quickly, wondering if he'd felt it too. It was obvious the atmosphere between us had changed. Neither of us could keep eye contact for any length of time. As hard as it was, I managed to keep my professional teaching head engaged and gave Josh the feedback he needed for his work, before talking to Steven.

Poor Steven didn't get my full attention for the first few minutes at all. I was trying to calm myself, wondering if I looked as flustered as I had felt while talking to Josh. Steven was asking me a question about his plan. "Do you think that would work, miss?"

Annoyed that I hadn't heard, I had to ask him to repeat his question, with the excuse that I wanted to make sure I'd understood what he had meant. Steven, seemingly oblivious that I wasn't giving him my full attention, was happy to ask me again.

Talking to Gemma was like talking to the younger sister I'd never had. She was so excited and pleased with her plans and the concept she had decided on. I had been surprised when Gemma had chosen to link her work to the idea of 'dance and movement'. Mainly because it was something that Gemma didn't seem interested in at all. Nevertheless, she had decided on her theme and organised visits to the dance lessons, where she had chosen a dancer from year ten as her muse. Although drawing wasn't her best skill, Gemma was still better than most and had done some very decent sketches of the dancer. She captured her movements well. Gemma intended to incorporate photography, her drawings, and some sculptures within her exam work.

I had a soft spot for Gemma. We shared the loss of a mother, but for different reasons. My mother had died when I was ten through illness, whereas Gemma's mum, Heidi, had walked out on her when Gemma was a toddler. Gemma's dad, Jed, had done his best in rearing his only child and had supported her as much as possible. However, he left her to her own devices much of the time, which probably was why she was such a free spirit.

When I first met Gemma, after a slightly rocky start, we had started to talk, soon recognising we had common ground. Over these last two years of the sixth form, Gemma had become aware that, in me, she always had someone she could turn to for support, particularly when it came to her passion and chosen career path.

Drawing the lesson to a close, I gathered everyone around my desk. "I'm very pleased with how well you've all got on with this. You have taken a completely individual approach to the theme, so I'm excited to see what you do during the practical exam. I won't be able to help at all at that point, so if any of you have questions about anything, you need to ask me before then. I'll read through all your commentaries to see if I can make any suggestions to improve them. Although you have to make the changes – I can't write it for you, Josh, Sam." I glanced over to the two students, who both hated the writing aspect of the exam, trying not to make eye contact with Josh. It was easy, as I also included Sam, so I could direct my comment to him when speaking. Not looking at anyone in particular, I continued, "I'll see you all on 10 June. Please spend the next two weeks finishing any preparations you have and keep those creative thoughts flowing in your heads. You guys are going to smash it!"

As they were packing away, I asked, "Has anyone got time to help me move some heavy stuff in the storeroom?"

"I'll help, miss, no problem." It was Josh.

My heart missed a beat. Wishing that anyone else had answered, I could only say, "Thanks, Josh."

The rest of the group left, shouting their goodbyes, and I walked into the storeroom, followed by Josh.

The stacked packs of acrylic paint and other materials that had arrived took up a lot of space. In the state I was in, I had to take care not to trip over them. I turned around to smile at Josh, ready to tell him what needed to go where and on which shelves. He was much closer than I had expected and had shut the door behind him, which I hadn't even heard. Then, without warning, he leaned towards me and kissed me full on the lips.

"Josh, what…?"

I pulled away in surprise, but before I could respond further, he pulled me back towards him, kissing me again, his arms holding me closer. I tried to draw away despite the softness of his lips and his body gently pushing against mine. I knew I should stop, but I couldn't. I yielded to his warmth, holding him against me. What had started as a gentle kiss was becoming more passionate. I could feel the excitement rushing through my veins. This didn't feel like kissing a boy – a man was kissing me. My brain and logic were fighting a battle with my body's reactions. Although I wasn't fighting very hard and, however much I knew it was wrong, I wanted more.

We almost fell from where we had been standing in the middle of the room to a place where I was leaning. My back was against the shelves, with Josh pushing against me, much closer than before. I could feel every shape of his body beneath his clothes. First, he had started kissing my neck. Then, holding one of my breasts, he leaned down to kiss the part of my flesh exposed above my blouse. We were both breathing heavily, and I could feel a rising ache between my thighs as his muscular body pressed against me.

"Rhi, are you ready for lunch?"

Our moment of passion was rudely interrupted. It was Ali. Panicking, I pushed Josh away and put my finger to my lips, signalling him to be quiet. Then, madly trying to calm my breathing, and scared that Ali might come into the storeroom, I shouted back, hoping not to sound as flustered as I felt, "Hang on, I'll be out in a minute. Just sorting some stuff on the shelves."

"Do you want me to come and help?" Ali immediately replied.

"No! No, no, it's fine. You can't get in until I've moved some stuff. Anyway, I'll be out in a sec."

Josh was smiling at me – his eyes were laughing. He didn't seem at all fazed by the whole event. He gave me a gentle kiss and, without making a sound, moved back across the storeroom, standing behind the door so that Ali wouldn't see him when I opened it. I smoothed down my skirt, checked I'd fully buttoned my blouse, and ran my fingers through my hair, so it wasn't so dishevelled. Smiling at Josh, I walked out of the storeroom.

"Wow, what were you doing in there? You look a right mess," Ali commented. Unfortunately, it seemed I hadn't managed to tidy myself up as well as I would have liked.

"Moving that stuff around in there is hot work," I answered, trying to sound casual, as though nothing had happened or I hadn't been in a passionate clinch with a student for the last 'however many' minutes.

I was desperately hoping Ali hadn't noticed how flushed I was and wouldn't question me further. I felt guilty, so surely, I must look it? Evidently not, as Ali started chattering on about what had happened during her morning before asking me how I felt about the readiness of my exam group. As head of department, Ali also had practical exams to organise over the next few weeks. In her case, the students had performance-focused exams. Either she or Megan, her second in the department, had to accompany several of the students on the piano. In addition, they had to rehearse with each student – an extra activity that had to be timetabled on top of standard teaching time.

By the time we reached the dining hall for lunch, I had visibly calmed down, although my mind was racing. My head was full of questions. What if someone saw Josh follow me into the storeroom, but only me coming out? What if he hadn't tidied himself up before leaving the room? What if his friends had put him up to a dare, or it was some way for him to prove himself? Would he tell other people? I put down my knife and fork, stopping eating. Suddenly I felt sick.

"What's wrong – you look pale?" Ali looked at me.

"Nothing, I'm just not hungry. I don't really fancy it. I'll catch up with you later, OK?" I got up and walked away while Ali was still speaking to me, leaving my half-finished meal on the table. Ali must have noticed I hadn't even cleared away the tray. Ironically, usually I was the first to remind people to take their dirty plates to the serving hatch.

I almost ran towards the creative art block. People were a blur, and I wasn't even sure I was going in the right direction. I kept waiting for someone to pass comment or to hear some of the older lads sniggering or giving me knowing looks. Nobody did anything out of the ordinary. Maybe I was panicking too much and blowing it all out of proportion?

When I got to the art room, I walked back into the storeroom and shut the door. I was surprised. Before leaving, Josh had cleared away all the paints and other art materials that he had supposedly come to help me move. I couldn't believe that he'd had the presence of mind to tidy up. I made myself a cup of coffee and sat down. Shutting my eyes, I recalled the feeling of Josh's lips on mine and sighed deeply. The memory was –

the only words I could think of were deliciously sexy. But I knew that as a teacher, I should have pushed him away and remonstrated with him. How could I have been so stupid? Everything was upside down – what was I doing?

CHAPTER 6

RHI

Following the storeroom incident, I found it hard to settle to anything for the remainder of the day. During lessons, my mind kept wandering. I felt tense, waiting for a comment or someone to start nudging their mate and whispering when I walked past. It hadn't happened. Not yet. But still, there was plenty of time. While I was pretty certain Josh wasn't the kind of lad to spread rumours, what if he couldn't help it? What if he let it slip to a mate that he'd 'snogged' Miss Dobbs? I felt sick even thinking about what could happen.

As my teaching day finished, I felt great relief. Then, I knew I'd be able to spend time alone in the art room, tidying up, and preparing for the next day's lessons. Keeping busy would be the best thing.

Ali popped her head around the door, just as I had finished and was about to leave. "Are you feeling better?" she asked.

"Yeah, sorry about lunchtime. I think I must have eaten something last night that didn't agree with me."

"That's OK. I just stopped off on my way to rehearse with some of my exam people – I wanted to make sure you're all right. See you in the morning."

As soon as I got home, I opened all the windows to let some air into the cottage. Immediately, my black cat, Tibbs, jumped in through one of the open windows and started rubbing himself against my legs.

I picked him up and snuggled him in my arms. "What have you been up to today? I bet your day wasn't as interesting as mine?" Not unexpectedly, he didn't answer, so I continued tickling him under the chin. Instead, Tibbs purred his answer, and after a while, jumped out of my arms, padding off towards the kitchen. It was his way of telling me he was ready for food. Following him, I got a tin of his favourite cat food out of the cupboard and prepared it. Meanwhile, he padded backwards and forwards impatiently at my feet, meowing noisily. He soon quietened when the dish was placed in front of him.

"That'll keep you quiet," I said, tickling his ears. But Tibbs wasn't interested – he was too busy devouring his feast.

I went upstairs to change out of my school work-clothes and returned wearing shorts, a T-shirt, and flip-flops ready for the beach. I opened the front door for Tibbs, who was sitting waiting to exit, licking his lips to ensure he hadn't missed one single morsel of his meal. Then, I noticed a large bunch of flowers sitting in the porch. I certainly hadn't seen them when I arrived home. I leaned out of the front door to see if anyone was there. Not a soul was in sight. Picking them up, I noted that as usual there was no message attached or anything to say who they were from. I hadn't been able to find out where or who they were coming from, never having caught anyone delivering them. My secret admirer's identity was a puzzle. It seems I'm doing well for admirers this week.

I had a sudden memory of the softness of Josh's lips on mine. Automatically, I touched my fingers to my lips. Carrying the flowers into the kitchen, I put them in the only vase I owned. At least it got a lot of use these days. I thought of Aunt Jinny and smiled, remembering how she had always had flowers around the cottage when I came to stay with her. Even in winter months, she had still managed to find something floral to display. I preferred my flowers outside in the ground where they belonged, so never bought them for myself. Since moving into the cottage, I hadn't needed to. Besides, my secret admirer was supplying me with flowers almost regularly.

It was on summer days like these that I was grateful to Aunt Jinny for leaving me the cottage in her will. Grabbing my sunglasses, notepad, and a pen, I walked out of the front door. Tibbs and I both headed off across the garden towards the cliff path. The sky was a brilliant blue, with a few fluffy clouds here and there. A gentle breeze blew, occasionally catching the wildflowers, making them nod back and forth as though in welcome as I passed. Tibbs had quickly disappeared and I couldn't see him anywhere.

For a cottage, it was quite an imposing house. Over the years, Aunt Jinny had extended what had been the original cottage into a more spacious dwelling. When visitors drove to the property from the road, it looked even more imposing. The gravel pathway stopped short of the front garden, from where you had a sea view, and the fields leading down towards the cliffs to the west. Aunt Jinny had married late in life, and after moving away ensured that whatever happened the cottage would belong to 'her Rhi'. She had wanted to guarantee that no one else could get their hands on it. For a few years after her marriage, Aunt Jinny had often returned for short holidays. I had always tried to be there at the same time as her, even when I'd been studying in Cheltenham. In my childhood, I had visited regularly and the visits continued into my teenage years. Now, this was my home. I felt blessed.

The cottage had a small garden to the front, enclosed by a low wall, with the gate I had just come through to enter the field. Halfway across the field, I turned to my right as I heard something rustling in the hedgerow. Expecting to see someone on the other side, I was surprised when Tibbs sprang from the hedge, landing in front of me. He also appeared spooked. It was almost as though someone had thrown him, but there wasn't anybody there. The cat was perfectly all right and began moving in and out of my legs, purring loudly enough to wake the dead – well, at least a dead mouse!

"I thought you'd gone off hunting?" I bent down and tickled him under the chin. As if he understood, he looked up and, rolling over, offered his tummy to receive the same treatment. With little reluctance, I acquiesced, and he began purring even louder than before. I needed to make a move. "Come on, I've got some planning to do. I can't keep you happy all day."

Tibbs rolled over back onto his feet and decided to follow. Together, we reached the corner of the field where the cliff path started to meander down to the beach below. I turned to Tibbs and gave him a last tickle behind the ears. I knew he wouldn't follow me. He was already lying on his back, rubbing himself among the grasses.

I walked down to the beach, found my favourite spot, and sat down, leaning against the rocks ready to start work on my planning. It was fairly quiet – only a few locals walking their dogs. It was going to be a few more weeks before the holidaymakers started arriving. Even then, Whittingbury Bay didn't get as packed as the town of Whittingbury. After a while, I looked down at my notepad. It was still empty. I couldn't focus. I needed to concentrate, but I couldn't. What was I going to do about Josh? How was I going to deal with it? I shut my eyes and started to plot my actions.

Then, waking suddenly, I felt chilly. I'd fallen asleep, which is not what I'd intended. As I stood up, I thought I noticed movement to my left. I turned to see who it was. There wasn't anyone there. Perhaps I'd imagined it while I was still partly asleep. I'm getting paranoid. First, more flowers, then a leaping cat, and now I'm imagining people watching me! Before leaving the beach, I had another quick look around, but couldn't see anyone. On my walk back to the cottage, I decided how I was going to handle the Josh situation. I felt a small weight lifted – at least for now.

The next morning, when I arrived at school, I went to the main office to find out where Josh would be during period three while I was free. Mrs Pevensey, the school secretary, was trying her hardest to find out why I needed to know about Josh Campbell. She was particularly nosey and loved to know what was going on around the school. Of course, Mrs Pevensey said she could have one of the 'runners' deliver any message. The runners' job was to deliver messages and collect students required by other members of staff. Thanking her, I pointed out that I needed to explain things personally. Eventually, the inquisitive woman seemed satisfied and gave me Josh's whereabouts for the period in question. As I walked away, I thought dealing with Mrs Pevensey was probably like trying to get travel permission from the Kremlin!

Period three arrived. I walked briskly to the room where Josh would be and then instantly felt nervous. As I stood at the door of the classroom, I suddenly lost all of my resolve. I was about to walk away when Mr Watts saw me through the little square window in the door. To my horror, he signalled at me to enter. I hovered partly outside and inside the doorway. Without letting my gaze wander, I looked straight at Mr Watts and asked if I could please have a quick word with Josh Campbell.

"Hope you've not been up to anything of an ill-nature, Mr Campbell?" Mr Watts always did like to be dramatic.

"Thank you, Mr Watts." I wished the floor would swallow me up there and then as every eye in the classroom was directed towards me.

As Josh appeared at the doorway, I'd already started walking away. "Can you just come with me for a few minutes, please, Josh?"

I knew that room 4D was free, so walked inside, Josh following me. Without turning around, I told him to sit down. Hearing the chair legs scraping on the floor, I knew he had, so felt I could turn around to look at him. I was shaking so much I was finding it hard to breathe and wondered if I'd be able to speak. Shutting my eyes, I inhaled and exhaled slowly and evenly. "Josh, the other day..."

Josh interrupted me. "I'm sorry, Rhi, I shouldn't have kissed you. I..." He paused and we both looked at each other hesitantly. "I couldn't help myself. I'll be leaving school soon and I needed you to know how I feel. I didn't expect you to return my kiss." And he looked into my eyes with a look that seared my heart.

"Josh, I shouldn't have kissed you back." Now I paused, before quietly adding, "But I couldn't help myself either." Josh was looking relieved. A huge smile appeared on his face and he looked as though he might move towards me. "But I'm your teacher, Josh. I can't do this. I'm supposed to be sensible, and responsible. I'm sorry, but we need to stay away from each other. And I don't want your exams to suffer because of something stupid that I've done."

Josh remained seated as we kept staring into each other's eyes. Finally, he replied, "I don't care that you're my teacher and I think it would be very irresponsible if we didn't see each other again. I need to get through my exams knowing I can see you again afterwards. What do you think? Can you give me something to look forward to?"

I was shocked. He was almost blackmailing me. Inside my head, I was saying, 'yes, yes, yes to everything. I don't care that I'm your teacher. I want you.' Instead, I answered as calmly as I could. "Let's wait and see. I need you to concentrate on your exams, Josh. Please. Don't let me ruin your chances of going to college. I care for you a great deal. So, please just think about work for now."

Josh was nodding slowly. "OK, for now." He smiled at me and all I wanted to do was kiss him and tell him how I really felt.

"You'd better go back to Mr Watts. Tell him we were planning the pick-up of your metal from Barnstaple." As I walked past Josh, he touched my hand and an electric shock went through my body. I rushed from the room, running down the corridor to get away from him. I managed to get back to my storeroom before breaking down and sobbing.

Despite my feelings, I got through the rest of the week with very little contact with Josh. I hadn't seen him around school that often either. On the occasion where I would have met with Josh, I had persuaded Mark, my assistant, into driving him to Barnstaple during lunchtime to collect the metal he had been promised for his exams. They had to take the school minibus. Therefore, it was easy to explain that Mark needed to go instead of me. I didn't drive the minibus, so Josh wasn't even aware that I had tried to avoid him.

Later in the day, I was leaving the art room when I met Jon, the drama teacher. I was surprised to see him at the art end of the corridor. He only normally visited when we had meetings or joint projects. "Hi, Jon."

As though he had read my mind, he said, "I was just taking a shortcut."

I was wondering where his shortcut was taking him, because once outside the end of the building he was headed towards, there was a dead end.

He continued speaking. "Thank God, it's Friday. I'm looking forward to my weekend."

"Are you doing anything?"

"Not sure yet. I've been invited to a barbecue on Saturday night, but don't know if I'll go. What are you up to?"

He wasn't usually interested in what I was doing. The way he had worded his question made it sound like an invitation to the barbecue, rather than a generic question about my weekend. I was sure I'd misheard him. "I'm out with Ali tonight and she's staying over, so we'll probably do something tomorrow. We'll see what happens. Have a good one then, bye." I smiled and walked under his arm, as he held the door open for me. I don't know what made me turn around, but when I did, he was still standing, watching me walk across the playground. I gave him a wave, feeling stupid having done so. It was a bit odd altogether, as Jon normally never gave me the time of day. And when he did talk to me, it was usually with a hint of sarcasm.

Arriving home, Tibbs, who, as usual, was waiting at the front door, ran up to greet me, meowing. I had too much clutter in my arms to stop and stroke him. "You only want me because you want to be fed! I know your game. Come on then." He trotted into the cottage, heading straight for the kitchen. Once I'd fed Tibbs, I went up to have a shower, and get changed before Ali turned up. The warm water was refreshing after my long day and it gave me time to mull over the day's events. With my eyes shut and the water running over me, I thought about Josh's eyes when he almost begged to see me again after the exams. It had struck me more deeply than I had realised. I felt cruel telling him I didn't want to see him, but I knew it was the right thing to do. However, a tiny voice inside my head was telling me that once the exams were over, we could, and probably would, see each other. After all, he'd be finishing school in a few weeks anyway, so what harm was there?

I was brought back to the present with a jolt as I heard a sound downstairs. I turned the water down so that I could hear better. Standing naked in the shower, I felt vulnerable. I remained quiet and still, listening carefully, but heard nothing else. Turning the water back on, I thought it must have been Tibbs knocking something over with his tail. Who could get into the cottage anyway? Continuing my shower, I then thought back to the odd conversation with Jon. It was rare to see him at the art end of the building, but then thinking about it, I had seen him a few times recently, seemingly hanging around for no reason. Weird.

When I finally got out of the shower there was a shout from downstairs. Ali had let herself in and had just arrived. "Put the kettle on. I'll be down in a sec," I yelled.

"Don't you want something a bit stronger?" she yelled back up.

"Later. I need coffee now."

I went into my bedroom and grabbed a blouse and clean pair of jeans from the wardrobe. I laid them neatly on the bed, along with the shoes and bag I was going to wear. Opening the drawers, I was madly searching for a scarf to take, just in case it turned cold later. Wearing a scarf always warmed me up. But I couldn't find it and began to lose my patience. So much so, I started throwing things out in case it had got tangled up with something else. In the end, I was so annoyed I gave up. Donning my summer dressing gown, I went downstairs for what was now a much-needed coffee.

Ali was waiting in the kitchen, hugging me before picking up her drink. Before leaving the kitchen, I had a good look around to see if the cat had knocked something over. Sure enough, unusually for him he'd knocked a pan from the work surface. At least I'd found the source of my fright. I felt a little easier. I followed Ali into the lounge where Tibbs was stretched out on the sofa. We scooched him up and joined him, though not stretching out quite as much as he. The three of us looked very relaxed together. Ali's phone rang, breaking the mood. So she went into the kitchen to take the call, leaving me drinking my coffee, and idly stroking Tibbs, who was revelling in the attention.

Ali broke my reverie. "Rhi, Rhi!" I was miles away and didn't respond. "Hey, Goggle Eyes."

"What did you just call me?"

"You heard!" We both laughed as we remembered the large round glasses that I had worn for a few years as a teenager.

"So, where were you off to in your head?" Ali asked.

"Nowhere important." I remembered Ali had a call. "Was the call important?"

"No, it was just Mum reminding me to get something for my brother's birthday."

"Which one?"

"Dan, he's thirty."

"Oh, getting on then."

"Yeah. Stop changing the subject. What were you so engrossed in?" she asked.

"Nothing, really."

"Mm, like I believe you. Anyway, as I was going to say before I was interrupted by the phone," Ali continued. "Tonight – you and me – the Plough. Speed-dating, remember?"

"Really? Do we have to?" I was looking forward to going out but wasn't that keen on the idea of speed-dating.

"Yes! You've got to do something to stop this mooning around. It's time you found a man you can stick with." I pulled a face. "No arguments, Goggle Eyes. Right, what have we got for tea?"

"Watch it! I have something quick we could put in the microwave."

After going back into the kitchen, we sorted out the food and opened a bottle of wine. While we were eating, I told Ali about my scare while I was showering, when all along it had been the cat!

She was surprised. "Why would you think someone was in the cottage?"

"Well, you know I keep getting those flowers delivered? I'm still getting them, and they are left inside the porch, so must be delivered by hand, yet I never see who by."

"That's odd, but not a reason to think someone's in the cottage."

"I know, but then I've been losing things recently. My scarf has gone – you know the one I often wear just to keep my neck warm. I've lost a diary, and some underwear went missing when I hung the washing out the other week. And I've felt I was being watched a few times when I've been down on the beach."

"Mmm. That is weird," Ali replied, looking genuinely worried. "You need to make sure all your locks are good and you shut the windows when you're out, and maybe when you're upstairs. Have you told the police?"

I gave her a look, before answering, "It didn't help much last time did it."

"That's true. But don't start thinking this is the same – it's probably just all a coincidence."

"Yeah, I know, I don't want to start getting paranoid."

We sat eating in silence for a while, and then to lighten the subject, Ali said, "So, when are you going to tell me who it is that you've got the hots for?"

Feeling as though I was blushing slightly, I changed the subject, saying, "Hey, look at the time. I'd better get dressed and get some make-up on. Otherwise, we'll be late for the 'cattle auction'."

"Ha, ha. You'll enjoy it when we get there."

CHAPTER 7

BEN

Ben looked in the mirror and smiled to himself. He wasn't bad looking really – some would say quite handsome. He was tall, slim, and had a good head of dark brown hair. A full head of hair was, according to his mum, an important attribute where women were concerned. What he was lacking though was an air of confidence, which his mum never failed to remind him.

As he walked out of his room, he bumped into Pam, arriving for her night care duty for his mum. "You look very smart tonight, Ben. Going somewhere nice?"

"Just going to try out a new pub for a meal," he said, shutting the door and rushing out before she could say anything more.

He was pleased she had noticed because he had taken great care in his choice of clothes. This was a special occasion and he wanted to look good. Ben had chosen a very different look to his normal jeans and hoodie. As he drove to town, he was certainly looking tidier than usual, wearing a pair of smart jeans and a colourful shirt under his casual jacket. He slipped his hand into his pocket, reminding himself that Rhi's scarf was there like a talisman helping him on his way.

Ben was nervous about the dating idea as his only date after leaving school had been a complete disaster! Having attended an all-boys private school, he had missed out on the normal exchanges of teenage life

56

and found he had no conversation. At least, not one that would make a connection with Anne, the student he had taken out. She was a film fan and loved music, but he couldn't talk about either subject. He had not heard any of the music she liked or seen any of the films. They had spent most of the evening in silence, trying to avoid each other's eyes. She had made her exit during a bogus visit to the ladies' room, leaving Ben sitting alone with his curry and glass of beer.

Tonight, as he strode towards the Plough from the car park, anyone noticing him would have told you, 'Here was a man on a mission.' He was going to the event for one reason only – to meet Rhi. After his previous near meeting, he was feeling confident that when he sat in front of her, she would remember him. He had never forgotten her smile or how kind she had been. She would be happy to see him and they would be able to see each other regularly. Then, after a reasonable time of dating, they would be together and neither of them would have to take part in this type of charade again.

Walking into the bar, he quickly scanned the room until he spotted her. She and Ali, her scatty friend, were busy chatting to the barman. Rhi was still wearing jeans, but this time, because of the better weather, a soft flowery top, which Ben thought suited her well. She had high heels on too. He realised he had never considered how tall she was. That was something he hadn't remembered. He was nearly six foot, so he thought he would probably be about the right height for her.

Suddenly, he was accosted by one of the organisers, Teresa, who wanted to check his registration and give him a name badge. She also took payment for the event and explained how the evening would work. Ben was listening only partially. "The ladies remain at their tables and you move from one to the next. You have about eight minutes for your 'date'. We also give you scorecards. Then, when the date ends you have a short time to fill them in before moving on to the next woman. You hand your scorecards in at the end and then we can help you contact anyone you'd like to meet for a second date. You…"

"I'm sorry, can you repeat the bit about the scorecards. I missed that bit?" Ben interrupted, not liking what he heard.

The organiser repeated, before finishing the sentence that Ben had interrupted. "You are not allowed to exchange contact details during the evening."

"OK, thank you." Ben felt disappointed, but he told himself when Rhi and he eventually talked, she'd be happy to meet up later. After considering the situation carefully, he wasn't worried. He attached his name badge, put his scorecard in his pocket, and went to the bar to get a drink. Rhi and Ali were no longer there. While the barman got his order, he looked around, seeing them sitting on two tables next to each other, a row apart.

The room was noisy as the participants for the date night arrived and started chatting and drinking. Ben worried if he would be able to hear if everyone was chatting at the same time. At the allotted hour for the event to begin, a bell rang and Teresa gathered everyone together, and yet again began explaining the rules of engagement. With scorecards and pencils in their hands, the men jostled to get near to the girl they fancied and quickly chose their seats. A few guys, who looked more uncertain than Ben did, stood in the middle of the room looking lost.

Not wanting to make his intentions clear too soon, Ben sat down opposite a dark-haired girl who was four tables in front of his target, Rhi. The girl, Jenny, was pretty in an old-fashioned way. Her voice was extremely quiet, so he had to lean in to hear what she was saying with all of the noise around them. To each of her questions, he mostly answered with one-syllable replies. He was trying to listen to her, but if he was honest, he wasn't concentrating on her at all. He felt a little mean because she seemed a nice girl, but he was watching his intended prize.

He thought, 'Eight minutes at each table, which means thirty-two more torturous minutes before I reach her.' The bell rang for the end of the first date and before Jenny could say anything more, he moved on. He wrote a cross on his scorecard and assumed that Jenny probably wrote the same on hers after his lack of attention. Ben didn't really care what the other women thought of him.

The next eight minutes passed in much the same way. The girl asked all the questions and he replied in his monosyllabic, disinterested tone.

This girl, Tracy, was far more assertive than Jenny and even had a list of questions she wanted to ask. Ben thought some of her questions were too personal. One was, "Do you want children?"

It elicited a more than one-word response, "I haven't ever considered it."

She continued her third degree, until eventually she asked, "Do you actually want to be here?"

"No, not really. At least, not with you."

"Well, you rude bugger! I don't know why you bothered. You're just wasting my time." But before he could reply the bell rang yet again. One step nearer.

His next date was a short, dark-haired girl called Amulya. She looked slightly exotic and he found himself staring at her eyes. He also had to ask her to repeat her name, as he hadn't come across it before. She began by telling him that her family had come to Britain from India, but that she was born here. She finished her short family history by asking, "Have you ever been to India?"

"Er, no. I've only ever been to Spain with my parents – in the past," Ben replied.

"Don't you like travelling?"

He was a little slow in answering. Having a sudden memory of the Spanish holidays his parents had taken him on as a child and later as a teen. They always stayed in beautiful villas, always with a pool. He remembered the hot lazy days and the fun the three of them had together. He looked up, to see Amulya waiting patiently for his reply, smiling encouragingly. "I've not been able to over the last couple of years. My mother has been ill, so I can't leave her for too long." He was suddenly aware that he was talking quite easily to this girl. She had a gentle way of asking her questions.

"I'm sorry to…" The bell rang, interrupting what appeared to be an apologetic reply.

He moved on again. Only one more person and then he'd be talking to Rhi. He felt a sudden quiver of nervous excitement in his chest. As he'd watched her during the evening, she had chatted to other dates, but he hadn't seen any real interest in her responses. When *he* sat down in front of her, she'd smile at him – he knew it.

The blonde in front of him was asking him something. "Do you like kittens?"

"Not particularly."

"Well, I just love them. Their cute little noses and ears," and she shut her eyes, "and when they purr." She stopped to take a quick breath and with her eyes still shut and her shoulders scrunched up around her ears she began to purr! He glared at her in horror. She was oblivious to his derisive stare and continued to ramble on about the joys of kittens, without taking any breaths whatsoever.

Ben was losing his patience. He had thought this would be a good idea – a way to meet Rhi. He hadn't considered how long it would take to reach her. Thank Christ, only a few more moments of this 'cat lady' bimbo with her dyed blonde hair and weird eyebrows that are about to join her hairline. Only a few moments more and I'll be sitting in front of Rhi.

As if answering his thoughts, the bell rang, and as he stood, a gang of young lads rushed into the bar, bumping into everyone and everything. They made such a racket that everybody turned to see what the rumpus was about. He also glanced at them, but when he turned back to take his seat in front of Rhi, his prize was gone. Panicking, he looked around the room in desperation. Neither she nor her friend was anywhere to be seen. Completely deflated and with a growing emptiness that was turning into anger, he forced his way through the heaving crowd to the door, bumping and knocking into people. Teresa yelled after him to leave his scorecard. But that was the last thing he was worried about.

Running outside, he looked anxiously up and down the street, but they had disappeared. At least outside in the car park, he could breathe, but he felt crushed. Yet again, he had failed. He had been so near and now it all seemed such a waste. He reached into his pocket and breathed in Rhi's scent from her scarf. With a heavy heart, he got into his car and drove home, feeling the complete failure that his mother had always told him he was.

CHAPTER 8

RHI

As the bell rang for the fourth time, Ali stood up and grabbed me by the arm. "We're going to the ladies' – grab your coat and bag."

Holding on to my hand, she led the way through the pub crowd, as we walked quickly to the toilets. Once inside, Ali said, "I don't know about you, but I've had enough. Let's just go. There's a back entrance – they'll never notice. What d'you think?"

"Yeah, that's fine by me." In truth, I certainly wasn't bothered either way. So, a few minutes later, we walked out of the back door of the Plough and along the High Street to 1745, the cocktail bar. It was always busy and a good venue for meeting people.

The two bouncers on the door smiled and let us in. I always found it amusing that Whittingbury pubs and clubs needed bouncers. It was a necessity I had come to expect in larger towns, but not here. Then, on reflection, I suppose you could have troublemakers anywhere. Inside, 1745 was small and dark. The walls were painted a deep purple with black leather seating set against the walls. Placed in front were glass-top tables and gold chairs. Above the wall seats were gold-edged mirrors. The lighting was subtle, supposedly to suggest an atmosphere somewhere classier than it was or looked in broad daylight. To be fair, the place was popular, although when we entered it was still relatively early for a Friday night and quieter than usual.

We ordered four cocktails, two espresso martinis, and two margaritas, as there was a 'buy two for one' offer. "Here's to a better night," said Ali, clinking her glass against mine. "I could *not* believe the duds that were there tonight. What were yours like?"

"OK," I answered, not having listened properly to the question.

"What do you mean OK? They were so boring. I had one guy who was going on and on about his Mini Classic. In the end, I told him I was surprised that he was bragging about it. He didn't even get the joke!"

I heard that comment and started to giggle. "You didn't say that did you?"

"Yeah, I mean why not? He was so dull. I needed to get some enjoyment from my date. So, what were your guys like?" she asked again.

"I wasn't impressed by any of them. There was one called Christophe. At least, I think that's what he said. He was quite good-looking but didn't have much conversation."

"I don't think any of them had a conversation. That's probably why they were there. Oh, well, it was a bit of fun, but I couldn't have stuck it out all night. There's got to be a better way to meet men. Well, decent men."

"I suppose so." Unfortunately, I'd lost interest in the conversation again and was daydreaming.

"Hey, Earth calling Rhi! Did you notice the tall guy who was going to be your next date when we left? I'm sure I've seen him before but can't work out where."

"No, not really. To be honest, my mind wasn't concentrating that much on the guys. You're right, though, like you said earlier, they were a load of duds!"

We settled back down to our drinks, with Ali all the while scanning the bar to see if there was any talent present. Two guys did join us later and we had a good laugh, although I wasn't that interested in Jack, even though he seemed keen on me. Ali had already swapped numbers with his mate, Mitchel, who was just her type – sporty and fit.

Much later that night, we almost fell through the front door of Starfish Cottage. Once inside, we both flopped down onto the large sofa in a heap. We were glad we had taken a taxi to and from town because we knew that neither of us would have been in any fit state to drive. Ali was staying over, which she often did when we had a night out together. She even had her own room waiting for her. Kicking her shoes off, Ali said, between hiccups, which she had been trying to get rid of for the last five minutes, "Oh my God, what a night."

I hit her hard and suddenly on the back – the shock tactic for hiccups. It worked for about a second until she hiccupped again. We both burst out laughing, which meant I suddenly had to rush to the loo. When I came back, Ali had already found a bottle of wine, opened it, and was one glass ahead. "What a night, indeed," I said, collapsing onto the sofa beside her. I had left my shoes somewhere between the loo and the sofa.

Ali poured me another drink. "I know. There were so many nerds and duds there. Where did they all came from?" It was a rhetorical question, and she wasn't expecting an answer.

"At least you managed to get a date, Ali. Do you know when you're seeing him?"

"Probably tomorrow night. He's sent me a text."

"Wow, he's keen."

"We'll see. All he probably wants is to get into my knickers." Ali smirked.

"Like that's not what you want. You have no morals, whatsoever," I retorted. But at the back of my mind, I was aware my morals were far worse.

After a few more glasses of wine, which was my Dutch courage, I felt ready to tell Ali about my encounter with Josh in the storeroom. I felt nervous, which was stupid because she was my best friend. We had been through a lot together over the years. However, this was different. I knew that this time Ali would have every right to tell me I was being an idiot. I also knew she wouldn't mince her words. Ali wasn't one for keeping her views to herself.

Tentatively I began, "Ali, you know the other day when I was in the storeroom, and you came to get me for lunch?"

63

Laughing, she answered, "Yeah, and you looked like you'd been wrestling a bear."

I managed to laugh, too. Feeling a little more relaxed and being fuelled by the wine, I continued, "Well, you know you always say I go for the wrong guy?" I paused. "Er, this time, I have and he's way off the mark."

"Oh, God, it wasn't Mark, was it?"

"No! Do you mind? I've got better taste than dating my second in department! Anyway, he's creepy."

Ali was impatient. "Come on, out with it. Who?"

"Josh," I answered, very quietly.

"Josh who?"

"Josh Campbell."

Ali stared at me for what seemed like forever. "What? What the hell was going on?"

"He kissed me." Stupidly, I felt embarrassed telling Ali what had happened because I was guilty, and I shouldn't have enjoyed it. Before she could say anything else, I said, "I was hoping tonight might take my mind off him."

Completely ignoring my reply, all Ali was interested in was, "You didn't kiss him back, did you? You didn't encourage him?" I remained silent. Putting her drink down she said, "Please tell me you didn't, Rhi. Come on, you're not that stupid, are you?" And she stared at me, willing me to say 'no'.

"I've fancied him for weeks." I could see the shock on my best friend's face, as I continued. "I tried to push him away, but..." I shut my eyes, remembering again his lips on mine. "I couldn't help myself. I just wanted him."

The room was completely silent. Ali looked so stunned, it was as though I had just told her the world was about to end. On the other hand, I had surprised myself with my admission. I had said it out loud: I wanted him. I wanted him so badly my body ached every time I thought about him.

Suddenly, Ali stood up. "I'm sorry, but I'm going to bed. I can't cope with this right now. I don't know what to say. I'm going to talk to you in the morning when I'm sober. I just can't say anything helpful at the moment." At least she hugged me before leaving the room.

I sat alone on the sofa for a long time, partly wishing I hadn't told Ali. But I was also feeling a little relieved that I had been able to share my feelings with someone else. At last, I went up to my room, finally falling asleep on top of the bed, fully clothed.

Breakfast was a quiet affair, neither of us wanting to start the conversation about Josh. We both had slight hangovers from the night before, which meant we were being overly polite. "Would you like some toast?" I asked Ali.

"Yes, please. Would you like me to make some more coffee while you're doing that?"

"Yes, that'd be great."

Suddenly, she started laughing and pulled me towards her, to give me a hug. "We need to talk about the Josh situation and not pussy-foot around each other. You're my best friend. I'm not going to judge you. I was shocked last night and couldn't think what to say. I'm sorry."

I hugged her harder than I already was, feeling grateful that I had such a good friend. "Let's finish breakfast and go for a walk on the beach." Smiling at each other, we finished our breakfast-making tasks and sat down to eat. I also shared the weird conversation I'd had with Jon.

"I think he's fancied you for a while, so he probably was trying to ask you out. I'm surprised he didn't do a better job of it. He's never struck me as a man lacking confidence," said Ali.

"I know, the way he talks he has never appeared to be short of girlfriends."

"They all talk about that," Ali said, amid a splutter of toast and marmalade. Inelegantly, she wiped her mouth on the back of her hand, continuing with, "Perhaps you should take up his offer next time."

"If he asks again. He's not that unattractive." I paused, considering his attractiveness. "And I've always got on with him. He might take my mind off things for a bit."

We finished breakfast and went to the beach. The weather had been unsettled all week, but today it was warm. The tide was out, which meant we could walk along the beach to the most westerly end, up onto the cliff path, and back along the top of the cliffs to the cottage. It would take a good hour if we chatted as we walked, and, of course, it might take longer if we stopped at Whitend Café for coffee on the way. I often took this walk in search of inspiration for my artwork, to photograph or paint the changing sea and landscape around the area. But it was also a place I could escape to and think without the stresses of the modern world.

As we walked, I told Ali about the conversation I'd had with Josh a few days earlier, telling him we couldn't start a relationship as he had to concentrate on his exams. I left out the part when Josh almost begged me to see him after the exams. We both agreed that if Jon asked me out again, I would take him up on the offer. Deep down, I knew I didn't feel any attraction towards Jon but would go out with him if he asked – maybe just the once to see how I felt.

On our return to the cottage, there was another bunch of flowers, but this time with a typed, cryptic note attached. 'Sorry I missed you.'

CHAPTER 9

RHI

This week was the longest I had ever known. Walking around school, I felt on edge, waiting for someone to make a snide comment about Josh and me, and at the same time, hoping I would see him around the school. I knew I wouldn't, as he was on exam leave, along with the rest of the upper sixth. I had hoped I might catch a glimpse of him if he was in school for any of the other exams he was taking. As soon as I'd thought that I realised how selfish I was being. I remembered Josh's face when I had told him we couldn't see each other and that seeing me would probably have been as bad for him too.

I caught up with Ali in the canteen for lunch a day or two after her date with Mitchel. "What was he like then – did you get on?"

"It was a good night. He's quite sweet." Ali smiled to herself as she spoke.

"Sweet! When have you been attracted to 'sweet'?" I asked, surprised that she had made the word sound so positive.

Ali remained quiet, obviously remembering something. "He's just very thoughtful and gentle and funny."

"And? Is he good?" I looked around furtively to make sure there weren't any students too close. "You know..."

Again, Ali smiled, though this time with an even larger grin. "Oh yes. He is..."

I encouraged her. "Come on, details."

"You'll have to wait. I'm not sharing that here. Big ears and all that." We both laughed, looking around the canteen at everyone digging into their lunches. They were all making so much noise, I don't think they'd have heard anyway. But that really wasn't the point.

"So, you'll be seeing him again?"

"Yes, we're seeing each other tomorrow night."

I was pleased for Ali. It was early days, but her reaction to this guy was different than usual. Recently, she had just been having one-night stands before moving on. Maybe this was going to be the start of a relationship that would last a little longer.

"By the way," Ali added. "I won't be around this weekend either. We're spending time together. He's taking me to Bristol and says we might stay over."

"Ooh! Is he treating you?"

"Yep! He works for a big IT company, so he has a good job. It makes a change to meet someone with money. What are you doing at the weekend?" she asked.

I had just taken a large mouthful of salad but eventually managed to say, "Friday, I'm going on a date with Jon. You were right. He asked me out on Tuesday." I continued eating, trying to look blasé about it.

"I knew it! Mind you; I didn't think you'd go if he asked you."

"I didn't think I would either, but then decided I need to do something to take my mind off 'you know who'. It's only one date. It's not as if we're getting married!" I tried to sound casual about it, although I felt anything but comfortable when thinking about going out with Jon. As ridiculous as it was, I felt as though I was cheating on Josh.

Ali smiled. "We'll certainly have plenty to talk about next week then, won't we?"

Friday arrived. I had begun to feel nervous and wondered if I had made the right decision about going out with Jon. He was coming to pick me up around 7.30pm. We were going to a little bistro in Coombe, one of the villages on the outskirts of Whittingbury. After making several outfit changes, I was ready by 7.15pm. I had finally decided on a pretty blouse with jeans and a thin jacket in case it was cold inside the restaurant. I often found buildings were much cooler inside than outside during the summer and didn't want to be shivering. I wasn't sure if I wanted to give Jon a reason to get close to me – thinking he was probably the sort of guy to offer to keep me warm. Another reason for wearing my hair up – a little more business-like. It was a date, but a date on my terms. I'd already told Jon we were only going out as friends. I certainly didn't have any romantic feelings towards him.

When he'd asked me out, I had at least been honest with him. "I'm not looking for a relationship at the moment, Jon. And I'm not sure that it's good getting involved with people who you work with. However, a night out with a friend will be lovely, thank you." Jon had smiled, saying fine and that he was sure we'd have a good night together.

He arrived at 7.30 on the dot. There was a funny and awkward moment as I opened the front door, and Jon moved in for a kiss. I moved away, so he was left hanging, looking somewhat embarrassed. Then, regaining his composure, he said, "You look lovely and smell amazing. I love that perfume." Feeling awkward, I just smiled back in reply.

Once we got in his car, things settled down as we began talking about our day in school. It was a good thing we had that in common – at least we wouldn't be short of conversation.

The Bistro in Coombe was in an old building and felt very cool, so I was glad I had thought about the jacket. Inside, there were low beams, although it was larger than it appeared from the outside. Near the entrance was a bar with a seating area for people who just wanted to drop in for a quick drink; this led into the dining area. The décor was tasteful, with modern furnishings and fittings in contrast to the age of the building.

After perusing the menu for a while, we ordered before quietly sitting and drinking the wine Jon had chosen. While sipping our wine, I looked around the room, taking in who else was there. When I turned back, I caught Jon looking at me a little too intently – I found it a little disconcerting. Breaking the silence, I said, "I was surprised when you asked me out, Jon, as you've never been that interested in talking to me in the past."

He smiled back. "I've wanted to ask you out many times but couldn't pluck up the courage."

"Come on. I can't believe that. You're always talking about your girlfriends. You come across as quite 'the stud' when we're all chatting in the meetings." I laughed, trying to make it sound more of a compliment than it was.

Jon looked serious. "It's true. Yes, I have had a lot of girlfriends – I own up to that. But I've wanted to ask you out for ages, and it's taken me time to pluck up the courage."

"Why? I'm not that scary, am I?" Strangely I was intrigued. How could someone who had the confidence to ask loads of girls out fear asking me?

"I wasn't that bothered about the other girls," he replied.

I looked away, not knowing what to say, and again felt uncomfortable. Finally, Jon must have realised, explaining, "I'm not a stalker or anything. I just wanted to spend an evening with someone who I…" he seemed to struggle for the words, "I find interesting." At that moment, to my relief, the food arrived. We both dived hungrily into our food, and the silence between us resumed for a while.

After a long pause, I decided to try a more casual conversation, asking him about films. I thought that as a drama teacher, it must be something he was interested in. I was right. Once I'd started him off, he was in his element, chatting about the latest films he'd seen and what he thought of them. At least I had managed to steer the conversation away from me! By the time we had finished our dessert, we had both relaxed a little and were chatting with more ease.

Over coffee, we were talking about school when Jon suddenly leaned over the table. He pushed an escaped curl out of my eyes, saying, "I've often wanted to do that. I've watched you walking down the corridor during lesson changes. I love your curly hair – and I've noticed it often falls out of your clips. You wouldn't believe the times I've had to stop myself from putting it right for you."

The intimacy of his statement surprised me. Endeavouring to lighten the moment, I tried making a joke. "I thought you said you weren't a stalker?" I gave an uncomfortable laugh. For a split second, Jon stared back at me in silence with a look I could not interpret fully. Was it anger or disbelief?

"Hadn't you realised that I've always liked you? Since you first arrived at school, I've wanted to ask you out, but you always seemed out of my league. I was so pleased when you agreed to come out tonight."

Shocked by his admission, I replied, "Thank you, that's a real compliment, but not at all true." I paused to think of the right words before answering. "If you remember, when you asked me, I did say I would only come out with you as a friend. I'm not looking for a relationship right now."

"Why? Is there someone else? I could understand it if there was, but if you're not seeing anyone, why can't we just see each other? I'm sure I could change your mind about how you feel."

I looked around the dining room at the other tables where couples were leaning towards each other with the intimacy that lovers do. During the entire date, I gradually became more aware of how much he liked me – more than either Ali or I had considered. The last thing I wanted to do was to lead him on. How could I be interested in him? The only person in my head and heart, try as hard as I might to stop and push those feelings aside, was Josh. I was madly trying to think of something to say to let Jon down carefully. Finally, I said, "I'm sorry, Jon. I've had a lovely evening but as your friend. I don't want to take things further."

Looking deflated, he replied, "I'll just have to wait for you to change your mind."

The drive back to Whittingbury Bay was awkward. We hardly spoke, and I spent the journey looking out of the car window. Had we not had the previous conversation, I might have kissed him lightly on the cheek to thank him for the evening. Instead, I got out of the car, thanking him as I went and hearing him say under his breath, "I'd expected at least a kiss after spending all that money on you!" I pretended I hadn't heard.

I quickly walked to the cottage without responding, letting myself in, locking the door behind me. Hearing Jon's car drive away, I felt relieved and made myself a hot drink before going to bed. Settling down to my drink, which included an added shot of rum, I thought about the evening's events. Had it been any other weekend, I would have rung Ali as soon as I got home to update her on how it had gone. Instead, I started wondering why the men I met became too serious, too soon. Several had been overly attentive to the point of obsessiveness. Perhaps it wasn't the men; maybe it was me? Churning this over in my mind, I finished my nightcap and went upstairs to bed.

I woke the next morning from a vivid dream about Josh and Jon fighting over me, which seemed bizarre. Tibbs was waiting for his breakfast when I went downstairs. "Where were you last night? Out on the tiles, mouse-hunting?" I bent to tickle his ears. "I could have done with you to talk to." I put some food down for him and grabbed my camera before setting off for a walk along the beach.

Today was a little cooler than it had been the previous week. The blue sky was full of fluffy clouds, and I knew from experience they would be reflected in the wet sand. There was something magical about those reflections that had always fascinated me. I had started to build up a collection of images that I would either paint or sell as photographs. I knew how lucky I was to have this beautiful scenery literally on my doorstep. Someone waved to me from a distance, and I instantly recognised Doris, one of my elderly neighbours. Doris Hufkins' cottage stood several houses away from mine, where she lived alone with her little dog, Horace, a Scottie. I always thought that her surname should have been a character in a Beatrix Potter story. She was a small woman with a mass of thick white hair, which almost matched Horace's wiry coat. As much as I liked Doris, I didn't feel in the mood to talk today, so I gave a quick wave back and turned away in the opposite direction. Walking at a much quicker speed, I was soon out of Doris's sight.

In my solitude, I began photographing the wonderful cloud reflections in the virgin sand. Luckily, it seemed no one else had ventured out this way yet, so the sand looked pristine. The only patterns were the swirling ridges left by the waves, the odd flash of white where shells were wedged in the sand, and the imprint of the gulls' claws. I wandered along slowly, stopping to take pictures, changing angles and heights so I could capture a good range of images. Then I stood for a while, breathing in the fresh sea air and gazing around the bay.

Suddenly a flashing light caught my eye. I looked up towards the rocks where whatever was catching the sun was situated. The light disappeared, and not seeing anything out of the ordinary, I carried on along the beach. A few minutes later, out of the corner of my eye, I once again noticed a light glimmering. Somebody or something was definitely in the rocks, and I knew they had either binoculars or a camera. With determined strides, I began to walk in the direction of the flashes. As I was trying to walk firmly across the sand, I wondered who it was and why they watched me. As I got closer, I saw a man hurrying away and clambering over the rocks, but I wasn't close enough to see who he was.

"Hey, can I help you?" I shouted after him. I couldn't run fast enough, for as soon as I reached the softer sand, my feet sank deeper with each step. By the time I arrived at the rocks, he had gone. Whoever it was, they hadn't wanted to talk to me. But why? They didn't appear to want to hurt me as they could quite easily have approached me on the beach. But, I thought, he must know the beach because in a few hours it would be full of locals and the dedicated tourists who knew its location. He was either a local or a returning tourist. Plenty of people to choose from! I finished my walk but kept checking now and then that nobody was following me, at least as far as I could tell.

It was around 11am when I got back to the cottage, deciding to cook as I felt in need of comfort food. Even though it wasn't winter, I felt a chill. So, to keep my mind occupied with thoughts other than those about who was spying on me, I decided to cook cheese and potato pierogi for my lunch. I had always loved them and remembered my Polish grandmother cooking them for me. Sadly, Babushka D had died long ago but, still, I could recall the wonderful aromas of her cooking and how good she was at giving hugs.

I'd only seen Babushka D a few times when I was little. Strangely I had managed to say Babushka but had never managed to say my grandmother's surname. This was particularly odd, as it would have been my surname, too. However, Dad had changed his name by deed poll when he was twenty-one after realising that English people couldn't say it. So by the time he met and married my mum Megan, Stefan Dubkowiecki was Stefan Dobbs.

Megan Jones from the valleys of South Wales was relieved when Stefan revealed to her his birth name. She was keen, though, that any children they had would be taught about their Polish and Welsh history. Ensuring that she followed her advice, when I was small, her bedtime stories were a mixture of Welsh and Polish stories and folk tales. Stefan didn't seem as proud of his heritage as Megan was of her Welsh lineage, as I rarely heard Dad speak Polish. The only time I did was when he phoned relatives back in Poland. He travelled there for his mother's funeral, but Mum stayed at home with me, deciding I was too young to attend.

There was a delicious smell coming from the kitchen. The pierogi were ready. Pouring myself a glass of wine, I sat in the lounge listening to music while I ate. A combination of the wine, pierogi, and the fresh air from earlier in the morning made me sleepy. Soon, I had fallen asleep on the settee, waking sometime later.

Feeling wholly refreshed from my sleep, I went outside to my studio to download the images from the camera. One of the most amazing presents Aunt Jinny had ever given me, apart from the cottage itself, was to have the garage converted into a fully equipped art studio. It wasn't a huge space. It was slightly larger than the single garage it had been initially, with natural light pouring into the building through the large windows placed on two sides. There was an area of tables set out for teaching small groups of up to six, which I used when running my summer workshops, plus space for easels and, lastly, a desk for my computer. On the windowless walls, there were shelves housing paints and other art materials. There was space to display my artwork, too.

I spent the rest of the afternoon editing the images I'd taken that morning, deciding which I would use to create paintings and keep as photographs to sell. Finally, I locked up and walked across the drive to the cottage. There, on the porch, was another bouquet. How on earth had anyone got them there? I hadn't heard a thing while I had been working. If someone had come in from the road, I would have heard them walking over the gravel, but I had heard nothing. That could only mean they had walked up from the beach or the beach path, across the field and through my garden. I had no idea how long they had been there, but they had undoubtedly arrived when I had been working in the studio.

After going into the cottage, I put the flowers in water. As before, there was nothing on the flowers to say who they were from or which florist shop they were brought from. Absolutely nothing to trace! I wasn't worried about my safety – flowers are hardly dangerous. But I did feel extremely uneasy that someone was both watching me and being furtive about their existence. Then there were the objects that disappeared – my diary and my favourite scarf had gone missing. As none of these things was serious enough for me to report them to the police, I couldn't imagine they would be likely to take my flower stalker seriously.

CHAPTER 10

BEN

He needed to fit in when he walked into the bar, not be noticed or remembered. Ben had thought carefully about what to wear. His choice of clothing for the evening was dark jeans, a black T-shirt, and a black hoodie. He thought he wouldn't look too out of place with the tattooed metalheads he'd seen in the bar. In anyone else's eyes, even with the stubble and dark clothing, he didn't look particularly mean or threatening, which is how he saw the people in the Black Raven. However, he was still feeling a little nervous because the pub had a local reputation as one of the rougher venues in the area.

Pam, his mum's carer, seemed to be taking longer than usual to get her settled for the night, and he was ready to go out. He didn't want a conversation with her about where he was going or why he looked so rough. He had not shaved intentionally that day or the day before, so he had great stubble which, in his mind, made him look cooler than the normal Ben Brooks. Pam would have expected him to shave before leaving his room, let alone going out of the house. So, not wanting to disturb either of them, Ben crept out of his room while Pam was still busy upstairs. He left the house, shutting the door quietly, before setting off to the bus stop. He had decided against taking the car in case he had too much to drink. He didn't want the police to stop him for drink-driving.

Several months ago, he had seen two kids he immediately recognised as Rhi's pupils going into the Black Raven. He had been surprised then, because he'd seen them at Rhi's studio a few months earlier when he had been walking by her cottage in the hope of seeing her. The first time he saw them at the pub, he noted the time and evening, checking on that day and time the following week to see if they were there again.

When Ben arrived at the Black Raven, it was already beginning to fill with a noisy, jostling crowd despite being relatively early in the evening. He looked around to see if the two kids had arrived yet, but he couldn't see them. Entering the bar, Ben bought himself a drink. He found a dark corner where he could stand, hidden by the crowd of drinkers who were now squeezed into every inch of the room, and slowly sipped his beer. Between sips, he looked around. At one end of the bar, the musicians had set up their kit and were busy doing a last-minute sound check. As he glanced around, he saw the 'arty kids' arrive. The girl sat down at one of the few free tables while the boy went to the bar to get the drinks.

The band started. Many of the people around him were moving around in time to the beat, which meant he could only occasionally catch glimpses of the kids who were deep in conversation. At one point, the girl leaned across the table and slapped the boy on the head. He prodded his finger back at her. Then, after both taking a drink, they settled back into their conversation, laughing, and smiling. At one point, the boy bent forwards as if telling the girl a secret, and she, obviously surprised by his comment, looked visibly shocked. She leaned back towards him, waving her arms animatedly and talking excitedly, and ended up giving the boy a whack on the arm while keeping a giant smile on her face. Ben was intrigued about the conversation's content but couldn't hear a thing from where he was standing.

He noticed the boy was much more smartly dressed than most people around him, but he didn't seem fazed by it. He was wearing smart jeans, a floral shirt, and a casual leather jacket. Perhaps he wasn't going to stay? About half an hour into the evening, Ben's thoughts were proved correct. The boy got up and walked out, turning to say something to the girl as he left. She shouted after him, and he was gone. From where Ben was standing in his corner, the loud music and babble of voices drowned out any chance of him hearing what they had said.

Continuing to watch the girl, Ben built up the courage to go and chat with her. A few other guys had stopped to talk to her on their way by, but none of them stayed for long. The speed-dating had given Ben more confidence to approach a girl, and after the conversations that night, he thought that surely this couldn't be any worse. He moved from the shadows nearer to where she sat until, at last, he made his move. He had a plan. Walking past her on the way to the gents', he would find some context to talk to her on his return. As he passed, he noticed she was engrossed in texting someone on her phone. On the way back, he 'accidentally' bumped her table, knocking over the remains of her drink onto both her and the tabletop.

"Sorry." He hoped he did look sorry. "Can I get you a new drink?"

The girl glanced up with a look of frustration, but then her face softened. "OK. Yeah, a lager."

When he returned with the drink, she was still checking her phone. "You waiting for someone? I've noticed quite a few guys chat with you – is one of them your boyfriend?"

"No, on both counts."

"You on your own then?"

"Might be." She glanced up at him again. "You gonna sit down or what?"

Surprised at how easily she had invited him to join her, he sat down, taking a closer look at her. He'd seen her plenty of times with the 'arty boy' but had never really taken much notice. She was pretty in an excessive way. Everything about her was the complete opposite to him. She had a vibrancy about her – the pink hair, her clothes, jewellery, even her tattoos all shouted confidence. She was what his mother would have dismissed as 'alternative'. He had to agree, although his mother would have meant it negatively, and he found himself oddly fascinated by her. She didn't seem worried about him being older than her.

She finished her text and asked, "I've not noticed you here before, and I'm here most Fridays. You new in the area?"

"No, I've been in a few times," he lied.

"So, what's your name? I'm Gem."

"Er, Mike," he lied again, not knowing why he hadn't used his real name.

He usually found it hard to talk to women, but he had been right. The speed-dating had helped him, at least a little. He soon found himself responding and interacting with her conversation on this occasion, led by her easy manner. Surprisingly, she didn't seem to notice his lack of finesse. The fact that the music was so loud also helped. When there was a lull in their conversation, the live band covered it. Also, whenever the band played something she liked, she stopped talking and sat tapping her feet and nodding her head in time to the music. She was so engrossed. Luckily, she seemed unaware of how long he sat watching her. He hadn't met anyone like her before. At the end of one song, he asked, "Was that your boyfriend earlier then?" The drummer interrupted his question with a final ear-splitting cymbal crash.

"What?" She was shouting as the cymbal's reverberation ceased. He repeated his question.

"No, he's my best mate. Anyway, he's way too pretty for me!" She laughed, although she hadn't commented with any hint of complaint. It was more a statement of fact.

"What do you mean – is he gay then?"

She nearly choked on her drink and, when she could speak again, said, "Definitely not. Josh is on a hot date tonight."

She gave him a quick sideways glance. "You jealous then, do you fancy him?"

"Do I look gay?" he almost shouted at her and then relaxed when he realised that she was joking.

"Anyway," she continued, the effect of the alcohol beginning to kick in, "what are you interested in him for? You're here with me."

Knowing the answer before she replied, Ben asked, "Do you two often come here together?"

"Not both of us, no. I'm here more often than Josh. We're often each other's alibis."

Ben looked quizzical. "What?"

"For the parents! It's not like my dad doesn't give a shit; he does – he just doesn't know how to deal with me." Ben was still unsure what she meant. "Me being a girl and him a single dad. You know." Ben nodded, although he didn't know what she meant, but gathered that they both lied to their parents about their whereabouts.

The band had stopped for a break, so the only noise now in the pub was the loud chatting and laughter of everyone around them. Gem asked, "So, what do you do?"

"I'm a graphic designer." He had decided not to lie about his job. Being an artist might also allow him to turn the conversation to art. She looked genuinely interested when he said what he did.

"Wow, that makes a change. Most guys I meet in here are mechanics or work in offices and come here for a bit of excitement on a Friday night. I'm studying art too. I've got a place at Brighton Uni later this year, starting in September. I can't wait."

"Brilliant. What sort of art do you do?" Ben tried to mimic her enthusiasm.

"Sculpture is my thing."

"So, are you still at school at the moment?"

Gem laughed. "Just about to leave in a few weeks. The only thing I enjoy is art. I won't miss the rest."

Ben needed to be careful while wanting to get her talking more about school. "Is your teacher any good?" he asked.

"Yeah, Rhi is brilliant. I wouldn't be going to uni if it hadn't been for her." Gem smiled to herself as though she imagined something.

"Oh, why do you say that – what did she do?"

"She's just a great teacher, but also she's become like a friend and real support to me."

Just as Ben was beginning to hear what he had come here for, Gem picked up her glass, realising it was empty. She pretended to pull a sad face, and it dawned on him he had almost missed the cue to get another round. So, he decided against pursuing his questioning. Managing a smile, he asked, "You ready for another drink?"

"Yeah, one more, and then you can walk me home."

He walked to the bar, feeling more than a little panicky. The whole point of coming to the pub was to find out about Rhi from the two kids. He hadn't intended to spend the evening with one of them, let alone walk her home. It was a scenario he certainly hadn't considered. However, she was much easier to be with than he had imagined. Of course, Gem could never replace Rhi, but this was the first time he'd had a night out with a girl since his school days. And that one had been a complete disaster. He was beginning to relax. Although he had to push down the feeling that he was cheating on Rhi.

Returning from the bar, he put Gem's drink down in front of her and started up the conversation again as casually as he could, asking what sort of things they'd done during art lessons. Her reply couldn't have been more helpful if he'd given her a truth serum, as she started waxing lyrical about the amazing time that they'd had with Rhi, how she had taken a few of them under her wing, getting them ready for college. He listened intently, making a note of any information that might prove useful in the future.

By the time they left the pub, which was still packed to the rafters, Gem was pretty drunk and more than a little wobbly on her feet. They walked towards one of the older established estates near the edge of town. She led the way, turning into a poorly lit alleyway that ran between back gardens. While it wasn't completely dark, there was still the odd bit of light from the gardens they passed that had some lighting. Trees lined the alleyway, and in her tipsy state, Gem tripped over the uneven surface where a tree root had risen through the concrete. Ben grabbed her arm to stop her from falling. Unexpectedly, and with more strength than he anticipated, she pulled him into the darkness between the tree trunk and the garden fence.

Taken unawares, he fell against her. She began kissing him, but he tried to pull away. Then, pulling him closer to her body, and between kisses, she said, "Come on, Mike, you're up for it aren't you? That's why you agreed to walk me home, right?"

His mind couldn't cope. Gem didn't repulse him, but he certainly hadn't intended to kiss her, never mind anything else. Still clinging on to him, she pushed her tongue into his mouth. It was a completely new feeling to him, but it wasn't that unpleasant. Taking hold of one of his hands, she guided it up inside her crop top, and he felt her firm young breast cupped within it. Now his mind was racing. He was feeling hot and confused. He had never been this near to a girl's body before. He had certainly never touched one. Suddenly his body took control. Breathing heavily, he could feel himself getting aroused. His erection pushed against her body. In response, she was also breathing heavily, and he felt her nipple harden in his hand. At the same time, he felt her hand on his jeans, trying to undo the zip. At that moment, his breathing became short and quick, his whole body shook, and involuntarily, he groaned as he ejaculated. Instantly, he felt the sticky wetness in his crotch and quickly backed away from her. She tried to pull him back.

"Seriously! You might have waited until you got it up?" She laughed at him.

Something in his head screamed. He pushed her away, causing her to fall against the fence and slip downwards. Trying to pull himself together, control his anger, and push down his feeling of utter failure, he bent down to help her up off the floor. But to his horror, there was something wet and sticky around her head. It was blood! Lots of it. She had hit her head on the low brick wall at the bottom of the fence.

Standing up, he began to panic. "Oh, God help me, what have I done?" Then, almost immediately, he thought, 'No, it was her fault – she shouldn't have laughed at me.'

He was torn between taking responsibility and guilt, and panic built in him. If he called for an ambulance, they might think he'd attacked her, but if he left her, then...? While he was wondering what to do, he heard a dog bark – it sounded close.

That decided it for him. Leaving Gem lying on the floor, he ran off down the alleyway, trying to stay in the shadows. Behind him, he heard a dog barking and someone shouting for help. He made his way back towards the main road, crossed over to the other side, and walked back towards town. An ambulance, blue light flashing, sped past him towards the alleyway.

As Ben walked home, he felt shaken. He was trying to keep his breathing even to calm himself. He kept in the shadows as much as he could, hoping no one had seen him. At one point, when he was far enough away from the area and still checking nobody was watching, he took a tissue from his pocket. After trying to rub her blood from his hand, he pushed the soiled tissue into his pocket, reminding himself he needed to burn it when he got home. Up ahead, he could see the service station and realised how thirsty he was.

Before walking onto the forecourt, he rechecked his hands to ensure there wasn't any blood. They looked clean. He walked past the pumps, keeping his head low, and entered the shop. For a moment, he couldn't think where the water was, even though he stopped there regularly to buy petrol. Seeing the fridge, he walked over and grabbed a bottle of still water, then took it to the till. There wasn't anyone else in the shop, surprising him that he didn't have to go to the hatch to pay from outside. He decided they probably stayed open later at the weekends. Standing and waiting for the guy to come in from the back somewhere, he glanced around, furtively took a chocolate bar, and put it into his pocket. A moment later, the shop assistant came in. Ben paid for his water then left, feeling smug that he'd managed to get the chocolate for free.

Continuing to walk as casually as he could, Ben's mind raced with thoughts and questions about what had just happened with Gem. He felt more in control now. He had enjoyed talking to Gem but hadn't been expecting her sexual advances. Sex hadn't even entered his mind. Still, he kept remembering the feel of her body against him and how she had laughed at his inexperience. He thought he had only given her a slight shove. He hadn't meant to hurt her. By the time he was several streets away from home, his breathing was almost back to normal.

'She had started it. She had instigated the sex. If only she hadn't laughed.'

CHAPTER 11

RHI AND JOSH

Tonight, was the night. I was as nervous as I had been on my first-ever date! I poured myself a second glass of wine – all I could do was wait patiently. If that was possible. I thought back to the party the night before.

Initially, I had been angry with Ali for arranging the exam after-party, but when I saw her face drop, I knew she realised what she had done. On the day of the last exams for all of the arts subjects, which happened to be art, Ali had invited everyone on the spur of the moment. She was feeling proud of all the students for getting through their exams, and the relief of how we, their teachers, felt at having got them this far. I hadn't been pleased, because I had tried to keep apart from Josh and knew it would be difficult for us to be in the same room together. But how could I stay away? After all, there were other pupils in the group apart from him. I was proud of how hard they had all worked, so I wanted to celebrate with them. At least the party was only for a couple of hours and I wouldn't have to stay till the end.

The best thing about the party was that I had time to catch up with Gemma. We talked for ages about college and what she was going to do afterwards.

"I'm so excited!" Gemma had a habit of gesticulating with her hands when she wanted to emphasise something, which always made me smile. "I just can't wait to get away and start my own life." She paused, and surprisingly, because I had never seen Gemma cry or show any emotion outwardly, she had tears in her eyes. She continued, "But I'm worried about how Dad will get on without me on his own."

I stretched out, taking hold of her hand. "He'll be sad at first, but he'll get over it. His little girl is going off to follow the passion she loves. You must know how proud he is? How can he not be pleased? He's looked after you all these years and now you're following your dream. Besides, he's probably secretly looking forward to getting the house to himself – having some peace." I smiled at her. This last bit made Gemma smile, her tears fading as she had hugged me, thanking me for all of my help. We had continued to chat about where she was going to live and what her course would entail during the first year. She didn't appear to be nervous about anything. She was ready to embrace it all.

Apart from this long chat with Gemma, and a few conversations with Ali and some other students, I had tried to avoid Josh. However, every time I looked up he seemed to be there, hovering, waiting to talk. He looked so sad it pulled at my heart. Yet, each time I stopped myself from meeting his gaze and quickly found someone else to talk to. But it wasn't only Josh who I had been avoiding. I was also keeping well away from Jon. Luckily, he seemed far more engrossed talking to the girls from his drama group who were hanging on to his every word. In the end, I told Ali I was leaving to have an early night.

As I walked out of the arts block, I heard the door shut behind me, followed by the sound of footsteps. It was Josh. "You haven't spoken to me all night, apart from saying 'hello'. Are you trying to avoid me?" he asked, moving towards me.

I automatically put my hands up, gesturing for him to stay where he was. "We said we'd keep away from each other and..."

Josh interrupted, "Until the exams were over. They are! We're finished!"

We stood a little apart, looking at each other intently.

"I need to see you, Rhi."

Before answering, I glanced around quickly to see if anyone was close by. "Come over to the cottage tomorrow night, 8.30." And, turning,

I quickly walked away. I almost missed seeing Josh do a happy dance but happened to glance around.

And now the moment was here. It was Friday night, it was 8pm and I was already halfway through drinking my second glass of wine as I waited for Josh to arrive. I was beginning to wonder if I was doing the right thing. I'd never been out with anyone younger than me before – well, not this young. Did I honestly expect us to have a romantic evening? And, morally, what on earth was I doing? If anyone found out, I'd be in big trouble. I know it's technically not illegal because he is eighteen, but it's so wrong in every other way. I'm supposed to be the adult, acting in *loco parentis*. But, a parent certainly wouldn't be thinking about what was going through my mind! I had another sip of wine. What was I expecting to happen? I tried to be sensible. Whatever I was hoping for, I had to take control and keep things platonic.

I had done my best to keep away from him at the party, but all along I knew my whole being wanted him. When he had said my name, all my resolve for us to stay apart completely slipped away. Now, I was waiting for the boy and pupil that I was incredibly attracted to with the intensity of a schoolgirl crush. 'Don't we ever grow up?'

The doorbell rang, and I jumped. Walking towards the front door, I practised the slow breathing technique, trying to control my nerves and excitement.

Opening the front door, I was met with Josh's glorious smile. He looked good. He wasn't wearing the usual baggy weekend outfit I had often seen him in. He was wearing smart jeans, a floral shirt, plus a casual leather jacket. I ushered him into the lounge, following slowly. He stopped suddenly, turned, and kissed me full on the lips. He certainly wasn't wasting any time! Feeling both relieved and relaxed in my surroundings, and after two glasses of wine, I responded enthusiastically. Every part of my resolve to hold back was blown away. My emotions were leading me, not my brain. We eventually pulled apart, both breathless, as we came up for air and laughed.

Trying to lighten things, I asked, "Do you need a drink after that?"

"Yeah, go on. Have you got a lager?"

I walked into the kitchen to get the lager from the fridge. Josh followed, leaving his jacket in the lounge. "This is really nice. I haven't seen inside the cottage before, only the studio." Josh was looking around the room. "It's brilliant."

"I suppose you haven't. I'm lucky to have it. I love living here."

I handed him his drink. "You'll have to show me the upstairs, too." He smirked.

He walked over to me, took my glass from my hand, and pulled me close to him. My whole body relaxed, as if I was melting from within, when he started kissing me again. We were both breathing heavily and with each kiss our breaths became shorter. In between kisses, he managed to mumble, "You should take me upstairs now and show me your bedroom." Managing to prise myself away from his lips, I grabbed his hand and, pulling him after me, I led the way upstairs.

Once inside the bedroom, Josh continued kissing me and began to unbutton my top. Moving his attention from my lips, he ventured to my breasts that were somehow now free of my bra. I couldn't stop myself from quietly moaning as he began to lick my nipples. I wanted more. Pulling away from him, I couldn't get his clothes off him quickly enough, almost ripping his shirt in the process. I moved my hands over his taut, beautiful body. Looking deep into his eyes, as if asking for permission, I undid his jeans and slipped my hand inside. Feeling his hardness, I gasped. He removed his jeans, before pulling mine off. At last, entwined in our nakedness, we fell onto the bed. As he continued to kiss me, I felt his hand slip between my thighs and was surprised to hear myself moaning and breathing in short gasps as his fingers caressed me. I hadn't felt this level of desire for a long time. My body ached to feel him inside me, and when he eventually entered me, pushing hard into my body, I felt our joined excitement. At last, passion filled me completely.

Afterwards, unlike many of my previous boyfriends, Josh held me in his arms, continuing to kiss me. He looked directly into my eyes. "Thank you, that was amazing. I can't believe I'm here with you. You're so beautiful." He kissed me gently, tracing the shape of my face with his fingers. His face held the same look as mine – one of contentment.

"It was amazing, Josh. I wanted you so much, you have no idea. I'm sorry I didn't talk to you last night – I just couldn't."

He kissed me again. "It was odd not being able to talk to you, but I understood. I just needed to see you. The exams seemed to take forever, and it was mad not being able to see you. It doesn't matter now. We're here!" Josh held me close, as though he never wanted to let me go. Our bodies were still warm with the exertion of our first lovemaking. When Josh kissed me again, I could feel him becoming aroused. The second time we took our time, caressing each other so our lovemaking was slower, gentler, but no less intense.

Sometime later, we went downstairs to get some food. "I'm always hungry after sex," Josh said, as though it were something quite natural that happened every day.

Laughing, I asked, "It happens often then?"

Josh almost looked embarrassed. "No, but when I do have sex, it seems to make me hungry."

I began to prepare some food – cheese omelettes and coffee. I hadn't eaten much either. "At least I know I've not led you astray and taken your virginity." I smiled at him across the kitchen. "It was pretty obvious that wasn't your first time." It wasn't a question as such, but I was allowing him the option to comment further on his love life.

"I've had girls before. Anyway, how could you lead me astray? I made the first move, remember?"

"Mmm, the art cupboard. You know Ali nearly caught us? Can you imagine if she'd walked in?" I paused, as I finished cooking. "Seriously, I could lose my job over this." I handed Josh his omelette, and we sat down at the kitchen counter to eat. Tentatively, I said, "I was worried after that day that it might have been a dare you'd taken. I spent the rest of the day waiting for someone to pass a snide comment."

"Seriously? I thought you knew me better than that!" Josh looked hurt, and nearly spat out the bit of omelette he was eating.

"I'm sorry." Reaching across the counter, I touched his hand. "I was surprised and confused. You're my pupil. I'm not supposed to have the feelings for you that I do. Until that moment, I didn't know you felt the same. I hadn't even imagined that you would be interested in me." I paused, trying to find the right words and not wanting to sound too serious and frighten him away. "I was so happy and excited, but it had opened up a whole load of emotions I'd not allowed to surface for some time. I admit I found it hard to believe you wanted *me*." Josh was looking down at his plate. 'Oh God, I've ruined it,' I thought. 'I've come on too strong.' Inside, I was panicking. Out loud I said, "Sorry, was that too much?"

Josh finally looked up and smiled. "No, I suppose making my move was a bit sudden." Gently laughing, he continued, "I'd been thinking about you for weeks and knew I had to do something before the end of term. I hadn't thought about it from your point of view." He leaned across the counter to kiss me. "I would never do *anything* to get you in trouble."

Relieved, I sighed inwardly. I hadn't ruined things. We finished our past-midnight snack, then I took his hand and led him back upstairs. "Let's go get some sleep."

"That's not what I had in mind." Josh kissed me on my lips, then began moving down my neck. I knew we wouldn't be sleeping – well, not just yet.

When I woke, it was around 9am. Josh was asleep, so I lay looking at his body. Any uncertainty about the wrongness of us disappeared. This was a man lying next to me, not a boy. As if on cue, Josh opened his eyes and smiled.

"Breakfast?" I asked.

"Not yet," he said and he pulled me towards him.

We eventually dragged ourselves out of bed for breakfast. While eating, we talked about how we were going to keep our new relationship to ourselves. And, how important it was that we did, at least until the end of term. Sitting together, drinking another cup of coffee, with Tibbs sat between us enjoying an extra body keeping him warm, we were chatting about what we might do that morning.

Suddenly, Josh sat up abruptly, scaring Tibbs, who leapt off the sofa. "Oh, God! I can't stay. I'd almost forgotten, it's my nan's birthday. We're all going over this afternoon, so I need to get back." He leaned over and kissed me. "You know I want to stay, but I can't."

I tried not to look disappointed. "No, your nan is far more important. You need to go and celebrate with her. I hope she has a good birthday." I wanted to say, 'give me a ring and we can catch up later,' but didn't want to push things too far, too quickly.

As I watched him walk away from the house, a little voice in my head kept saying 'please, please turn and smile.' If he did, it was a good thing – maybe last night was more than just sex. At the last minute, just as he reached the road, Josh turned and smiled at me before disappearing to catch the bus home. My heart did a little somersault – I felt like a sixteen-year-old!

CHAPTER 12

THE MORNING AFTER

Staring out of the bus window at the passing houses, Josh was re-running last night in his mind. He took a long breath, to calm the excitement that passed through his body as he remembered the feel of Rhi's body against his. He couldn't believe it had finally happened. He could feel himself smiling and quickly looked around to see if anyone had noticed – he must have looked manic! He turned his phone back on. His mum had probably been trying to get in touch to see why he wasn't home yet. As soon as the phone came to life, it buzzed incessantly with the number of messages that had arrived while it had been switched off. 'Wow, they're angry,' he thought, looking at all the missed messages from both his parents.

He rang his mum, who was always more forgiving than his dad. "What's up, Mum?"

"Where have you been, Josh? We've been trying to get you since last night!" Before he had time to answer, she continued, "Love, I'm sorry, but Gemma's had a serious accident. You need to get home."

Josh felt sick. His happy mood disappeared in an instant. "What happened? Is she OK? I'm on the bus, I'll be home soon." He finished the call, looking out of the window to see where he was. Not far from home now, so he'd find out soon enough. 'Please be OK, Gemma.'

Josh's mind was working overtime. He couldn't think what had happened to Gemma. She was fine when he left her in the pub. Then he realised he would have to think of another lie to tell his parents about where he was. He had already lied, telling them he was staying at Gemma's. They would know that wasn't true. What a nightmare! He was silently praying that Gemma was going to be OK. She was his best friend – the person he turned to when he needed to talk and the closest friend he had ever had, even though she was a girl!

Finally reaching his stop, he ran towards the house, unaware of the police car parked a little way down the street. His mum hugged him as soon as he got in the house. "She's in a coma, and they can't say much else now. We can't do anything but wait. We've got to hope she'll pull through this." Sue looked at her son. She knew what Gemma meant to him, but also, she wanted to know where he had been last night. He certainly wasn't where he had said he was!

"Where's Dad?" Josh asked, feeling nervous about the reception he would get from him. Patrick hated lies, and he wouldn't be happy with Josh for lying about his whereabouts the night before, even when he knew how much Josh would be hurting from the news. Before any of them could say anything else, the front doorbell rang. Sue opened the door to find two men standing on the doorstep.

"Is Josh Campbell here? I'm Detective Jackson and this is Detective Owen." Both policemen showed their warrant cards.

Sue turned to look at Josh as he moved towards the door. Patrick suddenly appeared, placing himself between Josh and Detective Jackson. "Can I ask what you want with my son?"

"We'd just like him to come down to the station to answer a few questions about his whereabouts last night, sir."

Patrick paused for a minute, looking as though he was about to say something else. Seeming to change his mind, he nodded at the policeman. Turning to Josh he said, "I'll come with you." Patrick then grabbed his coat, kissed Sue, and said, "Don't worry, we'll soon get this sorted. I'm sure Josh can help them with anything they need to know."

When Ben arrived home after fleeing from the accident with Gemma, he was surprised to see lights on in the hallway. He didn't usually leave the hall lights on, but then he remembered that Pam hadn't left before him, so maybe she had forgotten to turn them off. As soon as he had opened the front door, he heard someone running down the stairs. It was Pam. "What's going on? Why are you still here?" he asked.

"Don't worry, but your mum took a turn for the worse. She wasn't too good when you left, but it's rare you have a night out, so I didn't want to worry you. Her condition has worsened over the last half hour, so I thought it best to call for an ambulance. They should be here at any minute. I was just about to call you." Pam looked at him closely. "Are you OK, Ben? I'm sure once she's in the hospital they'll be able to sort her out."

Ben was aware that he probably looked ruffled and worried, and although it wasn't about his mum, it was a good excuse for his appearance and he wouldn't have to give any explanations. "I'll get changed and help you with anything we need for the hospital."

In his room, Ben sat down. His legs were trembling. His adrenaline had kicked in, probably in shock from the incident with Gemma, and now this. He leaned forwards, putting his head in his hands – he felt like weeping. 'Pull yourself together, man.' He made himself stand up and get changed. In the bathroom, he splashed cold water over his face, washing his hands several times. He was worried there might still be blood on them.

The ambulance arrived, and together he and Pam followed in her car. They arrived at Whittingbury Hospital around twenty-five minutes later. By the time they arrived, the hospital staff were taking care of his mum. They told them they would come and tell them when she was settled. He thanked Pam and told her to go home – she had done more than was required of her already. Sitting in the waiting room, it occurred to him that Gemma might be somewhere else in the hospital. He wondered how she was doing. He knew that the dog-walker must have found her a few minutes after he had fled. Why hadn't he stayed? After all, it had been an accident; he hadn't meant her to slip. He hadn't borne her any malice – she had just embarrassed him. Maybe he should go and see if he could find out how she was doing. But there would be questions about why he hadn't stayed. So, he remained where he was.

93

Several coffees later, and in what seemed hours, a nurse finally came to fetch him and take him to his mum. She was in a room on her own, linked up to more machines than he was used to. He gasped involuntarily when he saw the tube helping her to breathe – how frail she looked in the hospital bed. She never looked this frail attached to the usual machines at home. He sat beside her gingerly, not wanting to wake her. Gently, he touched her hand.

"You can stay here as long as you like," said the nurse. "If there's any change, we'll know straight away, so don't worry. We can't do anything more now. We just have to see how she reacts to the medication."

Ben realised he hadn't asked what had happened to his mum, but he also knew it didn't really matter. He had never seen her look so grey and pale. There was nothing he could do. He suddenly felt an overwhelming weariness. He leaned forwards to put his arms on the bed, laid his head down, and without any more thought about Gemma, he fell asleep.

On arrival at the police station, the detectives took Josh through to an interview room, leaving Patrick striding backwards and forwards in the reception until he was told to take a seat by the duty sergeant, who also offered him a cup of tea.

"I don't want a cup of tea. I want to see my son – he's only eighteen!" Patrick replied.

"I'm sorry, Mr Campbell, but at eighteen he is legally an adult, so we can talk to him on his own. He's just helping us with our enquiries at the moment. Have a cup of tea or coffee if you prefer and sit and wait for him. We can tell him you're here waiting."

Patrick sat down, resigned to the situation, but still unhappy about it. Before moving here, he had lived in London for most of his life and he knew that the police always blamed black kids. His Josh was *not* the sort of kid to get in trouble!

His cup of tea arrived with, to his surprise, several biscuits. After a few sips, he calmed a little. Maybe here in the sticks, they weren't quite so prejudiced! He rang Sue to tell her what was happening, and she suggested he gave their solicitor a ring, which was not easy on a Saturday morning. She also told him she would get in touch with her mum to say they may not get over for her birthday. Patrick had forgotten about Lizzie's birthday. He knew she'd understand. She loved Josh – after all, he was her only grandson. He went outside to ring the solicitor, Geoff Bevan, but, as he thought, there was no one in the office at the weekend. He recalled a business friend contact who often played golf with Geoff, so he gave him a ring to see if he had Geoff's number. His hunch paid off, and he was soon explaining the situation to the solicitor, who agreed to come to the station.

Detective Owen, the younger of the two detectives, led Josh into the interview room and asked if he'd like a drink – water, tea, coffee? Completely dazed by the whole situation, he answered, "Coffee please." The detective sent the young constable who was standing by the door out of the room. Josh looked around. The room had a table with chairs on either side and a recording device on the table – exactly as he'd seen in movies and TV programmes. The other detective joined them in the room, carrying a folder, which he placed in front of him and Detective Owen.

"Why am I here?" Josh asked.

"Why do you think? You're a friend of Gemma, aren't you?" asked Detective Jackson.

"I don't know. Is she OK? I haven't seen her yet."

"She's in a coma," the detective replied.

Josh felt sick. What on earth had happened to her? She's got to be OK, she has just got to be. The constable brought Josh his coffee, and he drank quickly, despite it being too hot. He needed something to be real. He burnt his tongue.

The other detective, Owen, turned the recorder on and said who was in the room, the date, and the time. Jackson, the older detective, was in charge. Opening his folder, he started to ask questions, while Owen had his pen at the ready to take notes. "So, were you with Gemma last night?"

"Yes, at the beginning of the evening, we went to a pub earlier for a drink, and then I left around 8pm," Josh answered.

"Where did you go?"

"To meet someone. I had a date."

"Can you tell us who, so we know where you were when Gemma had her 'accident'?"

Josh looked up from his coffee in shock. "You can't think I hurt her. She's my best friend. I'd never do anything to hurt Gemma."

"Well, somehow she's ended up in the hospital with a fractured skull. She's had an emergency operation, but the doctors don't yet know the extent of her injuries, and whether or not she'll recover."

Josh's hand trembled so much he thought he was going to drop the cup. Placing it carefully on the table, he put his hand over his mouth to stop himself from making a sound. Inwardly, he gasped. He was trying to breathe and take in what the detective had told him.

"The thing is, the last text message on Gemma's phone was to you. It sounded angry. Was she jealous?" Jackson handed Gemma's phone over for him to read the text.

ARE YOU STILL WITH HER!!!

Josh put the phone down and smiled.

"Why are you smiling? Did you enjoy the fact that she was jealous? Is that why you went and found her later and argued with her?"

Josh's smile quickly faded, and he panicked. "No, of course not. I told you, we're best friends. She doesn't fancy me – it isn't like that between us. We're just friends." He shouted the last few words, to reiterate the fact. "She's the only person who knew who I was with."

Sarcastically, Detective Jackson said, "Of course she is, and we can't ask her."

Josh shut his eyes and, looking down, shook his head. He hated adult sarcasm at the best of times, and this certainly wasn't that.

"Detective Owen, tell Josh all the information we have about last night."

The younger detective opened the file and started to read the information. "Around 11.30pm last night the local hospital contacted us to inform us that a young girl had been brought in with serious head injuries. A dog-walker out for a late-night walk in the alley behind Poppyfield Avenue found her and immediately dialled 999. Her belongings were recovered from the scene, so we could contact her next of kin. We spoke to locals around the area to see if there were any witnesses. One witness said she saw a young couple embracing against the fence when she drew her curtains around 11pm. Later she heard someone running down the alley. She looked out of her window again, only to see him disappearing into the distance. The dog-walker arrived a few minutes later to discover the girl with head injuries."

Josh looked dumbfounded. "Do you honestly think I'd have left her there if I'd been with her? I keep telling you, she's my best friend." He paused. "I wasn't there."

"So, I'm asking you again. Where were you last night if you weren't with Gemma?"

There was a knock on the door, and the constable from earlier signalled to Detective Owen who, after talking to him, came back into the room. He whispered into the other detective's ear, turning off the recorder. "It seems your dad has got you a solicitor, Josh. He obviously thinks you need one. Stay here, and we'll bring him in to you." The constable stepped back into the room and guarded the door.

Josh felt all life draining from him. He covered his eyes, which were filling with tears. He didn't want them to see him cry. How could they think he could do anything to hurt Gemma!

The constable left as Geoff Bevan walked into the room and started to inform Josh about the procedure and what to expect next. From his questions, he elicited from Josh that he wasn't with Gemma and tried to persuade him to say where he was, but to no avail. Josh wasn't going to give up Rhi. He knew she would lose her job if he said he had spent the night with her. Around 2pm, three hours after he had been brought into the police station, Detective Jackson walked back into the room, asking Geoff Bevan to step outside. They both returned, looking serious.

"What's happened?" Josh asked, his concern growing at their grim expressions.

"We've just had news that Gemma has died, so now we are looking at a possible murder inquiry."

He looked hard at Josh, watching for a reaction. He got one. Josh breathed in hard, gasping for air as though someone had hit him in the stomach. His hand automatically covered his mouth to try to stifle the sound of his sobs. His solicitor put his hand on Josh's shoulder in an attempt to calm him.

Detective Jackson passed him a glass of water, which Josh drank gratefully. The detective was practising his kinder tactics. "Right, Josh, when you've calmed down, we'll get back to some questions again. Is that OK, Mr Bevan?" The solicitor nodded.

Detective Owen joined them and switched the recorder back on. Detective Jackson continued the questioning. "Josh, this is more serious now. We are potentially looking at a murder inquiry."

"I've told you; I didn't touch her. She's...she was my friend."

"I'm going to ask you one more time. Where were you last night around 11 to 11.30pm?"

Silence in the room.

"I was on a date."

Mr Bevan said, "It would be in your best interest to say who with, Josh."

More silence. Josh's mind was full to bursting with the terrible information he'd just been told. He was trying madly to remember the words he'd heard people say when they were being questioned on TV programmes. They suddenly popped into his head. "No comment." Geoff Bevan sighed.

"Right, my lad, I think a night in the cells will do you good, and we can see if forensics backs up your story or not. We'll see how you feel in the morning."

Josh looked dumbstruck. He had only ever been in a police station once before, and that was when he was working on a project at school in Islington. He'd never been arrested in his life!

"I'll go and tell your father the news, and I'll see you in the morning. You'll be all right, they'll look after you," said Geoff Bevan, as once again he put his hand on Josh's arm, his idea of a comforting gesture, then he walked out of the room. After telling Patrick the news, Geoff almost had to drag him out of the station, he was so angry. Patrick was also worried about telling Sue that their boy was in a police cell.

After Josh had been taken to a cell and given something to eat, a constable brought him a blanket and left him for the night. As soon as the cell door was locked, panic set in. Josh sat on the bed with his feet up, hugging his knees tight, as if they would keep him warm and stop him from shaking. He was innocent, but he also knew that giving away where he was would cause massive problems for Rhi. Eventually, he lay down to sleep, but try as hard as he might, he could not relax enough to fall into a state of unconsciousness.

Josh's mind kept going over everything. He was still trying to come to terms with the fact that Gemma was dead. He felt deep sadness and annoyance at being unable to see her. A numbness was invading his emotions. Anxiety joined the melee of feelings, and he began to wonder if he was doing the right thing. Maybe he should tell them where he had been, but then his subconscious mind told him not to be so selfish. Sleep wasn't easy to come by, as much to do with his whirling mind as the slamming of other cell doors when other people were locked up for the night. Many of them were drunk and shouting and swearing at the police. Josh had been too shocked to put up any resistance when he had been led to the cells. Now sleep was resisting him too, and he lay awake for what seemed hours.

The following morning at 8am, when Detective Owen started his shift, he put his head around the door of Jackson's office. "What time are we talking to Josh again, Steve?"

Detective Jackson looked up from typing, using the one-finger method of bashing the hell out of the computer keyboard. "Leave him to stew until later this morning."

It turned out to be nearly lunchtime before the constable collected Josh from his cell. He was beginning to think they'd forgotten him. Surely, forensics would have told them it wasn't him? So, why hadn't they let him go?

The constable led Josh into the interview room, where his solicitor Geoff Bevan was waiting, along with Detective Jackson, who again led the questioning. "We know where you were Friday night, Josh." Josh looked shocked, wondering how on earth they could know.

"You're a lucky young man. Rhi has been in to see us." Josh didn't know how to respond – he tried hard not to look surprised. What was she thinking? She'll lose her job! He looked down at his hands. In his confused state, he didn't know whether to cry or scream.

"You're punching way above your weight there, aren't you?" Jackson added, giving Geoff Bevan a knowing wink. Josh raised his eyes just in time to catch the look passing between the two older men. He felt sick. "Also," Jackson continued, with more than a hint of annoyance in his voice, "there was no evidence of your DNA found anywhere on Gemma. Therefore, you're in the clear, so I'm releasing you to your solicitor. But, before you go, I want you to think about the time you could have saved by saying where you were. You've wasted a lot of valuable police time and public money!" He glared at Josh. "Mr Bevan, can you take Josh to collect his belongings and see he gets home safely? Thank you." And Detective Jackson stormed out of the room.

After collecting Josh's phone, and other belongings, Geoff Bevan led a bewildered young man outside, straight into the arms of Patrick, who was waiting at the police station's entrance. Patrick pulled his son into his arms, holding him tightly as Josh, at last, began to sob, letting out the tears he had fought to keep back throughout the last twenty-four hours.

"Let's get you home to Mum."

CHAPTER 13

SATURDAY NIGHT, SUNDAY MORNING

After Josh left, I decided I'd go for a walk. The weather was bright, although not particularly warm, for a typical British summer. I grabbed my phone, made sure it was set to vibrate just in case Josh called, and dropped it into my pocket. I wouldn't hear it if there was a lot of noise from the waves breaking on the beach. I was hoping he might have time to call, even though he was at his nan's birthday party.

Later, returning from my walk, my mood was less buoyant. I felt let down that Josh hadn't rung me. I was hoping it was more than just sex for him – adding another notch to his belt. Was I right or wrong? Then, I berated myself. Why was I beating myself up? How could I be so stupid? I mean, why would a boy eight years younger than me want to be serious! I'm kidding myself if I think that. Despite the voice in my head, there were a few times when I couldn't resist picking up the phone ready to ring him, but in the end, I didn't dial. I didn't want to look desperate.

The doorbell rang. I glanced quickly at my watch, which said 5pm. I hurried downstairs, hoping more than anything it was Josh. Unexpectedly, it was Janice, the school's headteacher. "This is a surprise. Come in. Do you want a coffee or something stronger?"

Janice didn't appear her usual, calm self. She looked uncomfortable and upset. "Please. Yes, coffee's fine."

Busy, making the coffee, my mind was working overtime as I tried to work out why Janice had turned up. I glanced over to where she was sitting. "I don't usually see you at weekends. Is there a problem at school?" I was imagining all sorts of mishaps. Maybe there had been a break-in or a fire. I had no idea. What on earth would bring Janice around at 5pm on a Saturday? She had always been friendly to me, but we were never friends in the sense of seeing each other outside school hours, so there must be something going on.

As I sat down with the coffee, Janice said, "Brace yourself. I'm afraid I've got some bad news. I thought I'd come and tell you in person, rather than you hear it from the local news or when you get into school on Monday."

I panicked. "Has something happened to Ali?"

"No, no, Ali's fine. It's, erm, Gemma Smith. She had an accident last night. She died this afternoon."

Janice looked at my blank face. Had I heard correctly?

"I'm so sorry. I know she was a special pupil of yours."

I was grateful I had already put my mug down on the table. I was so shocked, I couldn't speak. It was as though someone had punched me in the stomach. All I could feel was a dull emptiness opening inside my chest. My eyes filled with tears. "Not Gemma," I whispered. "What, what happened?"

Janice continued, "The police aren't sure. Now, they are treating it as murder, and that's the next shocking thing." Janice stopped to take a deep breath. "I can't believe it of him, but they are holding Josh Campbell."

I went cold. My heart froze and I couldn't breathe. It took some time to regain my composure, and even then, all I could manage to say was, "What?"

"I know, it doesn't seem conceivable, does it? They were best friends, and I can't see any way that Josh would hurt Gemma, but he hasn't got an alibi for last night. And, he won't say where he was."

I thought I was going to throw up there and then. I knew Josh wasn't guilty, but I couldn't tell Janice why I knew. Not at this moment. My shock must have been obvious to her because she leaned forwards to put her hand on mine in a gesture of comfort.

"Have they got any proof it was Josh?" I was grasping at straws, hoping I wouldn't have to own up to knowing his whereabouts.

"No, they're still waiting for DNA results, but they are suspicious because he won't say where he was. Apparently, there is also a text from Gemma to Josh, which they think is damning." Janice drank her coffee, as we both sat in silence for a while.

"How did you hear?" I asked.

Looking awkward, Janice stood up to leave. "Mr Campbell rang me. I'm sorry, I need to go, but I wanted to bring you the news personally and prepare you for Monday. I've got to go round to see Gemma and Josh's form teachers. I'm holding an extra early staff meeting at 7.30 to talk about how we are going to handle the situation with the pupils. Many of the girls will be very emotional about this. I've got to go round to see the governors tomorrow for a meeting to talk about how to deal with the press, too." Janice let out a long sigh. She was finding all this too hard. She had never had to deal with anything like this in her whole career and was hoping this would be the first and last time.

I didn't move – I couldn't. As she left, Janice said, "Why don't you give Ali a ring? I rang her earlier, so she knows. I'm sure she'll come over."

"Yes, maybe," I whispered in a barely audible voice, sounding nothing like my own. Janice let herself out.

I remained where I was for some time, completely still. I couldn't move. I felt light-headed – my heart was racing. It was as though I couldn't breathe. I felt sick. I didn't even react when Tibbs brushed against my legs, meowing to be let out. Suddenly, I felt bile rushing upwards. Putting a hand over my mouth, I rushed to the toilet where I was violently sick. I retched for some time. Once my stomach settled, I went to the kitchen for a glass of water, which I drank in one go. Cleaning myself up, I refilled the glass, went back into the lounge, and rang Ali, asking her to come over.

Since Mitchel and Ali's romance, we hadn't seen much of each other, but Ali was still the person I could turn to for support. I was happy that things with Mitchel seemed to be going well for her. It was a long time since I'd seen her in a settled relationship, so it was wonderful to see her so happy. While I waited for her to arrive, I sat absently stroking and cuddling Tibbs, who still hadn't been fed, but appeared to know something was wrong with his human.

I kept thinking about Gemma and the life she was about to start. There was something so completely incomprehensible about death at such a young age. Gemma had her whole life ahead of her, and now all her dreams were gone in one short moment of what? I didn't even know how she had ended up with her head injury. I tried not to dwell on that too much. I couldn't bear the thought of Gemma trying to fight someone off and the fear she must have felt.

I picked up the coffee I had made when Janice arrived, which by now was cold, yet I couldn't manage to get off the sofa to make myself a new one. All of my energy had suddenly left me. My thoughts turned to Josh as I imagined him in a cold police cell. I had no idea what a police cell would be like, but I had seen enough TV shows to visualise something grimmer than they probably were. Now, I understood why he hadn't rung me. On one hand, I was shocked he hadn't told the police where he was, but on the other, surely that proved our night together had meant something to him. Why else wouldn't he admit where he was? God! How can I be so selfish, thinking about myself after what's happened!

Lost in my thoughts, I didn't hear Ali arrive, so was surprised when she spoke. "Rhi, are you OK?" Then realising what a stupid question it was, she went on, "No, of course, you're not." Ali hugged me tightly, noticing how pale I was. "I'll make you a drink – you look as though you need one."

"Can I have another coffee? This one's gone cold."

After going into the kitchen, Ali made us both coffees, all the while glancing over at me. She probably thought I'd taken Gemma's death far harder than she had expected.

"What am I going to do, Ali? Gemma is dead and Josh arrested. I just can't…" My words trailed off.

"I know. I can't believe it either. Josh wouldn't hurt her. You've heard he won't tell the police where he was, which, of course, in their eyes makes him a suspect?"

"Yes, but he didn't hurt her."

Ali went quiet, obviously thinking about something. Quietly, while not wanting to ask the question, she asked me, "Rhi, why are you so certain Josh didn't hurt Gemma…? Tell me he wasn't with you?"

I didn't need to answer. She could tell by my face. "Oh, my God. Are you a complete idiot? No, don't answer that. What were you thinking? You do know you can lose your job if they find out?"

I sighed, shooting a look of exasperation at her. "What do you think I've been thinking about? I tried to keep away from him, but after the exams, when we had that party, it was torture for both of us. He followed me out when I left, and I told him to come round."

Ali looked mortified. After all, the party had been her idea.

I continued, "It's not just sex. It sounds stupid, but it feels right – us being together. We talked for hours, too."

"But he's a kid. A student. Whatever were you thinking?" Ali stared at me, then putting her arms around me, she pulled me towards her in a warm hug.

I clung to her as though fighting for my life and I started to cry loud, heaving sobs. Tears for Gemma, tears for Josh being locked up, for mistrusting him, and tears for myself. I had sabotaged my career. The career I had always dreamed of, was so proud of, and loved with every fibre of my being. I felt selfish, but I couldn't help crying for my loss, too. I knew Ali would be busy wondering where this was all going to lead. But still, she held me tightly, knowing there was little else she could do for now and it was what I needed most.

When I was able to control my sobs, I said, "He's virtually left school now, and I didn't think anyone needed to know. They wouldn't have if this awful tragedy hadn't happened." Ali nodded. It was true: there were only a couple of weeks left till the end of term, and we could have got away with it, even if we had carried on seeing each other. I continued, "How can they ever think that Josh hurt Gemma anyway?"

"You and I don't think he could, but the police don't know him. They're just looking for a suspect." Ali grabbed her phone. "I'm going to phone Mitchel and tell him I'm staying here with you tonight, OK?"

I nodded gratefully. I needed my friend, now more than ever. I certainly didn't want to be in the house alone. Even Tibbs' love wasn't enough to comfort me. Not tonight. I had a heartbreaking decision to make.

Going upstairs, Ali lay down next to me on the same bed on which Josh and I had earlier made love. She remained hugging me until I fell asleep, before creeping out to her bed in the spare room. In reality, I only slept for a short time. Most of the night, I lay awake deciding what I was going to do. I knew I needed to make the right decision. Not just for me, but Josh as well!

As soon as it was light, I got wearily out of bed, opening the bedroom curtains to weather that completely matched my mood. It was a dull day – both the sky and sea looked grey. It was not that unusual for a British summer, but a sunnier view might have made me feel better. The thought of Josh being locked up for something he hadn't done upset me most. I was grateful for him trying to protect me, but he wasn't doing himself any favours. I had to go to the police and tell them. Sadly, I knew exactly what that would mean for me. For the first time since Paul, I'd allowed myself to give in to my desires, and as such, I had ended up sabotaging my career. No one else was to blame. After all, I was supposed to be the adult in the situation, but I had behaved like some lovelorn teenager.

I went down to the kitchen, despite it still being early for a Sunday morning. Ali, still in her pyjamas, was already there, making coffee and toast. She pulled me towards her and gave me a big hug. "I heard you get up. You look like shit! Did you sleep at all?"

"Not much. I've spent all night thinking."

Ali put down a mug of coffee in front of me as I sat down at the kitchen bar. "About what?"

I saw Ali take a step back in her mind as she realised what a stupid question that was. Even she knew there was only one thing I would have been thinking about! "I'm going to the police."

"You're what? Are you mad? If you own up, you'll have to resign."

"I have to!" I took a deep breath, trying to control my emotions and push away the grief growing inside me at the thought of giving up the career I loved and had always wanted. "How can I not? I've broken the in *loco parentis* trust. I stepped over the line."

Ali looked at me in desperation. "But do you really want to ruin your career, Rhi?"

Tears started to seep from the corner of my eyes again, as I began to cry quietly. Ali put her arms around me, holding me until I had calmed down. Eventually, I answered Ali's last question. "I know it will, but I have to do it. I cannot ruin Josh's career before he's even started. He's already an amazing artist. He needs a chance at finding out what he can do. Besides, I do care for him. This isn't just some quick sex…" I stopped, searching for the word.

"Romp?" Ali suggested.

Despite everything, the silliness of the word made us laugh. "Exactly, it's more than that," I replied, desperately hoping I was right.

Although Ali offered to go along to the police station with me, I told her I'd rather go alone. Besides, Mitchel would be missing her. I knew Sunday was their day. They always spent it together no matter what else came along.

Walking into the police station, I felt more awkward than I'd ever felt in my whole life. It brought back too many memories of the situation with Paul. The reception was empty, apart from a uniformed policeman behind the desk. I asked him if I could talk to the person in charge of the Gemma Smith case. The policeman told me to take a seat, and he rang through to another office. I sat waiting in the reception area, watching the shadowy shapes of people moving behind the glass partition until eventually, someone appeared. He introduced himself as DI Johnson. Taking me into an interview room, he asked how I thought I could help. The interview room reminded me of an empty classroom, sadly in need of posters, class photos, and pupils to make it come alive.

"I think I may be able to help you," I began. "I'm a teacher at Whittingbury Academy. Josh Campbell's parents told the Academy that he won't say where he was on Friday night." I faltered, feeling embarrassed about the confession I was about to make. "Well, he was with me," adding, so that he fully understood how Josh was with me, "the entire night."

If Inspector Johnson was shocked or surprised, he showed no emotion whatsoever. "And what is your relationship to Josh Campbell?"

I took a long deep breath before answering, "I'm his art teacher."

This time the Inspector did look at me, just for a second, before continuing to write. I saw and felt all the disapproval and judgement in that one look and found myself flushing. "Can you prove he was with you?" he asked.

I was taken aback by this question. "Er, yes. I've not washed the bedding yet, so I'm sure there'll be his DNA. And I will have to resign my position as I have had sex with a student." With the hint of annoyance I was feeling, I asked, "Is that enough proof for you?"

It obviously was because the DI thanked me for my help and ended the interview.

During the interview, DI Johnson had taken notes as I had spoken. Once finished, he asked me to sign the declaration. As he showed me out of the room, his parting shot was, "We are releasing Josh Campbell today, as there was no match to any DNA on Miss Smith's body, so there was no proof he was ever there." Then smiling, he thanked me for coming, before seeing me out of the station.

I walked to my car in a trance. Sitting inside, I felt numb. What had I done? They were going to release Josh anyway. That smug bastard of a policeman! Perhaps I needn't have come to the police station after all. But...if I hadn't told them where he was, there would always have been a question mark over his innocence. People could imply he'd got away with it and that would stay with him his whole life. I breathed out slowly. No, I had done the right thing. I wanted Josh to be clear of all this.

After driving home, I went back to bed to try to catch up with the sleep I had lost the night before. It took a long while, but, eventually, I managed to drop off, waking up a few hours later feeling more refreshed.

My next job was to tell Janice I was resigning.

CHAPTER 14

SUNDAY AFTERNOON AND MONDAY

After a good sleep, I at least felt fresher. I gave Ali a ring to tell her how it had gone at the police station and thank her for her support. I explained to her that I would call Janice when I got off the phone with her and that I might see her tomorrow when I dropped into school to collect my belongings. This upset Ali more than I'd imagined, but once she'd calmed down, she offered to bring home anything I couldn't carry. I couldn't believe how relieved I felt knowing that Josh would be going home without a record hanging over his head. Below that, though, I had an underlying feeling of utter loss.

Suddenly I realised how hungry I was feeling. I'd only had a slice of toast to eat all day, so I shuffled into the kitchen to find some food. Tibbs appeared from nowhere, and I remembered I hadn't fed him either. Poor cat. On reflection, I wasn't sure he'd been fed last night either – given the desperate way he was gobbling his food, probably not!

As I prepared myself a sandwich, which was all I thought I could face, I started thinking about how I would break the news to Janice about what had happened. When I had arrived at the Academy four years ago, the head of department, Ralph Peterson, who was in his fifties, had become my mentor. He was exactly the sort of teacher I wanted to be – inspirational, always ready to listen to his pupils. As an artist, he was brilliant in his own right, always seeming to know how to encourage his students to get the best from them. When it came to discipline, he was fair but firm; never what you would have called strict. For example, with his sixth form students, he would allow them to play music in the background while they worked. Not so loud that you couldn't be heard when having conversations, but loud enough to add to the environment, helping them relax. He'd even managed to create an ethos where everyone valued each other's different musical taste – a remarkable feat indeed with teenagers of that age.

Ralph had a vision for the department, which I was glad I had been on the way to helping him achieve before his untimely death. When the head of department post was advertised, even though I was only at the end of my third teaching year, my boss, Janice, the head of Whittingbury Academy, encouraged me to apply. I remembered with pride the feedback Janice gave me after the interview. She told me that although I'd already been acting head of department, and it still hadn't been a foregone conclusion I would get the position, they wanted to offer me the post. They recognised I had a clear vision, ambition, skills, and knowledge to fulfil Ralph's shoes. I was so happy. Then she had said, "I know you'll make us proud and build the department into one of the best in the county."

Heading a department had been my dream, but I had thought it would be years until I could be in charge. I'd hardly expected it to happen so quickly, although the sadness of Ralph's death marred my gain.

Once I was in my role as head of the art department, and despite the educational cuts, Janice allowed me to set up two empty classrooms as a distinct workspace for the upper sixth art pupils. It had been part of Ralph's vision for the department, and so, The Peterson Art Hub became his legacy.

Each room was divided into six individual work hubs, which meant that every student could leave their work out in their space, ready to work on at any time. They could also display the work on the walls of their cubicle. In addition, there was a smaller space where the students could work at easels, either painting or sketching, and a supply cupboard and study for the staff. This way of working prepared the students for the type of working space they might encounter at art college, should any of them consider that career path.

A sharp pang of guilt hit me as my thoughts pulled me back to the present with a jolt, knowing I had let both Ralph and Janice down. I certainly wasn't going to be building the department any longer. A tear fell onto my hand, and I quickly wiped it away, trying hard to keep my emotions in check. I didn't want to cry anymore. I felt all-cried-out!

After eating, I was a little more fortified to talk to Janice. She took ages to answer the phone, nearly making me lose my resolve to speak to her before the morning. Then, just as I was about to stop the call, Janice answered.

I began talking straight away before I could change my mind and turn the phone off. "I'm sorry to ring you on a Sunday evening, Janice, but I need to give you some news. Please, can I come and see you first thing in the morning, before school and any of your meetings?"

She hesitated. "Yes. Though, can't it wait until later in the morning? First thing, I need to meet with the governors to work out what we're going to say to the school."

I could hear someone shouting impatiently in the background at Janice's end of the phone. I heard her yell back at whoever it was, "Hang on, I'll be down in a minute," before continuing to talk to me. "I'm sorry, Rhi, but I can't talk now – we're just going out. Jim's got a 'work do', which we can't miss."

I was silent for a moment, trying to find the best way to tell Janice that what I had to say would also impact the governors' meeting. I couldn't think of an easy way to have the conversation, so I said, "I'm sorry, but no. I need to talk to you before you speak to the governors. I'm so sorry, Janice. I don't want to hold you up, so I'll see you first thing. What time works for you?"

"It sounds ominous...how about 7.30?"

"See you then. Have a good night out." And I quickly switched my phone off, feeling a bit of a coward, but relieved that Janice was going out. I hadn't wanted to tell her the news over the phone. It felt disrespectful.

Going into my study, I pondered how to write my resignation letter.

'Study' was a grand title for the small, snug-like room to the right of the front door. It was where I worked on planning and those things that required concentration. I had decorated it with a minimum amount of fuss and detail, so that I wouldn't be easily distracted. I'd also situated the desk so that I sat with my back to the window. I knew had it been facing the seascape outside – I would never have got any work done.

Sitting down, I stared at my laptop. What could I say? There were so many things I wanted to write, but in the end, after a lot of procrastination, I decided to be as brief as possible. I would first explain to Janice, face to face, then hand her the letter, making it official. After printing the letter, getting it over and done with as quickly as possible, I signed it, placed it into an envelope, then dropped it into my bag, ready for the morning. Now I needed a drink, something stronger than coffee.

After going to the kitchen, I poured myself a large glass of wine, returned to the lounge area, then turned on the TV and sank onto the sofa. Tibbs ran across the room and jumped up beside me, rubbing his head against my arm to grab my attention. Absentmindedly I stroked his ear as he stretched out across my legs. We stayed like that for some time, the cat sleeping while I stared vacantly at the TV without noticing what I was watching. I couldn't settle to watch anything. My mind was too busy, asking too many questions but getting no answers. "Sitting here isn't doing either of us any good, Tibbs," I said to the cat. Gently pushing him off my knee, I went into the hall, grabbed my jacket, and walked out of the house. I thought maybe getting some air might blow a few thoughts free, helping me sort out the mess in my brain.

The light rain that had been around the previous night had gone. The skies had cleared a little compared to how they had remained for most of the day. Now there was a pink glow covering the horizon, and the waves were breaking gently on the shingle below. I walked along the cliff path, occasionally looking out to sea. I loved this view, but tonight, it was a good job that I knew the way well because my mind was anywhere but present. Those questions I had tried hard not to consider during the day would just not go away.

I loved my job, and the thought of losing it was devastating but it was my choice, I reminded myself. Would I ever be able to teach again? Possibly not in a school. What I had done was wrong in so many people's eyes that it would take a brave person to give me a job. So, what was I going to do without my job? That question wasn't a total panic in terms of earnings. I owned the cottage, so I only had to find enough money to pay the bills, run my car, and eat. I was confident I could cover that because I already ran workshops during the school holidays, which were quite profitable. So I could run more. But would I be able to earn enough? I could always buy a smaller car – the big one was only a status symbol, which in all honesty, I didn't need.

I stopped to remind myself that I would still be teaching, even when running workshops. The only problem was that the adults I worked with rarely had my young students' potential. Mind you; adults probably wouldn't care about why I had been forced to resign. Many of my clientele were women, with many returning each year. Knowing them quite well, I knew they would probably be playfully in awe, possibly wanting to pass smutty comments such as, 'go girl', and 'you cougar!' They certainly wouldn't be judgemental. At least, it would be an income for the time being. The thing that worried me most was what the other teachers would think. Would I lose their respect after what I'd done?

I stopped and stood staring out to sea. Listening to the sound of the waves, I allowed myself to relax. I couldn't help but slow my breathing to match their ebb and flow. The light had quickly begun to dim, and I turned back towards the cottage, feeling a little calmer. What would happen would happen. All I had to do was work hard to build a new career. Nothing big at all! As I walked back towards the cottage, the warmth of the lamps I'd left switched on glowed in the early dusk, and I smiled to myself, secure that it was my home.

Having spent the previous night with little sleep, I decided tonight I wouldn't go to bed late. While getting my things together for the morning, I heard someone knocking on the door. I felt a rush of excitement; maybe it was Josh. It wasn't. As I opened the door, Mr Campbell, his dad, stood in front of me, and my feeling of relief instantly disappeared. I had met Josh's dad a few times at parent–teacher evenings. He had always been very supportive of his son's love of art, which was a pleasing change to the often negative idea many dads had of the 'arts'. Today, though, Mr Campbell didn't even have a smile when I greeted him.

He silently followed me into the lounge. I decided against offering him a drink but did ask him to sit down. Neither of us spoke; the silence in the room was deafening. Eventually, not looking at me, his eyes focusing somewhere far behind me, Patrick Campbell said, "I don't know what you thought you were doing. My son is your pupil." The words hung in the air as I desperately thought of what I could say. There wasn't any appropriate answer that I could find. Finally, Patrick brought his gaze and focus back on me. "What on earth made you think it was OK to make a move on a boy?"

"Your son made the first move, Mr Campbell." As soon as the words were out of my mouth, I knew how childish they sounded. But it was the truth. He looked shocked, seeming to find it hard to reply. I continued, "That's not an excuse, but it takes two, and yes, I know I should have ignored him. In a few weeks, he's not going to be my pupil. We thought nobody would know. Besides, we love being together." I could see that my answers were falling on deaf ears.

It was apparent Patrick was trying to contain his anger, as he answered, "Maybe so, but you are the adult here. You should have turned him down gently, not led him on and certainly not had sex with him." Before I could reply, he continued, "As though it's not bad enough that he's just lost his best friend, he's now embroiled in this, this scandal with you, his teacher!" Patrick paused. I noticed his hands, which he clenched so tightly his knuckles had turned white. He exhaled loudly and relaxed his grip. "However, I want to thank you for going to the police and owning up that he was with you. I understand what that means for your career but…just keep away from him! I don't want you ruining his future."

"I don't intend to, Mr Campbell; that's why I went to the police. Josh is an amazing artist, and I too want him to be able to develop his career." I took a deep breath, trying to calm myself as I was beginning to get outwardly upset. "I promise not to get in contact with him, but if he contacts me, then I'm not going to turn him away. At eighteen, he's a man, and he can choose who he wants to see. I want him to do well. I care for him."

Patrick stood up. "Well! Thank goodness he's off to college soon. Then he can forget you and get on with his life. You just stay away from him!" And he walked out of the house, leaving me sitting in the echoing silence.

Early Monday morning, I woke to the sound of my alarm intruding into my chaotic dream. Not surprisingly, after Patrick Campbell's visit, I'd had a restless night. Now I had to prepare myself to face Janice and admit to what I had done. But I felt completely drained and not at all ready to face the day ahead.

As my car pulled up to the school gates, I was surprised to see a whole array of flowers, teddy bears, and letters stacked against the railings near the entrance. In retrospect, I shouldn't have been so shocked. Sadly, I had seen this numerous times on TV when young people had died. Yet, for some reason, I hadn't expected to see it here, and so soon. The other surprise was the presence of a few local photographers. When they saw my car drive into the school grounds, a couple of them ran towards me, but luckily, I managed to escape them. I wondered how on earth they could do their job, bothering people when they were at their lowest emotionally.

I made my way to Janice's office, feeling extremely nervous and sick to my stomach. This was going to be one of the worst things I'd ever had to do. The conversation with Janice was awful, even though she was more understanding than she needed to have been. After her initial shock, she had comforted me when I had broken down, almost reassuring me that I hadn't done anything illegal, as Josh was eighteen, but I had done something extremely inappropriate. The only thing Janice could do was to accept my resignation. However, she suggested that I wait until the first lesson started before collecting any of my stuff from the staff and art rooms. After making sure I had a coffee and some pastries, Janice settled me into one of the study rooms, telling Mrs Pevensey that no one was to bother me. She then went back to her office, ready for the governors' meeting and to inform them of the latest bad news.

I sat in the room, sipping my coffee, although I didn't feel like eating anything. I could hear the school coming to life. The noise of the teenagers as they walked, chattering along the corridors; doors slamming; the occasional raised voice of an adult shouting some indistinct direction – the usual busy life of a school, which I was going to miss. I almost couldn't bear sitting in that room, having to listen to the sounds I would soon no longer hear – all because of my selfish actions.

By 9am, everyone was in their first lesson. Quietly I opened the door to see if there was anyone around. Only Mrs Pevensey was in the office, who thankfully had her back to me, as I hurried past. Walking across to the art room, I saw the odd pupil, but no one from my art group, for which I was grateful. I couldn't have coped with their grief and my own.

Once in the art room, I looked around, taking in every space. Trying to etch the shapes, colours, and smells onto my mind. For the second time this morning, the real impact of what I was doing hit me. This had been my dream job, and I had thrown it away by one ill-considered act. But I had chosen to sleep with Josh – no one had made me, least of all him. I was the adult and could have said 'No.' I told my subconscious to 'shut up' and get on with collecting my most important things. There were certain objects and art paraphernalia that I knew I couldn't carry by myself, so I put them together all in one place in the storeroom. Ali would bring those back for me. I packed up as quickly as possible, not wanting to stay any longer than was needed; it was too painful. I didn't even want to wait until break time to see Ali; it would mean having to face my colleagues in the 'arts' department. I couldn't face them; not today, maybe in the future. Taking one last look, I walked out of the room.

I was almost out of the art block altogether when I saw Jon. He was making a beeline for me. Pushing his face closely into mine, he said, "So, you don't like to date people you work with? Huh! But it's OK to sleep with a student. You, you bitch!" The first part of the sentence had been almost a whispering hiss, but he'd shouted the last word.

I looked around, horrified, to see if anyone had heard. Fortunately, there wasn't anyone in the corridor. Shaken by Jon's sudden attack, I amazed myself with my comeback, which I managed to throw at him as I pushed past him and headed out of the door. "Yes, and he's more than half the man in bed that you could probably ever be." Jon stood staring, his mouth gaping. It most certainly wasn't the answer he had expected.

I rushed across the playground, hoping Jon wouldn't dare confront me there, where anyone could have seen us. However, he kept his distance. Going back to the office, I handed Mrs Pevensey my keys and passes for access to the school, mentioning that Ali would be collecting the rest of my things. Then, as quickly and carefully as I could, I piled everything in the back of the car and drove off, escaping the clamouring reporters and photographers, who had grown in number since I had arrived earlier.

Once I arrived home, I emptied everything from the back of the car into the studio. For now, I didn't want to be reminded about the school or see it in the house. Out of sight, out of mind. Walking backwards and forwards to the car boot, I felt dazed. I didn't even remember driving home, which was worrying. Finally, I went inside the cottage and straight upstairs to my bedroom. I was incredibly tired.

As I lay on the bed, the feeling of grief that had been beneath the surface all morning broke free. I started to cry. I was weeping for Gemma and what could have been in her life. I kept thinking about her laugh and how she always made jokes in lessons, keeping everyone entertained. I cried for Josh, having to go through the whole experience of losing his best friend and being wrongly arrested for her murder. And lastly, I cried for myself – for what I had thrown away. I didn't just weep, I howled. It was a good job that the cottage was isolated! At one point, Tibbs came into my room and jumped on the bed. He kept putting his paw on my mouth as if to quieten me. I think he was trying to comfort me. Unfortunately, it had the opposite effect, as I just howled even louder, scaring him away. Exhausted, I fell asleep.

Somewhere my phone was ringing. I woke with a start and managed to pull myself off the bed. I searched for my bag, finding it on the floor in the hall where I'd dropped it when I got home. But by the time I reached my phone, it had stopped ringing. There was a missed call from Ali. I rang her back.

"How are you doing?" she asked.

"Better than I was. I've had a good sleep, so feel a bit better."

I asked her about the stuff I'd left at school, and she agreed to bring it over later in the week. She told me all the staff were devastated I'd left. Even though the exams were done and dusted, Mark was panicking about having to take over. Ali said Janice would have to advertise for a new head of department because he wasn't ready yet to take charge. I sighed. I'd completely forgotten about Mark in my concentration on freeing Josh and my guilt about the situation. I should at least have warned him about what was happening. When I mentioned this to Ali, she replied that it would probably do him good to cope. He might learn to take on some responsibility. I knew what she meant. He had always just gone along with everything I suggested, meaning I usually had to remind him to do things.

Ali had asked me if I'd heard from Josh. I told her about his dad's visit, and she understood why it was a 'no'. Suddenly, she went very quiet, then after a while, she said, "Have you seen tonight's *Chronicle*?"

"No, I don't get a paper. Why?"

Ali sighed, preparing herself for what she had to say. "They have a story about Gemma on the front page, but on the inside, there is a story about you resigning." I thought it couldn't be that bad, could it? Ali continued, "I'm so sorry, Rhi, it refers to you seducing a student."

Instantly I felt sick. "Does it mention Josh by name?"

"No, Rhi. No, it doesn't, just yours." More to add to my grief and worry. I couldn't think of an answer. What could I say? Nothing was going to make this go away or make it better. "Rhi, do you want me to come over? Mitchel will understand."

"No, I'd rather be alone. Thanks, though." I desperately wanted her to come over, but as much as I would have loved to see her, I knew, if she came, we'd probably drink too much wine, and I'd end up crying again. So instead, I asked her if she'd come over the next night. Tonight, I wanted to spend on my own. I had some serious thinking to do, and I'd rather do it alone.

CHAPTER 15

RHI – 2 JULY

As promised, mid-morning, Ali phoned to say she was coming round later. As I didn't have to go into school, I'd got up later than usual. Besides, I hadn't slept well. Most of the night I'd been turning things over and over in my head. Thinking about what I was going to do now I wouldn't be teaching. I was feeling sorry for myself until I had an epiphany. I didn't need to stop teaching. There were plenty of other ways I could teach. I just wouldn't be teaching at Whittingbury anymore. Surprisingly, I managed to cheer myself up a little.

Luckily, I had always had an optimistic streak in me. Even when things were at their lowest with Paul, I hadn't given up completely. Oh, I'd cried a lot. I can always cry, but I hadn't become deeply depressed. I knew how lucky I was because lots of people can't be positive. When I was younger, if Aunty Jinny had seen me moping about, she would always say to me, 'There are always people worse off than you. Pull yourself together and remember all the good things you have.' She had instilled that into me, and it had stuck.

Looking on the bright side, I knew I had some teaching in the pipeline. I'd already got twelve people booked onto my summer school art workshops. I'd been running them for a couple of years now. There was a regular group that came back each year, with the numbers made up by new people. It was an easy two weeks where I earned well. Thinking about it reminded me that, with everything going on, I'd forgotten to organise the lunches. I made a mental note to myself to do that later, once I'd double-checked the numbers. There might even have been a few more bookings over the weekend. What I needed to do was make myself do everyday chores, to stop myself from wallowing in my situation. 'Keep thinking about the positives,' I told myself.

There was one thing I had been putting off. I needed to sort out my stuff from school that I'd dumped in the studio. After feeding Tibbs, I went out into the studio. It was hard sorting through everything – there were so many memories attached to them. Pleased with myself, I managed to tidy up, finding a new home for everything. After double-checking the bookings, I rang Beyond Bread, the local catering company that I'd used for the last two years. Sally, who ran it, had also been a teacher at the Academy when I first started but she had left to start her own business. She was making a success of it and had picked up regular contracts from a few local companies. I don't know who I'd use if not her.

Once I'd finished tidying away the art stuff from school, I decided to go for a short run along the beach to Whitend Café, then back along the cliff path. There was something I was trying hard not to think about and maybe a run would help me come to terms with it. The elephant in the room, or should I say in my head, was Gemma's funeral. Should I go? I needed to think whether my presence would be too embarrassing for everyone, me included. Locking up, I ran down to the beach.

It was incredibly quiet. OK, it wasn't the school holidays, but still surprising. There were usually at least a few people on holiday by now. The feeling of the sea air on my face, as I ran along the harder sand nearer the water's edge, was wonderful. My head cleared, and for a few moments everything that had happened this weekend disappeared completely. Not for long, though. A fleeting memory of Josh crossed my mind – his body against mine, kissing his lips, and laughing. My heart sank. We had spent just one night together and it had felt so right! I wondered how he was coping with his best friend's death. The trouble was, I couldn't get in touch with him to find out. Mr Campbell had made it clear I was to stay away from his son. Unless Josh contacted me, it would be difficult to get in touch with him without his dad knowing.

My problem with Gemma's funeral was that I would be bound to see Josh and his family. Other teachers from school would be there, and by now everyone in Whittingbury who read the local paper would have seen that embarrassing article in the *Chronicle*, plus those who had seen it on Facebook! I couldn't believe how quickly the news had found out about us. I'd only resigned yesterday, yet there it all was in last night's newspaper! I didn't read the newspaper but had seen it on my Facebook page, where some kind person had shared it. I was surprised by the image, which one of the photographers at the school gates must have captured on the morning I resigned.

The headline, too? ART TEACHER RESIGNS AFTER SEDUCING TEENAGE LOVER! These were typically salacious words to draw in people. When I first read it, I almost laughed. As if I was some kind of femme fatale. If only they knew it had been Josh who had made the first move! To be honest, there was very little information, but the damage had been done. It was something else I had to contend with. Would it influence how people saw me? That was a rhetorical question to me. As soon as I thought it, I realised that it was a stupid question. Of course, people were going to think differently about me. That was another of the reasons why I shouldn't attend Gemma's funeral. Maybe I wouldn't stop at the café today after all. I didn't fancy being gawped at, so I ran past, continuing along the cliff path towards home.

As soon as I got back to the cottage, I got into the shower. Ali arrived a little while afterwards. She hugged me for ages – just what I needed. I clung to her, grateful for some warm human touch, and the fact that she was there for me. Once we had settled with drinks, I told her I thought it best I didn't go to Gemma's funeral.

"Why not? She adored you, and surely you want to say 'goodbye'?"

"I think it would be too much trouble. Especially after the article in the *Chronicle* last night and shared on Facebook, too. You saw it?"

"Yes, I did. Mitchel showed me; he always reads the paper online. How on earth did they know about it?" Ali took a swig of her coffee. "The paper must have someone at the police station who gives them information or maybe someone at school?"

"Who do you think would be that mean?" I asked her.

We both sat thinking about that for a while. "What about Mrs Pevensey? She can be a nosey cow at times, and she might have remembered I was looking to find Josh the day after he kissed me." I had suddenly remembered, when I'd gone to the school office, she had asked why I wanted to find Josh.

"I don't think she's that bad, Rhi. Do you honestly think she could have worked it out or even remembered? She must have so much going on in that office." Ali looked sceptical.

Thoughtfully, Ali said, "I hate to say it, but I think I do know who it might have been."

"Who?" I wanted to know who had been so mean.

"Oh my God! I think it was Jon. I saw him chatting to some reporters later in the day, after Janice had spoken to us all. It didn't click what he was doing at the time, but now – it must have been him. What a bastard!" Ali was angry, to say the least.

"I'm not completely surprised, when I think about his comments to me. He probably is the vindictive type," I replied, remembering his vicious words when I'd met him that morning.

"So, what should I do about the funeral?" I asked Ali again.

"Why don't you go to see Gemma's dad? See what he thinks about you going to the funeral. You've always got on well with him."

I thought about her suggestion. It wasn't a bad idea. If he thought it would be disruptive having me there, at least I would have seen him and given my condolences personally. "You're not as dumb as you look!" I said, smiling, waiting for Ali's response.

Laughing, she replied, "Glad to be of help, Goggle Eyes."

I felt relieved. Going to see Mr Smith was something I needed to do anyway, and it made perfect sense to ask him what he thought.

"What's it like at school? How is everyone coping?"

Ali told me how people were reacting to Gemma's death, and what the teachers thought about my resignation. According to her, they were in total shock on both accounts. Of course, there was far more interest than there should have been about my 'affair' with Josh. She said Janice had dealt with everything brilliantly. She had told the staff at the early morning meeting she went to after I had resigned. According to Ali, Janice was very calm, saying she didn't expect any sensationalism of either news stories from any members of staff. Then she had talked to all the students in the morning assembly, without any mention of Josh and our 'affair' or my resignation. I had known that Janice would be fair, but I also knew it wouldn't be long before all the kids knew about what Ali had cheekily referred to as 'Josh-gate'. I'd hit her playfully when she had said that, but at the same time, her comment had lightened things a little.

I asked her how things were going with Mitchel. For a while, I wanted to get my mind off school, funerals, and Josh.

As Ali talked about Mitchel, I was seeing a new version of my friend. It was such a change to see her talking seriously about her feelings, without making jokes about moving on or finding fault in everything he did, which was her usual style when talking about boyfriends. She told me where Mitchel had taken her over the last two weeks, how they'd spent their time walking and talking, as well as having sex, and how much she loved being with him. It appeared things were becoming serious, and I said as much to her.

"I know it's still early days, but I think this could become something very serious." She beamed at me, happier than I'd ever seen her. Then she stopped smiling. "I'm so sorry. I wasn't thinking. Here I am babbling about how wonderful everything is, and you've had the most disastrous weekend, ever!"

"It has been, but it's good to know how happy you are. Just because my life has turned to shit in five days, doesn't mean yours has to. I can feel vicariously happy through you." I don't know who I was trying to kid, but it was true, I was happy for Ali.

The next morning, I went round to see Mr Smith, Gemma's dad. Standing at his front door after I rang the doorbell, I panicked, nearly turning to run. Just as I was about to make a move, he opened the front door. "Miss Dobbs!" He seemed surprised to see me, but not in an angry way. I hadn't thought about what I was going to say and was still trying to think of the right words to start the conversation when he invited me in. "Would you like a drink – tea, coffee?"

I said yes to coffee, and he disappeared to the kitchen to make the drinks. As I sat on the settee, I looked around the room. Gemma's work was all around. Pieces of pottery she had made, and even some of her drawings, framed, were hanging on the wall. Her dad was obviously very proud of her work. In contrast to the bright colours and designs of her work, the mantel above the fireplace was covered with sympathy cards. What on earth was I going to say to this man who had lost his only daughter? Five minutes later, I was drinking my coffee, and Jed, as he had asked me to call him, was busy talking about Gemma. I didn't have the chance to say how sorry I was, realising Jed probably didn't want to hear that yet again. People mean well, but in the end, it ends up sounding like some trotted-out platitude. I remember thinking that when Aunt Jinny died.

I needn't have worried about not knowing what to say – Jed just needed the opportunity to talk about Gemma. And I was only too happy to listen. He talked about her as a young child, telling me about the scrapes she had got into, and how he always dressed her in pink, which is why he thought she probably wore so much black as a teenager. Her rebellion against the 'girlie' pink of her childhood. He told me about what happened when his wife Heidi left him. He thought they had got married too soon, although they had got married because Heidi was pregnant. At the time, they thought they could manage anything, but when the baby arrived, he told me, his wife found it difficult being tied down. When Gemma was around two years old, Heidi went out one day, leaving Jed with the toddler, and never returned. She sent him a letter explaining everything a year or two later!

I'd known that Jed had brought Gemma up on his own after her mum left, but I hadn't ever considered how hard it must have been for a single dad, especially with someone as strong-willed as Gemma. Over the years, her personality had developed and when she became a young woman, Jed had allowed her to choose how she led her life. Maybe that was why she hadn't rebelled against him, as many of the other girls her age did with their parents.

Eventually, I managed to get up the courage to ask him what he thought about me attending the funeral, considering I had resigned from the school and the circumstances.

Having spent this time with him, his reply didn't surprise me. "She would want you to be there. You know you were her favourite teacher, don't you? It wouldn't be right if you weren't there. I don't care what other people think."

My eyes suddenly filled with tears. I felt embarrassed as I tried to wipe them away without being too obvious. I felt selfish crying when he had suffered such a great loss. Jed leaned across, touched my hand, and said, "You will come, won't you?"

I nodded, not trusting myself to speak. He had such an easy-going way about him, I understood why Gemma was so confident and relaxed about things. I left Jed, deciding that whatever anyone else thought, I would attend the funeral with his blessing.

I rang Ali and told her I would be going to Gemma's funeral. As she was going as the art department's representative from school, I suggested perhaps we could go together. I needed an ally to sit with. Ali agreed, saying she would pick me up on the day of the funeral, driving us both there.

The morning of the funeral arrived. After eating a breakfast I didn't particularly want, I spent ages trying to decide what to wear. I mean, what do you wear to the funeral of an eighteen-year-old girl? In the end, I decided on muted colours. Nothing too dull, as Gemma's style was Emo meets Goth. She always had flair, so my choice wasn't going to be black. Ali arrived on time, and I clambered into the car beside her, feeling somewhat subdued. We were both quiet, hardly speaking on the journey to the crematorium. She understood how awkward I felt about attending the funeral, so she didn't try to gloss over my feelings by being over-talkative or falsely happy. Typically, it was a dull day. One of those July days when the sun was fighting hard to appear between the darkening clouds that were blocking the sun. Everything appeared grey.

We decided to sit near the back of the chapel, which was a good choice as there wasn't much room left when we arrived, and it wasn't as if we were late. The chapel was full of Gemma's friends and relatives, along with several representatives from the school, including Janice. As I sat down, I caught a glimpse of Josh, sitting beside his mum and dad, only a few rows behind Jed and what I assumed to be members of his family.

My heart leapt when I saw Josh. I instantly felt disgusted with myself for allowing my thoughts to focus on my feelings, rather than the enormity and tragedy of why we were all there. At the very moment I noticed him, he turned to look around the chapel and our eyes met. I think he smiled, but I looked away, staring down at my feet to regain my composure and calm myself. Ali must have noticed, feeling my discomfort, so she held my hand. How could I be so selfish in this situation? I had to get a grip on things. We all sat for some time, listening to the music being played – a song with some guy gently singing and strumming a guitar. It was a tune Gemma had liked, although I didn't recognise the singer as I thought her passion had been rock music. On reflection, it wouldn't have been that appropriate at this moment. The music changed and someone asked us all to stand. As we did, Gemma's coffin was borne into the chapel. As her coffin passed us, I was surprised to see both Jed and Josh as the lead pallbearers. The last time I had noticed them, they were seated at the front of the chapel.

The service passed in a blur. My attention seemed to come and go. I noticed some of the eulogies given by family members, and even one by Janice. But however hard I tried, I could not concentrate. Today, there was no escaping the reality that I would never see Gemma again. Never hear her lively chatter or her raucous laughter. I couldn't even comprehend how Josh was feeling, losing his best friend.

The time arrived for the committal. Somewhere in the back of my mind, I could hear someone speaking. It was the celebrant. "Now we come to the time when in love and gratitude for her life, we reverently begin our final goodbyes to Gemma. We honour the way she lived her life and the love she gave to all whose lives she touched. We cherish her memory, as with respect we bid her farewell. Into the freedom of wind and sunshine –

we let you go. Into the dance of the stars and the planets – we let you go. Into the wind's breath – we let you go."

I was thinking what beautiful words they were when someone at the front of the chapel let out a gut-wrenching wail, which clutched at my heart. By the sounds of the sniffling and people blowing their noses, I wasn't alone as my eyes filled with tears. All around the chapel, people were sobbing while trying, yet failing, to contain their emotions – the typical British stiff upper lip. I don't know why we are always so embarrassed about showing our feelings, but we seem to be.

At last, the service was over, and we all filed out, each stopping to talk to Jed, who was standing at the entrance. Standing beside him was a blonde-haired woman, maybe a few years younger than him. Even today, you could tell her lifestyle was alternative to his, merely by her choice of clothes. I guessed this was Heidi, Gemma's estranged mother.

Outside everyone was standing around the crematorium gardens. The sun was beginning to win its battle with the sky, being far less grey than it had been when we entered the service. Janice gestured for us to join her. Much to my surprise, she hugged us both. I thought she would have preferred to keep her distance from me. In retrospect, that was disingenuous of me. Janice hadn't said anything negative to me about my situation. She had been upset about my resignation and the reasons for it, but she hadn't been as critical as she had every right to be. She asked me how I was getting on, and what was I doing with my time – pleasantries without much substance, but considering where we were and the situation, it didn't call for the third degree.

There were many people standing around close together. Ali nudged me to look around. Josh and his parents were standing next to us, talking to some other people, whom I didn't recognise. Josh was almost in touching distance. He moved slightly towards me, still in conversation with his parents and their friends, then he touched my hand with his. Instantly, it was as though an electric shock had passed through my body. He squeezed my hand, suddenly letting it go. His parents, well Mr Campbell specifically, had just noticed who they were standing near to. He ushered everyone away as quickly as he could.

"You OK?" Ali asked.

"Yeah," was all I managed. It had been nearly three weeks since my night with Josh and Gemma's accident. I was feeling relieved that he was still interested.

Everyone had been invited back to a local pub for drinks and some food. I wasn't sure I could cope with that, but reminded myself, Jed had wanted me there, and he was having a far worse day than me. Ali had the morning off work, so she didn't need to be back until around 2pm for her next teaching session. She offered to drive me home before returning to school, but I told her I might not stay at the wake that long anyway, so I would get a taxi.

The pub had organised a private room for Gemma's wake, and when we arrived there were quite a few people already sitting around drinking and chatting. Jed had tried to make the event a celebration of Gemma's life, as was apt for someone her age, rather than a morbid remembrance. He had put photos around the room of her growing up and hung some of her artwork on the walls, along with a display of her pottery on a large table. Someone had put together some photo albums that were on each of the tables for people to browse through while they chatted. It was a lovely idea and helped to remind people of the living Gemma and all she had achieved in her short life.

Ali and I grabbed a drink and some food, before sitting down at an empty table. As we looked around the room, there were a few parents we recognised from school, but not many other people. We presumed they were relatives. All the other staff from school had returned, as they had teaching commitments. Janice was the only one who had stayed, along with the chair of the school governors, Rob Peters. They made their way over to join us. Under my breath, I said, "Oh God, Ali. Rob Peters. I'm not looking forward to this."

I hadn't seen anyone from school since resigning, least of all any of the governors. The atmosphere was going to be strained to say the least! But Rob surprised me. He sat down and smiled at me. "Good to see you, Rhi. I'm so sorry you had to resign. You are, and will continue to be, greatly missed." Then, turning to Ali, he spoke to her for a moment, before tucking into his food. What could have been a tense moment turned out far better than I could have expected. I was grateful for his understanding – especially today. After about three-quarters of an hour, I'd had enough, so I mentioned to Ali I was going to the loo and then leaving.

As I walked out of the ladies' toilets to go back into the private function room, I met Josh walking towards me, obviously on his way to the gents'. "Rhi, I'm sorry. I needed to see you, but my parents have…" He stopped abruptly mid-sentence, as the door from the function room opened and his dad appeared.

I smiled at Josh and walked past him, brushing my hand against his as I passed. "Hello, Mr Campbell."

"Miss Dobbs." He continued walking past me towards Josh.

I almost ran back into the function room and over to our table. "I'm off, Ali. I'll get a taxi, you don't need to drive me. Bye, Janice, Rob." After grabbing my coat from the back of the chair I made a quick exit.

Ali came rushing after me. "Rhi, what happened?"

"I just bumped into Josh and Mr Campbell."

"Come on, let's get you home. What did he say? Josh, I mean."

"He was saying sorry and that he needed to see me when his dad arrived. Mr Campbell came to see me after the accident. He told me to stay away from Josh, but it seems as though he's been keeping tabs on Josh."

Ali ushered me out to her car and drove me home. She wanted to come in with me but, after telling her I was fine, I hugged her, went in, and crawled upstairs to bed. I felt completely drained of all energy. I needed to sleep.

CHAPTER 16

BEN – 3 JULY

It was three weeks since Ben's mum had been taken to hospital. He had visited her every day, although she didn't know he was there most of the time. She passed away a week after being admitted, without ever regaining consciousness. The night his mum went into hospital was also the night of Gemma's accident, but apart from thinking about her briefly when he arrived at Whittingbury Hospital that evening, he hadn't given her a thought since. He had presumed she had recovered and was fine.

Ben was sitting in the kitchen, drinking a cup of coffee, looking out at the garden, and absently watching the birds splashing around in the bird-bath. He was ashamed that he felt relief. Relieved that his mum wasn't suffering anymore, but also for himself as now he wasn't going to be tied to the house. It seemed wrong to admit this, but he had spent the last six years putting his life on hold while he looked after her.

Ben realised, that since the age of eighteen, all he seemed to have done with his life was spend time in hospitals or looking after his mum. He'd not had any real freedom to make new friends or meet girls like most young men of his age. Mum had been far too demanding, and had a way of making him feel guilty most of the time. After the car accident, when his dad had died, Ben had spent most of this time at the hospital with Mum. She had remained in the ICU for weeks, before eventually being moved to another ward, where she had a room of her own. By the time she left the hospital, with help from the staff, Ben had been put in touch with an agency that would help him organise the equipment needed for his mum's home care.

Initially, he had been terrified. What if he accidentally gave her the wrong medication or moved her in a way that hurt her? He was, therefore, relieved when the agency suggested a regular carer. Unfortunately, the first six or seven carers didn't last long. His mum had been very rude when the mood took her, which was often. Some of them left in tears, others left swearing at her, telling Ben on the way out that he'd never get anyone who would put up with her behaviour. Luckily for him, the next person that came along was Pam. As a carer, she had been wonderful, soon managing to deal with his mum her way. Sadly, in the days following, apart from the odd visit by the doctor, Pam had been the only person who ever came to the house. It was as if he had pressed the pause button on his life.

The few friends he did have disappeared. In the early days, after his parents' accident, his friends had rallied around, but whenever they asked him out, he had refused, as he couldn't leave his mum. In the end, they had stopped asking. Thinking back, he realised that he had probably pushed them away, but what else could he have done? He was on his own. None of his parents' relatives had been of any help either. Apart from his aunt, who had collected him on the day of the accident to take him home, they had all kept away. His memories of visiting relatives were not happy ones. His mum had usually ended up causing a scene with someone, while his dad would try to smooth things over. This inevitably resulted in the visitors leaving earlier than planned. Over the years, he saw less and less of his dad's family until finally they stopped making any effort to keep in touch.

Ben had often wondered why his dad had married his mother. Deep down though, he knew why. She was beautiful, and he imagined that when she was younger she would have been able to wind any boy around her fingers. Dad worshipped the ground she walked on. But surely, he thought, his dad must have known how she treated people. However, right up until the accident, Ben had never heard them have a real fight.

They had argued, but she had always managed to get around his dad, smoothing things over. Now she was gone, and for some reason he couldn't explain, he felt guilty to be free.

A few days after his mum had died, Pam came around to help him dismantle the medical equipment his mum had relied on, as well as help arrange the return of some that could be reused. At least it meant someone else would benefit from it.

His mum's funeral had been a very quiet affair at the crematorium on the outskirts of Whittingbury. The memorial gardens, surrounded by trees, had small, hedged areas where people could sit in privacy to remember their loved ones. He knew his mum would have thought it the right calibre of place for her remains. Sadly, only Pam and a few neighbours attended. Ben wasn't surprised. Most of his parents' friends had disappeared soon after his dad died. It was only then that he had realised it was his dad that people liked. His mother was certainly not everyone's cup of tea!

Ben had been grateful to Pam for taking the time to come along to the funeral, asking her back to the house. He wanted to give her something. After their cup of coffee, he surprised her by asking if there was anything from his mum's room that she would like. To start with, Pam wouldn't say. However, he pushed her, telling her he was happy for her to choose anything as he would be getting rid of most of the stuff – it wasn't his style. And besides, he'd rather she had it if it was what she wanted. After getting over her embarrassment, Pam chose an ornament that his dad had bought his mum when he was born – a Lladro porcelain figure of a mother and baby.

As Pam was leaving, Ben thanked her for all the help she'd given him. He told her there had been many times in the past when he wouldn't have coped without her. In her usual, generous manner, she replied, "It was my job, but thank you for saying that. Keep well. Maybe now you can do the things you want to do with your life?" As she left, hugging her gift, she turned and kissed him on the cheek – something she had never done before.

During the next few days, Ben started changing the house around.

He had money, so could now do exactly what he wanted with it. His dad had always provided well for his family when he was alive. After he died, thanks to how well he had built his business, the mortgage was paid, leaving more than enough money in the bank to pay for his wife's care. Ben started by altering his mum's room. It was, after all, the master bedroom, which included an en-suite and built-in wardrobes.

After getting rid of the dressing table, feminine furniture, and soft furnishings, Ben changed the colour of the walls and bought blinds for the windows. He had a good sense of design, so created a room that suited his personality. He moved his bed from downstairs into the room and placed his clothes in the wardrobes. Looking around the completed room, surveying his handiwork, he was pleased. Considering he had spent every day in this room, looking after his mum, it could have been a depressing thought to be sleeping there, but with the new paint and furnishings, it was a completely different space.

Downstairs, he altered his former bedroom into a large office. He bought a bigger desk, which went in the same place as his previous one, meaning he could still look at his images of Rhi. He kept his settee and TV there, so he had a relaxation space when he felt like a rest from his computer work. Ben also had big plans for developing the kitchen, wanting a kitchen/diner with a TV area and bifold doors leading onto the garden. However, he decided to pay someone else to do that for him, as he didn't think his DIY skills went quite that far.

While Ben had managed to keep himself busy, the reality that he was now on his own gradually kicked in. He'd always thought that when his mum wasn't around, he would feel more confident without her constant put-downs. However, he hadn't thought about how quiet the house would be. Not that she had made lots of noise, but there had been the constant hum from the machines keeping her alive. He had rarely played music, apart from through his headphones. But now, he could play music as loud as he wanted. Who was going to stop him? There was enough space between him and the neighbours for him to be as noisy as he liked. The problem was, he had spent so long being quiet, having to think about Mum, that he was finding it hard to be himself.

With his jobs finished, Ben decided he'd catch up with the local newspapers Pam had brought him. He grabbed a tray, made himself something to eat, plus another coffee, and took them into the front room. After placing the tray next to him on the settee, with the pile of papers on the floor, he started reading the first one as he munched away on his sandwiches. They were dated back to that awful weekend in June when his mum had gone into hospital. It was now July!

His first shock was seeing a photo of Gemma and reading that she had died from her head injury. Police inquiries had found no evidence of foul play, claiming it was a case of accidental death. Ben put the paper down. He was sorry Gemma had died. He hadn't wanted her to get hurt, having only pushed her gently. In another edition, he found an article about her funeral, which he was surprised to read was the same week as Mum's. Fleetingly, he wondered if Rhi had been there. For a moment, he thought about the lively girl sitting opposite him in the pub, remembering how excited she had been when telling him about college. The fact that wasn't going to happen made him feel particularly sad. Placing the paper on the floor, he sipped his coffee, thinking about what Gemma would be missing. This made him move on to thoughts of his own life and all he'd missed out on.

Picking up another of the papers to read, he realised they weren't in date order. 'That's annoying,' he thought, 'but then, as it's past news, it doesn't matter that much.' However, when he picked up the next paper, he nearly dropped his mug as he saw a picture of Rhi staring out at him with the headline:

'ART TEACHER RESIGNS AFTER SEDUCING TEENAGE LOVER!'

Ben read the article, then reread it. Angrily, he threw the paper across the room and stood up. He began pacing up and down, shaking his head, screaming questions out loud to the photos of Rhi. "What have you done? How could you have been so stupid? Throwing away your career for a boy!" He'd been living his career vicariously through hers, every step of the way over the last four years. How could she do this to him? Ben had never felt so angry about anything. 'She just hadn't been thinking. Why on earth had she been so rash? Surely this kid wasn't worth all she had worked for?'

Over the last few weeks, as he'd been sorting the house out, his dream about a time, sometime soon, when he would invite her over and cook her supper had helped to keep him going. He'd imagined the scenario. Rhi would be impressed, and they'd plan to build a business together. Then, eventually, when he'd finished his plans for the house, she'd move in with him. He didn't expect it to happen straight away, because they had to get to know each other again, but now – she'd thrown all of that away.

Ben stormed out of the front room and ran upstairs to the room he had been decorating. After grabbing a hammer, he ran back downstairs to the kitchen and started hitting the wall. Hard, heavy strokes, putting every ounce of anger he felt into each one. He screamed at the wall as he released his anger. It was nothing coherent, just an animalistic sound that crawled up from deep within his gut. Finally, he stopped. He was sweating but felt much better. He placed the hammer on the kitchen top, looked at his handiwork, then went back into the front room.

Sitting back down he stared into space, cradling his now tepid mug of coffee in his hands. He needed to find out more about this boy. He needed to know if Rhi was still seeing him, wondering all the time what could be so alluring about a teenage boy. What if it was that boy who was in the bar with Gemma? Was he the one? The good-looking, smart, smiling boy, who couldn't wait to leave because he was on a date. Ben was devastated. He'd seen him on the night he was going to see Rhi.

In his mind, he could hear his mother's imaginary words. 'You're useless. You let some young lad like that snatch your girl from under your nose. You're worthless.' What joy she would have had making fun of him. Well, she wasn't here now, so he would deal with it in his way!

He wandered out to the kitchen to tip the last dregs of his cold coffee away and looked at the wall he had just made a hole in. He needed to get someone in to do the alterations.

CHAPTER 17

BEN - 10 JULY

Since he had read the newspapers, Ben's every waking minute had been consumed thinking about Rhi. He had already started making changes to the house for when they would be together. It would need modernising in some parts, but the house was spacious, and over time she would be able to put her stamp on it. He was sure with her feminine ways she would easily make suggestions for changes! Having already painted his mum's room and moved in there, he had decided that he would re-do it. It was only now that he realised it was too masculine. But the first move was to find out what Rhi was up to with her life, and if she was still seeing that boy!

Ben was still getting used to the silence in the house, so found it hard not to wake as early as he had when taking care of his mum and preparing her meals. Sitting eating his breakfast, he was trying to keep his mind occupied. Thinking about Rhi was the best thing to think about. By his calculations, and having read the article in the newspaper, it was nearly a month now since she had resigned from the school. He knew she had her summer art workshops coming up soon, which would keep her busy. Last year, he had seen her on the beach with some of her group, and recently he had seen her talk about this year's workshops on her Facebook page. At least she was keeping herself occupied. When he had been wandering around the bay, he hadn't seen Rhi with anyone else, apart from the annoying friend she'd been with in the café. She always seemed to be at Rhi's.

Hugging his cup of coffee, he gazed out of the window. The garden was looking untidy. He would have to do something about that too before Rhi moved in. The pathways were overgrown and the borders were full of weeds. Sadly, what had been his mum's favourite part of the garden, the patio and pergola, were now totally overgrown. She had spent hours out there in the summers getting her tan before the accident had happened. Perhaps he could pay someone to sort it out for him? He didn't fancy doing it himself – gardening wasn't his thing at all!

By the time he'd finished his breakfast, he had decided to take a drive to the bay and see what was going on. He was hoping he could catch a glimpse of Rhi. As he drove, he was mulling over her behaviour of the last couple of months. He had stopped sending her flowers – she didn't deserve them anymore. And he still couldn't reconcile the fact that she had resigned from the most amazing job. It was one in which she excelled but she had thrown it away, because of some young lad. Never mind the fact that she had slept with the boy when she should have been saving herself for him. It made him seethe with anger. She had disappointed him beyond anything he could have imagined.

Arriving near Rhi's, Ben parked and walked towards the beach. He always walked down the old slipway that ran beside Starfish Cottage. He couldn't be seen from the cottage, because of the hedge that grew alongside the path. Arriving at the end where the path began a gradual incline down to the sandy beach, he heard voices. He had found a viewpoint where he could watch but not be seen. He sat on the low bollard that had been placed there to stop cars from gaining access to the beach. To any passerby, he looked as though he was just relaxing, looking out to sea.

Ben could hear Rhi and her friend laughing. He glanced round to the cottage. They were sitting outside on the grass having a drink. Rhi's cat was with them, lying stretched out full length beside her. She occasionally rubbed its tummy as she chatted to her friend. There was very little noise, so he could just about hear what they were saying without having to strain too hard. He managed to find out that Rhi was going away to Italy for a week from tomorrow and Ali, her friend, was going to feed the cat. The most encouraging thing he heard was that she was going alone. He felt some relief. Maybe the boy hadn't been anything important after all. Just a fling, a one-night stand. He smiled to himself, feeling a little lighter inside.

Then he heard Rhi tell Ali not to forget her key, asking if she could remember where the spare was if she did. Ben's heart leapt with excitement. With Rhi away, if he could find where the spare key was hidden, he could get inside and see how Rhi lived. He'd been able to see through the windows and on one occasion had even stolen her diary, which had been on the windowsill. But the thought of getting inside the cottage was exciting. Feeling much happier than he had when he arrived, Ben walked down to the beach, then along to Whitend Café where he had a celebratory coffee and cake, gazing out to sea while imagining himself inside Rhi's cottage.

Three days later, around 10am, Ben arrived at the cottage. He decided that Ali wouldn't be feeding the cat at that time of day as she would be teaching. That thought reminded him to check when the school term finished. He didn't want to bump into Ali. During the conversation he'd overheard, it seemed that Tibbs would be fed each day, early evening. To his advantage, the front of Rhi's cottage was not overlooked by anyone. However, if someone was walking on the cliff path, they would be unlikely to know that he shouldn't be there. Just to be on the safe side, he had brought a spade and gardening gloves with him. He laid the spade on the floor next to the flower bed beside the front door. To any passerby, it would look as though he was either the gardener or the house owner.

Ben looked at the front of the house. He thought about the common places most people hid keys. He tried the top of the door and inside the roof structure of the porch with no luck. Then he searched under and inside the pots around the door and under the mat. Lastly, he had noticed a pile of stones and remembered having seen a picture of a 'safe rock' in a magazine. Bending down he began checking them all. Eventually, he found the right one. It was a clever idea because it looked like a normal rock, and unless you knew about it you'd never guess. Ben removed the key, putting the rock back in place. He tried the key in the door. Success!

Ben looked around before walking into Rhi's house, putting the key in his pocket. Standing in the hallway, he shut his eyes and breathed in the smell of her home – her cottage. From the hallway, her lounge was to the left. He knew this because he had seen inside when he had delivered Rhi flowers. He walked in, slowly looking around at her things. Her photos, ornaments, of which there were only a few, and very different to those his mum had owned. Rhi appeared to love candles, as there was an assorted collection on the coffee table. He was surprised she had a wood burner. He hadn't imagined her collecting wood, although there was often wood washed up on the beach. He wondered if it was any good for burning, as he'd never seen a wood burner in use.

Ben walked into the open-plan kitchen and was surprised by the lovely little garden she had at the back of the house, accessed through bifold doors. He had never walked around to the back garden. He was surprised at how modern the inside layout of the cottage was, considering how it appeared on the outside. After walking back into the hallway, he opened the door that was to the right of the front door. It was a small office. For some reason, he felt surprised she had an office, especially as she also had the studio. But then he supposed she probably did her school planning in here. He dismissed that idea angrily, as she wouldn't be doing any more school planning! He shut the door and headed upstairs.

As there were only two bedrooms and the main bathroom, it didn't take him long to find Rhi's room. Ben just glanced into the spare room. His interest lay in Rhi's. He felt incredibly happy. He was standing in *her* room. Like his mum's, it was very feminine, but it was a fresher, brighter room, filled with a clean, wonderful scent. She didn't have a dressing table like his mum's old-fashioned one, but there were perfumes and jewellery on the top of a chest of drawers with a mirror on the wall above. Ben was taking notice of the colours and style of the room. He started thinking ahead for when she moved in with him.

The furniture was all pale wood, maybe ash, but he wasn't sure. Her bed had a soft headboard made from some sort of synthetic material. The

139

colour of the room was predominantly pale grey, with one wall painted a pale lilac. The matching curtains and duvet cover were in an abstract pattern containing blues, pinks, and lilac colours. It was what he would call a 'girlie' room, but still tasteful. Just what he had expected of Rhi. The whole cottage was tasteful. He would have to up his game when it came to decorating his parents' house. Suddenly, he said emphatically out loud, "No! It's my house now," telling himself off.

Walking around the room, Ben ran his fingers over the surfaces. Touching her bed, her 'dressing table', her bedside table, the trinkets on top of the chest of drawers. He wanted to touch anything she had touched. Picking up her perfume bottle, he pressed the top, releasing an instant spray of the aroma into the room. Leaning into the spray, he inhaled. Breathing in the beautiful floral smell calmed him, and he knew this must be how Rhi smelled. He took a photo of the perfume bottle with his mobile. Mentally kicking himself, he made a note in his head to take pictures of all the rooms before he left.

Ben was about to open one of the drawers when he heard something. Someone was at the front door. He panicked. Surely Ali wasn't coming to feed the cat already? It was too early. Looking at his watch, he realised it was actually noon. He had been wandering around Rhi's house for two hours. He stood still, listening. Then he heard the letterbox ping, as someone posted something inside. Relaxing, he breathed a sigh of relief. For a moment Ben thought it had been Ali arriving extra early, maybe in a free period to feed the damn cat!

Ben walked back downstairs, relieved to see it had been the postman. He was about to pick the letter up and place it in the lounge, stopping himself just in time. He went back into the kitchen and looked for the key to the bifold doors, eventually finding it hanging inside the small utility room. Only then did he realise that the doors might not open from the outside. Better still, he noticed the backdoor and a key hanging on a hook next to it. He put that key in his pocket, alongside the front door key, and went back to the front door. Stepping over the post, he went outside. Next time, he would stay longer.

Returning to his car, Ben drove into town to get the keys copied, after which he returned and replaced the originals in their normal places. Afterwards, he went for a long walk along the beach, stopping again at Whitend Café, where he had lunch, and then sat reading for some time. He was reading a Jack Reacher thriller, which he was enjoying. The sun came out, making it warmer than it had been earlier in the day. He went back to the beach, found a sheltered spot, sat against a rock, and continued reading. Ben wanted to hang around until Ali came to feed the cat. He needed an idea of what sort of time she would arrive. Then, when he next visited the cottage, he would know how long he could stay there safely.

The next few days had been busier than Ben had expected. One of his regular clients had sent some design work over to him. They were on a deadline. Then, a day or two later, he had received an urgent call from his mum's solicitor, asking him to go in and sign some papers. It had all been a bit tedious, but, over the next week or so, everything was going to be finished in terms of paperwork, and his mum's will would be settled. All his parents' money would be signed over to him, along with the deeds of the house. He was their sole beneficiary. At last, in his mother's words, he 'would be a good catch for any young woman'. Although he had wanted to get back to Rhi's cottage as soon as he could, he knew that in the long term he now had more than just his affection to offer her. He had a home and money.

A few days later than he had imagined, Ben walked back into the cottage, having let himself in with his key. He felt good – almost as if he had the right to be inside her home. After going into the lounge, he sat on the sofa and looked around him, soaking up the room's atmosphere. This time, he noticed more detail, such as the photos, which he presumed were of family members. He got up and went into the little office on the other side of the hall. One wall had shelving, which was full of art and photography books and what looked like files of schoolwork. On inspection, he found he was right. There were lesson plans and other stuff she needed for her job, or, as he reminded himself, had needed.

A couple of shelves had reading books and he began looking through them, wanting to see what type of books she enjoyed reading. Ben had presumed she would read romance or whatever girls liked reading. Surprisingly, although there were a few romantic novels, there was far more crime fiction. He pulled one out – an Ian Rankin thriller. He'd never read anything by him, so, taking the book into the other room, he put it on the coffee table. Next, he went over to the kitchen where he searched through the cupboards until he found some coffee. Finding the mugs, he put the kettle on, then opened the drawers until he found a spoon. She wouldn't have left milk in the fridge for a week, but he could drink his coffee black. Once the kettle boiled, Ben made a coffee, then settled on the settee with the book. He felt at home.

The story was good; he would have to look for some Ian Rankin books for himself. After reading for a while, Ben put the book down, washed his mug and spoon, and put them away, checking he hadn't left any traces of his having been in the kitchen. He wandered upstairs, wanting to spend time in Rhi's bedroom and be as close to her as possible. Walking into her bedroom again, he smiled. It was so beautiful and suited her perfectly. The last time he had been there, the postman had interrupted him, but today he could stay longer. Her friend wouldn't be over until much later – she would still be teaching.

There was a door in the corner of the room that he hadn't noticed on his previous visit. Opening it, he discovered the door led into a dressing room, with an en-suite through another door. Ben was imagining what a large room this must have been before being modernised. What great use of the space though. Walking into the dressing room, Ben was slightly amazed as he hadn't seen anything like this before. His mother would have been impressed – it was something she would have envied!

Rhi's clothes were hung along rails, surrounded by shelves for shoes, jumpers, handbags, and anything else she wanted to store. Ben ran his hands over her clothes, feeling the soft textures. He noticed the blouse she had worn to the speed-dating night. Carefully pulling it towards him, he inhaled, imagining the soft scent was that of Rhi. He ran his hands across the material of her tops and dresses, trying to visualise her wearing them. Next, he walked into her en-suite. Like her bedroom, it was beautifully decorated, continuing the colour theme of her bedroom and with matching towels. He looked inside her bathroom cabinet to see what was there. Not sure what he was expecting to find, there wasn't anything that surprised him.

Wandering back into the bedroom, he opened some of the dressing table drawers. Finding her underwear drawer, Ben pulled out the delicate, flimsy panties. Unable to stop himself, he held them to his face, shutting his eyes, breathing in the idea of Rhi. He put them back, all apart for a pink lacy thong, which he put in his pocket. She probably wouldn't notice it was missing. The bed looked inviting and, feeling tired, he decided to lie down, just for a while. Removing his shoes, he lay down on top of the bed. He shut his eyes and began to dream. The sun was shining into the room. Rhi was lying next to him, her beautiful red hair fanned out on the pillows. Suddenly, she turned and smiled at him. They looked into each other's eyes. He could feel her love warming his whole being. She leaned in to kiss him.

Ben woke with a jolt, as a bang startled him. He leapt off the bed, freezing on the spot. Was somebody in the house? Moving quietly, Ben looked out of the window. Then he sighed with relief – it was the damn postman again! Looking at his watch, he realised he had been in the house all morning – it was almost 12.30. He needed to go. He had work to finish off for one of his clients. Smoothing the bed cover, so no one would know he had been there, Ben checked the doors were shut and that nothing looked different from usual. Going back downstairs, he checked the kitchen and lounge. Everything looked fine. Stepping over the post, Ben walked out of the house, feeling contented. There were a few more days before Rhi came home, so he knew he could visit again.

On what Ben knew would be his last visit, everything seemed to go wrong. First, he took a cup of coffee up to the bedroom, spilling a tiny drop onto the duvet cover. Panicking, because he knew that coffee could stain, he quickly got a tissue and dabbed hot water on the spot. It seemed to do the job. However, he couldn't relax until the duvet had dried. It was almost indiscernible – a tiny little stain. Surely, she wouldn't notice that? Ben walked out of the room, then back in, gazing at the bed. But he knew where the stain was – he could see it. In the end, he decided it was so small she wouldn't notice or she would think that she had done it. Finally, he relaxed.

Downstairs, having finished reading the Ian Rankin novel he had started to read on the previous visit, he replaced it and 'borrowed' another one. Leaving, he decided to walk down to the beach. As he walked across the grass, he saw Rhi's cat. Bending down he picked Tibbs up. At first, the cat seemed quite happy, but he must have done something wrong because, without any warning, it sunk its claws into his bare arm. Ben flinched with the pain and grabbing the cat by the neck, he managed to extricate it from his flesh. Violently, he threw the cat away from him and stood cradling his arm where the cat had scratched him, drawing blood. He heard a sickening thud. The cat was lying lifeless at a strange angle, against the low wall that demarked Rhi's garden from the field. Ben shuddered: another wall, which tragically this time the cat's head had hit!

Bending down, Ben prodded the cat. It appeared lifeless. He considered his options. He could take it to the vet, but it was probably dead or past saving. If he went to the vet, how would he explain what happened? Cats are supposed to have nine lives. They were known for being able to land after jumping from all sorts of angles. He must have thrown it far harder than he meant to. The cat wasn't going to be saved by anyone. On closer inspection, he saw that it had hit its skull. There was a lot of blood. "I'm sorry, cat, you shouldn't have scratched me." Thoughts of Gemma ran through his mind, and he shivered again.

Ben looked around, checking if anyone was about. Luckily, there wasn't. Feeling a little queasy, he picked the cat up and walked across the field. After laying it under a clump of weeds, he wiped the blood from his hands on the long grass, before walking back to his car. Once in his car, Ben looked at his arm. The cat had left him with a nasty scratch, which he knew he should see a nurse about. He remembered reading somewhere that cat scratches could be far worse than expected. It was beginning to throb, so he decided it might be a good idea to drop into the doctor's surgery on his way home.

Arriving at the surgery, he was very lucky to see one of the nurse practitioners. She cleaned and dressed the wound, and gave him a prescription for antibiotics. By the time he arrived home, Ben was feeling both angry and upset. He hadn't meant to harm the stupid cat. If it hadn't stuck its claws in him, he wouldn't have pushed it off. Ben couldn't believe it. How could he be so accident-prone? First, Gemma, who he had only shoved very gently, and now this bloody cat! Rhi would be upset, and it was his fault. He went into the kitchen and began to take his anger out on the previously damaged wall. As he smashed the hammer against the wall, each hit released some of his pent-up anger. But, as the wound on his arm began to become excruciatingly painful, he threw the hammer on the floor. Taking his antibiotics, he went into the lounge. Feeling tired, he lay down on the settee, eventually falling asleep, only to dream of cats with extra-long claws, chasing him.

CHAPTER 18

RHI – 20 JULY

Driving towards the cottage, despite having wanted to escape from Whittingbury a week ago, I felt relief and happiness as I saw my sea twinkling in the sunlight. Although it was a lot cooler than the weather had been in Italy, I was happy to be home.

After emptying the car, I dumped everything in the lounge and made myself a coffee. I walked out into the front garden, breathing in the familiar air, and gazed out to sea. It was beautiful. Different from where I had been – a different beauty. Looking around, I wondered where Tibbs was. He usually came to meet me whenever I'd been away. Maybe he was off mouse-hunting.

Italy had done its job. I felt more relaxed and calmer within myself. My problems hadn't gone away, but the change of scenery had given me time to think, without the constant reminders of Gemma and Josh around me. On arrival in Italy, I'd hired a car and driven to the small village where I had rented a tiny villa. It was in the Umbrian countryside, just outside the city of Orvieto. I had spent the whole week walking around the narrow streets of hilltop villages, photographing sunflowers, olive groves, and the beautiful countryside. Interspersed with good, local Italian food and wine, I couldn't help but feel better. I'd taken hundreds of photos that I would use either for creating paintings or selling as pure photography. Plus, of course, I'd taken my sketch pad and a small selection of pastels. As an artist, you can never travel far without the tools to create!

It began to feel chilly, so I went back inside, got rid of my coffee mug, and took my cases upstairs to unpack. As I walked into the bedroom, something felt different. I couldn't decide what it was, but it was strange; I had an odd feeling. As I put the case on my bed, and slowly looked around the room, something felt wrong. Everything looked the same, but I had this creeping feeling inside me that someone had been in the room. Nothing appeared to have been moved as far as I could see.

Then, I noticed one of the drawers was slightly open. I hated seeing drawers not completely closed. When I had lived with Paul that was something that had always got on my nerves. And even on the occasions I had shared a room with Ali, I always noticed when she didn't quite shut drawers properly. I looked inside the offending drawer and as far as I could see nothing was any different. Although, that was pretty stupid, because how could I tell if my knickers had been moved or not? It wasn't as if they were all neatly folded – they were too small for that! Maybe it had been Ali, but why would she be going through my drawers while I was away? What would she have been looking for? It was bugging me, so I decided I'd ask her later, just to check.

Leaving the case on my bed, still packed, I walked into the other upstairs rooms to see if anyone had been there. Nothing! I went back downstairs and checked around the lounge and kitchen. I couldn't see anything, but it still felt as though someone had been in the house. Yet nothing looked out of place downstairs either. Maybe I'm just being paranoid! I'll definitely ask Ali if she has noticed anything when she came in to feed Tibbs. I needed to give her a ring anyway. I was hoping she could come round a little later – I'd bought her a present to thank her for looking after Tibbs. I went back upstairs and unpacked. For only one week away, I had a lot of washing to do, but I decided it could wait until tomorrow. I rang Ali to see if she wanted to come over for a drink.

Arriving about 8pm, she came bounding into the house. "You look great! How was it? Was the villa OK?" Ali threw lots of questions at me as we hugged. You'd think we hadn't seen each other for ages, rather than a week ago.

"It was what I needed. The villa was lovely, just the right size for me, and in the perfect location. You should take Mitchel. You'd love it. The food is to die for and the wine isn't bad either! Guess what I bought you?" I held out the bottle of wine I'd bought her.

"Ooh looks good. Mitchel and I can share it tomorrow."

"I bought you this, too." I gave her a little box.

Being Ali, she almost grabbed it off me saying, "What is it?"

She had opened it by the time I opened my mouth to say 'open it.' I had bought her a pair of silver earrings in the shape of sunflowers. She has a thing for earrings and when I saw them, I knew she'd love them. Ali pulled me towards her and kissed me. "I love them, they're so beautiful." She took out the ones she was wearing, put the new ones in, then rushed into the downstairs loo to see what they looked like in the mirror.

"There was a local silversmith in Orvieto – her jewellery was superb. When I saw them, I knew you'd like them."

"Thanks, Rhi, they're perfect."

I poured us some wine, and we went to sit in the lounge, where I told her about the rest of my week. We were both trying to keep off the subject of school, but we both knew it would come up at some point.

"Don't your workshops start next week?"

"No, the week after. I've got a few more things to get ready, but not much. Are you going away this week after you finish?" I knew school finished this week, but couldn't remember, with all that had been going on, when Ali and Mitchel were going away.

"We were going away the same week as your workshop, but we altered it and we're going after the exam results are out. I like a week or two to get sorted after school finishes, but I can't wait. It'll be our first proper holiday away together. Makes me feel quite grown-up!"

"You'll never grow up. It's great though, seeing you two getting on so well."

"I know, I can't believe it. Everything seems to have fallen into place. Mind you, Mitchel hasn't seen the bad side of me yet." Ali laughed.

"What bad side? You're a nutter, but that's all." I was incredibly happy for Ali. I hadn't known her in a serious relationship for years. Maybe this one was going to last.

"Where's Tibbs?" Ali looked around the room. "I thought he'd be all over you when you got back."

"I don't know, I haven't seen him either. He must be off wandering around, mouse-hunting somewhere." I wasn't that worried. It was unusual for him not to come and greet me, but I knew if he was on a serious hunt, then I probably wouldn't see him for a couple of hours.

We carried on chatting about holidays, and eventually, when I asked, Ali told me about the school and what had been going on. People were still shocked that I wasn't there and the reasons I left. Ali hadn't seen Josh in school at all, although that wasn't that much of a surprise, because there wasn't any reason for him to be there anyway. She promised me that when the A-level results came out around the 13th, she would get in touch to tell me how everyone had done. I asked how Mark was getting on leading the department. Ali said he was just about coping, but she knew Janice was going to advertise for a new head of department soon. Ali had been reluctant to tell me that last bit, and I felt sad hearing it. I still couldn't quite believe that I had walked away from my dream job. I quickly turned the conversation back to holidays and told her more about Italy.

After several more glasses of wine, Ali decided she ought to go. I suddenly remembered I was going to ask her about the open drawer. "Erm, you didn't go into my knicker drawer for any reason, did you?"

"No! Why would I? Your knickers wouldn't fit me, and I'm not so weird that I'm into sniffing your knickers!"

"Don't be gross," I managed between fits of laughter. "It's odd, but when I got back it felt as though someone had been in the house other than you. Then I noticed one of my drawers left open, just a little, and you know how much that annoys me, so I'm certain it wasn't me."

"Maybe Tibbs has found a way of opening it. Anyway, how can anyone get in?"

"Yeah, I didn't find any evidence of anyone else, but it was odd."

"I shouldn't worry, you're safe here."

"Yeah, I've got to stop being paranoid. Paul certainly had a lasting effect on me."

Ali hugged me. "All that's happened over the last few weeks is getting the better of you. Your holiday was supposed to help that. Drink some more wine and look at your holiday pictures!" She waved as she went out of the front door. I stood in the doorway, watching her drive away. Then I called for Tibbs a few times, but to no avail. He wasn't ready to come home.

Tibbs still hadn't returned a couple of days later, which was unusual for him. He would always come back for food. I thought maybe he had found somewhere else to get fed and was enjoying hunting too much, but that was unlikely. Why would he suddenly find somewhere now? He'd always come home before.

I talked to Ali about it, and she said sometimes old cats crawl away somewhere to die. That wasn't something I wanted to hear; besides, Tibbs wasn't that old. Then, when I thought about it, I realised that he was quite old for a cat. Aunt Jinny had him a few years before she left for Hong Kong, which I always forgot, so he was older than I always remembered. I tried to put it out of my mind and imagine him enjoying himself, off somewhere hunting for mice, and being fed by some lovely old lady.

My week was busy, getting the materials organised in the studio and arranging the food for lunchtimes in preparation for next week's workshop. I'd emailed everyone with details to remind them what to bring with them and where to park. They had all managed to get booked into local B&Bs, which a few of the regulars had stayed at in previous years. I went for my daily run, later in the day than usual, and made a mental note of a few places where I'd take the group sketching. The main plan was to keep my mind busy, so I didn't have time to think about the last few weeks, and to keep my mind from wondering if I would see Josh again. After Mr Campbell's pleas, no, demands, that I stay away from Josh, I wasn't going to be the one to make contact. Apart from which, I didn't want to look desperate, as if I was chasing a young man!

In my saner moments, I could persuade myself that it was for the best if I didn't see him again. After all, he was so much younger than me. As a relationship, where the hell was it going? But there was still a glimmer of hope when I remembered lying in his arms and the feel of his lips on my skin. I ran harder, and by the time I got back to the cottage I was ready for a good shower and some food.

The weekend before the workshops started, I went out for a meal with Ali and Mitchel. We went to the pub where they had met at the speed-dating night. The new owners of the Plough were doing well. Their ideas had upset some of the old regulars, but they had soon drawn in new, younger customers, so the place was buzzing.

Earlier in the day, as I'd stripped my bed, I'd noticed a tiny stain on the duvet. I hadn't spilled anything on it. In fact, it was rare for me to have a drink in bed, and even if I did, the spill would have been nearer the top of the duvet. I'd have been sitting up in bed drinking. Why on earth was there a spill nearer the bottom of the bed? I mentioned it to Ali, while Mitchel was at the bar. I hardly thought he'd be interested.

"Are you still being paranoid about someone being in the cottage while you were away?" asked Ali.

"I know it sounds paranoid, but I rarely drink coffee in bed. That's what it looked like, a coffee stain. I only drink in bed if I'm ill – otherwise, I get up. I never see the point of getting up, making a hot drink, and then going back to bed."

Ali interrupted, "Don't you ever take a drink to bed with you at night?"

"No, not usually. That's why it's so odd. You weren't walking around the house with coffee, were you?"

"No! I certainly wasn't going through your drawers or drinking coffee in your bedroom. Come on, Rhi, you're being over-dramatic. I'm positive no one was in your house. Surely, I'd have noticed when I went to feed Tibbs?" She paused. "Talking of which, has he come home yet?"

"No, he hasn't. I'm beginning to think he's either done a runner to another home or he has died somewhere."

Ali put her hand on mine for comfort. "I'm sorry." Mitchel came back with drinks and we carried on the rest of what turned out to be a brilliant night, with no conversation about people breaking into my house, or Tibbs.

I slept extremely well after our night out, more likely because of the amount of wine we drank than anything else, luckily without a hangover. I felt rested. Over breakfast, I was mulling over the conversation with Ali about the coffee stain. I decided I'd check through my knicker drawer, just to see if anything was missing.

I tipped the whole of its contents onto the bed. The bed was covered in an assortment of frilly knickers, thongs, and what I considered my everyday boring ones. All were pretty small, taking up little space on their own, but together they filled the drawer. I went through them. As bizarre as it may sound, I have my favourites. Pairs of knickers that are either very comfortable or I think are particularly pretty or even sexy. There was only one pair missing. A tiny, delicate pink lacy thong. Ali had bought them for me as a 'birthday joke' present. She was surprised I liked them so much, but I thought they were cute and they were one of my favourite pairs. Now they weren't in my drawer. I checked in the washing basket. I couldn't remember wearing them recently but thought I'd make sure they hadn't got pushed to the bottom. I went downstairs to check inside the washer-drier. They weren't anywhere.

The paranoia kicked in again. Someone must have been in the house. I ran back upstairs and checked through the drawer again. I even pulled the other drawers out in case they had fallen behind them. They weren't to be found. They were missing – strange.

Then there was the spilt coffee stain on my bed. Someone had taken my knickers and had been drinking coffee in my bedroom. I felt physically sick. As I sat on my bed, quietly contemplating that someone had been in my house, the front doorbell rang. The sound jolted me out of my thoughts and I nearly fell off the bed.

After running downstairs, I opened the door and was met by George, the local farmer, holding a dead Tibbs in his arms. I could tell he was dead by the awkward way his head fell. "I'm so sorry, Rhi," George was saying. I gagged, leaving him standing there as I rushed into the toilet where I was violently sick. When I managed to control the spasms, I cleaned myself up and went back to the front door. George was no longer holding Tibbs, having placed him on the grass.

I was still shaking as I spoke. "Sorry, George, it was a bit of a shock. Where did you find him?"

"He was hidden under some grass and weeds at the side of the next field. He didn't put himself there, Rhi. This wasn't an accident." He let that sink in for a moment, before continuing, "What do you want me to do with him? Are you going to call the police?"

I couldn't think. "Leave him on the grass for the minute, George. Come in. I need a drink. Would you like something?"

George removed his boots and followed me into the house. "Can I have a coffee please, Rhi?"

In automatic mode, I filled the kettle, got two mugs from the cupboard, and made us both a coffee. "Have you got any whisky, Rhi?" George was looking around the kitchen. "I think it would do you good to add a little to your coffee."

"Yes, in that cupboard," I answered, pointing to where I kept my spirits. George got the bottle of whisky and poured a good measure into my mug.

George was someone I'd known forever. From the time when Aunt Jinny lived here, he had always cut the grass in the field next to the cottage, keeping the grass low on the other side of the garden wall, and cutting the hedge. He continued doing the same for me. I was grateful he had found Tibbs.

We sat in the kitchen, silently drinking our coffees. "Are you going to tell the police?" George asked.

"I'm not sure. I think they've got far more important things on their hands than dead cats."

"Sadly, that's true. It was probably some yobs. Hopefully, it was no one we know," George replied. "I don't know what the world's coming to these days."

Inwardly, his last comment made me smile, despite how I was feeling. He sounded just like Babushka D, who had always been bemoaning the changes in the world compared to when she had been younger.

"Would you like me to help you bury him in the garden?"

"Thank you, George, that's very kind of you. I wasn't sure what I should do."

"Have you got a spade?" I told him I had and walked out into the back garden to get the spade from the shed. George smiled. "That's a lady's spade, that is. Don't often see those."

"It was Aunt Jinny's, but it works well for me for the amount of gardening I do, which is very little!"

"See if you can find something to wrap him in and we'll put him in the ground. Have you got a cardboard box we could put him in, too?"

Leaving George to finish his coffee, I went out to the studio where I had plenty of boxes, having recently received lots of art supplies ready for the workshops. I found one that was the right size for Tibbs. As I picked it up, tears began to stream down my face. I sobbed, trying to muffle my sounds from George, who I was sure would hear me even back in the house. I blew my nose, managed to calm myself, and went back into the kitchen.

"Come on, girl, let's go and put him to rest." George patted my shoulder and walked to the front door, carrying the spade. I followed with the box and a large cotton scarf to wrap around Tibbs' body.

George suggested burying him near the flowers, because he said when his body degraded it would add to the soil and help their growth. I found it strangely comforting that Tibbs would become compost for the plants. Also, at least I knew where he was now.

CHAPTER 19

RHI – BEGINNING OF AUGUST

I had completely forgotten about the missing knickers until I got up to get ready for the Monday workshop. They had been the least of my priorities after burying Tibbs. But it was far too late to dwell on that now. I had to concentrate on my workshop attendees. Several of them I'd met before. They were very loyal and came along each year. The first few times they reappeared, I had wondered if I'd done my job well enough, but I realised that they just loved the whole experience, not minding if I went over things they'd learned the previous year.

Everyone started arriving at the workshop around 9.30 and helped themselves to hot drinks. We had an introductory session where each of them introduced themselves, saying what their experience was and whether they'd been before. Out of the eight, half of them had been in previous years, so it was a good mix. The first session was a creative activity to help them settle in with each other and to get used to the studio, finding out where everything was and discovering their environment. After the mid-morning coffee, but before lunch, we went for a walk to the beach. I wanted them to find something they could use as a starting point for an abstract work in the afternoon. They could find a shell, a piece of rock, seaweed – anything that took their fancy.

I felt exhilarated. I was teaching again, suddenly realising how much I'd missed it over the last couple of weeks. There were some very good artists who had come along before and two of the newer members of the group were very good, too. The others were people who loved art and could produce some pleasing work but would never go much further. However, that didn't matter; the whole point was for them to enjoy the experience.

One loyal member of the group, who was here for the third year in a row, was John. He was in his late forties, single, and had a job in the City. The workshop had become part of his regular summer activities and holidays. He was a good-looking guy, though slightly too earnest. He worked for a large architect's company in London, earned a high salary, and had told me on his first visit that this was his time to unwind and become truly creative.

I had always held high regard for architects. It was something that, had I been better at maths, I might have considered. Buildings had always fascinated me. As a child, back at home in Didsbury, whenever I got bored in school, I would often be sketching designs for houses, much to my teachers' annoyance. I think for John, this was a different kind of creativity, where he could work more abstractly. I did wonder, though, why he was still single. If he lived in London, I don't think he would have stood much chance of remaining so. Although, on further reflection, I wondered whether he hoped he might meet someone at the workshops, because he had been the only man on every year he had attended.

This year, the other returnees were Julia, Tracey, and Angie. Julia and Tracey were best friends who lived in Birmingham and were good artists. They were both teachers in a primary school. Angie worked in an office in Weston-super-Mare. She had started painting views around Weston and had been successful in selling some of her artwork since attending the workshops. The newbies were Leanne, Helen, Bonnie, and Rachel. I'd have to see how they got on during the week. During the first session of the day, Rachel had proved to be the most competent in terms of drawing skills, but Helen had shown her creative side. I would have to see how Bonnie and Leanne got on. I thought that, of the group, they would perhaps be the two who might struggle a little. But as long as they enjoyed what they were doing, that was the main thing.

I had been worried that people might have been put off the workshop if they'd read about my resignation from teaching, particularly Julia and Tracey. But, of course, I was blowing the impact of my behaviour out of all proportion. As it had only been in the local newspapers, it hadn't made the national news. Thank goodness! I decided I wouldn't mention losing my job unless someone asked about it.

As we walked back from the beach, I was expecting to see the caterers' van outside the studio, but the driveway was empty apart from my car and two belonging to the group. I unlocked the studio to let everyone in, telling them to make themselves a hot drink if they wanted. I then went to ring Sally at Beyond Bread to see what was going on.

"I had a phone call saying you didn't want lunch today," Sally replied to my query about the food.

"What? No, I didn't cancel, Sally. I've got eight hungry artists here, expecting lunch." I was trying to keep calm.

"Oh my God. I'm so sorry, Rhi. I've got this new kid working with me for the summer. He took the phone call. I'll get the food over, but it will take a little longer – is that OK? I'm so sorry."

"That's fine, Sally. Can you find out who it was that rang?" I couldn't think who on earth would phone and cancel the lunch, but at that moment I didn't have time to dwell on it. After going back into the studio, I explained what had happened, suggesting if they couldn't wait for the food to eat a few biscuits and have some more coffee. In the meantime, we would start work on the ideas with what we'd found on the beach. Despite any disappointment and anger, they were all very understanding.

The food arrived about an hour later, which wasn't that bad, considering it was a busy time for Sally. The news about the phone call was that the 'kid' said it was some guy who had rung saying that lunch wouldn't be required. The 'kid' hadn't thought to ask for a name or to query it, but then why should he? Whoever it was, it wasn't very helpful and didn't make a good impression on the new attendees or the workshop. However, once they got stuck into the food, if anyone had been feeling annoyed they soon forgave me. Sally's catering was delicious and had been worth the wait. Fortunately, the rest of the day went off without any hitches and the group all went away happily, ready for the next day.

After tidying up and locking the studio, I went into the cottage and cooked myself a meal. As I ate, the whole lunch debacle was going over in my mind. I couldn't imagine who would cancel the lunch! Nobody from school would be that petty, and apart from anything else, what would they gain from it? The only other person I could think of was the one who had, up until recently, been sending me the flowers and who I suspected had been inside the cottage. But again, why on earth would they do it? What did they have to gain from messing up my day? On reflection, I realised that maybe the whole point was to cause me problems and make my life difficult.

When I finished eating, I rang Ali and told her what had happened with the lunches, Tibbs, and the missing knickers. I hadn't told her earlier about Tibbs, so she was almost as upset as me. She said she'd be around in thirty minutes. Good as her word, she turned up twenty-five minutes later, along with Mitchel. I was surprised to see him, but not unhappy about it.

"I brought Mitchel with me. I thought he might have some ideas about how we can sort this stuff out," Ali said, stating the obvious as soon as she walked in the front door. We all hugged, and they followed me into the kitchen.

"Wine?"

"When have I said no?" Ali answered.

"Have you got a lager?" Mitchel asked.

I knew I hadn't got any cooling in the fridge as it wasn't something I drank. I had a quick check in the lobby, where I kept the drinks, only to find I was completely out of lager and beer.

"I'll have a wine then, but only a small one, as I'm driving," he said, before going to flop down on the sofa.

"I'm so sorry about Tibbs. What happened?" Ali asked, giving me a big hug.

I poured out our drinks and we joined Mitchel in the lounge. Then, tearfully, I recounted how George had brought Tibbs home the night before. I hadn't had time to grieve as I'd been too busy preparing for the workshop. I also told them about the missing underwear and the coffee stain on the duvet. I added that unless Ali had been having a party, wearing my underwear, then someone else had been inside the cottage. After initially making smutty comments at the thought of Ali in my underwear, they both went quiet.

"I've told Mitchel about your secret admirer who leaves you flowers," Ali began the conversation, "but we need to try to work out who he is, although it's going to be tricky without any clues."

Mitchel suggested I make a list of everyone I'd been out with who might be feeling annoyed I'd broken up with them and who might have a grievance against me. Although it wasn't funny, that made me laugh. I was the one who had finished with most of the guys I'd been out with. Mind you, since Paul I hadn't got a very good record when it came to relationships, although there hadn't been that many, especially when I took the one-night stands out of the mix.

"So, we're discounting the one-night stands, are we?" Mitchel asked.

"Yeah, they weren't relationships, they were just someone I fancied on the night!"

"But they might have fancied you more than you did them," Mitchel said.

Feeling a little ashamed, I answered, "Maybe, but I can't remember some of their names. There weren't that many – I'm not a tart, you know," I added, for clarification.

Mitchel and Ali both laughed. "Mmm, I'm not so sure about that!" Ali managed in between her laughter. We didn't even list Paul. Ali had already told Mitchel about him and that he was completely out of the picture. Mitchel made a note of the shortlist of names.

"OK. Mike Wood was the parent I went out with for a couple of weeks. I ended it. But everything was amicable. He didn't seem bothered. We've seen each other since at school dos and he's been perfectly normal with me. Anyway, he's met someone else, and I'd heard they'd moved in together."

Ali agreed. "He always seemed pretty level-headed to me, too. He's never caused any problems at school at all. And if he's moved in with his new girlfriend, I think we can cross him off. What about Peter?"

I pulled a face. Peter had been someone I met when I'd been out with Ali. We'd been out on a couple of dates, but he was another of those guys who got too serious, too quickly. He kept buying me presents and texting me every hour of the day. I couldn't hack it. Men like that make me feel uncomfortable. It's nice to get presents, but not all the time. I think it's a bit smarmy. And it made me think of Paul, who had appeared very attentive when I'd first met him. We all knew how that had ended. Peter had been upset when I'd finished with him, but I hadn't seen him since and he hadn't even texted me.

"No, I'm certain it's not Peter."

We crossed two other names off. I'd only been out with them for a very short time and had completely lost contact with them. That left Jon, the drama teacher from school.

Ali started, "I think it could be Jon, you know. He is weird sometimes."

"How?" Mitchel asked.

Ali took her time to answer. "Well, he's incredibly arrogant for one thing, so I think he'd expect girls to fall over themselves for him, and Rhi didn't. And..." She paused for effect. "I've noticed him hanging around the Art Hub a few times when he didn't need to be there. I've caught him staring at you." And she looked straight at me.

"You haven't told me that before," I said. "I agree he is arrogant, but I can't imagine him going out of his way to deliver me flowers. I have to admit, he was pissed off with me after our date, and you should have heard what he said to me when he found out about Josh."

"You didn't tell me about that – what did he say?"

I recounted the meeting I'd had with Jon, the morning I'd resigned. "In some ways, it could be him, he's vindictive enough, but the flowers – no, that's not him at all," I added.

Mitchel said, "The flowers could be from someone else. I mean that's a caring thing, sending flowers. It could be that the flowers guy isn't the same guy who is following you."

Ali nodded in agreement. Then, as though she'd had a second thought, she said, "Though why have the flowers stopped? When did they stop, Rhi, before or after you resigned?"

I had to think about that. When had the flowers stopped? So much had happened since the weekend of Gemma's death – everything was one big jumble. "I think just before I resigned. I haven't had any flowers for weeks. Do you think the timing is relevant?" I looked at them both. You could almost hear all our brains working overtime trying to find an answer to the question. Not having a clue about who it was made it hard to know whether there was a link between the two events.

Mitchel changed the subject. "If someone got inside, and I'm not ignoring what you think, how did they manage to get in?"

"There's a key inside a stone by the front door that I leave for Ali. Thinking about it, I suppose if someone has been watching me, they might have seen Ali pick it up from there. I should have thought about that."

"Seriously, girls, you've got feathers for brains. Well, the best thing would be to ditch that and get your front door lock changed." Mitchel ducked as he said this, as he received verbal and some physical abuse from Ali, who was nearer to him than me. "The thing is, whoever it is, he hasn't hurt you in any way. He hasn't put you in danger, has he?" Mitchel asked.

Ali answered before I could say anything. "No, he hasn't yet, but he is causing Rhi stress. How would you like it if someone was rummaging through your stuff?"

Tentatively, Mitchel answered, "We don't have any real proof that anyone has, do we? You only know you can't find some things, which there could be an explanation for. Change your locks and see if things settle down."

Ali looked at me. I could tell she was annoyed with Mitchel's comment. Keeping as calm as I could, I smiled at her, replying to Mitchel, "You're right, I don't have proof. But someone is watching me. Someone killed Tibbs and cancelled the lunches for my workshop, and I'm ninety-nine per cent sure someone has been in the house. He hasn't hurt me physically but it's incredibly unsettling knowing that someone out there is messing with you."

"I'm sorry, Rhi, I'm not dismissing how you are feeling or what has happened, but if you went to the police, at this moment in time they'd want more proof than you have." Mitchel reached over, took my hand, and smiled at me.

I smiled back. "I know you're right. The police were useless last time. It's hard to prove someone is controlling you or stalking you. I know you're not disregarding my worries. However, I'll take your advice, ditch the stone, get a locksmith out later this week and get the front door locks changed." Replenishing our wine, I changed the subject to talk about something lighter, asking them about the holiday they planned. By the time they left, the mood had relaxed.

After Ali and Mitchel had gone, I finished off my glass of wine. My mind returned to our earlier conversation about trying to think who my 'admirer' might be. It had to be someone who knew me from somewhere, though I still had no idea who it might be. Strangely, although I found this situation unnerving, it was less scary than when I knew Paul had been watching my every move. Then I had known what he was capable of, and he had known where I was all the time. Whoever it was now couldn't possibly know everything about me or where I would be all the time, could they? I certainly couldn't face going through a repeat of my time with Paul. Despite being blasé, it still felt a little like it was starting all over again. Every time I turn around I am expecting someone to be watching me. One thing I know for sure: it won't be Paul. He can't come back from the dead.

CHAPTER 20

FOUR YEARS EARLIER

I was standing by the bar, drinking my mojito, and watching people dance when I noticed a guy watching me. He was good-looking, had sparkling eyes, and was tall. I returned the smile he was giving me, which he took as an invitation to join me.

"Hi, I'm Paul. Can I buy you another drink?"

"I've not quite finished this one yet, but I suppose I could knock it back and have another. Thanks."

He managed to catch the bartender's eye easily, annoying several guys who had been waiting at the bar longer than he had. Then, after ordering himself another lager, he came back with the drinks and suggested we find somewhere to sit. Amazingly, in such a busy bar, we managed to find a free table and sat down. He was funny, and I laughed with ease at the little quips he dropped into the conversation. When he leaned in to talk to me, I could feel the frisson of attraction between us, and after a few more drinks, when he leaned in again, he kissed me. Before I could react, he grabbed my hand and pulled me after him towards the dance floor.

Paul was surprised I had only just finished college. For some reason, he didn't think I looked like a student, although he didn't give me a description of what he thought one might look like. At the end of the evening, he walked me home. We spent some time kissing, hidden in the darkness of a large tree in the front garden of the house I had just moved into with other teachers from where I was about to start teaching. I couldn't invite him in after only just meeting him. I didn't want the other people in the house to get the wrong impression of me, especially as I found it hard to stop things from going beyond the kisses and some general petting.

When we came up for air, Paul asked, "Can I see you tomorrow? We can go out for a meal if you like, then you could come back to see my place." It didn't take me long to agree, and the next night he took me for a meal at a little bistro in the middle of Cheltenham – one I'd not been to before, as it had always been way out of my student spending league.

Going back to his flat, I was surprised, as I'd expected him to live in a rented flat – perhaps in an older house instead of the modern, beautifully decorated apartment that he lived in. While Paul was getting us drinks, I wandered around the room, looking at his books, music, and the décor. "It's beautiful, Paul. Is this all your place, or do you share?" I asked. I was unaware of how rude the question might have seemed and only understood by his answer that Paul had taken it that way.

"Of course it's mine. Why wouldn't it be?" He sounded a little indignant.

"I'm sorry, I just meant that for some reason it's not what I expected. I'm used to being with teachers and we don't earn huge amounts. What do you do? You haven't told me yet."

"I work at GCHQ. I'm an IT programmer. It's well paid, but I can't ever talk about work, we're not allowed to."

"Ooh, very hush-hush." I laughed.

Paul pulled me to him, and kissed me, saying dramatically, "If I tell you anything, I'll have to kill you." I stayed that night. If my housemates couldn't see what I was up to, well, they needn't know. I was so attracted to Paul; I just couldn't help myself.

I'd not had much time for guys during my teacher training year, so I felt ready for some love and romance. And Paul appeared to be the perfect boyfriend. After that night, we saw each other regularly. He often turned up with little presents. To start with, chocolates, flowers, pretty candles, and then little pieces of jewellery. I loved it. No one had ever treated me like this before. It made me feel good, knowing that someone cared so much. He made me feel secure too, as when we were out, he always looked out for me.

After only six months, Paul suggested I move in with him. "It makes sense. I wouldn't expect as much rent as you must pay for your share of the house. I know I want to have more time with you, and we do enjoy being together. What do you think?"

He was right; it did make financial sense to move in together. I loved being with him, so why on earth wouldn't it work? And I was spending more time at his place than I was at the house. I agreed, as it seemed to be the best idea and a great decision. After a few weeks, spending every day together, I was glad that I didn't have to talk about his work. The only times I had seen him working, or heard snippets of his conversations with work colleagues, made me think that I couldn't imagine anything more boring. Sadly though, he also wasn't very interested in my teaching, though he loved my artwork. If I didn't bring it home.

Paul was banging around in the lounge. "Rhi, I've asked you before not to bring your messy paints into the flat. I've just found a blob of paint on the wooden floor." I could tell he was angry, not only by his voice, but he had a little vein in his head that throbbed. "I don't want your artwork at home, keep it at school. Please!"

"I'm sorry, Paul. I'll take more care, but sometimes I have to bring work home. Some of it isn't just for work. Where am I supposed to do my work?" I was annoyed. Where did he expect me to do my work?

Paul went quiet for a while. "I suppose you could draw or work on your photos, but just no paint or paraphernalia to do with it," he replied.

Upset by his comments, I went into the bedroom, put my headphones on and sulked. That is, until he came in and started kissing my neck, which led to more intimate kissing, and we'd soon had the best-ever making-up sex.

Apart from the issue around my artwork, living together worked out well. Paul didn't usually arrive home from work until around 7 to 7.30pm, so I stayed on at school to mark work or to catch up on my personal projects. Most evenings we ate out at one of the many wine bars or bistros in the town, as neither of us overly enjoyed cooking. After moving out of what Paul referred to as 'the teaching house', what I missed most was time to catch up with my friends. There was never enough time during the school day, so about a month after I had moved out, we decided to meet up one night after school.

I rang Paul, mentioning in passing that I would be late getting home that evening. He went very quiet, and the rest of the conversation was very one-sided, with his responses being cold and monosyllabic. Noticing the change in his mood, I tried to placate him, promising, "I won't be back too late and it is only one night. You see me every day."

"Have a good time without me, then," he replied, turning his phone off abruptly. Feeling a little guilty I was leaving him on his own, I put his mood down to having had a bad day at work.

We had a great night out, starting with a meal, followed by a couple of drinks at Wetherspoons, although nobody wanted to drink much or stay out too late, as the next day was a teaching day. When I arrived home, sadly, Paul's mood hadn't changed. I went to kiss him, but he turned away, and when he asked me about my night, it was more like an inquisition than casual interest. Even when we went to bed, he turned his back, ignoring me, which was completely different from our usual nights. However, after a few days, things were back to normal, and he was the loving, caring Paul he had always been. I decided it had been a one-off, that he must have had an extremely bad day at work, hence his behaviour.

My friends decided it would be a good idea to meet up once a week if we could. I made the excuse of having a prior engagement. I thought it was possibly too soon following Paul's previous reaction. Though the following week, when they planned to go out, I agreed to go too, deciding that surely Paul wouldn't be bothered this time. It was three weeks since the last time. It wasn't as if I was out on the town every night. Besides, things had been good between us. He had been spoiling me with presents and been very attentive and loving – particularly in bed.

I decided that this time I'd ask him well in advance, rather than tell him I was going out. I wanted him to feel he had a choice in the decision. Over dinner at the Petit Bistro, one of our favourite haunts, I broached the subject. "My mates have asked me out again this week. I told them I didn't think you'd mind." I said it as casually as I could. Paul didn't look up from the steak he was carving. I noticed that his knuckles had turned white as he pressed hard with his knife.

"Paul, surely you don't mind. It's been three weeks since I last went out. We never have time to catch up at school, and you must get sick of me all the time." I gave him one of my best smiles.

Putting his knife down, Paul met my gaze. I could see he was trying hard to control himself, although I couldn't quite decide whether it was anger or he was upset. "Am I so boring that you need to go out all the time? Don't I look after you? Give you things?" He was raising his voice, causing people to turn and look.

Feeling embarrassed, I leaned across the table, putting my hand on his to calm him. "Paul, it's not about that. Of course, you look after me, and you're always spoiling me, but I need to see my friends too. Seeing them doesn't reflect at all on my feelings for you. I wouldn't mind if you wanted to go out with friends from work."

Quieter and calmer, looking at me intently, he replied, "All I need is you. I don't want other friends." He took my hand and kissed it before returning to eating his food. Again, I felt uncomfortable. He may have meant his answer to sound reassuring, but for the first time his voice had a menacing undertone that unsettled me.

CHAPTER 21

RHI – THE PRESENT

As I ran along the beach, I was thinking about last week's workshop, which had been a success, despite the debacle with the lunch. I had received some great reviews from the two friends, Julia and Tracey, who said they would return for next year's workshop. John surprised me, telling me he was taking a bit of a longer break this year, intending to have this week free. He was looking around the area, before coming back for next week's workshop. Bonnie, one of the new attendees, also booked onto next week's workshop at the last minute. The fact that John and Bonnie had booked for next week meant I had to change some content, otherwise they'd be repeating what they had already done. Not that I was bothered, as I could easily create some alternative activities.

It was a most glorious morning, with the tide on the turn, meaning I could run along the sand almost all the way to Whitend Café. I say almost, but not quite, as there were a few places where a shallow pool hadn't quite dried out yet. I managed to sprint across most of them, landing on drier spots of sand. Despite all that had happened over the last few months, life felt good here and now. There was something wonderful about the sea air and the space between the sea and sky that seemed to talk to my spirit.

When I reached the café, I turned and ran back along the cliff path. I was wearing my new shiny front door key around my neck, so it wouldn't get lost. The locksmith had come around one day last week while I was running the workshop, changing the front door locks for me. Hopefully, that would keep whoever was getting into my house from visiting again! I must remember to tell Ali I had followed Mitchel's advice.

After showering, I made myself a coffee and was just about to start work on the alternative activities for next week, when my mobile rang. I was surprised to see it was Janice. "Hi, Rhi, are you well? I thought I'd let you know that the A-level results are in. I wanted to tell you how good the results are and to thank you for the amazing job you did." She paused. "I am right? You do want to know the results?" she asked hesitantly.

"Yes. Yes. I'm pleased to hear they all got good results." I was at a loss to know what else to say. While I was glad that they had all done well, still, everything was tinged with sadness because of Gemma and the fact that I was no longer teaching them. The fantastic mood I had felt during my run suddenly disappeared.

"Steven did extremely well, possibly better than even he had expected. Fantastically, no one got below a grade C, with most getting Bs and As, including two A-stars." Janice sounded very upbeat. It was as though she had forgotten I was no longer teaching. But, for her and the school, the results were important. Not that they weren't for me. One part of me was proud of what the group had achieved, but mostly it just reminded me of what I was missing and would be missing next school year.

Janice was talking again. "I'll get Ali to bring you a printout of all the results, so you can see." Then, almost as an afterthought, she asked, "How are things going? Have you had your workshops yet?"

"Everything's OK. Thanks, Janice. Last week's workshop went well, and next week I'm fully booked, so thanks for ringing."

I sat hugging my coffee cup, feeling a mixture of emotions. I was proud that everyone had done so well, but in my heart I was very sad that I wasn't going to be working with a group of new students next year. I hoped that Josh was one of the two A-star results. Most likely Gemma would have been the other – yet another reminder of the tragedy of her death. As I thought about how much she had been looking forward to college and a life of art, the tears began to well up in my eyes. It was then the front doorbell rang. Wiping my eyes, I was thinking it must be Ali, although, in the same instant, I realised it couldn't be as she was getting ready for her holiday with Mitchel. They were due to leave any day now.

Through the door glass, I could see the shape of a male figure at the door. It was Josh! Opening the door, I was transfixed to the spot, until he put his arms out and began hugging me. We stood in the doorway, hugging for dear life, as if we hadn't seen each other in years, which is what it felt like. Finally managing to pull myself away, I said, "Josh, I can't believe you're here." Only then did I realise how stupid that sounded.

He looked ashamed. "I'm so sorry I haven't been in touch. I wanted to talk to you properly at the funeral but Dad was watching me all the time. He told me I had to stay away from you."

"I know," I interrupted. "He visited me the day you'd been in the police station. He came to thank me for saying where you'd been, and then warned me to stay away from you."

It seemed Josh wasn't aware of that. Pulling me towards him, he kissed me. "Oh God, I'm so sorry, Rhi."

"It's not your fault." I managed to pull away from him and walked into the kitchen.

"Do you want a coffee?"

He nodded.

"How come you managed to escape your dad today?"

"He's away working for a few days. Mum isn't as obsessed with where I am."

While I made Josh a coffee, and myself another one, he sat watching me. "So, I hear you've had your exam results?"

Beaming, he said, "Yes, I got an A-star."

"I'm not surprised. That's great news. Did Gemma get the other one?"

"I don't know. I only saw my results, Steven's, and Georgia's. How do you know there are two A-stars?"

"Janice rang me, just before you arrived. What did Steven and Georgia get? Don't keep me in suspense!"

"Sorry, they both got Bs. Steven is so pleased with his results, he couldn't believe it. They were upset that you weren't there. They both wanted to thank you." He glanced up at me as if checking my reaction.

"I'm sorry I wasn't there too, but I'm very happy you all did so well."

"All down to your teaching." Josh looked away from me.

I handed him his coffee and sat opposite him at the kitchen counter. "Josh?" He couldn't meet my eyes.

"It's all my fault that you're not teaching. You didn't have to say where I was – they would have found out that I was innocent! I've ruined your life."

I grabbed his hand. "No, you haven't. It takes two, you know. I could have said 'no' to you that night, but I didn't. I wanted you. I want you. I can get a new job – it's not the end of the world, you know. It's not like I'm over the hill and old!" I smiled at him, trying to get him to look at me. "Did you hear what I said? I want you, if you still want me?"

That made him look up. "Yes." Then, his face broke into a broad grin. "But I'm going to drink this coffee first."

Josh took two sips and then walked around to my side of the counter. "I lied," he said, breathing coffee as he started kissing me. All the pent-up emotion we both had inside erupted, as we made love against the kitchen counter. Afterwards, we went upstairs, where we made love again, slowly, no rushing, enjoying the comfort of my bed and each other. Now, I knew Josh felt the same way I did – that we wanted each other equally.

After showering together, which took some time, as it was hard to keep our hands off each other, we went back down to the kitchen to get something to eat. I remembered Josh saying how sex made him hungry and had to agree that I was feeling peckish, too. I put on shorts and a camisole, while Josh wandered down in his boxers. I opened the bifold doors onto the enclosed garden, leaving Josh to sit in the sun while I prepared the food. He hadn't seen the garden before and was surprised at how quiet it was.

The holiday home behind was a bungalow, but it didn't overlook me at all. It meant the garden gate kept the garden enclosed from the cliffside of the house. It could be quite a suntrap, and on days when the wind was blowing in from the sea, a great shelter too. One of my favourite things about the garden was the pair of seats Aunt Jinny had commissioned from a local carpenter. They were made from two rowing boats, cut in half then upturned, the prow of the boats being the top point, with a seat set in the middle. They were painted different shades of blue and had our initials, R and J, painted at the top. Oddly, I hadn't thought about the significance, until Josh noticed.

"This one's got my name on it," he said, sitting on Aunt Jinny's seat, with his plate of chicken salad. I smiled, telling him the story about the seats.

He told me how, after returning from the police station, he had been incredibly low for days and couldn't stop thinking about how Gemma died. "You know, it was a regular thing for her on Fridays. She often picked guys up at the pub. I was always telling her to be careful, but she didn't seem to care. She used to go to the pub without me all the time, so I couldn't have stopped her." Josh paused. "I didn't tell the police about her and the guys she picked up. I didn't want her to sound like a..." He was looking for the word.

"People judge too quickly," I interrupted. I leaned over and kissed him. We both ate quietly for a while.

"Anyway," Josh continued, "after the funeral, Dad drove me down to stay with my sister, Alisha, for a couple of weeks." He took another mouthful of his salad, before continuing. "I told her all about you. She was a bit shocked at first, but the more I told her, she understood. It was she who encouraged me to come and see you today. I was worried you might not want to see me."

"I'm glad you came. Do you want another beer?" I walked back into the cottage, feeling elated, and pleased that I'd bought more beer since Mitchel and Ali visited. Josh was here, the sun was shining, and, I smiled to myself, his dad was away.

Our morning was spent sitting in the garden, talking about everything and anything. The music we liked, the films we'd seen. He told me about the girlfriend he'd had in Islington, and I told him about my bad luck with men in the past, without going into too much detail.

I'd tell him about Paul another day. It was late afternoon by the time we went back inside. The air had cooled a little, so Josh went to fetch his T-shirt from upstairs.

When he came back into the lounge, he stopped to look at a photo sitting on the bookshelf. "Is this you?"

I was busy putting the dishes from our lunch into the dishwasher, so glanced over my shoulder. "Yeah, that's me."

"Who's the lady?"

"That's Babushka D."

"Baba who?" Josh asked, looking puzzled.

"Bab-u-shka," I repeated slowly. "She was my dad's mother, my grandmother, but Babushka because she was Polish."

Josh looked at the photo more closely. "You were cute."

"What do you mean, I looked cute? I'm still cute, if you don't mind!"

He put the photo back and came over to kiss me. I could tell he was thinking about something. Then he asked, "So, why haven't you got a Polish surname?"

I told him the story about Dad changing his name because ours was too hard to say. "You try saying Dubkowiecki."

Josh tried, without much success. "Try it in bits – Doob-kov-etski. Does that help?" He tried again, with more success. "You can imagine the combinations I'd have got with kids trying to say that at school. Although I don't like it that Dad got rid of our Polish heritage, I understand why he did it."

"I like the word Babushka; I can manage that at least."

"Well, don't you start calling me that. I may be older, but I'm certainly not your grandmother."

Laughing, Josh pulled me towards him and started kissing me again. He managed to mumble between kisses, "No, you're certainly not!"

When we came up for air, it was my turn to ask a question. "I've always wondered how come your dad has a Scottish surname."

"Slave owners," Josh replied, in a matter-of-fact way, as if I should know what that meant.

"You need to explain a bit more – my history isn't that good."

"What lots of people don't know is that most Caribbean people are descendants of slaves. Slave owners gave their slaves their surnames, taking their real names away. So, way back in history, my dad's family were owned by the Campbells."

"Oh, God! I hadn't thought about that before."

"One of Dad's friends changed his name by deed poll because he wanted to choose his name."

"I don't blame him. Didn't your dad want to change his?"

"No. He says, he's comfortable with who he is, and as that was years ago, he can live with it. All the family he knows have that surname, so in his eyes why would he want to change it?"

"Well, we've both got interesting backgrounds, then."

He told me he couldn't stay too late, otherwise his mum would start to wonder where he was. He'd told her he was celebrating with some mates, having just got the exam results. They were going to have a family celebration when Patrick, his dad, got back from his business trip. Before he left, he told me he wouldn't be able to see me for a couple of weeks, as his parents were taking him to Jamaica to visit his dad's mother and family. They wanted him to have a holiday before starting college.

"I promise I'll come round before I go off to Cheltenham, but we can see each other at weekends – that is, if you want to?"

"I want to, but once you get to college, you'll meet some girls your age. You might not want to bother seeing me anymore." I tried keeping my voice light, not letting him hear how scared I was that he might meet someone in his age group.

"You needn't worry. That's not going to happen." Once again, he kissed me passionately, before grabbing the rest of his clothes, getting dressed, and disappearing into the night.

CHAPTER 22

ALI AND MITCHEL

Ali couldn't believe how early she was getting up – it was still dark! She had stayed over at Mitchel's because Bristol airport was that bit closer from his place. This was going to be their first holiday together, which was amazing, as she had never gone away on holiday with a boyfriend before. This was a first, and she couldn't wait. Mitchel had kept most of the details of the holiday a secret. Ali knew they were going to Italy, to the area around Umbria, but she didn't know where they would stay. He had told her what to pack in terms of clothes – some smart outfits, casual, and sunbathing stuff, so she knew it wasn't going to be purely a poolside holiday.

Neither of them felt like eating – 5am was far too early for breakfast. After a cup of strong coffee, they set off for the airport, knowing they could get a snack before the flight. The flight went smoothly and amazingly was on time, meaning it wasn't long before they had arrived at Fiumicino Airport, Rome. They picked up their hire car, which, to Ali's surprise, was an Alfa Romeo convertible. Mitchel smiled at her as he tied the suitcases onto the luggage rack on the boot before putting the rest of Ali's bags on the small back seat of the car. He told her the drive would take between an hour and a half and two hours, depending on the traffic. He also explained they were taking the motorway because it was quicker.

It had been a busy time to arrive, but it wasn't as though they had to drive through the centre of Rome. But once they'd left the airport, Ali was grateful they hadn't had to drive through the city. She had never driven in Italy, and to her, the standard of driving was something to be witnessed. People hooted, yelled, and generally didn't seem to take much notice of traffic signs or rules – if there were any. Mopeds passed on all sides. Whenever there was the slightest gap, they'd aim for it. It appeared to be complete chaos, and yet everyone narrowly missed everyone else. Once they got out of Rome, the traffic was a little less manic.

As Ali had only ever been on trips to cities, she had visited Rome and Florence. However, on both occasions, she had travelled by train to her destinations. Occasionally, Mitchel would point out landmarks, such as the River Tiber, which at one point was on their right, next on the left. It continued to meander, changing sides as they drove along the motorway. The land was varied, with sloping hills leading down to the valleys below, where Ali could make out olive groves and vineyards, some of which spread back up the hillsides. The land looked like a patchwork quilt of different greens made by the trees, fields, and the variety of crops.

They didn't talk much as they drove along, although occasionally, Mitchel held Ali's hand, making contact in their silence. She was in a world of her own, fascinated by the landscape. Ali was also feeling a little nervous because she had no idea where they were going to stay. Considering they had only met in May, things were moving fast for her. She hadn't been serious about anyone for a long time – if she ever had. Her love life had always been pretty good, but she wasn't very good at keeping relationships going. However, with Mitchel, everything seemed to click into place. They felt comfortable around each other, whatever mood they were in, and could quite happily sit in silence for hours. She hadn't met any of his family yet, but he had mentioned that he'd probably take her to meet his parents when they got back from Italy. He'd already met her family and had got on well with everyone. Ali hadn't considered that he wouldn't get on with them. As far as she was concerned, what wasn't there to like!

She already knew that Mitchel's mum was Italian, but they hadn't talked about how that had impacted him, if at all. Now, here they were in Italy, and it was obvious that Mitchel knew his way around well and that he could speak perfect Italian too. This had been a bit of a surprise because she had never heard him speak anything apart from southwest English. She had mentioned how good it sounded hearing him speak the language when they first started on the drive. "You've kept that quiet. I didn't know you spoke such good Italian. You should have used some Italian chat-up lines; they would have sounded much sexier than in English. You might have got your leg over quicker." She laughed lightly.

"I don't think it could have been any quicker, do you?" They both laughed. Mitchel promised to use some Italian chat-up lines later.

Ali replied, "That might be safer. I don't want to get excited and drag you off for a quickie while you're driving."

Mitchel took his eyes off the road for a short time to wink at Ali. "Quindi vuoi una sveltina?"

"What?"

"So, you want a quickie, yeah?" Mitchel ran his hand up her nearest leg.

"Just keep your hands on the wheel," she managed between giggles.

As they drove out of Lazio and into Umbria, the land became hillier. Ali could see tiny hilltop settlements. When they turned off the motorway for Orvieto, the River Tiber was on their right. Bypassing the town, Mitchel told her they'd be back to visit over the next few days and he drove south down the Via Della Castagneta. The road was a long winding road, making it appear as they were sometimes almost coming back on themselves. Mitchel clearly knew the way, for the road ran down from the town and then climbed back up. As they drove along the treelined road, they passed several small tracks and roads which disappeared into the trees. Each time, Ali would strain to try to catch sight of buildings, but to no avail. They passed one entrance to a very beautiful villa, which she caught a fleeting glance of before it disappeared.

The light was beginning to fade a little as they went around another right-hand bend before suddenly turning off onto a track. A few hundred yards along, there was a secure, modern gate. Mitchel swiped a card, and the gates opened, closing after them once they had driven through. On the other side of the gate, to the left of the private road, the land fell away in lines and lines of vines, for as far as the eye could see. The route they drove on finally opened up to reveal the front entrance of a beautiful Italian villa, built in typical Italian style, with a near-flat roof and a central tower topped by a dome.

"Welcome to Villa Geisomino," said Mitchel as he turned the car engine off.

Ali looked around. She was astounded. It was breathtakingly beautiful. "Is this the hotel?"

Mitchel opened the car door to help her out. "No, it's a family home." Ali was shocked as he continued, "I'll tell you all about it later, but for now, let's get inside and have some food."

Ali was starving, so she decided to eat and then ask all the questions flying around in her head later. As they walked towards the main entrance, the front door opened, and an older man rushed out and hugged Mitchel, speaking to him in Italian.

Eventually, a little reluctantly, he let Mitchel go and walked over to Ali. "Welcome, Ali. I'm Mitchel's uncle Guglielmo. Come in, get yourselves settled, and we'll have something to eat."

Mitchel grabbed the suitcases, helped by his uncle, and together they led Ali upstairs to the bedroom they would be using. "Have a freshen up, then come down for an apéritif before dinner," said Guglielmo as he wandered back downstairs.

"Wow, Mitchel, you didn't tell me your family owned something like this!" She didn't know what else to say, being so taken aback by the grandeur.

Although the villa was an old building, the interior had been tastefully decorated in a modern, unfussy style. Walking to the entrance, Ali had straight away understood the architectural significance of the dome. Light flooded the entrance hall and the beautiful stairs that circled leading to the first floor. Their bedroom and en-suite were stunning. Far better than any hotel she had ever stayed in. It dawned on her that his family had money.

Mitchel could tell she was too shocked to say much. "Perhaps I should have given you a heads up, but I didn't want to put you off coming."

"Put me off? This is superb." Then pulling him towards her, she kissed him the way she had wanted to do all day.

They both had a quick shower, and although Ali was worried that they might be taking too long, Mitchel suggested they had time for a *Quindi vuoi una sveltina*. She decided after he had brought her to such a beautiful place, it would be rude not to.

It was, therefore, about forty minutes before they went to join his uncle downstairs, although he didn't seem bothered that they had taken their time. He handed them a glass of white wine each. It was a warm evening, so Guglielmo led them out onto the terrace, where he offered them some hors d'oeuvres. Ali hoped the real food wouldn't be too long, because now she was so hungry, she felt she could eat a horse!

Sipping her wine, Ali looked around as Mitchel and his uncle chatted away. Even though he was at least in his late sixties, maybe early seventies, Guglielmo was still an attractive man. Ali smiled to herself, thinking about the 'silver fox' title that people often used to refer to one of the TV presenters in the UK. Here was a prime example. There was no stoop of old age, no apparent signs of him being overweight, just beautiful white hair and sparkling eyes that had surely seen life. They both turned to look at her. Ali felt as though she had been caught out, hoping she hadn't been staring too much!

"I'm so sorry, my dear, it's very rude of us talking in Italian. My apologies." And the most beautiful smile radiated from Guglielmo's eyes.

Hoping she wasn't blushing, Ali replied, "Don't be. It's lovely to hear, although I don't have a clue what you're saying. Besides, I'm enjoying looking around your beautiful home."

"Thank you; I'm glad you like it. Isabella, my housekeeper, will call us when supper is ready." He took a sip of his wine. "What do you think of our wine?"

"Your wine?" It slowly dawned on Ali that all of the vines she had seen must belong to the villa. Both Mitchel and his uncle nodded. "It's wonderful, thank you. I love white wine," she replied, hoping the food would arrive soon, as she was feeling a little light-headed. As if mind-reading, Isabella entered, saying supper was ready.

"Buon appetito!" Guglielmo said as they began their meal and gently clinked their glasses. Isabella had prepared a plate of assorted cold meats, vegetables, cheese, and pasta. Ali was pleased it wasn't a large meal – too much food would have made her feel even more sleepy than she already did. A mixture of travelling and the heat had finally caught up with her.

During the meal, Guglielmo told Ali how he and his wife, Lucia, had moved to the villa when his father had died, and he took over the business. That had been over forty years ago. Sadly, Lucia had died a few years ago, leaving him alone. She had been an artist, so the tasteful and exquisite decoration was all down to her. Never having children of their own, they considered Mitchel their child. Ali could see the close bond between the two of them.

"When he told me about you, I asked him to bring you to meet me. It is important for me to see him happy," Guglielmo said, putting his hand on Mitchel's shoulder. "He tells me you're a musician and play the piano. Will you play for me while you're here? We have a beautiful grand piano, which is hardly ever played these days."

"Of course, I'd love to," Ali replied, hoping the piano was still in tune if it wasn't played that often.

After the meal, although not large, which had taken far longer than any English meal Ali had ever eaten, she felt deliciously full and relaxed. Nevertheless, she was embarrassed when she nearly fell asleep while sitting on the luxurious sofa. Guglielmo suggested they get an early night, and perhaps tomorrow Mitchel could show her around the vineyard and then take her into Orvieto.

Once in bed, Ali started to ask Mitchel some of the questions running around her head. "So, Guglielmo is your mother's brother – are there any other brothers and sisters?"

"No, not now. They had another brother, but he died when he was quite young."

"Is this a family business or just Guglielmo's?" She was intrigued because she hadn't thought Mitchel was well-off; she just thought he had a good job. Yawning, she snuggled closer to him.

Mitchel took his time answering. "Well, sort of, but I'll tell you more tomorrow. You can hardly keep your eyes open." And he kissed her as she yawned, already beginning to fall asleep.

The next morning, Mitchel woke Ali by kissing her before he leapt out of bed to open the curtains, allowing the bright Umbrian sunshine to stream into the room. They joined Guglielmo out on the patio for breakfast. He had been up some time and was busy reading the newspaper and drinking coffee. Ali was excited and couldn't wait to see around the vineyard. Wine was her go-to drink, although she had no idea what to expect when it came to how it was made. So, she was surprised when Guglielmo, saying "Goodbye, see you later," disappeared off to a meeting. Ali had thought he would be showing her around. It was, in fact, Mitchel, who was even more of a surprise because at home, he always drank lager. Besides, he worked in IT, so what would he know? It turned out to be quite a revelation, as Mitchel knew everything about wine production.

As Ali followed him through the working areas of the vineyard, Mitchel took her through the process of how the wine was produced. First, he explained how the harvest was usually done in early September to October – when the grapes were picked by hand. It was done this way because it was important to Guglielmo that his grapes weren't damaged by machinery and it made the wine taste better. Next, Mitchel led her through the fermentation room, where the maturation took place, and where the resulting wine was bottled. Lastly, he took her into the shop where people could taste and ultimately buy the wine.

Hand in hand, they walked between the vines, Mitchel wanting her to see the grapes, experience what it was like to walk between the rows of beautiful, ripening fruits that each year yielded their much-valued prize. "What do you think?" he asked quietly.

Ali gazed at the rows and rows of grapes clinging onto the vines, their lush leaves a delicate green in the sun. "It's truly beautiful and amazingly peaceful."

Mitchel bent towards her, gently kissing her. "I'm so glad you like it."

As they walked through the vines, Ali noticed that some of the grapes differed in colour, which surprised her. She thought they would all be the same, so she asked Mitchel about the differences.

"That's because several different grapes are blended to create the wine."

"How come you know so much about this? Have you taken part in the harvest?"

"Yes, I come over every year."

"Wow! And I thought you were just an IT guy – there are so many things I still don't know about you." Gently, Ali kissed him.

Mitchel held her tightly. "I hope you're liking what you find out?" He smiled, kissing her, before releasing her; then, grabbing her hand, he pulled her after him, further into the vines.

Later, Mitchel drove them into Orvieto for lunch. After parking, they wandered through the narrow streets, which were bustling with people, with the occasional van or small car trying to get through the space between people and buildings. Ali was amazed any traffic could get down the tiny streets. There were plenty of cafés, bars, and pizzerias, but they kept walking until they reached the Piazza del Duomo. They found a seat outside a café, opposite the old cathedral. Ali had never seen a building like it. The cathedral dominated the piazza and the surrounding buildings. Its façade was highly decorative, but unlike any cathedral she had seen before, the sidewalls of the building's structure were striped. The brickwork created a horizontal, light, and darker brick striped pattern. The inside, which they visited after their lunch, was incredibly ornate, with gloriously coloured paintings on the walls and vaulted ceilings. The columns holding up the arches echoed the striped walls outside.

Because Mitchel knew Isabella would be preparing a substantial meal later, they had pizza for lunch. To this, they added some wine. As they ate, finishing the full bottle of wine, they watched the world go by. Afterwards Mitchel showed her all of his favourite spots around town – unsurprisingly, he made a great guide.

While walking down one of the streets, Ali noticed a jewellery shop, something that always drew her. On further inspection, she realised it was the one where Rhi had bought her sunflower earrings. She went inside and, after some time, chose a necklace for Rhi. Ali wasn't surprised Rhi had had such a good break a few weeks back, managing to find some calm. Orvieto was incredibly different from Whittingbury – a different world. They wandered a little longer before returning to the villa, where Ali spent a couple of hours in the pool before changing for dinner. As requested, she played the piano for Guglielmo. She was pleasantly surprised to find the piano was perfectly in tune, despite not being played regularly.

Much to Ali's sadness, the rest of the two weeks seemed to rush by. They spent their time visiting other places around the area, sunbathing by the pool, or walking around the vines and the land around the villa. Mitchel disappeared on quite a few occasions with Guglielmo, leaving Ali swimming happily, reading, or relaxing in the sun. She didn't feel abandoned but did wonder what they had to talk about that was so important when Mitchel was supposed to be on holiday.

By the time they left, Mitchel had taken Ali to Perugia for the day, and they had travelled to Rome on the train rather than drive. But her favourite trip had been to Civita di Bagnoregio, a hilltop village where the only access is by a pedestrian bridge at the bottom of the hill. It was the most stunning place she had ever visited, and Ali thought it incredibly romantic. Looking out from the hilltop, she could see for miles around. She hoped that Rhi had visited when she had been in Italy a few months ago and reminded herself to ask when they got back. Had Rhi been there, she would have captured some great photos, much better than she or Mitchel could manage.

Ali had the feeling that Mitchel wanted her to love it all as much as he did. It wasn't difficult. She'd loved Orvieto, Villa Geisomino, the vineyard, and everywhere he had taken her. She smiled as she remembered Rhi telling her she should take Mitchel to Orvieto when she had returned from her week away. Ali couldn't wait to share everything with Rhi when she got home.

On the day they left; Guglielmo hugged her as if they had known each other for years. Ali was sad to leave him but, as he reminded her, he'd see her again, and he hoped soon.

CHAPTER 23

ALI AND MITCHEL

On the journey home, Ali was still on cloud nine. The holiday had been wonderful. Different in every way to any other holiday she had ever been on, and she had loved it. She had visited Italy before, mostly with girlfriends, partying, spending time sunbathing, or lying around the pool. Mitchel had introduced her to the real Italy, and she was sad to leave. Usually, at the end of the holidays, she was glad to be going home to get a rest, but this time she was looking forward to visiting again. She was sure Mitchel would take her back.

When they arrived home, however persuasive he tried to be, smothering her with kisses, Ali had to extricate herself from his arms. She couldn't stay at Mitchel's, as she had a meeting in school the next morning and needed to be refreshed and prepared. Even though it was the holidays, as head of the art department, she had some organising to do. She and Janice, the headteacher, had to plan the teaching timetables for the new art teacher taking over from Rhi.

After spending most of the morning and early afternoon in school, Ali went to see Rhi. She wanted to give her the necklace she had bought her. But she also couldn't wait to tell her all about the holiday. Also, she wanted to see how Rhi was doing, whether she was coping. She felt a little guilty because she hadn't given much thought to her while she'd been away. She also hadn't seen much of her since the evening she and Mitchel had gone round to support her after Rhi had found Tibbs' body.

When she arrived at Rhi's, she was pleased to see her friend in a happy mood. Rhi loved the necklace, and sitting in the front garden, Ali told her all about the holiday over a coffee. Rhi couldn't get a word in edgeways as Ali rambled on about everywhere they had visited, the vineyard, Mitchel's uncle Guglielmo, and several times she mentioned the size of the house. "And he can speak perfect Italian!" she said, as though it were a huge surprise.

"Well, you'd have been even more surprised if he'd spoken Swahili." They both burst out laughing.

"You know what I mean. I've never heard Mitchel say anything in Italian. I didn't know he spoke it."

"Well, I don't suppose there's much call for it in Barnstaple. I can't believe that Mitchel managed to keep all that quiet. He must be good at keeping secrets," Rhi said, as Ali stopped for a breath and to take a drink of her coffee.

"I know. He didn't say anything until we arrived. I thought it was a posh hotel; it was stunning."

"I hope you took pictures."

"Yes, but they won't be as good as yours. Every time we visited somewhere, I kept saying that to Mitchel. 'I bet Rhi got better pictures than we will.' Finally, I think he got fed up with me saying it."

"At least you know your limits," Rhi said cheekily. Ali hit her playfully on the arm, nearly knocking her coffee over in the process.

"So, what have you been up to while I was away?" Ali asked.

Rhi smiled. "Well…I had a visitor."

Ali looked at her in surprise. "You didn't…?"

"I did. Several times."

Ali opened her mouth to say something, but before she could, Rhi continued, "Josh came round to tell me about his exam results. We talked about Gemma, cried together, and then one thing led to another and…" She sighed. "I just can't forget him, Ali."

They sat in silence for a few minutes. Ali spoke first. "Well, at least he's left school now, so it's all legal! But he's going off to college soon.

How's that going to work?"

"I know. We talked about that, and he's adamant he's going to continue to see me, but I don't know. He's going to meet girls his age..." Her voice trailed off.

"You don't want to hear this, but he probably will. However, if you are happy for now, then maybe just go for it knowing it will end. Can you cope with that?"

"Honestly, I don't know. There is a connection between us, which sounds stupid because Josh is so much younger! Yet! It just feels right. I can't explain; we fit together."

Ali tried to lighten the atmosphere. "Gross, too much information."

It was Rhi's turn to hit Ali. "Do you have to bring everything down to sex?"

"Mmm, yes!" They both laughed, the mood changed, and Ali switched the subject, telling Rhi about the upcoming weekend trip to meet Mitchel's parents. She was feeling a little nervous, especially after finding out he was much better off than she had thought.

Rhi told her, "He's obviously pretty serious about you, so just be yourself. He wants you to meet his parents. You'll be fine."

The following Saturday morning, Ali held on to Rhi's words as Mitchel drove them through the Devon countryside towards Lynton. She'd be fine. He had told her his parents' house was in the country, outside Lynton, with a view across fields looking out to sea. It sounded lovely and having already seen the place in Italy, Ali certainly wasn't expecting a three-bed semi! She had been right not to.

When they arrived, they pulled into a drive that disappeared down a slight rise so the house couldn't be seen from the road. The house itself was one of those modern glass designs Ali had coveted when watching the TV programmes about building your dream home. Mitchel's parents' house fit the bill perfectly. And to top it off, it was built in a position most people could only fantasise over. Once inside the house, you understood the need for the glass. The house faced the coastline, and on a sunny day like today, the view was glorious.

Mitchel's parents were lovely, making her very welcome. His

mum, Gina, was almost how Ali had imagined her; dark hair swept up beautifully into a neat chignon, so you focused on her beautiful face. She was every bit the sophisticated Italian mamma. After the fantastic lunch, prepared by Gina, they sat on the patio drinking wine, chatting, and relaxing while taking in the sea view. Neither Gina nor Martin, her husband, made Ali feel the slightest bit uncomfortable. Happily, they seemed to accept their son's choice of girlfriend. They talked about the vineyard, and Mitchel broke into Italian at one point, which his mum told him was rude, even though Ali loved listening to him talking to Gina in her language. Later in the afternoon, one of Mitchel's sisters turned up with her husband and children. The house was suddenly much noisier as the children ran around playing with their toys. No one seemed to mind, leaving them to it.

The conversation was buzzing when Mitchel's sister Gabby began to ask him, "So, when are you moving to..."

Before she could continue Mitchel shut her down with a curt comment in Italian that sounded angry to Ali, without her even understanding what he had said, and with a look that would wither the most strong-hearted. He quickly changed the subject, talking about the children, asking how they were doing at school. Ali could see that Gabby had suddenly realised she had made a mistake and went very quiet.

Not able to contain herself any longer, Ali asked Mitchel, "Where are you moving to, Mitchel?" At that point, everyone seemed to stop talking. Mitchel glared at Gabby.

"I'll tell you on the way home. I've been waiting to tell you about it."

Ali didn't want to let it go. "If you're moving, why haven't you told me? Is it local or further away?"

Gabby couldn't contain herself any longer, blurting out, "He's moving to Italy to take over the running of the vineyard." Mitchel released another furious torrent of Italian at his sister.

Ali asked him what he had said. "I just told her she should learn to keep her big mouth shut. She always must have the last word. I was going to tell you, Ali, when I was ready, but now is not that time!" He was furious. Ali had never seen him angry before, not seriously angry like this. He had pretended to be mad on occasions, but he had gone red today and clenched his hands. Now everybody was quiet, even the children.

Gina came across, quietly said something in Italian that sounded like an admonishment. Then, taking Ali by the hand, she led her down the garden. "Come for a walk with me, dear."

Ali glanced behind her to see Mitchel still laying into his sister and his dad, Martin, trying to calm them both down.

"I apologise for my children's behaviour," said Gina. "They have always fought. Plus, Gabby is annoyed that Mitchel is going to run the vineyard rather than her and Bobby."

"He hadn't told me he was moving." Ali could feel herself becoming upset. Everything was going so well. They had just had a fantastic holiday. Today had been lovely; up until now. She turned away, hoping Gina hadn't seen her eyes filling with tears.

Gina was incredibly empathetic. She took Ali's hands in hers. "I know you two haven't been together that long, but he cares greatly about you. It is extremely rare for him to bring girlfriends home; in fact, I'd say you are only the second." She smiled at Ali. "He should have told you, but I don't think he knows how."

Ali tried to return Gina's smile. "I thought he knew me well enough to tell me something this important. I don't know how a long-distance relationship is going to work."

Gina smiled back. "I understand, especially when you care for him so much too. I can tell, just seeing the pair of you together. Come, let us try to enjoy the rest of our afternoon. You two can talk about it when you are back home. Let's continue enjoying this sunshine while it's still here. The one thing I don't like about living in the UK – summers don't always remain summery."

Ali couldn't help but smile back at Gina. She had been very gracious in the way she had reacted. Gina linked her arm into Ali's, and arm in arm, they slowly started to walk back towards the others. Halfway down the garden, Mitchel joined them. Gina kissed him before walking away towards the house, leaving them alone.

"I'm sorry, Ali, I didn't mean you to hear like that. Do you want to leave now so we can talk?"

She did, but at the same time, she couldn't desert his parents after they had been so kind. "No, we'll talk about it later when we get home, but I think we should drive home tonight, not stay. Will your parents understand?"

"I know they will." Mitchel leaned forwards to kiss her, trying to take her hand. She responded to his kiss but ignored his hand. For the rest of the afternoon, Ali felt like she was watching everything through a lace veil, as if it was all slightly muted. By playing with the children, she managed to forget, for a short time, the feeling of creeping dread that was slowly filling her heart.

They left around 8pm, with Gabby whispering an apology to Ali as she hugged her and Gina and Martin telling her they hoped to see her again soon. The atmosphere on the drive home was cold. Ali didn't trust herself not to cry, so she kept quiet. Mitchel focused on driving, although she saw him glance across at her a couple of times from the corner of her eye, a look of concern on his face. Finally, when they arrived back at his flat, she couldn't contain her tears any longer, and with a mixture of anguish and anger, spluttered, "Why on earth didn't you tell me you are moving to Italy?"

"At least sit down, Ali." Mitchel took a deep breath. "Because I knew this would happen." He paused. "That night I met you, I wasn't looking for a relationship. I was out for a fun time."

Still wandering around the room, Ali flashed him an angry look and was about to say something, but Mitchel continued, "Then I got to know you, and I realised I liked you more than I was expecting to, and it…you were more than just a bit of fun. I love being with you."

"How long have you known you were moving to Italy?"

Mitchel couldn't meet her eyes. "Since becoming an adult, I've always known that at some point I'd take over from Guglielmo, but I didn't think it would be for ages yet."

Ali fell on the sofa. "So, why start a relationship with me? Did you know when we went to Italy? Was that why you went there?"

"No, I didn't know Guglielmo was going to talk to me about moving over. I just wanted to take you there to see where I would be moving to in the future, to see if you like it, let you meet Guglielmo. I was thinking about our future." Mitchel looked at her hopefully.

"Our future! Since when do you make plans for my future?" Her anger now fuelled Ali's tears.

Mitchel looked hurt. "I'm sorry, but it has all happened too soon. I've fallen for you, Ali. I love you, and I was hoping that we'd have time together for our relationship to grow even stronger before moving to Italy together."

"You love me?"

"Yes, I do," Mitchel's face brightened up, looked more hopeful. "I hope you feel the same."

Ali sighed. "I love you too, Mitchel, but my life is here; I'm not sure I'm ready to move to Italy or have someone else organise my life for me."

Completely missing what she had said after 'I love you too', Mitchel had pulled her towards him and kissed her. "We can work this out, Ali, we can!"

Ali returned his kiss but then pulled away from him. "I need to think about things. This is all too much. I'm sorry, I have to go." Reaching the door, she looked back to see Mitchel's hopefulness fade from his face as, deflated, he sank back onto the sofa.

CHAPTER 24

BEN

As Ben entered the house, the silence hit him. Over the last few weeks, after the initial grief of his mum's death and the release from his carer duties, the house had started to feel empty and too big. He felt lonely as he rattled around the space. He didn't have any friends he could catch up with; they had long gone after his parents' accident. Most of them didn't know what to say to him, with caring for his mum taking up most of his time. He was used to being alone in many ways, but recently his loneliness had begun to invade his whole being.

Ben's morning had been busy delivering some designs to a client, which he'd managed to take longer over than was required. It had given him an excellent excuse to get out and about, meaning he hadn't been in the house alone the whole day. Ben didn't think he had ever felt so alone. He wandered into the kitchen to make himself a coffee, which he drank while staring out into the garden. He was picturing Rhi's little garden – how inviting it had looked. Very different from the overgrown, untidy jungle in front of him. He decided there and then to find a local landscape gardener to come and re-do it for him. Next time he visited Rhi's, he'd take a picture of her garden and use it as a model for ideas for the makeover of his own. Ben was pleased with this idea.

Another thought struck him. He wanted to update the kitchen, so that he could add bifold doors too. He could alter the whole layout on the ground floor if he knocked the wall out between the lounge and the kitchen, creating one ample, open living space. It would make the layout almost the same as Rhi's cottage, just on a larger scale. His office would be to the right of the front door, and then from the hall on the left, the new open-plan lounge and kitchen. Ben smiled to himself. When Rhi moved in, she would recognise the similarities with the layout of her own home, which would help her settle into the house. He could feel his mood lifting. So, after his coffee he decided he would start searching for gardeners and builders, knowing he couldn't manage all the alterations himself.

Sitting down at the kitchen table, he continued to read the book he'd 'borrowed' from Rhi's on his last visit. Ian Rankin's *Saints of the Shadow Bible*. He was enjoying the dour character of Rebus and the grittiness of the settings. He wasn't a big reader, but he was certainly enjoying reading this book, and not just because it was Rhi's. With his coffee finished, he marked where he was in the book and went into his office to research gardeners and builders. Ben felt much better than when he'd walked into the house earlier. Keeping busy – that was the answer. He still had so much to do to the house to get it Rhi-ready, as he had termed the makeover. By the time he'd finished his research, he had found a couple of gardeners and builders to contact. First, though, he wanted to revisit the cottage.

He hadn't been around to Rhi's house for a couple of days. Now she wasn't teaching, and opportunities were few and far between. He couldn't get inside her space and enjoy breathing in her air, her scent. So, Ben logged on to Facebook and checked her profile to see if he could gain any information about what she was doing this week. After a few seconds, there it was, posted earlier this morning – just what he was looking for. He read her post: 'Excited to visit the exhibition in Bideford, where I've got some work on show. Drop by and see me at "Artistry Co" in the high street. I'll be there all day.'

Rhi was being very helpful. If she was going to be there all day, he could visit the cottage in safety. He decided he'd go to the beach and check to make sure she had gone. It was a bright day, and it would do him good to get out into the fresh air.

Rather than park near Rhi's cottage, Ben thought he'd park closer to Whitend Café, where there was plenty of parking. It also meant he would have a good walk along the coastal path. The views were perfect today; he could see for miles. There was no heat haze, just a beautiful blue sky causing the sea to glisten in the sunlight. He could see Lundy clearly, and to the south, towards Westward Ho! Rhi was lucky to live this close to the beach. Ben suddenly felt a little nervous, wondering if she would ever want to leave this view and her cottage. Maybe he could move in with her. It wasn't something Ben had considered before, and it upset his equilibrium for a minute. He had been planning for her to move in with him all along, whereas maybe she would prefer for them to live in her cottage. He stopped in his tracks. Why was he wasting his time making all the changes to his home? He thought about this quandary for a while, and then answered the question. He would still need to do his house up if he was going to sell it, so he wasn't wasting his time. Continuing to walk, he was nearing Rhi's cottage. Her car wasn't there, so she had gone out.

He put the key into the front door and got a shock. It wouldn't open! Rhi had changed the lock. He found the backdoor key in his pocket and, walking around to the side of the house, prayed she hadn't changed that lock too. He held his breath as he gingerly put the key into the lock. Then, breathing a huge sigh of relief that the key still fit, he let himself into the house. For a while he stood perfectly still, listening to make sure there wasn't anyone home. He was right; the house was empty.

Ben knew how upset he would have been if she had changed all the locks. He would have been exasperated. After putting his jacket on the settee, he walked over to the kitchen to make himself a coffee. Part of his plan for this visit was to photograph the garden, but first he needed to see if Rhi had a spare front door key for the new lock. He thought about where he would keep spare keys, initially searching through the kitchen drawers, but found nothing. Next, he went into her study to look. They weren't in a drawer, but she had left a couple of copies sitting on one of the bookshelves. She must have intended to give them to friends. 'Not very security minded, Rhi,' he thought. Ben smiled at the hypocrisy of the situation. He removed one key from the keyring and put it in his jeans pocket. He'd get a copy cut later and return it on his next visit.

Looking out at the garden, he decided he'd go out for a closer look after he'd been upstairs to visit Rhi's room. This time, he was careful not to spill any coffee on the bed. He put the coffee cup down on the bedside table before lying on the duvet, breathing in the scent of Rhi. With his eyes closed, he felt the warmth of the sun on his face, imagining she had just got up, leaving him resting a little longer after spending the night together, their bodies close. He began to fantasise about her naked body next to his. Abruptly, he sat up, breathing heavily, aware of his erection. He felt ashamed and horrified with his body. He didn't want to think of Rhi in that way. Not as something smutty. He wasn't one of those men who read girlie magazines to turn themselves on. He had always prided himself at being able to contain his sexual feelings. Then thoughts returned to the night he had met Gem and how her touch had so easily aroused him. Angrily, he got off the bed. His erection had subsided as he walked into Rhi's en-suite. He ran the cold tap, splashing water on his face. He didn't want this memory here in Rhi's room!

Slowly his anger subsided, and he returned to her bedroom to collect his coffee. He took a drink, but it had cooled down and was now tepid. Walking back into her dressing room, he began to run his fingers over the different materials of her clothes. She didn't have a lot of dresses, mostly jeans and tops, with a few short skirts. He liked the way she dressed. She always looked smart and modern, but never what his mother would have referred to as 'tarty'. After a while, he was beginning to feel too hot, so he decided he'd go out and take pictures of the garden. He grabbed the mug from the bedside table, looked around the room to make sure nothing looked disturbed, and walked back downstairs.

After washing his mug, he put it back in the cupboard. Then, having worked out how to open them, he slid the bifold doors back and walked out into the garden. It was incredibly peaceful, very sheltered, and private too. The garden was a suntrap. The fact that no one overlooked it was great – perfect for naked sunbathing, should you be into that sort of thing. Ben got out his mobile and took pictures from several angles to show a gardener the effect he was after.

There were two large seats to the left of the garden, which Ben hadn't initially recognised as being the shape of upended boats. Someone had very cleverly cut up the bow ends of two craft, retaining the seat. Or they had created the shapes from scratch. Either way, the two seats were perfect. They were painted white and shades of blue, with soft cushions on the seating. He sat in one of them to get a different view of the garden. He imagined Rhi sitting there with her coffee, relaxing in the sunshine.

His daydreaming was rudely and suddenly interrupted when he heard a vehicle coming into the drive. Panicking, he rushed to the side gate to look through. Relieved to see it wasn't Rhi, he wondered how he would explain his presence in her garden to a gardener. The vehicle was a truck full of gardening tools. He sat back down on the seat, trying to look as though he should be there.

The gardener, a guy in his late fifties, carrying a collection of tools, walked into the garden and looked a little startled to see Ben. "Oh, I wasn't expecting anyone to be here. Rhi didn't mention she had someone visiting." The gardener didn't look suspicious, just surprised.

"Hi. No, she didn't know I'd be here. I dropped in last night – I'm an old uni friend, just popped down for a few days." Ben extended his hand, wanting to appear friendly and normal. The gardener put his tools down and returned Ben's handshake.

Ben stood up, saying, "No worries. I'll go back inside. I need to pop out to the shops anyway, so I'll leave you to it."

"OK. Have a good visit." The gardener picked up a hoe and started to attack some of the weeds.

Ben walked back into the house as nonchalantly as he could, hoping he could shut the bifold doors easily. He needn't have worried. They slid shut with ease. Locking them, he checked again he had left the kitchen as he had found it. Slipping his hand into his jeans pocket to assure himself the key was still there, he felt the coolness of the metal. Then, smiling, he walked out of the house.

CHAPTER 25

RHI

The second workshop had been a huge success, with no problems or interruptions. I was relieved as I had quite a few new people attending. When we finished, several attendees said they were booking for next year, so I finished the week feeling buoyant. Although there was a subtle move of things in the studio, I wasn't sure if it was one of the other students or my unwanted visitor! Besides, unless someone had got into the studio while we'd been on the beach, it would have been impossible to get in at any other time because of the alarm. And after the positive week I'd had, I wasn't going to worry about it too much; I wouldn't let someone else ruin my time. After all, I had seen Josh and was feeling a lot more pragmatic about life in general. And in two weeks he'd be back from his Jamaican trip.

Much to my surprise, I'd also had a call from a local private girls' school – The Beeches. They were looking for someone to take over for a couple of weeks because of maternity leave. The teacher they had organised to take over had been in for several months but had been taken ill, so now they needed someone else just for the last few weeks. I asked them if they knew why I had left my last job, which they did, but they still wanted me. I agreed to go along and visit for an informal interview. They offered me the job there and then. The headteacher, Miss Hopkins, had already spoken to Janice, who had generously given me a glowing reference, so they knew about my work at Whittingbury Academy. And despite my resignation, they knew I was hardly going to be a threat to their girls!

The job was only for three days a week, from September until mid-October, which meant I had time for any projects I wanted to work on. They had a pretty good setup in terms of their art room. It was nowhere near as spacious or as well-equipped as Whittingbury, but still adequate. As far as small private schools go, it wasn't bad. However, it was nothing compared to the amazing setup at Cheltenham Ladies' College, where I had visited as part of a short placement while at art college. Things were certainly on the up. Two successful workshops and a well-paid job for a couple of weeks. Life was improving.

I hadn't done any real cleaning around the house for weeks as I'd had too many other things on my mind to bother. Besides, it was always a chore, certainly not an enjoyment! I was therefore almost grateful when the doorbell rang. It was Ali, who I wasn't expecting and hadn't seen since she had been to meet Mitchel's parents. Thinking about it, I was surprised not to have heard from her when she got back, but I'd been too caught up doing my stuff, so had not thought about it. As soon as I saw her, I knew something wasn't right. Her eyes looked blotchy, her hair lank, as though she hadn't washed it, and she wasn't wearing make-up. She looked completely dishevelled. Normally, she never left the house without at least mascara. This was not the lively friend I was used to seeing.

"What's happened?" I asked, my first thought being she and Mitchel had broken up.

Almost throwing herself at me, Ali burst into tears. I put my arms around her, hugging her tight until she had calmed down a little, managing to push the front door shut behind her at the same time. Once she'd settled, we walked into the lounge where she fell onto the sofa.

"Do you want a coffee?" She nodded. "Then you can tell me what's going on," I continued.

After a few sips of her coffee, Ali finally managed to control her sobs and, noisily blowing her nose, she told me about the weekend visit to Mitchel's parents and the revelation of his move to Italy. When she finished telling me, I smiled at her. "I know it must have been a shock, but isn't it a good thing that he loves you? You love him, don't you?" I asked.

"You know I do, but I'd not even considered moving anywhere now. I'm building my career." She stopped abruptly. "I'm sorry you've lost yours…"

I interrupted, "Don't be silly. It's not about me. Go on."

Ali continued, "I'm still developing the department. I've got so many plans and you know how much I love my job. I am serious about him, and yes, I do want to be with him, but I still have so much I want to do at school. He's expecting too much!" She took a long breath. Tears started rolling down her cheeks again. She wiped them away, now feeling anger as much as anything else, and drank more coffee.

We sat in silence for a moment. I was trying to think of what to say next. It was a difficult situation. I knew Ali loved Mitchel, but things had happened very quickly. "Did Mitchel know he was going to be moving to Italy so soon?" I asked.

"No, I don't think so. I think he said that it wasn't supposed to be yet, but I wasn't completely listening. I was so angry that he expected me to give up everything just like that! And I was confused, because I do love him and maybe in a few years, but this is not the right time." Ali looked at me, as though imploring me to give her the answer.

All I could think of was, "When is the right time?" It was a rhetorical question; I didn't expect Ali to answer, and she didn't. She just sat opposite me, looking lost and confused. "You need to go and talk to him," I said, trying to be encouraging. "If you don't talk, you can't sort anything out." She didn't reply, just nodded silently, continuing to drink her coffee.

I told her about my part-time job at The Beeches, thinking it might take her mind off things for a while. By the time we'd both finished our coffees, she had relaxed and looked more like the normal 'Ali'.

"What are you doing for the rest of the week?" Ali asked.

"I've got to go and collect my stuff from Bideford, then…"

Ali interrupted, "I'm sorry, how did the exhibition go? I forgot to ask."

"It was OK, thanks. I only sold one piece, but that's better than nothing. They never get a huge footfall, but sometimes people get in touch afterwards wanting to buy something they saw but couldn't afford at the time. It's always hit and miss," I explained. "Then the rest of the week – tomorrow I'm going to start some planning for teaching The Beeches girls. I hope they're not too snooty. The ones I saw during my last visit seemed OK, but you never know."

"But it's not Cheltenham is it, darling?" Ali said, trying to sound haughty and laughing at the same time. It was good to see her smiling again.

"Do you want to stay for lunch? Then we could go for a wander on the beach for a bit," I asked.

"Yes, that'd be good. It will take my mind off Mitchel for a while and help me relax," she replied.

With some disappointment, I said, "Except, I wanted to hear about Mitchel's parents."

After a pause, Ali replied, "I think I could manage to tell you about that. They were lovely and their house is amazing."

We spent the rest of the day together, which was wonderful. We hadn't had this much time, hanging out, relaxing, and laughing together for ages. Not since the fatal weekend and all that had followed. Life had changed drastically for both of us, but at least we still had our friendship, for which I was incredibly grateful.

The next week seemed to pass far too slowly. I kept thinking about Josh, hoping he was having a good time with his parents in Jamaica meeting family. Ali was on my mind too, and I hoped she had spoken to Mitchel, though a few days after I'd seen her she still hadn't been to see him. I think she wanted to make him suffer, though of course she was inflicting pain on herself too. I'd also managed to plan several weeks' lessons for my part-time teaching job, so I was feeling pleased with myself that I'd managed to plan. It meant I could concentrate on my work for the couple of weeks I had left before the school term started again. I was surprised how easily I had relaxed into *not* thinking about Whittingbury. So many other things had kept my mind busy, which was a good thing.

I had started work on a new series of paintings and was busy in the studio when my mobile rang. "Hi. I'm Kyra Jackson, I'm a local journalist. I wondered if I could come and talk to you about an article I'm writing?"

I was suspicious. "Why do you want to talk to me? Is this anything to do with my resignation from Whittingbury Academy?" I asked, feeling a little annoyed that she should think that it was all right to intrude on my life.

There was a pause, before Kyra answered, "Only in a very roundabout way. Look, rather than talk on the phone, could I buy you a coffee and tell you about it? You don't have to agree to anything; just listen to what I'm writing about and see if you'd be interested in being involved."

I calmed down. She sounded pleasant enough, and if I didn't agree to anything, meeting someone new and having a coffee might be a good thing, so I agreed to meet her at Whitend Café the next morning.

Walking into the café, I looked around, realising that I didn't know who I was looking for. Of course, I needn't have worried as she knew who I was. After all, my photo had been plastered all over the local paper. Kyra waved to me across the room. She was around my age, which surprised me. I had imagined someone older, maybe because in my head journalists weren't young. Where had that idea come from? They had to start at some point! Kyra had an air of confidence but in a positive way. She leapt out of her chair, offering to buy me a coffee, then disappeared off to the counter to order it for me.

I made myself comfortable. Returning with my coffee, Kyra sat opposite me. "It's good to meet you. Thanks for coming." She smiled at me.

I decided to be honest: "I'm not sure what you want from me, and I am feeling a little suspicious, especially after being written about in the local papers without anyone talking to me about my side of the story."

"I can understand that. I suppose it was quite a sensational story for little Whittingbury, which of course didn't help you. I'm sorry about what happened. How are you getting on, now you're not at the school?" Kyra asked, with what seemed like genuine interest.

I thought carefully about my answer, as she still hadn't told me what she wanted to write about. "I'm doing OK. I hadn't wanted to leave, but circumstances overtook my needs." I took a sip of my coffee. "So, what do you want to talk about? What is your article about?"

Kyra smiled at me again. She did have a lovely open face. I realised that in my head I had a stereotypical idea of what a journalist should look like. It was nothing like her. She continued, "I'll talk to you about that in a minute. But I'd just like to get to know you a little first. How long have you been in Whittingbury?"

I relaxed, telling her about Aunt Jinny. About how long I'd been visiting for holidays before moving here a couple of years ago. I also told her about my unknown follower. She seemed genuinely concerned about the latter. In return, I asked her how long she had worked as a journalist and had lived in Whittingbury, if she did. Kyra told me she was born in Bideford and lived there still, although she worked between there and Whittingbury. She often wrote for the *Chronicle* but was at pains to say she hadn't written the story about me. Interestingly, Kyra's mum was from Jamaica, but her parents weren't together anymore. Her dad, who was Bideford born and bred, had brought her up. She reminded me of Gemma. She appeared to have a sense of independence and self-confidence that so many women I know don't have. Kyra didn't need to follow fashion trends, having her own unique style. Looking at her made me think I was quite boring in my dress sense. I tend to stick to the same styles I like, which aren't that individual and, upon reflection, are not very creative for an artist.

As we chatted, I began to relax more. "So, what is this article you're writing?" I asked.

"Well, it's not for the local press, but an article for a national magazine. It's about people who are in relationships with younger partners." She stopped, when she saw the look of horror on my face, before continuing, "I know it might seem a bit thoughtless of me after what happened, but I thought you might like to get your side of the story out and it would be interesting for people to hear."

"Yes, it is thoughtless, and far too soon," I replied, thinking it would always be too soon. I felt angry. I was enjoying talking to her, but that she had even considered asking me broke the generosity of my mood.

I began to stand to leave but Kyra, putting her hand on my arm to stop me, gently said, "I'm sorry, Rhi. I have misjudged this. I was being over-keen; putting my journalistic hat on. I truly wanted people to hear your story. I couldn't believe that someone who had such a good career and a great reputation with both pupils and staff would throw it all away for a quick fling. I honestly thought you must have had a good reason."

Slowly I sat down, finishing the last of my coffee, which was beginning to go cold, and giving myself time to calm down and consider my answer. "I did have a good reason, and you're right, it wasn't a quick fling. Well, it has turned out not to be. But I'm not ready to talk about it publicly, not yet. It is too soon, and it wouldn't be fair on Josh."

"That's OK. I understand. I wanted to ask you, but maybe in the future when things have quietened down. Perhaps then you might want to share your side of the story? Please stay. Let's just sit and chat. I'm enjoying getting to know you. Would you like another coffee?"

Kyra had a great manner, having managed to calm me. "Thank you, yes I would. I appreciate you not being too pushy."

"Do you fancy a cake with it? I think we need to have something a bit gooey to lighten our mood, don't you?" Kyra was very persuasive, so I agreed to a chocolate muffin.

She asked me more about my 'secret admirer', and whether I'd been to the police or made any other enquiries. I told her briefly about my previous issues with Paul and how, although the police had been involved, it hadn't been that useful in the long run. She made some suggestions of things I could do, along the same lines that Mitchel had spoken about. By the time we had finished our second coffees we had settled into a comfortable chat about everything and anything, with Kyra even telling me about her latest man. We got on well, finding we had quite a bit in common when it came to what we liked to read. Before we left, we made a date for another catch-up for a drink one night the following week. I felt good having made a new friend; someone who wasn't connected to my previous life in school, and I was looking forward to spending time with her again.

As much as I understood what both Kyra and Mitchel were saying, stubbornly, the idea of having cameras around my house annoyed me. Especially when it was because of someone else who was intruding into my life. I knew I was being my own worst enemy, but I wasn't ready to make my home into a fortress, which is how I considered cameras. Besides, this didn't feel like the situation I had with Paul. This time, I didn't know the person. That was the weird part. Surely, if someone was interested in me romantically, they would speak to me? Unless of course, he's incredibly shy but, on the other hand, he hadn't done anything to hurt me. What I did know was I couldn't face going through that feeling that my life wasn't my own as I had with Paul. I'd made the decision back then. Nobody else was going to control how I lived my life!

CHAPTER 26

FOUR YEARS EARLIER – BREAKING POINT

In the end, I decided to go out despite Paul. I wanted to celebrate Jackie's birthday with the rest of them. We were having a great night, laughing, catching up on the latest gossip about what was going on at school and trying to get Jackie slightly drunk. Jackie's boyfriend, Johnny, suddenly said to me, nodding in the direction of the entrance, "Isn't that Paul over there?" I turned to look. Sure enough, I just managed to see the back of him disappearing out of the door. Feeling awkward and embarrassed, I said, "He must have had a drink with some mates after work."

We carried on our conversation as I tried hard to put him out of my head and enjoy the rest of the night. However, I was annoyed that he had been there and had a niggling suspicion that I would pay for it when I got home.

And I was right, for as soon as I got through the door, Paul started on at me. "Who was that guy you were sat next to?" he demanded.

Not having remembered speaking to any men, I was going to say, 'what guy?', when I knew he must have meant Johnny, one of the other teachers. "Johnny's a teacher – he's just one of my mates from work."

Paul didn't look happy. "So, why was he sat so close to you if he's just a mate?"

"Come on, Paul. He's seeing someone, and even if he wasn't, aren't I allowed to speak to colleagues? Surely you have women that you work with and talk to. Or don't you think you can have women friends?"

"Of course, I work with women, but I don't see the need to spend time with them outside work and I don't see why you have to, either."

I was shocked. Trying to keep calm, I took time to think about my answer. "I enjoy having conversations with my friends outside work because they are just that – friends. Don't you trust me to behave, Paul?"

"Of course, I trust you, but I don't trust them. You are my girlfriend; I don't want other men drooling over you."

I couldn't believe what I was hearing. Paul seemed to be suggesting that I shouldn't be out with male friends or even talk to them. He was behaving like my father, not my boyfriend. And on reflection, even my dad had never been that paranoid about who I was seeing. "Paul, yes, I am your girlfriend, but you don't tell me who I can be friends with and who I can talk to."

Paul pulled me roughly towards him. "If I say you won't go out with your friends, you won't, do you hear?"

I pushed at his body, struggling to get out of his arms. "Who made you the big 'I am'? Let go of me, you…you…bully. You don't own me – get off me."

Paul slapped me hard on the side of my cheek. It happened so quickly, we both stopped in our tracks. I was stunned by both the reaction I had elicited from him and the painful slap. Paul appeared to be shocked at what he had done. Immediately after he'd hit me, he tried to pull me back towards him, saying, "Oh God, Rhi, I'm sorry."

Ignoring him, I ran out of the room and went up into the bathroom, where I locked the door before bursting into tears. No one had ever hit me before, not my parents and certainly no man. I sat on the loo seat and sobbed. How could Paul be so cruel and then, on other occasions, be so kind? I blew my nose, trying to control my sobs.

After a while, there was a gentle knock on the bathroom door. "Rhi, please. I'm sorry, please come out. Rhi? Please, Rhi, I'm sorry, I didn't mean to hit you. My anger got the better of me. Please forgive me."

I made him wait a little longer, then gingerly opened the door. He was sitting on the floor. Instantly he stood up and put his hand out towards me to hold mine. I looked at his big brown eyes. He looked sorry, and at that moment, I would have forgiven him most things. He pulled me towards him and gently kissed my cheek, which was still sore and was now very red. "I'm so sorry, Rhi; I just love you so much."

Again, the attraction between us took over, and we ended up in the bedroom. That is, we just about made it to the bed where we had the most amazing make-up sex – again. While we had sex, there was not a single hint of the cold, cruel, controlling person I had seen earlier. Despite an underlying feeling of foreboding, I pushed all the thoughts away, wanting to believe this was the real Paul.

Over the next few weeks, I felt like I was treading on eggshells. If I said the wrong thing or suggested anything that Paul could turn into something twisted in his mind, I waited for him to hit me or start laying into me verbally. The sad thing was that I always gave into him when he begged forgiveness afterwards. When holding me close, making love, he was the gentlest man you could ever meet, but he had another, darker side that he couldn't always keep at bay.

A few months later, though, things turned from bad to worse. I had continued to meet up with my friends, although often I didn't stay too late because that didn't seem to make Paul quite so angry. This night, Johnny was celebrating a promotion at school, so I couldn't not be there. We were laughing and having a great night when, suddenly, Paul turned up.

"What are you doing here, Paul?" I hadn't told him where I was going.

"I tracked you on your phone. I wanted to find out what you are really up to, and I can see." He almost spat his words out. He strode towards Johnny with a determination that scared me. I managed to stand between the two of them. Paul, pointing his finger at Johnny, shouted, "You leave my girlfriend alone; stay away from her."

Everyone else in the party froze in shock. Finally, Johnny started to reply, "Mate, she's just…"

"Are you listening – she's not just anything of yours! I don't want you touching her or even speaking to her again. You hear?" Paul's face was ugly when he was angry, and I could see the vein in his temple beating hard. I thought he would hit Johnny, but instead, he grabbed me by my hair and almost dragged me out of the pub. I could hear my friends shouting in the background. Someone was phoning the police.

Once outside, Paul pushed me down an alleyway, keeping a tight hold on me as he frogmarched me to his car, which wasn't far away. He pushed me into the passenger seat, and before I could get out, he had got into the driver's side and locked all the doors. As we drove off, I saw a police car arriving at the venue we had just left. I didn't dare say anything. I kept quiet, not even venturing to look at him. Once we got home, while Paul was locking the front door of the flat, I managed to get away from him, running into the bathroom before he could take his rage (which was now at boiling point) out on me. I was terrified. I could hear him banging around the flat. Then he started banging the bathroom door. I thought it would give way.

Luckily for me, one of the neighbours called the police, who turned up at the flat. When they arrived, I felt safe enough to come out of the bathroom. After talking for some time, they took Paul down to the station for questioning, asking me if I wanted to press charges. All I wanted was to get away, so they took me back to 'the teachers' house' and my friends.

CHAPTER 27

RHI – FIRST WEEK OF SEPTEMBER

Monday morning and the last week of school holidays had arrived. What had seemed impossible was going to happen – I would be teaching in a school again; only a few days a week but better than nothing. I felt a mixture of trepidation and excitement. I loved being in the classroom, helping my students create their work and improve themselves. But even so, The Beeches would be very different from Whittingbury Academy.

Even though I'd had a week's placement at Cheltenham Ladies' College during my art college year, I'd never taught for long at a girls' school, and I was sure The Beeches would be very different. Cheltenham Ladies' and The Beeches were poles apart. The only similarities were they both only taught girls and were private schools, but that's where any comparison stopped.

Cheltenham had pupils from all over the world, outstanding facilities, and parents who had to be wealthy to afford the termly fees. In contrast, The Beeches had fees, but at a different level and all the pupils were from the surrounding areas. They were the daughters of people who didn't want to send their little darlings to what they saw as rough state schools. Part of me didn't agree with private education, but as I'd seen on my visit to The Beeches, the only real advantage the pupils had was smaller classes. Their facilities were no better than Whittingbury's.

The actual teaching didn't start until next week, but I had a staff training day on Thursday, which was where I'd meet the rest of the staff and spend some time in the art room to prepare. Josh would be back from his family holiday and I was trying hard to keep him out of my mind as I knew he would be off to college this coming weekend. The thought of not seeing him again was heartbreaking, but at the same time, I knew I had to be realistic. I was fooling myself if I thought we'd manage to have a long-term relationship. But deep inside, I couldn't help but hope.

Rushing around, I grabbed my denim jacket, as I was going to meet Ali in town for a coffee. I wanted to hear if she had made up with Mitchel. I hoped they had, as I knew they loved each other. They just needed to talk about the move to Italy without getting heated. We had decided to meet at Watson's Café on the high street. Our last visit had been weeks ago. We both liked it there, as it was quieter than most of the other cafés in town, thanks to the owner's policy of asking mums to leave their buggies outside. This seemed to put most off from bothering to go inside, so generally there were only a few children in the café. It made a change from the others that were often filled with screaming babies and toddlers running around. I don't dislike children, but when I'm relaxing I prefer to be able to hear myself think and speak! The cafés near the beach were always noisy and packed with tourists when the season was in full swing, and out of season it was where most of the mums' groups met. Looking around Watson's, I noted it was mostly full of older couples and a few businesspeople sat here and there. As usual, I arrived first, grabbing a table near the window. Ali arrived a few minutes later, and I bought us both coffees and cakes.

"Have you spoken to Mitchel yet?" I asked Ali, as we both sat cradling our coffees. I should have guessed by her mood that she hadn't.

"No. I think he's the one who should get in touch with me after springing the move on me like that!"

"Oh, Ali! If one of you doesn't make the first move, you're going to regret it. You know you love each other, so surely you must be able to sort something out?" I told her. Ali didn't reply. I could see she was beginning to get tearful. "I'm sorry," I said, reaching out to hold her hand. "I didn't mean to upset you, but you've got to do something about this, otherwise you're going to be stuck in this stalemate."

Ali blew her nose, loudly. "I know. I think I might go over and see him this week. I don't want to lose him, but I'm…I'm just so angry with him for springing this on me." She had another drink of her coffee. "When we went to Italy, I loved it, and I loved his uncle. I just hadn't realised that he wasn't coping with the vineyard. I'm being selfish, aren't I? All I can think about is my career and Mitchel must be hurting because he loves Guglielmo so much. I liked him too; that's what makes it so hard."

I couldn't think of anything useful to say. Only Ali could decide what she should do, but I did know that she and Mitchel needed to talk, otherwise they'd not get anywhere.

We chatted about the new school term, which wasn't so hard now that I could also talk about my teaching job. Then I told her about meeting Kyra and how she had backed up what Mitchel had said about a camera for the house.

"Is your secret admirer still visiting?" Ali asked. I nodded, as I'd just taken a mouthful of cake. "So, why are you so much against having a camera?"

I sighed. "I don't want to be ruled by a man again. This situation is annoying, but it's not like Paul. I don't know who this is and, so far, he hasn't done anything to hurt me. I won't be made to feel like a prisoner in my own home."

"Yes, so far. Don't you think it's more dangerous that you don't know who it is?" Ali asked.

"I don't know. I have no idea who it can be, but having a camera on my house makes me feel I'm giving in to fear. That's how I felt with Paul, always scared. I'm not doing that again!"

"OK, I get it, but you need to do something, especially if he starts invading your privacy."

We sat in silence for a while. Ali asked if I wanted another coffee, and when I said 'yes' she went off to order them. As she put the coffees on the table, she asked tentatively, "Have you heard from Josh?"

"Not yet," I answered, trying to suggest confidence in that he would get in touch. "He only got back from Jamaica at the weekend."

"Are you wanting to hear from him?" Ali asked.

I tried not to sound too desperate, answering, "Yes," as casually as I could.

The next morning as I was on the beach gathering some shells and pebbles for teaching props, my mobile buzzed. My heart leapt with excitement when I saw the text – *Can I come over tonight? Josh x.* He wanted to come over later that evening. He'd only been back a few days and he'd got in touch! I felt so relieved. It was as if I'd been walking around holding my breath for the two weeks he'd been away, without my body realising it.

I replied. *Can't wait to see you x.* Then I deleted it. *Missed you, see you later x.* I deleted that too. Finally, I sent, *See you later x.* I was so scared of appearing to be pushy.

The rest of the day dragged, meaning I couldn't settle or concentrate on doing things. I did a little cleaning, then I went into the studio for an hour or so to spend time on the painting I was working on, but my mind wasn't on the job. Later in the afternoon, I decided to take a bath. After pouring myself a glass of wine, I added a bath bomb to the filling bathwater and, finally, relaxed, soaking in the water's warmth. I didn't usually take baths, but it was just what I needed. My mind completely relaxed. When I emerged, although a little wrinkly in places from the warm soak, I felt much calmer. I chose one of my few matching bra and knicker sets, deciding it looked sexy. My body ached as I thought about the coming evening.

Unexpectedly, I heard the gravel crunch in the driveway around 5pm. Intrigued, I went to see who it was. Any calmness I had managed disappeared. When I opened the door, it was Josh. I almost flung myself into his arms. So much for being grown-up about this, I thought. Josh held on to me as though it had been years since we last saw each other, before eventually letting go so I could close the front door.

"It's so good to see you," he said, his beautiful smile embracing his whole face. Echoing my thoughts from earlier, he said, "I can't believe I've only been away for two weeks." He began kissing me again and I just melted inside.

"How long can you stay?" I wondered.

"All night if you want, but I need to get back in the morning."

Of course, I wanted him to stay, but there was a little niggle in my head. Wouldn't he be missed overnight? After all, I'm sure part of the reason his parents took him to Jamaica was to get him away from me.

"Won't your parents be worried? Where do they think you are?" I asked, then felt stupid for asking.

Josh laughed. "Dad is away working, and Mum isn't as paranoid. She just accepted that I was meeting up with friends and that I might stay over with them. I am eighteen, remember?" We both laughed, as he kissed me again.

"I know, that was a stupid question, but I know how angry your dad was about us."

"Well, he can't be that angry with me, because he bought me that car, so I can drive myself back and forth to Cheltenham."

I looked through the window at the bright red Clio sitting on the drive. By its number plates, I could tell it was second-hand but in good nick.

"Wow, lucky you." I closed the curtain and pulled Josh further into the house. "Do you want a drink?"

"No, I was hoping you might have other things in mind."

"Is that all you want me for?" I said, laughing that I didn't need any further encouragement. By the time we reached my bedroom, our clothes were abandoned on the steps of the stairs.

Later, going down to get some food, Josh told me about his holiday in Jamaica. I had assumed they'd stay with family, but they'd stayed in a hotel, visiting relatives throughout the two-week stay.

"Dad doesn't like staying with family, it's too much hassle, and Mum likes the hotels. It means they've got all the luxuries, including a swimming pool, and they spray the grounds, so she doesn't get bitten by so many bugs. The last time they stayed with family, she was almost bitten to pieces!" He laughed gently. "The lifestyle out there is very different to here – for most Jamaicans. If you're wealthy, it's fine, but it's not like living here. Getting any internet is a nightmare if you're not in the right place. I couldn't live out there, apart from the weather."

"I've never been to the Caribbean. I've always thought it would be too hot for me," I told him. I'd never considered it, especially with my colouring, I tended to burn easily in the sun.

Josh continued to tell me about his relatives who sounded interesting characters. "The other thing is, that the locals know you're not Jamaican. They call you 'English'."

"How do they know, you're not Jamaican?" I asked, surprised by that.

"Well, I'm way lighter-skinned, but even with Dad, they can tell he's not Jamaican."

"But how?" I couldn't understand why.

"By the way we walk, how we dress, our accent when we speak. Mum has problems understanding what anyone says, especially when speaking patois, and I do too sometimes, which is another reason why we don't stay with family."

I interrupted, "Does your dad speak patois?"

"Sometimes, when he's with family. He can, but he doesn't most of the time."

"Can you?" I asked, intrigued.

Josh smiled. "Only a little, but even I have difficulties understanding relatives, sometimes. I didn't grow up listening to it, whereas Dad did when he was a child. It's just like when people go back home in the UK, they pick up their accent again."

"Yes, that's true, my mum did that when she went back to Wales. Her accent got much stronger. And although my dad spoke Polish, after his mum died, he rarely spoke it.

"When was the last time you went to Jamaica?" I asked him.

He thought for a moment. "I think I was about nine or ten. My sister has been back since with friends, but I wasn't that bothered. I enjoyed visiting some of the places that I hadn't been interested in when I was younger, plus we went to some bars in Kingston, which I hadn't been able to visit as a child. We went to Usain Bolt's cocktail bar – he wasn't at home though!" He laughed again.

After we'd eaten, we listened to music snuggled up on the sofa with our drinks.

"Have you got any pictures of you as a child? I've only seen that one of you and your grandmother," Josh asked.

"I might have," I said, getting up to grab the photo album from the shelf.

As we looked through the album, occasionally Josh would look at me, as though checking that I really was that little girl in the image. I hadn't looked at it for ages and it brought back a lot of memories of my parents, especially of Mum, before she died. As I turned one page, there was an image of Mum, dancing with me, somewhere in a field. I can't remember where it was, but I remembered the feeling of her holding my hands, singing, and us laughing as she swung me around. A tear slid down my cheek as I heard her laugh inside my head. Even now, all these years later, she was there.

Josh lifted my face towards him and kissed me. "I'm sorry, I didn't mean to upset you."

I wiped my face. "It's fine. I suddenly remembered that day. I don't think about her as much as I should. But I'm fine." I kissed him back, holding on to him. I couldn't explain it, but I felt safer than I'd ever felt before feeling Josh's arms holding me close. His age made no difference. He made me feel secure and protected.

When we went back upstairs, we made love before finally falling asleep, curled up together. I was woken early by the sunlight streaming into the room, where I hadn't quite shut the blinds completely the night before. Josh was still asleep but woke to find me staring intently at his face. Kissing me, he pulled me towards him, his body pressing into mine. We eventually got up around 9am and, after showering, we went down for breakfast. The air was heavy with our silence. Neither of us wanted to talk about the fact that at the weekend Josh was leaving for college. But we had to have that conversation. I decided to broach the subject. "When are you going to Cheltenham?"

"Friday. Mum and Dad are driving up in their car to see me settled in. I've got a room on the Hardwick campus. Where did you stay?"

"I was based at the Pittville campus – before they re-organised everything. You'll be closer to town than I was, which can't be a bad thing."

I didn't want to ask him straight out about us keeping in touch. He was young, and I knew he'd make lots of new friends. He'd meet girls his age. I remembered how close everyone got in my first couple of weeks. Those exciting new friendships, the freedom of being away from home, able to do what you want when you want. It had been the most exciting time of my life, until my relationship with Paul completely soured my memory of Cheltenham. My face must have been showing my thoughts.

"Hey, there's no reason to be sad," Josh said, kissing me.

"Sorry, I was just thinking about my last year at Cheltenham, which didn't go so well. And I was thinking about all the great new freedoms you'll have, being away from home. You'll be a dirty stop-out, partying every night. You'll soon meet someone your age and all this will be a forgotten memory," I managed to say, keeping my cool.

Josh smiled. "Yeah, there might be a different girl every night, possibly two at weekends." He was laughing, looking at me quizzically, and I realised he was teasing. Pulling me towards him, between kisses, he said, "I will be making new friends, but I will be saving myself for you. I'm not going to be looking for a new girlfriend. You're my girl…well, woman." He gave me a much longer kiss and I sank into his embrace, feeling both love and lust, as well as contentment.

CHAPTER 28

RHI

Josh eventually left around 11am, saying he'd ring me on Friday after his parents had gone. I hoped he would but thought it unlikely once he'd met up with some of the other students. I tried not to think about it too much, knowing I would have to resign myself to the fact that perhaps it was over, whatever it was.

After going upstairs, I tidied the bedroom. It looked as if there had been a catfight in the middle of the bed. The duvet was hanging off one side, and the bottom sheet was scrunched up. I decided I needed to put on some washing. As I was gathering the bedding together, something white, hidden slightly behind a photograph on my set of drawers, caught my eye. Pulling it out, I audibly gasped. "Wow!" It was a sketch of me. Naked, curled up, sleeping peacefully, the bedclothes abandoned, but still clinging to parts of my body. Josh must have sketched me earlier in the morning. The drawing was exquisite, and it was most obviously me. I couldn't believe I could look that beautiful. I placed it carefully on the bed and the soft sunlight fell on it, allowing me to see it more clearly. Josh must have found the sketchpad I kept in the house for the ideas I needed to draw before I forgot them. He must have crept downstairs while I was asleep! I had to get it framed – it was incredible.

I texted Josh to thank him rather than phone him in case his parents were around. He replied straight away. *I'm glad you like it. I was going to keep it but wanted to leave you a surprise. Speak Friday.*

Keeping myself busy for the rest of the day, I phoned Ali to ask her if she wanted to meet me at Whitend Café for lunch. She had been in school all morning, preparing for the new term, so was happy for a break. Initially, I didn't tell her about Josh's visit. Besides, I wanted to see if she had spoken to Mitchel, before sharing details of my happy love life. She had managed to have a conversation with him but said the atmosphere between them was still chilly. However, they were meeting on Friday night to have a good chat. I hoped they'd get things sorted out between them. I felt sad that Ali and Mitchel might split up when they appeared to love each other. It just didn't seem right.

She asked me about Josh, so I told her about his visit, and about the wonderful drawing he'd left. Then she asked me about my 'admirer'. I realised I hadn't thought about him during the last week at all, telling her, "I've been so busy, and haven't noticed anything unusual around the house, to be honest. I still haven't found that pair of knickers mind you, but I may have lost them somewhere in the house."

"I can believe that – they are pretty miniscule. I manage to lose socks, and never know where they go!" We both laughed.

"Maybe he's disappeared," I said, but I was not sure I believed that. However, I'd been feeling so much more positive this last few weeks after the new job, the success of the workshops, and, of course, Josh's visit yesterday.

Ali had to get back to school for a meeting with Megan, her second in the music department. Walking back along the cliff path, I gazed out to sea, which today looked like floating silk undulating in the breeze. My mind recalled how this time of year was usually manic for me, too. Although I still missed Whittingbury Academy immeasurably, a minute part of me felt relieved about not having the responsibility for all the lesson planning. I was beginning to enjoy creating my own artwork again, having time to paint without the pressures of timetables. I surprised myself with this recognition. Maybe I wasn't a career teacher after all, as much as I loved it. Perhaps I was embracing the fact that I am an artist.

I spent the rest of the afternoon and into the early evening in the studio, painting, finishing off the last of a series for clients who had bought one of my paintings at the recent exhibition in Bideford. I had been both delighted and surprised when asked to paint a series of paintings for them. The couple had recently bought a house in the countryside overlooking the River Torridge and, in their words, had several walls begging for artwork! How could I refuse? They were coming over to see the finished works next week, so I needed to get them finished.

Unusually for me, by 10pm I was feeling tired. It must have been the excitement of seeing Josh, and the small amount of sleep we had managed, catching up with me. I decided to go to bed early, curling up with a book to read. My eyes kept closing, and eventually, after waking up to find the book about to fall on the floor, I decided to mark the page I'd reached and go to sleep.

Suddenly, something woke me. Slightly dazed, I wondered if I'd overslept, and it was the postman or someone knocking on the door. But it was still dark. Someone was moving around inside the house. Slowly sitting up in bed, I kept still, trying to quieten my breathing, listening. Somewhere nearby a dog was barking, but nothing else – no other sounds, apart from the loud pounding of my heart. Feeling sick with fear, I put on my bedside light, thinking if there was anyone in the house the light would scare them off. Or not! I lay there for what seemed an age, holding my breath because my heartbeat was too noisy to hear anything. There was nothing. No more sounds – just the ear-beating silence of the night. Eventually, I turned the light off, managed to calm my breathing, and fell asleep.

The next morning, I wondered if I had been dreaming and if I did sit up in bed last night... After showering, I went downstairs for my breakfast. On the way down the stairs, I was suddenly aware of a familiar smell. Turps. I sniffed, inhaling to see if I was imagining it. I walked back to the top and down again. No, there was a definite, albeit very faint, smell of turps lingering on the staircase.

When I moved into the cottage, I had made myself a rule that I would never take my art paraphernalia into my living space. Anything art-related would stay in the studio. I even changed into my 'painting' clothes when I worked in the studio. And there was a bathroom where I could wash my hands before coming back into the cottage. My house never smelled of anything remotely to do with cleaning brushes!

Sitting down at the breakfast bar in the kitchen, I felt sick to my stomach. Someone had been inside the house. I know I hadn't been dreaming. This was my worst nightmare. Whoever it was that was watching me had taken things up a notch. Now, I knew they had been inside the house. Before, I had only been suspicious, because the odd thing had been missing, but now there was no mistake. Someone was stalking me!

I decided to ring Kyra. I couldn't talk to Mitchel now, because of his and Ali's situation. Besides, Kyra had suggested getting a camera too. I briefly explained why I wanted to talk, and we agreed to meet at Watson's. It was lovely to see her again. After I got us both coffees, the least I could do as I was picking her brains, we settled down to chat. I asked her about the best security camera to get.

"I'm no expert, but I can tell you a man who is. He owns a shop in Bideford and has a whole range of security cameras. Or if you don't want to drive there, you could look online. But I'm sure you'd have thought of that." She paused. "Did you really want to talk about cameras?"

I shouldn't have been surprised that she was so perceptive. After all, being a journalist, she probably had to see through the waffle and rubbish people regularly threw at her. "No, you're right. I just wanted to talk to someone about what happened last night. He's taken things to the next level."

"He hasn't threatened you, has he? You must go to the police if he has."

"No, he hasn't. But, on several occasions, I've thought someone has been in the house when I've been out. I've never had any proof; I've just felt it. I think I mentioned that the last time we met. But last night, I woke up in the night and I was sure someone was in the house. I put on my bedside light, but there was no one in the room. I sat for ages listening but couldn't hear a thing. I…"

'Oh my God, Rhi, that must have been terrifying," Kyra interrupted.

"How on earth did you manage to get back to sleep?"

"I didn't for ages, but then I just fell asleep, I was so tired. Anyway, this morning, when I got up, as I walked down the stairs, I could smell turps." Kyra opened her mouth to say something but I continued, explaining my rule about no art cleaning products in the house.

"And you still haven't phoned the police?" she asked.

"No. What's the point? They won't find anything and I have no idea who it is. You know that usually in these sorts of cases it's an old boyfriend or someone you've turned down, and there are neither of those in my life now. They won't have anything to follow up on," I answered. At that moment, Jon and his vitriolic comments when he found out about Josh leapt briefly into my mind. But both Ali and I had previously discounted him – he was too much of a narcissist to put himself out. Anyway, we knew he had plenty of other women and girls who adored him, including his young pupils. Despite his high and mighty ideals, he was just as vulnerable as me.

"That's true. The police won't follow up if they don't have any leads. But you need to be careful. Even though he hasn't done anything to harm you yet, he still might in the future," Kyra warned. I had just wanted to talk about it in the light of day when I could rationalise things. Already, I felt calmer talking with Kyra. She was right, though, I did need to take care. Whoever he was, he might have malevolent plans for my future.

We stayed and chatted a little longer, and then Kyra received a call and had to leave, saying we'd catch up soon for a night out. As she left, she said, "We can chat more when you've got your camera sorted – you might recognise him."

When I got home, I looked online, finding and ordering what I wanted. A wireless, weather-resistant (especially good for where I lived), HD security camera with motion detection. In the future, I'd be able to see my stalker, as I was now thinking of him.

CHAPTER 29

BEN

To Ben, it had seemed like weeks since he'd seen Rhi. He was missing her and being in her house. The last two weeks' work on the garden was beginning to take shape, and he'd been at home organising what was going on, plus he'd had to keep the gardeners plied with tea. He remembered that's what his mum had always done whenever she'd had tradespeople working at the house. Also, he'd had a large design job to do for one of his major clients, so he needed to spend time on that as he had a deadline that was closing in.

The kitchen was also having a makeover. After yesterday's fitting of the bifold doors, he had eaten his breakfast at the kitchen island, looking out at the garden. He knew Rhi would love it. In between his work, he regularly checked what she was doing on her social media. Now she wasn't teaching, he'd noticed that she wasn't quite so guarded about what she was getting up to. She had even mentioned that she was starting a part-time teaching job at a girls' school, although she hadn't said which one. His whole being had lit up at that comment because it meant he could visit her house during the day while she was out.

Recently, he'd decided to install some software on her computer. He'd found out on one of his recent visits that she didn't have a password, which he thought was a little careless of her! Once he installed the program, he could see everything on her computer, including her emails.

He'd know when she was talking to the boy, who he now knew was called Josh. Whittingbury Academy always posted images from the A-level results day, so he'd seen Josh among the kids collecting their results. That meant he'd soon be off to college and away from Rhi; Ben felt relieved. He'd have her all to himself. It was time to build up the courage to speak to her and spend time with her. He couldn't wait to see her face when they finally met and she remembered him. He was feeling particularly happy this morning, because Rhi had posted last night that she was off to visit the school today for a teacher training day. Her house would be empty. The gardeners would just have to look after themselves today.

As he arrived at Rhi's cottage, he noticed her car wasn't parked on the drive, so he knew the house was empty. Letting himself in, he went straight into her office, sat down at her Mac, and began to download the program that would give him remote access to everything she did. When the program had finished downloading, he hid it where he thought it was unlikely she would notice, turned the computer off, and then went into the kitchen to make himself a coffee. As he always did, mug in hand, he wandered upstairs, going into Rhi's bedroom.

The first thing he noticed was the beautiful sketch of Rhi in bed, naked. He couldn't take his eyes off it. Ben couldn't have clearly explained to anyone how he felt. It was a mixture of utter despair and hurt, knowing that someone other than him had drawn such a beautiful image of Rhi. He felt anger and disappointment with both her and Josh. Absently putting his mug down on the top of the drawers, he picked up the picture, which was incredibly well-drawn. It was a beautiful picture of the woman he loved. At that moment, Ben realised he loved Rhi, even though he hadn't spoken to her for years. Deep in his heart, he knew that's what he felt. Love. Oddly, he hadn't given his emotions for Rhi a name – until now.

Staring at the drawing, his eyes devoured every part of her body. The beautiful curves, the light as it fell onto her skin, and her beautiful serene, sleeping face with the curls of her hair framing each detail. He was in awe of the drawing, yet completely despondent that he hadn't been the artist. Placing the image back where it had been, he quickly took his

222

mug off the chest of drawers, panicking to see if it had left a mark. To his relief, it hadn't. He didn't want Rhi to know he had seen her drawing. There was a plan growing in his head. After washing up his mug and clearing up after himself, he left the house. He hadn't stayed for as long as he had planned but he intended to return tonight so he, too, could see Rhi sleeping.

Back at home, Ben logged on to his Mac to see if the remote program was working. It was! He sat for quite some time, looking through her files and emails. He didn't find any emails from Josh, but then, when he thought about it, he shouldn't have been surprised. Most people sent texts or WhatsApp messages. He only used emails for his business. Even so, it was useful seeing Rhi's calendar, which told him that he was right: Josh was off to college this coming weekend.

Ben slept for a while late that afternoon. Well, he tried to sleep. He was almost too excited about his planned night-time expedition. Around 1.30am, he drove over to Rhi's cottage, wearing all dark clothes, wanting to disappear into the shadows, although he hadn't accounted for light from the moon. Parking a street away from Starfish Cottage, he looked around to see if there were any late-night walkers around. He didn't see a soul, although one house still had its lights on. As he walked past, Ben wondered if they were partying or just a family who stayed up extremely late.

Walking across the gravel on Rhi's driveway, Ben was as careful and quiet as possible, not wanting to wake her, as he could see her bedroom window was open. He decided the front door would be the quieter of the two entrances, if he didn't make too much noise fitting the key in the lock. Gingerly, he pushed the key into place and waited. Everywhere remained quiet. Gently, he turned the key and pushed the door open. He waited again but heard no movement. He removed the key and placed it in his pocket, and, after closing the door as quietly as possible, he stood at the bottom of the stairs.

With care, he started to walk up the stairs, which he knew he could have managed blindfolded. Luckily, none of the steps squeaked, which was a bonus. At the top of the landing, he paused again, listening for any movement from Rhi's room. The door of the main bathroom had been left open slightly, lighting up the landing with moonlight. Ben took his time; he didn't want to chance Rhi waking up and seeing him. The last thing he wanted to do was to scare her – he just wanted to see what Josh had seen: Rhi sleeping.

To his relief, her bedroom door was open. He suddenly realised he hadn't considered that it wouldn't be. Had it been closed, his whole journey would have been a waste. After a few more carefully placed steps, Ben leaned against the frame of her bedroom doorway. Rhi was lying with her back to him, so all he could see was the mass of her hair. He was disappointed; he wanted to see her sleeping face, but he couldn't chance walking around the bed. As if she had heard his thoughts, she rolled over. Panic rose inside his chest as he wondered if she might open her eyes, but she had only moved her position, remaining asleep.

He couldn't help but smile. A streak of moonlight created by a tiny crack in the curtains fell on her face. It illuminated her beautiful face, which was framed by her red hair like a halo. She reminded him of one of Burne-Jones' pre-Raphaelite romantic angels. Her whole body was relaxed and peaceful as she breathed. The duvet had been pushed away from her body as she slept, and he could watch her breasts gently moving with each inhalation and exhalation. Standing silently in the darkness, he found himself trying to match her breathing. His mind slipped into an imaginary scenario, where he was lying next to her, holding her. He began to feel aroused, almost emitting an audible sigh.

A dog barked somewhere nearby, jolting him back to reality. He felt as though he had been standing in her room for ages, but it could only have been a few minutes. Rhi stirred and he wasn't sure if she had opened her eyes. Not wanting to wait and see, he moved quickly. He crept back down the stairs as quickly as he could and let himself out of the front door. Once out of the house, glancing upwards, he saw a light go on in her room. Keeping to the shadows as best he could, he lightly ran out onto the road and back to his car.

Once inside his car, Ben's breathing gradually returned to normal. He didn't know why, but he felt a mixture of elation and loss. He almost couldn't believe his audacity; that he had been brave enough to follow through with his plan. He had just been in the same room as Rhi, while she was sleeping in her bed! The loss he felt was, unlike Josh, he hadn't been sleeping next to her, holding her close. That Rhi was sharing herself with someone else made him incredibly sad. But tonight, being that close to her made him feel as though he were on a 'high' – not that he knew what that would feel like, having never tried drugs.

Now he had an image he could cherish and carry around with him.

CHAPTER 30

RHI AND JOSH'S WEEKEND

The security camera had arrived in the post yesterday. I wasn't sure I'd be able to put it up on my own as I wasn't too good on ladders. Usually I would have asked Ali, but she was still sorting things out with Mitchel. At least they were speaking to each other again, which was good.

I suddenly remembered that Rob, the gardener, was coming today. I could ask him to give me a hand. He arrived around 10am and said he was happy to help with the camera. We agreed he would do it after he'd finished the gardening, which wouldn't take too long today as there wasn't much to do. Finishing off, he opened the back door and yelled my name. While he was up the ladder screwing the attachments for the camera into the bricks, he surprised me by asking, "Did you have a good time with your university friend the other week?"

I wondered who he was talking about. "University friend? I'm not sure who you mean?"

"He was staying with you the last time I came round. I met him in the garden. Nice chap," Rob answered. He asked me to pass him the camera, which he fitted to the attachment, then climbed down the ladder.

I was still trying to think who on earth he could be talking about. Maybe it was my stalker? "Rob, have you got time for a cuppa before you go?" I was thinking that maybe I could get him to talk more about my 'uni friend'.

"Yes, I've got time. Mrs Chapman won't mind if I'm a little late. She won't notice, bless her, she's getting a little absent-minded these days anyway." Leaving his boots in the hallway, Rob followed me into the house.

While we were drinking our tea, I quizzed him about my 'friend'. I didn't want to tell him that no one was staying with me, otherwise he might feel awkward about the situation. So, I made up a lie. "I had a couple of friends staying that week; had a bit of a party."

"Ah! I thought it was odd you didn't know who I meant. Your friend shook hands with me and then went back into the house – said he had some shopping to do," Rob said.

I was trying to keep the shock off my face, that my 'friend' had kept so calm having obviously been inside the house. "Did he have blonde hair?" I asked, as though I was trying to differentiate between my non-existent visitors.

"No, tall, dark brown hair, quietly spoken. Pleasant guy, but I didn't talk to him for long. As I said, he had to go to the shops."

"That must have been Phil," I answered, surprised at how easily I'd lied.

At last, I had a little bit of detail about my stalker. He was tall with dark hair. Inwardly, I sighed. It could be absolutely anybody! In the future though, I was going to be more comfortable knowing I had the camera. If my stalker did decide to drop in, then I'd see him. With the way it was set up, I could see anyone standing at my front door and a few hundred yards on either side. At least I'd know if he'd let himself in the house.

To my amazement, Josh did ring me after his parents had left him at college. We chatted for a good half hour. He said his room was a little sparse, but OK, and he'd met a few other people who had moved in too. We decided next time we'd FaceTime, so we could see each other. I'd hoped he'd ring me but hadn't believed he would, so I was in a great mood for the weekend.

At last, I managed to catch up with Ali on Saturday. She told me she and Mitchel had made up, and that she was going to join him in Italy over half term, which was only a couple of weeks away. We were sitting in the Plough, where we'd been for the dreadful speed-dating event.

"Are you going to move out there or are you going to have a long-distance relationship?" I asked her.

"I don't know. What I do know is, I don't want to lose him, so we'll have to see how it goes," she replied.

"That's the only thing you can do, but I bet you'll end up moving there. Don't lie, you loved it didn't you? It was like being back on the farm," I teased her.

"What are you saying? You can take the girl out of the farm, but you can't take the farm out of the girl? Cheeky bitch!" And she laughed, before continuing, "It did remind me in some ways of the farm. Only with better weather and no animals, a vineyard, swimming pool..."

I interrupted, "No cattle shit or stinking manure!" I nearly choked on my wine. "Oh my God, do you remember when I managed to fall into a pile the first time I came to visit? I couldn't get rid of the stink for weeks." We both fell about laughing at the memory.

Managing to finally control my laughter, I said, "Seriously, I'm glad you've made things up, I didn't like seeing you so unhappy. Changing the subject, it's Josh's nineteenth birthday around half term, so I thought I'd take him away for the weekend. What do you think? Does it seem over the top?"

"Why would it seem over the top? I bet he'd love being taken away. Every young man's dream! No, I think he'd enjoy it. Where are you thinking?"

"I thought a cottage in the country, near the Tarr Steps in Exmoor, where we could walk, talk, listen to music, and spend some together time." I smiled at the thought.

"You're just a bad influence." We clinked our wine glasses together. "Sounds idyllic to me. I'll think about you when I'm lying in the sun by the pool," Ali replied.

I looked at my friend. "I'll miss you if you do move out there, but I'll be over for holidays." We clinked our glasses once more in agreement.

The weeks leading up to half term flew by. I was enjoying being back in the classroom. Only being there for a few days a week was great because it meant I had time for my own work. I had painted more since leaving Whittingbury Academy than I had for all the time I'd taught there. A huge positive, arising from a negative, which was another of Aunt Jinny's sayings: 'things always happen for a reason.'

I had been nervous when I told Josh I'd booked a cottage for a couple of nights for his birthday, as I didn't know how he'd feel about it. When he said he thought it was a great idea, I was relieved. Although I did wonder how he would explain it to his parents, because I knew his dad wouldn't be happy that we were still seeing each other. In the end, Josh told his parents he was going to stay with a mate of his for a few days, which they readily accepted. Why wouldn't they? It sounded so feasible.

Although I was looking forward to the days away, it would be interesting to see how we coped with each other all the time. Up until now, we had at the most only spent a couple of hours a day together. This way, we'd see how well our relationship stood up. If it really was a relationship, rather than just a fling! I still couldn't accept the possibility that this might not last. The age difference was something that kept nagging at the back of my mind. I was sure that he would find someone nearer his age now he was away at college. Yet, whenever we spoke about it, he would strenuously deny any interest in anyone else. I needed to put my fears behind me and just enjoy the time we had together.

Josh arrived in his Clio, and we transferred his stuff to my car, leaving his parked on the drive. He wasn't worried that his parents would see it as, according to him, they never came down to the bay. "I've been looking forward to this all week." Josh pulled me towards him to kiss me.

"Me too. I hope you're going to like it, a city boy like you?!"

"I'm not such a city boy since living down here, and Cheltenham isn't a city either. I'm enjoying it more than I ever thought I would." Josh smiled, and I realised how much he had settled into living in the south-west.

Just as we finished putting everything in the car, Josh noticed the camera above the front door. "When did you get the camera? Have you been having problems?" he asked.

"I've had a few unexplained things happen recently, but I haven't got around to linking it up with my computer yet. I'll do it when I get back after the weekend," I replied, lying rather too convincingly. My casual reply seemed to placate Josh, and we set off on our journey.

The small cottage I'd booked for us was a short walk from Tarr Steps. It was not so long a drive that time would be wasted getting to our destination, but far enough to escape normal life for a few days. When we arrived, the cottage was lovely – even better than I'd imagined from the photos online. It was clean, cosy, and perfect for our first get-away. Because it was on a farm, they had arranged for a hamper of food, so we'd have something to eat when we got there. It contained a fantastic selection of local goodies to go with the wine and some other bits I'd taken. We were all set up, although I'd thought we could eat out at local pubs.

It didn't take us long to christen the four-poster bed, and after a shower we set off to find the nearest pub, get some food, and then go for a walk. After an incredibly tasty but filling lunch, we needed a walk, so set off down to the Tarr Steps. Even on a chilly October day, what sun there was glinted through the trees, causing little flashes of light on the steps of the clapper bridge. I'd read somewhere that it was the longest of its kind in Britain. It must be a beautiful place to be in the summer.

We wandered along the footpath by the river, and then into the valley, eventually stopping to catch our breath after a bit of a climb. Sitting down, we found the ground was damp, but neither of us cared. Josh wasn't a hand-holder, but when we sat down, he pulled me close to him to keep me warm – well, that was his excuse.

"What do you think of the area?" I hoped it wasn't too boring for him.

"It's beautiful. When we lived in Islington, I'd never even thought about walking in the countryside – it just wasn't something I ever did. But now I'm here, it's lovely." He leaned in to kiss me.

"Do you ever miss London – the liveliness of it, and your friends?" I asked.

Josh went quiet. I was beginning to wish I hadn't asked as I wasn't sure I wanted to hear his answer. Eventually, he said, "No, not really. I sometimes miss the music events I used to go to, but I've made new friends here. Well, I had…" Suddenly he went quiet – he had meant Gemma.

I kissed him. "I miss her, too," was all I could say, knowing nothing else could help.

Josh returned my kiss. Continuing, he said, "I miss my sister, but I can always visit, and I talk to her regularly, so that's OK. But life is good here. I need to move forward."

We kissed again, before both getting up off the ground, which was now becoming a little too damp to remain sitting. We decided to head back to the cottage to get warmed up. As we walked down through a small, wooded area, I noticed a flash of light, a reflection, and, for a moment, had a feeling we were being watched. Josh nearly tripped and, as we both laughed, I soon forgot the intrusion as Josh chased me in between the trees.

The next day we drove over to Lynmouth and wandered down by the harbour, before having another fantastic pub lunch. On our last morning, we stayed in bed until almost 11am, eventually getting up and throwing everything into my car for the journey home. We had survived a whole weekend together!

As we drove into the drive, I knew there was something not quite right with Josh's Clio. It seemed to be lower on the ground. As we got close, we both saw why. Someone had slashed his tyres!

"Shit! Who in hell would do this?" Josh walked around the car, looking angry and flustered. "I didn't want Dad to know where I was, but now I'm going to have to tell him. I can't afford to pay for four new tyres!" He kicked one of the tyres in frustration.

Without thinking, I pulled him towards me, trying to calm both him and me. I was angry too. "Don't worry, I'll pay for them." I'd had the extra money from my teaching over the last few months, so I knew I was OK, although it would make a dent for a while.

Josh looked at me, his whole body relaxing. "Really? No. I can't ask you to do that. I need to stop my dad from telling me what I can and can't do. Having said that, he's an awkward sod at times, and knowing his temperament, he'd make my life a misery if he ended up paying for the tyres." Then he hugged and kissed me saying, "Thank you." As an afterthought, he asked, "Shouldn't we phone the police? I really don't want to, but if I'm going to claim on the insurance, don't I have to?"

"No, there's no point, and you don't want to have a claim on your insurance. We'll just get the tyres changed," I answered. I had my suspicions who had slashed the tyres, so offering to pay also helped removed some of my guilt. Besides, I didn't want to tell Josh anything about my stalker. I didn't want to give him something to worry about while he was at college or for him to be thinking about the extra baggage that he was being saddled with by going out with me.

"It's a shame you haven't linked the camera up yet, then we would have had some evidence for the police," Josh said, as he began to take things out of my car boot. Rather than lie, I kept quiet about the fact that I had set it up before we went away.

After unpacking, I rang a local garage where I often took my car, seeing if they would come and do a job on a Sunday. Amazingly, they said 'yes', although it took them a couple of hours to turn up. Josh was still wondering who on earth would slash tyres, especially around the bay. It wasn't the normal place for drunk tourists to visit. I made up a story about there being some rowdy local lads who had been around over the last few weeks, suggesting it might have been them. He seemed to accept that answer, and we settled into the cottage, like any normal couple at the weekend. We spent our remaining hours of the day listening to music, chatting, and relaxing. Around 7pm, after a long, amorous goodbye, Josh set off back to Cheltenham with his car sporting a new set of tyres. He promised to ring me when he arrived.

Feeling a little down now he was gone, I walked back into the cottage, and picked up the post I'd thrown onto the kitchen island. There were the usual bills and a brown envelope without a postage stamp, which I hadn't remembered picking up. Wondering what it was, I opened that one first. I couldn't believe what I was seeing. A couple of photographs of me and Josh walking in the countryside. Plus, one taken from a distance showing us inside the cottage. I dropped them onto the island top, as though they were infectious. I looked around the room, trying hard to notice if anything had been moved. I rushed upstairs where my bed looked as though a cat fight had taken place. My eyes slowly scanned the rest of the room, looking for anything unusual – anything out of place. I breathed in to see if there were any unexpected smells. Nothing. But then, Josh and I had been in the cottage all afternoon – the last thing on my mind had been my stalker. For the whole weekend, I'd forgotten about him. As soon as I thought that I realised it wasn't true. There had been that flash of light when we'd been out walking and when we were sitting in that field. He'd been there. He had followed me and had been watching us!

CHAPTER 31

FOUR YEARS EARLIER –THE INTERVENTION

Having witnessed Paul's anger, and heard about the arrival of the police, my friends tried hard to encourage me to move back in with them. But at that point, I didn't want to believe Paul would always be so controlling, so I moved back into his flat. For a couple of weeks, Paul was the perfect boyfriend, although I didn't push him over the edge by going out on my own or with any of my friends. I was beginning to feel like a nun, and without meeting other people I was beginning to waver about whether I should stay or move back in with my teaching friends.

Jackie suggested I invite Ali to stay with us, so she could meet Paul. While he was still in a contrite mood, I asked him if Ali could come to visit. Initially, he wasn't keen about having someone staying with us, but relented when I explained Ali was my best friend and we hadn't seen each other for over a year. However, he didn't know that we spoke regularly.

Jackie phoned Ali to explain the situation, so when I called her, she had already cleared her diary for the following weekend. She could come down a few days before the weekend too, which worked well. She arrived on the Thursday night, expecting Friday to just be the two of us during the day. But Paul surprised us both, saying he didn't need to go to work; he had the day off. They were doing a special upgrade of equipment, so instead of working they'd been given the Friday off. However, he would be working on the Saturday morning. He surprised me by being the perfect host. He took us both out for the day, showing Ali his best behaviour. There wasn't even a hint of his jealousy or controlling temperament. He was sweetness and light, the entire day. Yet again, I began to wonder if I was being rash in considering moving out.

When Ali and I were alone in the ladies' powder room, as it was called where we were having lunch, she mentioned that she had noticed how Paul watched me like a hawk. It seemed she hadn't been taken in by Paul's cloyingly attentive manner, which she had recognised as part of his controlling strategy. She told me I needed to leave him, and she was going to help me. Hearing my friend tell me what she thought woke me up, so together we hatched a plan.

On the Saturday morning, Paul kissed me, shouted 'goodbye' to Ali and left for work. As soon as I heard his car drive off, I leapt out of bed, got dressed, and grabbed my bags. Ali had already packed her overnight bag and put it in her car. She then set about helping me to pack the rest of my stuff. We didn't even stop for breakfast – there was too much to get organised. By 11am, we had crammed most things into Ali's car, with Jackie coming round to collect what wouldn't fit. I looked around the flat, checking there was nothing left. Despite the situation, I was still feeling sad about leaving the flat behind.

"Don't even consider changing your mind about this," Ali said, seeing the look of sadness on my face. "A leopard never changes its spots!"

I nodded. "You're right, I know, but it was so good when we moved in together."

"Well, it isn't now, so stop glazing over the bad bits. I don't want to be visiting you in hospital."

When we arrived at 'the teachers' house', everyone was there to welcome me home. They helped move my stuff back into my room before we all sat down to a massive lunch that Jackie and Bex had prepared. We opened a couple of bottles of wine, and a small party ensued. I felt as if I had never left. Ali had to return to Whittingbury on Sunday, but I was glad she had been there to witness Paul's true nature when he turned up that mid-Saturday afternoon. Arriving home from work, he noticed as soon as he walked into the flat that my things were missing.

My personality had been in every room. Fuming, he knew exactly where I was, and without any delay, he got in his car to drive over to the house. The girls had been prepared for this, having invited their boyfriends over. So, when Paul arrived, expecting to be faced with only a couple of girls, he found two large, burly rugby players opening the door.

"I want to see Rhi," he demanded.

"Sorry, mate, but she doesn't want to see you," said Roger, the larger of the two boyfriends, blocking the doorway, so Paul couldn't see past him.

"I'm not leaving until I see her," Paul continued. "You can't keep her from me."

"We can when she doesn't want to see you," said Rich, the other boyfriend.

Flustered, and getting redder by the minute, Paul stood at the doorstep, obviously trying to decide what to do. "I'm not letting you go, Rhi. I love you, and you belong with me," was his shouted parting shot, before he slammed the door of his car, and screeched off down the road.

Everyone in the house comforted me, reassuring me they'd keep me safe.

The texts began over the next few days. To start with they were innocuous, but over time they became more and more threatening. After that, I saw his car outside school, which became more common, so that in the end I travelled to and from school with one of the other girls. I was nervous when I went out as well because Paul would be there, watching me. Over the few months since I'd moved out of the flat, I had become a nervous wreck. I was the opposite of the confident young woman who had moved into the shared house. I'd never been so depressed in my life, and I began to go into a bit of a downward spiral. I felt both stupid and embarrassed that I had fallen for someone so paranoid. How on earth could I have mistaken the signs of his controlling personality with such a dramatic lack of awareness? Was I so desperate for the love of a man?

Finally, Jackie persuaded me to go to the police. The police asked me if Paul had ever been violent towards me, and when I mentioned the last incident, they found the call out to the flat. I told them he had been violent once and that on a second occasion I had managed to escape him, despite being terrified that he would harm me. I told them he had recently started following me, sending me threatening texts, and now I didn't feel safe. Sadly, in the end, it seemed the police could do very little unless he physically hurt me, which was ridiculous. As the weeks progressed, I changed my phone, removed myself from Facebook and other social media to the point where my life wasn't my own. I was just existing.

It was Ali who came to my rescue yet again. She told me there was a teaching job going at Whittingbury. I couldn't believe it – that would be the perfect answer, as I could stay with Aunt Jinny if I got the job. I went for the interview in May for a job starting the next September. Aunt Jinny was so pleased to see me, as I hadn't seen her for far too long. And I certainly hadn't told her about the issues with Paul – I hadn't wanted to worry her. Although, when she saw I'd become painfully thin, she kept going on about fattening me up. I was just grateful she didn't delve too much into the why.

Over the weekend after my interview, I took Aunty Jinny and Ali out for lunch. I felt the most relaxed I'd felt for months. The sea air and being with people I loved was the tonic I needed. The interview had gone well and I felt positive I'd done a good job. Now I just had to wait for the outcome. After a wonderful lunch, Aunt Jinny had to leave us to meet another friend who had dropped in to see her. Having paid the bill, Ali and I finished off the bottle of wine we were sharing and sat reminiscing about our youth in Whittingbury. Out of the corner of my eye, I suddenly caught sight of Paul. Instantly, I felt sick. It was obvious from my pallor that something was wrong.

"Whatever's the matter? You look like you've seen a ghost," she said.

"Look over by the shoe shop. It's Paul," I almost whispered, filling up with dread.

"Bloody hell! Come on, let's confront him." She grabbed her jacket; I followed slowly.

We started walking towards him, but he quickly disappeared down an alleyway, so we lost him.

"I can't believe it. He's even followed you here. Maybe we should contact the local police?" Ali queried.

"What's the point? It will take us so long to explain, and I'm going home tomorrow. He'll get fed up – I hope," I answered, sounding more confident than I felt.

We wandered around a few shops, and then Ali had to go too, so after browsing through some clothes, I decided to drive back to Aunt Jinny's cottage. As I walked towards my car, I saw Paul, leaning against the bonnet. "Can't you just leave me alone? Haven't you got anything better to do with your life, Paul?" I asked, trying to keep my voice level. He didn't move, so I decided to go a different way, perhaps get a taxi home and leave him there.

"You can't get away from me, Rhi. You know I love you. I need you. I can't live without you," he said, slightly louder than I wanted, as several people walking by turned to listen. Then he started shouting, "Rhi, you bitch, you led me on, made me believe you loved me. You were happy enough when I was fucking you, though I don't know who else you were with too."

I looked at him, in disbelief. "What the hell are you on about, Paul? You hit me – I had every right to leave you." I moved a little closer. I didn't want the whole of Whittingbury to hear our conversation, even though those around us certainly had. "Go home, Paul, and leave me alone. It's over!"

I started to walk away, looking for a taxi. Paul tried to grab my arm, but because he was leaning on the car, he hadn't got the leverage he needed, so I managed to pull free. I ran out of the carpark towards the centre of town where there were more people. I quickly glanced behind me, panicking as I saw him giving chase. Arriving at the main road, I edged out, stepped off the pavement between a parked car and a large van. I couldn't see what was coming but scanned the road, and although I saw a lorry further down it, I calculated I could get across before it arrived. So, I ran. Blindly, Paul followed me from behind the van, without looking. I was frozen in terror, so much so that I couldn't tell him to stop. He ran straight into the path of the oncoming lorry. His body was thrown into the air like a rag doll, then flung aside like litter. I could hear screaming – not realising that it was me.

All the witnesses said they saw the man chasing the girl. How she ran out across the road and he followed, without checking for traffic. It was no one's fault! It was deemed an accidental death. The poor lorry driver was in no way to blame either. Despite the ruling that it was accidental, and the fact Paul was stalking me, I felt guilty for a long time, wondering if I could have stopped him from running out in front of the lorry. The silver lining of the whole situation, if there could ever be one, was that I landed the second-in-department job at Whittingbury Academy.

After Paul, I had a tough time trusting any man or even changing my opinion of men. And yet, four years later, I now had a man I loved and another one, who I didn't even know, stalking me.

Is it someone who wishes me ill, or someone obsessed with me romantically? Is the latter even possible? Surely, he would try to speak to me. Unless, of course, he is incredibly shy – I just don't know. But I do know that I am not going to go through that feeling again where my life isn't my own.

CHAPTER 32

RHI – THE PRESENT, END OF OCTOBER

How could my stalker have known where we were at the weekend? The question was worrying me. He must have seen something in the house, though I didn't remember leaving anything around. The only information I had was on my computer. My mobile rang. It was Josh, letting me know he'd got back to Cheltenham. We chatted for a bit and then I could hear someone calling him in the background. A girl. I tried not to be jealous when he said he had to go, as a group of them were going out for a drink to celebrate his birthday. Try as hard as I might, I couldn't help thinking about the young girl's voice, imagining they might be more than just friends. Even though we'd just had the most amazing weekend together, and the way he always made me feel as though I was the only woman in his life, deep down, I still felt insecure, knowing I was older.

The next day, when I got back from school, I looked at the footage from the outside camera since I'd put it in place. Finally, I saw him. One morning walking towards the house, but he must have seen the camera as he turned his back towards it before I could get a good look at his face. He disappeared down the side of the house. Then, late on the Saturday night when we'd been away, I saw him approaching the cottage again. He was wearing a hoodie, with a scarf around his face. It was drizzling with rain, so I couldn't see him as clearly as I might, but I could tell he was tall and, by the way he walked, younger rather than older. As he reached the house he disappeared. He had a key! How on earth had he got a key? I'd already changed the locks.

When he reappeared, leaving the house, I saw him stop near Josh's car. The range of the camera didn't quite give me a complete view of the entire drive, but I knew that was when he was slashing the tyres. Enough was enough; it was time to do more. I'd investigate getting more cameras – I could put them inside the house, so that I'd get a better look at him when he next visited. Kyra had been right – I did need indoor cameras, though I was not calling the police; they've enough to do. It's not that big a deal, and this time, I was going to be in control, unlike with Paul. However, I wasn't going to put any in the bedroom. I didn't quite fancy filming myself, especially the next time I was with Josh. Suddenly the memory of the girl's voice leapt into my head – that is, if there was a next time.

Over the following days, I ordered three cameras for inside the house. I checked the outdoor camera footage regularly, finding 'he' had been inside the house on another occasion. I realised, while watching, that he knew the camera was there, so always kept his head down. I couldn't wait for the other cameras to arrive – maybe I'd be able to see who he was.

Josh rang me mid-week to ask if he could come down to stay for the weekend. I had been worried that he was ringing to say he was finishing our relationship, but the way he spoke didn't give any indication of that. "I'm missing you so much. I can't wait to see you again," he had said.

Trying to sound as casual as I could, I asked, "Did you have a good night out with your girlfriend for your birthday drink?"

"Yes, a group of us went out. Sian is on my course and has a room just along from mine – she's a good mate," he replied.

"Is she pretty?" I was annoyed by the lack of subtlety in my question. I couldn't have been more obvious.

Josh laughed lightly, saying, "Are you jealous, Rhi? You needn't worry. She's not interested in guys."

Smiling, I silently told myself off. "OK, I was a bit worried. But you can't blame me when you're surrounded by lots of young pretty girls."

Josh interrupted me. "Er…It's not as if you're ancient, Rhi. You're only a couple of years older than me."

"Eight years is more than a couple," I reminded him. "But I'm glad you don't think I'm ancient." He laughed. I suggested, "I could come up and see you instead if you want?"

"Oh, no. My place really is rough. I have a shower in my room, and I have to share the loo. Besides, my bed is certainly not as comfortable as yours. I don't think your old body would cope with it..." And he waited for my response. He didn't have to wait long.

"Cheeky! Yes, I remember the beds. I only lived in the halls for a year. I couldn't wait to get out. Yes, come here. I don't fancy sharing a loo with a load of students. So, when are you coming down – Friday or Saturday morning?"

"I'll see you Friday night." I couldn't wait.

The first thing Josh said, after coming into the cottage and kissing me, was, "Have you linked the camera up yet? Why did you get it – have you been having problems?"

I hadn't wanted to tell him what was going on but knew I couldn't keep it from him anymore. I poured us both a drink and we sat down on the sofa, so I could explain what was going on. Josh listened quietly, looking more and more shocked, particularly when I told him that whoever was stalking me had been in the house.

"Why on earth haven't you phoned the police, Rhi? He could hurt you. We can ring them now, while I'm with you."

"No!" My reaction was too curt, too loud. I took a breath, saying gently, "No, I'm not getting them involved. I have no idea who it is, and I don't want them poking around in my life. They couldn't do much last time when they did know who was bothering me, so I don't see how they can this time. I need to get a good image of him so I can show them."

Josh didn't look convinced. "But they deal with this sort of thing all the time. They'd be able to do something, surely?"

"I'm going to put some cameras downstairs inside the house, so I can catch him when he's here. He won't see them, so he won't be on the defensive. He's seen the camera outside, so he's hiding his face as much as he can. Then, if I get a good image, that will be the time to get in touch with the police," I told him, trying to sound reassuring, although I still wasn't sure that I wanted to go down that route. It hadn't ended well the last time. "I'm not going to let someone intimidate me again," I said, firmly.

Josh did a double take. "Did I hear what you said? What do you mean last time, and you're not going to let anyone intimidate you again? Have you had a stalker before?" He was seriously worried.

I let out a long sigh. I hadn't really wanted to tell him and was thinking about how much to say.

"Rhi? Tell me, please," he asked.

Without being overly dramatic, I told him the shortened version of how Paul had made my life hell, and how the police couldn't help. When I mentioned Paul's death, I saw Josh relax. Then I told him about my 'flower' stalker, and how recently he had become more aggressive by breaching my privacy and entering my house when I wasn't home.

Josh looked serious and asked, "How do you know he's not going to be here one time when you come home?"

"He hasn't approached me yet and he hasn't done anything to hurt me, which is why I have put cameras inside the house. I've shown his picture to Kyra, my journalist friend, and asked her to see if she can find out anything about him. Once I have captured a clear image on the cameras inside the house, then I can approach the police," I replied, trying my best to sound completely in control of the situation. "Besides," I added, "I'm considering buying a baseball bat, just in case."

Josh gave me a look of incredulity. "Seriously? Will you be able to use it?"

"I don't know, but I think if I meet him face to face I can get angry enough to at least threaten him." I tried to make a joke. "You know the saying, 'there's nothing worse than a woman scorned'." I was trying to sound brave and realised it wasn't quite the right quote for the situation. "Don't worry, I'll be fine."

"I don't like you being here alone. You need to contact the police soon. Promise me you will? Please?"

I promised, giving him a kiss to seal it. Josh still didn't look convinced, but I hoped I'd persuaded him for the time being. I soon managed to take his mind off it all, and we spent the rest of the weekend making love, chatting, and laughing. On the Sunday, while we were having lunch, a nervous-looking Josh told me he had some news. Suddenly I felt nervous. My paranoia about our age difference set in. I was sure he was going to tell me that this had been our last weekend; that he'd met someone else. I was tensing myself ready for his admission.

"I've had the most amazing offer through my professor," he began. I felt my whole body relax. "There is a company in the US which is interested in my work." He paused for effect, a huge smile on his face, before continuing, "They want me to go out there to do some work for them."

"Wow, that's amazing." I leaned over and pulling him towards me, I kissed him deeply. "I wasn't expecting that news. That's…" I searched for the word. "Incredible. So, are you going?"

"Hell, yes! I'm going out in a few weeks. I can't wait, but…" His face fell. "After what you just told me, I'm not sure I should go now."

"Josh, you have to go! You can't miss an opportunity like this. It's incredible to get noticed this soon in your career. Of course, you must go," I replied.

Tentatively he said, "I was hoping you'd be able to come out to see me while I'm there. I've been talking to them, and they've told me they'll pay for you to come out too." He looked at me, hopefully.

"You told them about me?" I couldn't believe how wrong I'd been about what I thought his news was going to be. "Wow, that would be wonderful." Josh kissed me, hugging me so hard I thought he was going to crack my ribs.

Full of excitement, he told me about the company, which was based in Santa Monica, California. They were a large design company that provided artwork for hotels. His professor, Jed, had an old friend who was the owner. He had mentioned Josh's work to him, sent some images, and the rest, as they say, is history. They were going to hire him an apartment near the beach for the entirety of his stay, which was basically all November. They had also agreed to pay for a flight out for one of his friends.

"Obviously, I chose you. I mean, who else would I want there with me? Definitely not my dad." Josh laughed.

I couldn't believe that he wanted me to go and to see him. I was also so pleased that he was being given the opportunity. "How come the college is letting you go, mid-term?" I asked.

"I thought that, too, but Jed says any work I do out there can go towards my degree, so it's all good. I can't believe my luck. So, I was thinking, why don't you come over for Thanksgiving, which is near the end of November. The 25th to be exact," he suggested. "It'll give me time to get my work done, and I'll have found the best places to take you."

It was my turn to hug him. "Yes, yes, and yes!" I couldn't stop hugging him. "I knew you were talented, but this is such a great opportunity for you."

Josh smiled, saying, "Well, I did have a great teacher, didn't I?"

As he was leaving to go back to Cheltenham, his mood became more serious. "I'm not happy about leaving you alone with this stalker around. You will ring me if anything happens or, more importantly, the police if things develop? Does Ali know what's going on? She'll help you too, won't she?"

I could see Josh was worried and I now wished I hadn't told him. "I'll be fine, and yes, Ali does know. Remember, I told Kyra too, so I'm not alone." Secretly, although I wasn't going to let my stalker take over my life, I wasn't quite as confident as I tried to sound. Especially as Ali had told me she was going to be spending more time with Mitchel in Italy, and that she was going to move there in the new year. But I still had Kyra who, with her contacts, could be a great ally.

October ended and November began, with Josh disappearing off to the US. I had only got a few more weeks teaching at The Beeches, as their teacher was about to come back, wanting to start back part-time, leading up to Christmas. Ali spent most weekends in Italy, while I existed alongside my stalker, who I was now able to see on my indoor cameras, although I had only seen him a couple of times. For some reason, he seemed to have quietened down.

When I did capture him on film, weirdly, he appeared to be an innocuous-looking type, apart from the fact that he was breaking into my home. I'd only captured him a couple of times and was madly trying to work out who he was. He looked vaguely familiar but I couldn't recall where I had seen him. I showed the footage to Ali, who was convinced he was the guy she had noticed at the speed-dating night. Neither of us could place him. I took a picture of him to show Kyra, wondering if any of her contacts knew who he was. She had asked around, but no one knew him, so he wasn't a known burglar or offender. There didn't seem to be anything to help us discover his identity. Now was probably the time to get in touch with the police, but something kept holding me back.

Instead, as I told Josh, I bought myself the baseball bat, just in case.

In case of what? He hadn't done anything to hurt me physically – he didn't even seem to be doing anything that intrusive when he was trespassing inside my property. Oddly, he seemed to enjoy pretending to live in my space. The only thing he had done that was destructive was to slash Josh's tyres. What worried me more than my safety was him hurting Josh. For now, I knew that Josh was safe in the US, so I only had myself to consider. Mmm. For now, the baseball bat was just a security blanket. At last, I decided. I was fed up knowing that someone else was in my home – that someone was following me. But for what reason? I set up the alerts on my phone, so the next time he was in the house I would know. I would come back, quietly creep in, and confront him. This had gone on long enough.

CHAPTER 33

BEN

Ben was feeling more upbeat than he had for several weeks, and it wasn't just the fact that he hadn't been alone. The house had been full of different tradesmen, as he'd watched over the final stages of the makeover to his house. He felt some pride each time he said that to himself. His house! It was now looking perfect for when Rhi moved in with him. The garden, the open-plan kitchen and lounge, the upstairs main suite, and modernised family bathroom. The remodelling was amazing; it looked like a completely new home. And the entrance downstairs was so much brighter, now the dark panelling had gone, and the walls had been painted. It was an inviting space to enter and had been worth every penny he had spent. Not that he couldn't afford it, because he could. He was happy to spend it, making it into what he thought would be Rhi's standard.

After the elation of seeing Rhi sleeping, he had hoped to get out to her cottage sooner, but then when he was celebrating the finished work, he went down with a virus, having to spend several days in bed. The doctor, who he had to visit in the end, said he thought it was a delayed reaction to his mother's death. Either way, it held up his plans. When he did visit the cottage, he was in for a shock. As he began to walk towards the front door, he stopped in his tracks, quickly looking down. Rhi had installed a camera, which was pointing directly at him. He turned his

247

back to it as if walking away, pulling up his hood, and keeping his head down, before turning towards the back door. Luckily, he always brought both keys with him.

He didn't stay for as long as he usually did, mainly because he came across a brochure for a cottage in Somerset. He went into Rhi's study to look through her emails. He quickly found the confirmation of a booking for two at the cottage for the weekend after next. Feeling angry, because he knew exactly who she was going away with, he closed the computer and, after slamming the front door, stomped back to his car. Back at home, he got online and looked for the place Rhi and that boy were going to stay at. He knew exactly what he was going to do.

The weekend arrived; it was miserable. On the Saturday morning, as he drove over towards Tarr Steps, the roads were filthy. The rain was pouring, with his windscreen-wipers having trouble keeping the windscreen clear. By the time he'd arrived near to where Rhi was staying, the rain had almost stopped. He got out to walk, eventually finding the cottage where they were staying. He walked past, glancing inside. He couldn't see anyone, and carefully trying to keep out of sight of any windows, he walked around to the back of the cottage where he saw Rhi's car parked. 'Perhaps they'd gone for a walk,' he thought. Suddenly, he heard voices. After quickly running back round to the road, he walked away from the cottage. A few minutes later, Rhi and Josh walked past him, holding hands, and giggling like a pair of teenagers. Ben could feel his anger growing but managed to contain it. They hadn't appeared to notice him, so slowing down, he dawdled along behind them.

After a while, they disappeared into the pub where they ate. He also went inside, but to the bar, finding a seat from which he could see them. It was making him feel sick. Watching them touching hands, occasionally kissing, and gazing into each other's eyes. 'It should be me,' he thought. 'Not some young kid. What are you doing, Rhi?'

After finishing their meal, they set off walking. At a safe distance, Ben followed. They eventually sat down in a field, which must have been damp after all the rain, but they didn't seem to notice. Ben stayed hidden among the trees of a copse. He had brought his camera with a long lens and was happily snapping pictures of them – that was until Rhi happened to look his way, and he panicked. After a while they moved on, but rather than follow them, he decided to drive home. He had a different plan in mind.

Arriving back in Whittingbury, Ben went home for some food and to print out the photos he'd taken. When it was dark, he drove towards the bay and, as he often did, parked a few streets away, walking the last bit to Rhi's cottage. He looked around, listened for the sign of any dog walkers or any lights from torches, but everything was quiet and still. It was drizzling with rain again. Partly because of that, he pulled his hood up, wrapping a scarf around his face. He wouldn't be recognised this time. After walking up to the front door, he let himself in and placed the brown envelope of photos on the kitchen top. He looked around, then walked back out into the drizzle. Taking a large hunting knife that he'd bought just for the occasion but checking first that there was still no one around to see him, he viciously stuck the knife into each of the little Clio's tyres, pulling it through the rubber as best he could.

Smiling to himself, he walked back down the road and drove home.

He felt a little reluctant to visit during the day now that Rhi had a camera in place. But on the days when it was pouring with rain, which had seemed to be quite regularly over the last few weeks, he just made sure he had his hood up and wore a scarf to cover his face. Once inside the cottage, he could relax and enjoy breathing in all that was Rhi. He was confident she hadn't recognised him from the camera because the police hadn't called.

A couple of weeks later, near the end of November, while perusing her emails, he found yet another confirmation that upset him. Why on earth did he do this to himself? If he didn't search through her things, he wouldn't find what he didn't want to know, but he couldn't help himself. He discovered Rhi had plans to visit America in a few days. She was counting down the days on her calendar. He panicked, not being able to work out why she was going there. That was, until he found a Facebook Messenger conversation between her and another friend, where Rhi was telling her that Josh had landed a fantastic job in California. He wanted her to go out and join him. For Ben, this was almost the limit to his patience. He could hear his mother's voice, telling him how useless he was. Why hadn't he spoken to her? The longer he had left it, the harder it had become. If he was honest with himself, he knew he had to do something. For God's sake – Rhi had been living in Whittingbury for four years and in all that time, he hadn't had a conversation with her. But how could he? He had been looking after an invalid, his mum, and a young woman wouldn't have wanted to be tied to someone with that responsibility. He was both angry and disappointed with himself for lacking the courage to face her instead of creeping around.

Going into the garden, he started kicking some large pieces of wood leftover from the house refurb. But kicking them didn't make him feel better, so he found the axe in the shed and started hacking angrily at them. That made him feel far better. With each strike, he tried to turn his anger towards Rhi, rather than be mad at himself. But try as hard as he could to imagine hitting her, he just couldn't. He got even more upset at the thought of hurting her. He loved her too much. Mind you, he wouldn't have minded hitting that boy, but he wasn't accessible. Ben had missed his chance.

After he had calmed down, Ben went back into the house and poured himself a beer. He had decided that tomorrow he would go around to the cottage, let himself in, and wait for Rhi to come home. Then he'd tell her exactly how he felt. How he had no responsibilities anymore and would look after her in the house he had created for her. Surely now he would be a good catch? He had the house, money, and he loved her. He would do anything and everything for her. She shouldn't be wasting her time on this boy. Ben was confident she would see the sense in what he was going to say.

CHAPTER 34

CONFRONTATION

The weather had been horrendous for the last couple of days and taking my normal run hadn't been enjoyable or particularly safe, as the cliff path had become incredibly muddy and slippery. Water had been running down the hill across the field next to the cottage, and in one place, the cliff edge had begun to crack and break away. The TV weatherman had given weather warnings for the area for the next few days. I didn't envy anyone out at sea getting caught in it. It also wasn't the best time to be flying either, so I prayed that the weather wouldn't affect my flight out to join Josh in the US. Only three more days to go and I'd be sunning myself in the lovely Californian sun.

I'd finished teaching at The Beeches. Their regular art teacher had started back after her baby was born, so I had more time to spend doing my work and getting myself ready for my trip. Having had to get up for school, I was still waking early, so was surprised when my mobile rang around a quarter to eight, while I was still eating my breakfast. I didn't recognise the number but hoped it might be Josh.

Tentatively, I answered, "Hello?"

I heard Josh's voice. "Hi, Rhi. I wanted to hear your voice. I'm missing you. You seem so far away."

I felt a warmth rush through my whole body. "I'm missing you too. How's it going? What time is it there?"

"It's amazing. I still can't quite believe I'm here, but I'm loving it. It's almost midnight, but I didn't want to phone earlier and wake you up too early in the day."

"Are you ahead of us or behind? I can never remember."

"You're ahead. It's Wednesday night here," he replied.

"That's so weird. So, what's it like?"

"I'm working in the company studio in downtown Santa Monica. It's totally mad. I get access to almost anything I need. It's better than college." Josh excitedly told me about what he was working on and the amount of support he was getting. I listened, my heart dropping with each sentence. He was so excited, and I was panicking as I realised how much he was loving it. I began wondering if he would ever want to come back. He had stopped talking and I realised he'd asked me a question I hadn't heard. "Wow, that sounds incredible. Cheltenham is going to be a bit of a disappointment after that," I replied.

Josh said, "I know. Did you hear what I said about the apartment?"

"Sorry, my mind was wandering hearing about all of the work. Tell me again."

He described the fantastic apartment where I'd be staying with him and the view it had of the sea. He added with excitement, "And, when you're here, Mike, the CEO of Katz Co., has invited us to spend Thanksgiving lunch with him and his family. How cool is that?"

"You're obviously doing something right, then. That is kind of him."

"I'll meet you at the airport on Saturday. I can't wait for you to get here. Sorry, this is a short call. I've got to go – I need my beauty sleep to keep my energy up for when you arrive." He laughed. "Love you, keep safe." And he ended the call.

I sat looking at my phone. He had said 'love you'. My heart was racing. I hadn't replied. That he had ended the call after saying it made me think it was just an expression but he had said the words!

Despite my happy mood after hearing from Josh, the weather outside was trying its hardest to dampen my spirit. It was dull, grey, and the rain was incessant. The sea looked forbidding and angry. However, in the afternoon, I decided to pop into Whittingbury to get some of the things I had forgotten when I'd done my main shop. I put on my waterproof and went out into the downpour.

Ben drove over to Rhi's and, as usual, despite the heavy rain, he decided to park a few streets away. He had his hoodie on to keep his hair dry. He pulled up his raincoat collar in the hope that he would keep his neck from getting too wet. It was far too windy for an umbrella, and besides, he always felt stupid carrying one. Keeping his head down to miss the camera, he let himself into the cottage and hung his coat up in the hallway, watching it drip onto the floor. It would soon dry, he hoped.

He was feeling more than a little apprehensive. He had decided that he was going to stay put when Rhi came home. At last, he was going to talk to her. Feeling slightly sick, he made himself a cup of coffee before settling on the sofa to read the latest book he had borrowed from her study. It was yet another Ian Rankin Rebus story. There was something about the character's dour take on life that he enjoyed. Glancing around the room, he could see Rhi was getting ready for her trip. He hoped she wouldn't be too long coming home, as he didn't want to lose his nerve. Soon, however, he was lost in the story he was reading, unaware of the raging weather that was building up outside.

As I stood in the queue at Boots, my phone pinged. After I'd paid, but before walking back out into the rain, I checked to see the notification. It was an alert from my camera system. I saw I'd also missed one from earlier. I logged in and saw my visitor in the lounge, sitting on the sofa, sipping a hot drink. 'The cheeky bastard,' I thought. Before I lost any of my determination to confront him, I marched back to the car, luckily having already bought most of the things I needed.

Reaching the cottage, rather than drive up to the front door, I drove very slowly, parking just inside the gateway. With the amount of noise that the rain and wind were making, I was certain I wouldn't be heard. It was beginning to get dark, so if he was still sitting reading, he wouldn't notice me pass the window. Quietly walking into the cottage, I saw his raincoat, which looked dry, so he must have been there for some time.

Putting my purchases down in the hall, I picked up the baseball bat, just in case…

My stalker was sitting on the sofa, reading.

"Is that one of my books?" I asked, startling him.

He looked up, slowly raising his head. "Hello, Rhi. What are you going to do with the bat?" he asked, about to stand up. But, using the bat, I signalled for him to stay where he was.

"Nothing, I hope. Do I know you?" I asked, ignoring the question I should have asked about what he was doing inside my home.

"Don't you remember me?" He looked hurt.

"Obviously not, otherwise I wouldn't have asked my previous question!" I stared at him. Did I know him? There was something faintly familiar about him, but I just didn't know what.

"Cheltenham Art College in your second year?" he said, as though I would remember immediately.

"Were you in my year? I don't remember you." Again, he looked hurt.

His answer sounded like a mixture of hurt and pleading. "Seriously, you don't remember? I was upset, well, crying, and you comforted me outside the principal's office. Do you remember now?"

I thought back, vaguely remembering the situation, but that was over four years ago. A lot had happened since then. "I'm sorry, but only very vaguely. Remind me what happened, and what's your name?" I loosened the grip on the baseball bat, although I wasn't ready to let go of it just yet.

He looked sad as he replied, "I had just been told my parents had been in a car accident. My dad had been killed and my mum seriously injured, and I was going to have to go home and leave college. You comforted me. You held me in your arms to calm me. I've never forgotten you, Rhi." He looked up at me imploringly. "My name is Ben, Ben Brooks.

When he mentioned the stairs, I suddenly remembered. He had been sitting underneath them, sobbing as everyone just walked past ignoring him. I don't know why, but I had stopped and hugged him. Afterwards, I hadn't known what had happened to him, nor ever wondered, to be honest. "OK, so that's where you know me from, but that doesn't tell me what you are doing in my home, and why you have been stalking me?" I looked at him with my angry teacher expression. "How have you been getting in? I changed the locks."

He smiled. "When I found the key under the fake rock, I also had a backdoor key cut. Luckily for me, you didn't change those locks." Looking smug, he continued, "So, when you changed the front door lock, I just came in through the back door, found the spare set of new keys, and had one cut. And here I am."

I lifted my bat, in what I thought was a threatening way. "Well, you can hand them both over, now!"

Surprisingly, Ben acquiesced, giving me the keys, which I quickly put into my raincoat pocket. I remained standing, feeling the dominant position gave me some control. If he started to move, I could retaliate quicker than he would. It was strange, even with him sitting in front of me, that I still didn't feel particularly scared. I thought I would be, but now he was here he didn't look like the dangerous stalker people always imagine. But then, on reflection, I remembered all the films I'd watched, and the saying of my mum's: 'it's always the quiet ones you need to be wary of.'

"Why are you here, Ben?" I thought the directness of my questions might help me cut to the chase. "Why has it taken you four years to talk to me?"

Ben seemed to take an age to answer, and I could see he was struggling. Finally, he managed to say, "I have wanted to talk to you so many times. I saw you earlier in the year in a café in town. I thought you'd recognised me, but you were waving at your friend. Then I saw you at a speed-dating night and I was going to talk to you, but you left early. So many times, I have almost managed to talk to you but then didn't. It knocked my confidence to say anything in the end."

"So, you've still not answered my question. Why are you here now, today?" I asked with a little more force. "Why shouldn't I phone the police and tell them there is someone trespassing in my house? Even if you leave, I now know your name." I was the one feeling smug now.

Ben looked nervous. "I…I needed to talk to you. To tell you you're throwing your life away on this boy. You need a man to look after you…"

I interrupted before he continued. "And you're that man?"

"Yes, I am!" He managed that with far more conviction than anything else he'd said. "I have loved you since I saw you that first day. I couldn't do anything about it because I had to look after my mum, but she died recently, so now…now, we can be together. I have a large house, which is mine. I've modernised it for you, and I have money in the bank. Enough for us to live comfortably. You are wasting your life on this kid. He isn't worthy of you! You deserve better." His voice got louder as he spoke, gaining more confidence.

I just looked at him, thinking, 'He's mad.' I needed to be careful what I said. Needed to get him out of the house. Maybe he wasn't quite as innocuous as he had initially seemed.

"I'm sorry, but I love Josh."

This time it was Ben who interrupted me. "How can you love him, he's not even a man yet? He hasn't got the money to look after you like I can."

"I don't need to be looked after! Why is it you men always think you need to look after us women? I have managed these last four years to look after myself. Even after resigning, I've managed to continue looking after myself, so I don't need a man." There was a long silence between us.

Suddenly, it dawned on me that if someone just dropped in, the situation would look ludicrous. Me, standing in my still dripping raincoat, holding a baseball bat, and Ben, sitting on the sofa, with his book and cup of coffee, looking as though he was the house owner and I had just arrived to beat him up.

"Ben, I'm sorry, but I'm happy with who I'm with. I'm sorry you have had these feelings for me, but just because you have them, doesn't mean to say I feel the same way."

All at once, his demeanour changed – he looked defeated. "Mum spent her time telling me how useless I was, and now you're telling me the same. Maybe she was right. I just wanted to be near you. That's why I have spent my time here, to be around you and your things. I even met your cat. I'm so sorry, I didn't mean for it to die."

"You killed Tibbs? Why on earth would you do that?" I couldn't believe that this seemingly gentle guy would have killed my cat on purpose. I tightened my hold on the bat. "Did you mean to kill him?"

"No! It was a terrible accident. The cat came up to me and I picked him up to stroke him, but he dug his claws into my arm suddenly. It was so painful. I sort of threw him away from me. He fell, hitting his head on the bricks of a low wall. I hid him in the long grass because I didn't want you to find him like that. I'm sorry. I didn't want to hurt you." He did look genuinely sorry.

"I suppose you meant to be kind, hiding him, but I still ended up seeing him."

The premise about psycho killers starting by killing cats suddenly leapt into my mind. 'Come on, Rhi,' I thought, 'he's no psycho. He's not threatened you.'

"So, how long have you been following me?" I paused, as something dawned on me. "Was it you who cancelled the lunches for my workshop? And why on earth did you follow me and Josh the other weekend?"

Ben sighed. He was beginning to look more beaten down than he had before. "I have followed your career since you got the job at Whittingbury. After I had to leave college, it was wonderful to follow what you were doing. Seeing you succeed helped to keep me sane. Looking after Mum every day was tedious, and I had lost my dream of being an artist. So, watching you was…" He struggled for the words. "… Helping keep me calm, making my life bearable. The more I watched you, the more I wanted to be near you, and feel your arms around me again. You were the first woman to show me any care. The only woman." He looked up at me.

"Surely, your mum hugged you, didn't she?" I was shocked. If what he said was true, I could only pity him.

"Not so much. Mostly, she denigrated me, made me feel useless. But, seeing you, being in your house, just being near you, helped to make me feel alive." Yet again, his voice was growing in confidence as he talked about his feelings for me. "I even met up with one of your students. I met up with…" He stopped abruptly, looking down at the carpet.

His words sparked a scary thought. "Ben, who did you meet up with?" I asked, a feeling of nausea rising in my stomach.

He raised his eyes. He realised he had said something he shouldn't have said.

"Ben. Who?" I asked, though I already knew. Very quietly I said, "Gemma?"

"Yes."

I backed away from him, He stood up abruptly. "Please, Rhi. That was an accident too. She slipped and hit her head. She was coming on to me, and I was embarrassed. I wasn't used to girls, not like that. I pushed her away, only gently, but she slipped and…" I could see he was ashamed. "I ran off. But I knew she was OK, because I heard the dog-walker approaching. I know he phoned for the ambulance. I didn't know she had died until weeks afterward, when I read it in the papers just after Mum died."

Up to that moment, I had had some sympathy for him. I felt sorry for the fact that he'd had his career curtailed before it had even started. But after what I'd just heard, I didn't know how to react. I was nearer the door than I had been, and still clinging onto the bat. I had a massive urge to hit him with it – I was so angry. He had killed Gemma. Even if it was an accident, he had been there. Because of me, and only because of me, he had been with Gemma. I had been the cause of her death!

I didn't trust myself not to use the bat, and I couldn't cope with being near him any longer. I turned towards the door, but he grabbed my arm. "Please, Rhi, I love you. I didn't want any of this to happen. I just want to be with you."

Pulling away from him, I dropped the bat, and ran towards the door, shouting, "Keep away from me." Blindly, I ran into the wind and torrential rain, uncertain as to which direction to go. If I ran towards the street, very few of the houses were occupied at this time of the year, as they were holiday homes. If I ran the other way, it would be along the cliff path. Stupidly, I ran towards the cliff path. I couldn't see Ben, but then I caught a glimpse of him standing in the doorway, lit by the house lights.

He had grabbed his raincoat and was trying to see where I had gone. The horizontal rain was making it hard to see anything. He was acclimatising his eyes to the darkness because I saw him start to run my way.

Even though I knew the path with my eyes shut, I was finding it hard to make much headway. The wind was strong, and the ground incredibly muddy and slippery. Eventually, Ben managed to catch up to me. He made a lunge for my arm, managing to grab me. He was shouting at me, but his voice, taken by the wind, disappeared into the darkness. We seemed to struggle for ages, although it was probably only a few minutes, if that. The muddy ground was more than either of us could cope with. We fell in a heap in the mud and water, which was continually washing down in little rivulets from the fields and hills beyond, before disappearing over the cliff edge.

"Rhi, I'm sorry." Ben's words were barely audible above the wind. At last, panic had set in, and I continued to wrestle with him, frantically trying to get away.

CHAPTER 35

THE END

The rain was blowing from all directions, and the ferocious wind came in from the sea. With some difficulty, weighed down by my fear and running, battling hard against the weather, I managed to stand up. I was unsteady on my feet because of the mud beneath us. Ben pulled himself to his feet as well. He reached out to grab hold of me again, but somehow, I pulled away from him and, in doing so, he lost his grip on me. The opposite force meant he fell backwards, his feet slipping in the mud. I looked up to where he had been standing. One minute he was there, shouting out my name, then suddenly he was gone. In the noise of the wind and rain, I didn't even hear him scream, which he must have done as he slipped over the cliff edge.

I fell to my knees with both relief and shock. I didn't dare go near the edge to see how far Ben had dropped. At that point, I would have put myself in danger of falling over the edge too. Besides, it would have been impossible to see down to the sea in this darkness. After running back to the house, I found my mobile phone. I had every intention of calling the police. But, as I began to dial, I stopped. How would my explanation sound to them? I could imagine the conversation: 'This man, who has been stalking me, was in my house. We had an argument, which ended up on the clifftop, and he just fell off.' I'd be their one and only suspect, especially if it were the indomitable DI Johnson who I'd spoken to when he arrested Josh. I turned my phone off.

Pouring myself a drink of whisky, which I only kept for specific visitors, I sat pondering the situation. From what he had told me, Ben lived alone. He was self-employed, so he wouldn't be missed straight away, even if he didn't contact his clients. They would probably be unlikely to phone the police, just thinking he'd forgotten to get in touch with them. I'd taken the keys back from him, so there was no evidence on him that he'd been in the house. I wondered if his phone would give away his locations? But, if he were walking on the cliff path, it would be close to the cottage anyway. Surprisingly, I felt calm. There was no reason why I should feel guilty. It wasn't as if I'd pushed him. It had been an accident. Now, I wouldn't have to worry about being followed or watched. My life would be my own.

After pulling off my muddy clothes, I stuffed them into the washing machine, cleaned my shoes, and left them out in the back lobby to dry out. While the washer was running its cycle, I cleaned the surfaces where I thought Ben might have touched – just in case I was questioned by the police, and they wanted to check for fingerprints. Then I realised it wouldn't have mattered if there were a few because I knew someone had been in the cottage. I just didn't know who. So, I didn't bother cleaning everywhere. I wished Ali was around. As much as it wouldn't have been a good idea to include her in what had happened, it would have been good to share it with someone. However, after a long soak in the bath, I felt more relaxed than I had for ages. After getting something to eat, I settled down to watch a video.

Incredibly, and despite the storm and my mind going over the events of that evening, I slept well. The wind had abated by the following day, and although it was still raining, it was nowhere near as heavy as the night before. I put on my wet running gear and went down to the beach. I couldn't run all the way along because there was a landslide where the cliff had given way – the spot where Ben must have fallen. I looked around to see if there was anyone out and about, which there wasn't, so I clambered gingerly over some of the rocks to see if I could see any evidence of a body. Nothing. Had Ben's ravaged, dead body been there?

I didn't think I'd be quite so blasé about it! Luckily, there was nothing to show of the tragedy of the night before. Who knows where the tides would have taken the body?

I spent the day packing and tidying things up around the house, so it would be OK to leave it for the couple of weeks I'd be in the US with Josh. Ringing the hotel where I was leaving my car, I checked to see if they had a room free if I drove down today. Luckily they had, so I piled everything into my car, locked up the house and studio, ensuring the alarm was set in the studio and set off for Heathrow.

Mid-afternoon, I emerged through customs and searched the people standing around in arrivals, looking for Josh. Then, finally, I saw his smiling face, and when I reached him, he pulled me towards him. I held on to him, not wanting to let go, trying hard to control my emotions. When I eventually released him, laughing gently, he said, "Wow, I can tell you're pleased to see me."

"You have no idea how relieved I am to be here. The weather back home was horrible, and I have missed you so much." I was trying hard not to cry, feeling as though a huge weight had been lifted from me. Even though I wasn't feeling guilty about Ben, I had spent some of the eleven-hour flight wondering if I'd be arrested when I landed because they'd found Ben's body with a piece of damning evidence suggesting my part in his demise.

Josh led me out to find a taxi, and after around twenty minutes, we were at his apartment. It was larger than I had expected, even following his description, which I thought he had probably exaggerated. "Do you want something to eat, or do you want to sleep?" Josh asked. "I know how tiring that flight can be. I've got a little bit of work that needs finishing, so you can have a nap. Then I'll come and wake you when I've finished."

He was right; I was more tired than I had expected, but I was also a little disappointed that he hadn't wanted to sweep me up in his arms. Though, when I saw myself in the bathroom mirror, I don't think I'd have tried to ravish me, either!

"Thanks. You're right. I do need it. I'll take a shower. Wake me when you're ready." Josh kissed me, leaving me to get myself settled.

My short nap turned into an hour, with Josh waking me with the attention I had been hoping for. When we emerged from the bedroom, he made us something to eat, which we ate sitting on the balcony looking out at the sea. It wasn't the quietest of locations, as you could constantly hear the hum of traffic, but seeing the sea was still special.

Thanksgiving lunch was quite an occasion. I hadn't understood the significance of it as a holiday. Mike, Josh's boss, and his wife Mia were lovely, and their kids Ava and Mikey were lively, articulate, and funny. I have never understood why American men name their male children after themselves. I just imagine the confusion in the household when you want to get either of their attention. At least when he's young, Mikey is fine, but I doubt he'll want to be called that as a grown man. Mia was also a creative though like Ali, she was a musician, so the four of us had plenty of common ground for the conversation, which flowed easily.

After Thanksgiving weekend, Josh had a few days off to be with me, during which he took me to the office to meet some of the team. They were all young – a great ethnic mix of people and lively. It was a fantastic atmosphere in which to work. It was apparent they all loved Josh and were impressed with his work.

On the fourth day of my trip, I was surprised when I got a text from Kyra, asking if we could chat the next day, 10.30pm my time. I was surprised to hear from her but knew she must have a good reason to ask, so I agreed. The next evening, I waited for her call, while Josh sat outside, listening to music.

My mobile rang, and Kyra said, "Hi, how's your trip going?"

"I love it, thanks. What's going on in downtown Whittingbury, then?" I asked. "You must have got up early to make this call – are you always up at this time?"

"Sometimes I am, so it's not a problem, but I thought I ought to give you a 'heads up'. A body was found and they think it went in the sea near your cottage on the night of the big storm."

Suddenly, I couldn't breathe. Luckily, Kyra continued, "They put his picture in the paper. It's the guy in the photo you showed me. So, I talked to one of my contacts at the station to see if I could find out more about him. She told me that they had found evidence that he had been stalking someone. My contact wouldn't say who; she didn't know…"

I interrupted her, "But you think it's my guy." I was feeling sick. Would they find anything to prove we met that night?

"Yes, it must be. I hope there aren't that many stalkers hanging around Whittingbury – though you never know. Anyway, I thought, maybe, your cameras might have captured him if he was near your house?"

Probably taking a little longer to answer than I should, my mind racing as I recalled the incriminating evidence on my cameras, both outside and inside. Finally, feeling grateful Kyra had phoned, I said, "Thanks for the information, Kyra. I'll check my cameras when I go home. It would be a bit of a coincidence if it were him. I presume the police will probably want to ask me if I saw anything or whether my cameras caught anything." I paused, wondering whether to ask my next question. In the end, I decided to, realising she was probably warning me, otherwise why ring me while I was away. "Do they know how he died?" I asked.

"They seem to think it was an accident due to the storm and water washing part of the cliff away, but the investigation is still ongoing." Then, she changed the subject. "So, how long are you out there?"

"Another week, then I'll be back. We'll have to catch up when I'm home. Thanks for letting me know the news," I said, trying hard to sound casual about it all.

We chatted a little longer about stuff she had going on, and after the call finished, I went over what Kyra had said. She was warning me that the police might come to check my camera footage. So, I needed to erase everything as soon as I got back and come up with a reason for not having any images on the outside camera. No one need know about the indoor ones – they were hidden, and I could easily remove them once I got home.

I must have looked worried when I went out to join Josh on the balcony, where he had a glass of wine waiting for me. Gratefully, I took a long drink. "How was Kyra? Everything OK, has something happened?" Josh asked.

I considered what to tell him. I could tell him most of the truth carefully without having to reveal the information about Gemma. Then, impressed by my calmness, I explained the body and that it might be my stalker, although it was uncertain. I also said the police would probably want to talk to me to ask whether I saw or heard anything.

I made a mental note that the first thing I needed to do upon my return was erase all the footage and destroy the indoor cameras. And, just in case, remove my baseball bat from the hall. But, for now, I was determined to enjoy the rest of my time with Josh.

CHAPTER 36

THREE YEARS LATER

Our little flame-haired girl, Ferne, ran towards her daddy, who was already on the beach. Josh scooped her up in his arms and swung her around. Watching from the house, I still can't believe we are here in this amazing place. The house has a gate that leads us directly onto the sunny Californian beach. We were incredibly lucky to find it, and thanks to the sale of Starfish Cottage and a large bank loan, we could buy this renovated beach house.

When I arrived back at Whittingbury after my Thanksgiving trip visiting Josh, I found a note through my door asking me to contact the local police station. Two officers dropped in to ask me questions. I'd already removed and thrown out the cameras from inside the cottage and deleted the images from the outdoor camera as well in case they asked to see the footage. Incredibly they didn't. They were satisfied by the evidence they had found in Ben's house, that he had been stalking me and had inadvertently slipped when the cliff subsided.

They asked me if I knew he had been inside my house and whether I knew that he had had access to my computer. I feigned shock and ignorance of both, although I did tell them I was aware that someone was watching me; I just hadn't been able to work out who it was. I also told them about some of the things that had gone missing. They surprised me by telling me some of the other clothes they had found in his house, which by the description were also mine, although I hadn't missed them. It just shows how much of our stuff we don't wear! After trying a key in the front door, they were satisfied that he couldn't have gained access since I'd changed the locks, which meant my version of events held fast. Satisfied, they left, thanking me for my time. I had felt a weight lift from my head.

At the end of that year, Josh and I spent Christmas with his parents, his sister Alisha, her boyfriend Sam, and Sue's mum, Lizzie. Sue and Patrick had eventually come around to accept our relationship. Although I think it took Patrick until the birth of Ferne to accept and trust that it was genuine. The agency, Katz Co., offered Josh a full-time job, and after getting everything sorted regarding visas and immigration, he left college and moved out to the US ahead of me. It meant lots of flights to and from there until I, too, managed to get my visa sorted. It hadn't taken long to sell the cottage. Although I was sad to leave because of all the happy memories it held, I knew it was time to move on. I also felt that if Aunt Jinny were looking down, she'd be happy for me.

Initially, Sue and Patrick hadn't been pleased about Josh leaving college, but when they realised how much he was getting paid and how well he was doing in the US, they understood why he had taken that route. Ultimately, a degree wasn't going to make any difference to him being the good artist he was, although the company had said they would support him by allowing him some time to spend at college in LA if he wanted.

The most exciting news of the following year, apart from the move, was our journey to Italy for Ali and Mitchel's wedding, where I was one of the bridesmaids. It was a happy time as I had just found out I was pregnant. Ferne was born surrounded by family, for which I was grateful. Sue and Patrick had flown out to spend a month with us after her birth, and that helped me find my feet as a new mum. These days, I was regularly selling work at a local art gallery, and occasionally, Josh and I did some art together. He was getting quite a name for himself and was fast developing into the amazing artist I always knew he would be.

Next year, we plan on getting married at Ali and Mitchel's vineyard in Italy, with Ferne and Lucia, their young daughter, as flower girls. We all appear to have suddenly grown into responsible parents!

However, I still have my secret. Although Josh knows my stalker was the person who died, I hadn't told him about my confrontation with Ben or that he was with Gemma when she had her accident. I can't bring myself to explain that she died because of me. That knowledge won't make him feel any better about her death, so I'm letting sleeping dogs lie. He never needs to know. That's all in the past.

Finishing off my job in the kitchen, I walk down to join Josh and Ferne on the beach. Holding hands, Josh and I wander along the edge of the sea, watching our daughter, happily, running in and out of the shallow, rippling waves as they wash onto the shore.

ACKNOWLEDGEMENTS

I have many people to thank. My two best friends, Fiona Scott and Helen Richmond, for their encouragement and belief in me, and their continued support. Teresa McGrady for reading through and giving feedback at the very beginning of writing. The wonderful Carolyne Crawford, Helen Richmond and Amanda Dear for taking the time to read through the first draft, giving me useful, critical feedback. Without the help of Lukasz Kudla I would not have known how to pronounce the Polish surname in the story. A huge thanks to Arthur Cole and Beverley Douglas for their help with police procedure. At one point, I wasn't happy with the ending, but Alex Hudd helped me with ideas that made it work. A special thanks to Julia Dickmann for information and wording for the crematorium service for a young person. Abbie Pagington for her help with understanding some of the psychological traits of someone with attachment issues. Ann Brady for the first edit and to the staff at SilverWood for their support getting my first novel published.

Lastly, my husband, Conrad who supports me in life, puts up with me disappearing to write, and then has to listen to my latest ideas, whether he is interested or not!

Lightning Source UK Ltd.
Milton Keynes UK
UKHW040649130522
402919UK00001B/24